1-26 ?

ALLEGIANCE

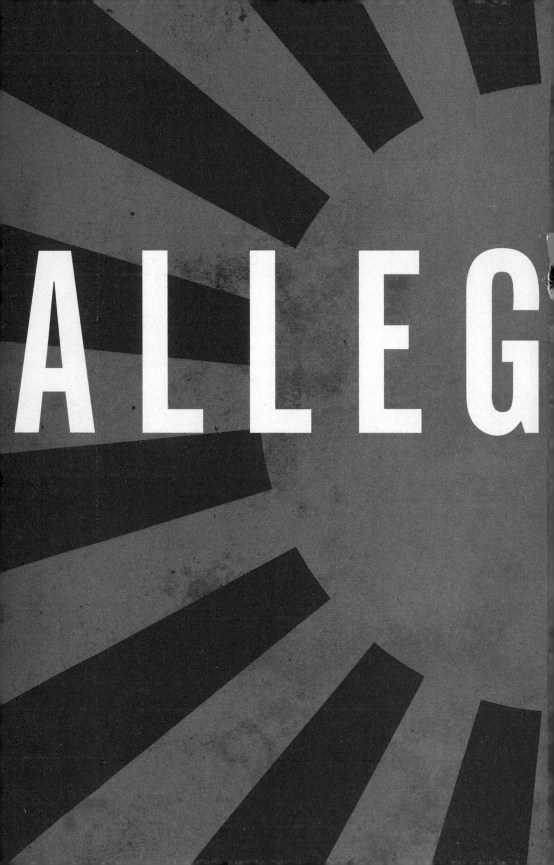

IANCE

A NOVEL

Regan Arts.

Regan Arts.

65 Bleecker Street
New York, NY 10012

First Regan Arts hardcover edition, August 2015.

Library of Congress Control Number: 2014955549

ISBN 978-1-941393-30-7

Interior design by PagnozziCreative
Jacket design by Richard Ljoenes
Interior photographs: pages 5, 6–7 by Dorothea Lange/US National Archives and
Records Administration; pages 166–167 by Clem Albers/US National Archives and
Records Administration; pages 308–309 by Francis Stewart/US National Archives
and Records Administration

Printed in the United States of America

10 9 8 7 6 5 4 3 2 1

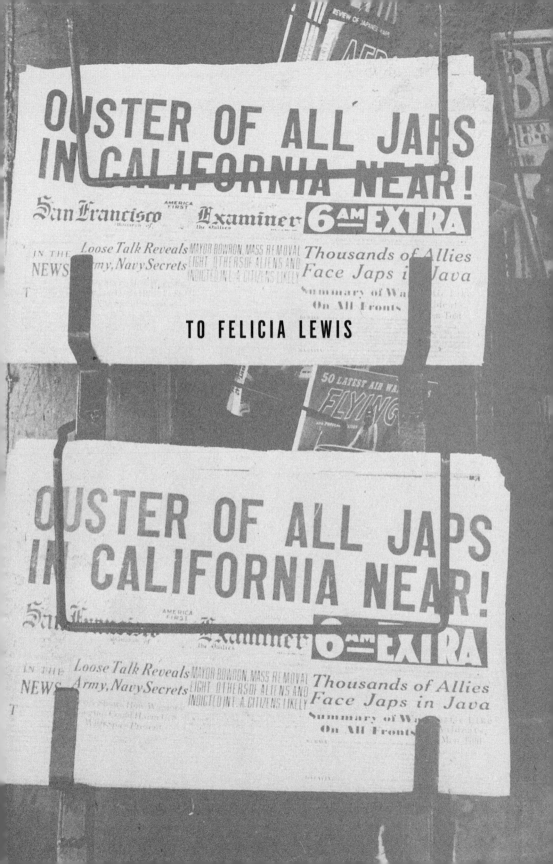

TO FELICIA LEWIS

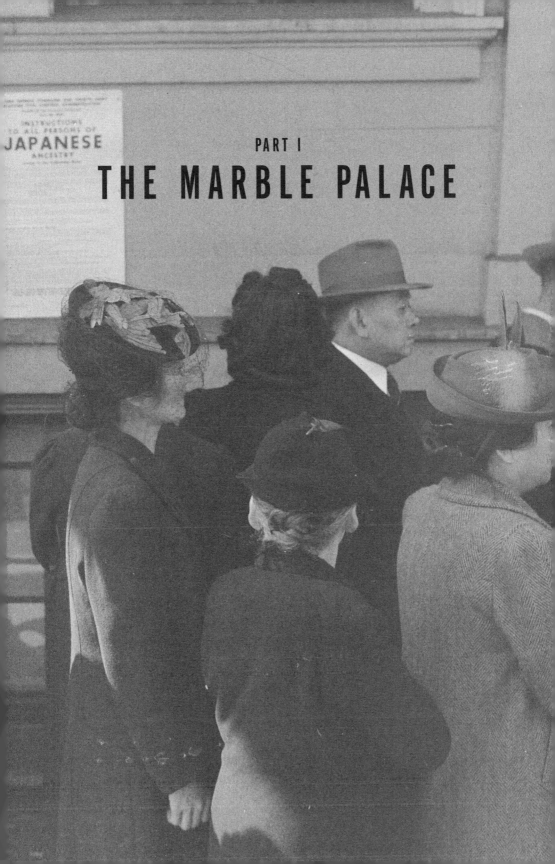

PART I

THE MARBLE PALACE

CHAPTER 1

EVERYONE REMEMBERS WHERE they were when they heard the news. I was in New York, the Beta house at Columbia, with constitutional law books on my desk and last night's drinks in my head. Law school final exams fought with the debutante season for my attention. A doomed struggle; even without the pounding hangover, which pushed academic thought past bearing, Herbert Wechsler's views on the Supreme Court could not stand against the white shoulders of Suzanne Skinner. They tanned honey-gold in the summer, with freckles like snowflakes of the sun. But as fall grew cold they paled to alabaster and in two weeks at the Assembly they would be white, as white as her dress, and you would barely see where the straps lay. And my hands by contrast would seem dark and rough as I steered her around the floor. And all about us the air would fill with . . . silence.

That wasn't the right thought. The air would fill with waltzes and songs plucked from strings. But in the room now there was silence. It had stopped the clack of Ping-Pong balls from below and crept up the stairs; it had stilled the traffic on the street and slipped in through the window. Now it surrounded me, as though the whole world was a movie stuck between frames.

And then there were new noises. Outside, horns sounded and raised voices called, shrill and indistinct. Inside there was a clatter of shoe leather through the halls. Excited Beta brothers hurtled into the room. "Turn on the radio, Cash." Exams and debutantes vanished; yes, and even Suzanne. The

1

announcer's words bred different images in my mind. Planes out of the blue Pacific sky, too fast, too low, too many. The sparkle of cannon fire from their wings, the smoke of ships afire at anchor, the red disc of the rising sun.

"The rats," said one of the brothers, stubbing out a cigarette.

"Well, damn it, I'm joining up," said another. Three of them rushed out, the echoes of their feet fading down the stairs.

For a blank second I sat there, watching the space where they'd been. Then everything came into focus in an instant, like putting on glasses for the first time, seeing suddenly all the sharp edges of the world, the crisp, clear lines of truth. "Wait for me!"

I dashed down the hall and took the steps four at a time, jumping off the top without thinking about where to land, launching myself again as soon as my feet touched down. We must have made quite a noise, but I heard nothing, saw only the boys ahead of me flying through the air. I burst out the front door onto the street. One of them—Jack Hamill, I remember the puzzled look on his face—was standing still on the sidewalk, head cocked as though an important thought had just occurred to him. The other two were rounding the corner onto 114th Street. I sprinted after them, threading through the pedestrians, darting past cars.

It took me only half a block to catch up. I was making good time, even in the crowd, and they were slowing down, turning their heads to exchange words, coming finally to a complete halt, faces as puzzled as Jack's. I pulled up, panting slightly. "Why'd you stop?"

Pete Metcalfe turned to me. "Oh, Cash." He sounded relieved and just a bit hopeful.

"What?"

"You don't know where a recruiting station is, do you?"

"No." I thought for a moment. "No, I don't."

Pete bit his lip. "Neither do we." For a moment he looked as if he might cry.

We stood like sleepwalkers, woken in an unfamiliar place, impelled by a vanished dream. The urgency of the sprint was fading, the cloud of certainty, the single purpose. I could think of other things now, other people; I could imagine Suzanne's reaction, and my mother's. Running off without a thought for anyone else. I looked down at the sidewalk. By my feet lay a silver gum wrapper, a cockroach mashed flat. "I can't do this."

"No," said Pete. "I guess not."

Our walk back to the Beta house was slower. The radio was still on in my room, the brothers still clustered round. The ones who'd stayed barely looked up as we entered. Jack Hamill had taken my desk chair, and I found a space on the bed. And we sat there in silence, not meeting each other's eyes, listening to the voices over the air and the metallic clanking of the radiators as the heat came on.

We sat there for hours, almost the rest of the day. But it wasn't that long shared vigil that stuck with me in the weeks that followed. I never told Suzanne about how I'd run out; I never told my parents, or anyone else at home. The reaction came to seem absurd, almost shameful. So thoughtless, so irresponsible. But that was what I remembered in those later days, the feeling I had at the top of the stairs. Before we went down to the snarl of traffic and the realization we had no idea where we were running, there was the purity of that moment when I stepped out into space. When we soared above the jagged steps, our coattails flapping like ailerons, arms outspread to grasp the empty air.

CHAPTER 2

"WHAT ARE WE going to do?" Suzanne asks. There is a tinny note to her voice over the phone, an unusual strain. It sounds like a wire stretched thin over the miles between us; it sounds like the leading edge of panic.

"Don't worry," I say. "Everything's going to be okay. I'll be back soon." I try to sound assured, but I am confident only about the last part of this statement.

"And I'm looking forward to seeing you," Suzanne says. "Of course. It will make me feel better, for a little bit. But how long will you be here?"

"Winter break," I say. "Till January fifth, probably, or—"

"That's not what I'm talking about," Suzanne interrupts. "Cash, I'm so scared I can't sleep. I just lie there trying to think of something I can do."

"You don't need to do anything," I tell her. "I'll take care of you. You're safe."

"Me? Of course I'm safe." Now she sounds impatient, another unfamiliar tone. "That's not what I'm afraid of."

"What is it, then?"

"Don't you understand, Cash? We're at war now. You're the one who's in danger. Boys like you are going to be drafted."

Of course, the draft. Consumed as I was with dreams of volunteering, I hadn't given the draft any thought. But now with Suzanne's words it enters my mind. She sees a grasping claw, but to me it is a hand stretched in invitation. It offers the liberty of compulsion: no one could blame me; no one could fault my choice. I pick my words carefully. "Maybe I'll get lucky."

"Lucky!" She doesn't understand what I mean, but still Suzanne repeats the word incredulously. "We're talking about your life, Cash. Boys like you are going to die."

. . . .

Winter break in Haverford. The Assembly is canceled, but there are other dances; there is the Merion Cricket Club. There are kisses on the balcony overlooking the Great Lawn; there is her mouth open to mine and the taste of champagne. We do not discuss the draft or the war. Instead, there is talk of what I will do in Philadelphia after graduation, of Center City houses and Main Line trains.

But in two weeks I am back in the Beta house at Columbia and the future we discussed seems increasingly distant. Meaningless, unreal, it follows the Assembly into the world of things that will never happen. What is real is opening the paper to see unfamiliar names. Wake, Guam, Bataan. We are losing. Radio announcers strain with the pronunciation. Sarawak, Rabaul, Bouganville. The Empire of Japan grows. It is hard to sit there and listen, harder to think of anything else, an agony to turn the radio off and go to class. I look out the window at the tangled street and see armored columns, massed infantry. The world hangs in the balance, somewhere very far from here, and fat, old Professor Hanson asks me to define a springing executory interest.

And then the draft comes. We cluster around the box on a chilly March day to hear the numbers read out. Back in October, they made an event of it. Henry Stimson stirred the balls with a spoon carved from the beams of Independence Hall, and Roosevelt read the first number. "We are all with you," he said, "in a task which enlists the services of all Americans." But only some are enlisting now, and the voice that tells us who is unfamiliar and brusque.

"You think you'll go west or east, Billy?" asks Joe Eisner conversationally.

Skinny and red-haired, William Fitch is still recovering from the shock of hearing 485. "Shut up," he says absently.

Eisner is unoffended. "Lots going on out West," he says. He has never liked Fitch. "I heard a Jap sub hit Santa Barbara. They could land any day. But there's bodies on the beach at Montauk."

Fitch swivels his long neck. "Shut up." His face is pasty.

"They tell you to keep the lights down on Long Island," Eisner continues. "But no one does. The freighters get backlit and the U-boats just line 'em up. It's a shooting gallery."

"Shut up," says Fitch. "Damn you."

"Don't get sore," says Eisner cheerily as Fitch storms out. "We're all going. It's just a question of when."

For another several minutes we sit with only the unknown voice to break the silence: "347. 852." And then it comes: 129. "That's me," I say, and as no one seems to notice, I repeat it louder. "That's my number."

Eisner pats my shoulder, his face somber. "Tough break."

I look down, saying nothing. Eisner suspects I am hiding tears, no doubt, but in truth I am trying not to smile. I did get lucky. Part of me is already hearing Suzanne's voice, already seeing the look on my mother's face. I'm not stupid. I know what war means. Dink Morris left an arm at Belleau Wood and watches each Merion dance with empty eyes. But still, the sentences that parade through my head are marching on light feet. I'm needed. I've been chosen. I am called. It may be west or it may be east, but that makes no difference. I have a direction now; I know where I am headed. I am going to war.

. . . .

Me and a million other American boys. So many the Army doesn't have doctors for all the physicals. The induction letter summons me back to Philadelphia, and on Friday I join a line of wan young men at Pennsylvania Hospital. Billy Fitch is a Philadelphia boy too; up ahead, I can see his red curls, the nape of his pale neck. Behind me a fellow with slicked-back hair snaps his chewing gum. "Ask me how I'm getting out of it," he says.

"Getting out of it?" I repeat, uncomprehending.

"What's that?" he bellows, cupping an ear. "Sorry, can't hear you."

I blink, and he turns away with a laugh.

There are no rooms for the examinations, just spaces made with hanging sheets. I fold my clothes and place them on one stool. The doctor sits on another and taps my folder against his knee. "Caswell Harrison," he says.

"Cash," I answer.

He circles a finger in the air. "Turn around for me." He makes a note in the file. "That's all right, then."

"What?"

The doctor strokes his beard. His smile says he knows something I do not. "So, Cash, you look like a fellow who's got at least half his teeth."

"Yes."

"Ever been convicted of a crime?"

"No."

The pencil moves, checking boxes. "Drink too much? Like boys?"

"What?" I can feel my face redden.

"Sit down." He takes my foot in his hand and flexes it. "How are your ankles?"

"They're fine. Couple of sprains."

"Mmm. Straighten your leg out. Knees?"

"Never had any trouble."

"You do any running?"

"I play squash."

He nods. "Get up and walk for me."

I go from my stool to the sheet. When I turn to come back, I see the pencil pressed against his lips. "Ever run straight? Or hike?"

"No. I did track once, but . . ." My voice trails off.

"Your knees hurt."

"No more than normal."

A small shake of the head. "It's not normal." He makes another note and closes the folder with an air of finality. "You're out," he says. "Go home."

"What?"

"Overpronation. You can't march."

"Of course I can." Part of my mind is insisting that I should feel relief, but what rises in me instead is anger. "I'm a varsity athlete."

"Side to side I bet you're grand." He smiles. "Like a crab. But you can't go forward. It's like flat feet."

Something is being taken from me. "I want to volunteer," I say. "There must be something I can do."

For the first time, he looks surprised. "I'm sure there is. But this isn't a recruiting center. It's a preinduction physical, and you've failed. Go home."

"But I can still volunteer?"

"I don't know why you're asking me." He shakes his head. "Look, I've got other men to see."

I button my shirt as I step out. Young men mill on the sidewalk, hands exploring new-mown hair. The gum-snapping slicker is there, both ears now prominently on display. Billy Fitch looks younger without his curls, all big eyes and pale, vulnerable skin. He looks at me. "What happened?"

"Ankles," I say.

His nod is unconvinced. "You always seemed okay to me."

"I thought so too. It was the doctor." He nods again and turns away. We are on different paths now, in different worlds. I take a taxicab to Suburban Station and ride the Paoli Local out to the Main Line. The first name the conductor calls triggers the whole familiar string in my mind. Overbrook, Merion, Narberth, Wynnewood, Ardmore, Haverford, Bryn Mawr. *Old maids never wed and have babies.* I never make it to the babies either, getting off at Haverford. From the station I can walk home down the wide and quiet streets. There has never been much traffic, but now there is even less. Almost anyone can get a B or C gas sticker from the local price administrators, but new tires are harder to come by.

The familiar houses sprawl back from the road, with low stone walls and long drives. I knock at a glossy black door and give my bag to James, who has been with us since before I was born. My mother kisses me and grasps my hands in hers. "You said they were going to cut your hair." She reaches up, as if to be sure it's still there, and runs her fingers across my brow.

I pull her hand down. "I failed."

"What?"

"I failed. Something about my ankles."

Her face lights up. "But that's wonderful. Charles, come here." My father does not stir from his study, or even deign to answer, so she pulls me with her into the room. Now he sets aside the *Bulletin* and rises from his chair. His back is straight, his grip strong.

"Cash. Will you be staying for dinner?"

"Yes, father. The weekend, actually. I need to make some plans."

"Now you can join Morgan Lewis after all," he says.

"Yes," I say. "I could. But——"

"You're not thinking of New York, are you?"

"No. I'm thinking of volunteering."

At my side, my mother gives a small gasp, but my father just blinks at me. His face suggests that he's not quite sure what I mean, but if it's along the lines he suspects, I must be insane. It's the expression I must have shown the gum-chewing dodger, and now I realize where I get it. "Volunteer?" he says, as though trying out a word in a foreign language. "For what?"

I have not yet given this much thought, and I manage only a few inarticulate syllables before my father speaks again.

"You don't know." He shakes his head as though his suspicions have been confirmed.

"I just want to do something."

"Drive an ambulance, maybe? Like Ernest Hemingway?"

"Why not?"

"I don't believe there's much need for that right now." He pauses, and a slow smile touches his lips. "And don't you know what happened to him?"

"Charles!" My mother turns to me. "Cash," she says. "Why would you want to leave? What about Suzanne? What about us?" She listens to the radio. She has heard that war will plow under every fourth American boy, that we will not put out the fires of Europe by setting our home ablaze.

"Do you remember the Easter egg hunts at Merion?" I ask. It is her turn to look puzzled. "When I was five," I say. "I'd just moved up into an older group, but I went after the toddler eggs by mistake. I got them all. I remember showing you my basket."

She shakes her head. "I'm afraid I don't remember that."

"I was very proud of myself. And you didn't tell me that they weren't for me, that I'd made a mistake. You just said, 'And what will you do with your bounty?'"

"I did? Bounty? That doesn't sound like me."

"Well, that's what you said. And then——"

"I certainly don't know what I meant by that," she continues. James places a glass of wine in her hand. "If I said it."

"Yes, you said it."

"Bounty?"

"Yes!" It comes out louder than I intended. My father coughs; my mother raises the glass to her lips. Age shows in her hands. The skin is thinner, tight over the knuckles and webbed with lines. The rings look heavy on her fingers. "And then you helped me hide them again."

"Would a five-year-old even know the word 'bounty'?"

My father coughs again. "That's charming," he says. "But I don't see what it has to do with your plans. Egg hiders are in less demand even than ambulance drivers, I should think."

"It's about doing something with what I've been given," I say.

"Bounty," my mother says again. "You know, I don't think that's a word I use."

I blink at her. "Maybe not. But that's how I remember it. And that's what matters."

"I think it matters what I said."

"I'm going to volunteer," I say. "For something. You can't stop me."

She looks at my father, helpless. "Indeed, you have been given things," he says. "Investments have been made. In you. What return do you foresee from this?"

"It's not about return," I say. "It's the right thing to do."

He raises his eyebrows mildly. "Because of what you owe your country? It was not your country that sent you to the University, that paid your way to law school. That fed and clothed you these years. Other people have a claim on you as well."

I look down at the dark waxed floor, my certainty melting. My brother is raising a family already; he trades stocks, went to Harvard. Each achievement made me feel less necessary, a fainter echo trailing in his wake. But my father is a banker; perhaps he loves his reserves better than I know. Or values them more highly. The firelight flickers over thinning Persian rugs. My mother lays a hand on my arm. "Just take some time," she says. "Talk to Suzanne. Talk to her father."

• • • •

Judge Skinner's house is another short walk down the quiet streets. Dusk is gathering in the trees; the birds have gone still, and a pale moon is emerging in the eastern sky. But when Suzanne opens the door, it's as though the sun is still high. Her skin has the glow of a spring day and her green eyes are full of light. "How are you?" she asks, and throws her arms around me.

"Not good enough for Uncle Sam," I say. Over her shoulder I can hear voices and the clink of glassware. The Judge is entertaining.

Suzanne squeezes me harder and then lets go. "I knew it," she says, and she truly doesn't sound surprised. "I knew you wouldn't leave me."

"I was thinking, though. That maybe there's something else I could do."

I can see her body go tight as she takes a step back. "What do you mean?"

"My number came up. I was supposed to go."

"That's not what the doctor said."

"I feel like I'm cheating. Like I'm not pulling my weight."

"Don't be silly. You work harder than anyone I know."

"Some guys at Columbia," I begin. The observation says more about her acquaintances than my work habits, but there's no point in pursuing it. "It's not about working. It's serving."

"But that's what you're doing. This is what's right for you. Oh, Cash, you don't belong in the army. You're going to be a lawyer."

"Billy Fitch was going to be a lawyer, too." I think of his pale face, the accusation in his eyes. "He's just as smart as I am. Works just as hard."

"I don't care about Billy Fitch," Suzanne says, and her arms are around me again. "I want you to be safe."

"But why me and not him? How am I different?"

"You big dummy," she says. Her voice is amused but patient, as though explaining something to a child. "You're different because I love you."

This will not be resolved in one conversation. I stroke her hair and she nestles into my chest. "Let's see a movie," I say, and she rubs her face up and down against me: yes. There will be time to talk to the Judge later. And certainly there is no hurry. I have a school year to finish out, one more round of exams to take. But still the idea grows inside me. My number did come up. It wasn't the call I thought, but it feels like permission. It is a sign, if you believe in that sort of thing. By May, law school will be done. By the end of the month, I can sign up and ship out; by June, I will be gone.

So I say, and Suzanne protests and remonstrates and finally weeps. And my father talks of investments, and my mother reaches out and lets her arms fall to her side. Even Judge Skinner has a word with me about the fine traditions of Morgan Lewis and the value of Center City practice. But as it turns out, June finds me someplace none of us could have expected.

CHAPTER 3

"DOING WELL, CASH?" the voice on the phone asks. It is Herbert Wechsler, who taught me constitutional law, or tried, and now sits at the Justice Department in Washington, DC He doesn't wait for an answer. "Good. Anyway, this isn't a social call. There's an opening at the Supreme Court. Hugo Black needs a new law clerk."

"Me?" I am taken aback. A law clerk sits at the Justice's elbow, discusses the cases, offers opinions on weighty and complicated questions. I am not an obvious choice for that role. Not all my exams were as disastrous as con law, but I am by no means one of the bright young things of Columbia. It seems quite possible that Wechsler is thinking of another man entirely. He is young and brilliant but somewhat distracted, and students have never been his chief focus. Perhaps, I suggest, he intends to reach out to someone other than Caswell Harrison.

"Of course I mean you, Cash," Wechsler says. "You're the right sort of guy for this."

"Really?"

Now he hesitates a moment. "It's a bit of a last-minute thing, that's all. Justice Black's just had a second clerk drafted out from under him."

I remain silent. The phrase puts me in mind of one of the glorious generals from the history books in Judge Skinner's study, battling to victory as a succession of mounts go down. It makes more sense now that Wechsler would call me, from one perspective at least. Word of the physical has gotten around: I am a horse that will not falter.

"You could start in June, couldn't you?" he continues. "And you play tennis."

This last is a statement, not a question, and it makes me wonder where he is getting his information. I am a competent tennis player, but not a star. "More squash," I answer. At Merion, lawn tennis is an arriviste that crowds out cricket. "I lettered at Penn."

"You could keep up with a fifty-five-year-old man, though," says Wechsler. Again it is not a question, and this time I let it pass.

"Actually, I was thinking," I say. "That after graduation maybe I'd sign up for something."

"Sign up? What are you talking about?"

"Volunteer. For the war."

"Justice Black needs a clerk," Wechsler says. Now he sounds annoyed, a tone I remember from class. I have failed to identify the principle underlying some judicial decision. "Your name came up."

He waits for me to complete the syllogism. I try to perform the audible equivalent of a shrug. A new future has appeared, neither perilous volunteerism nor staid Center City law practice.

Wechsler interrupts. "Stop it. No one likes a mumbler. Look, Justice Black will be in Chester this weekend at Owen Roberts's farm. Go home and talk it over with anyone you need. Then see him. Perhaps you'll hit it off."

· · · ·

This time I go to Suzanne's house first when I reach Haverford. She is watching from the window, evidently, for the door flies open before I'm halfway up the drive, and she runs to me with her arms outstretched.

"The Supreme Court," she says. "How wonderful!"

"I don't have the job yet," I tell her. "And I'm not even sure I want it."

She cups my face with one hand. "What are you talking about?"

"Washington," I say. It's not as bad as New York, but even Washington is really no place for a proper Philadelphian. It is filled with politicians, sharp dealers, people pulling this country away from its roots. "I just wonder if that's the right thing for me. You know, I was going to try to find some way to enlist."

Suzanne's face tightens. "Yes, I do know that." Then she softens. "But don't you see, Cash? This is perfect for you. This is how you can serve. It's what you trained for."

"But how is it serving?"

"You don't have to pull a trigger to be fighting, Cash. We're all a part of it. Like John Hall."

"I don't," I say. Hall was two years ahead of me at Episcopal, then went to Harvard, where he continued beating me at squash and visited Suzanne more than I liked.

"What?"

"I don't like John Hall. And anyway, he's in the army."

"He's an army lawyer. That's the best use of his talents."

"What talents?" I say. Hall always struck me as an idiot. But Harvard Law evidently thought otherwise, and now he has their stamp. Of course, a Supreme Court clerkship is a higher mark of distinction. At least in some circles.

"You told me you'd take care of me," says Suzanne. "Let me do that for you one time."

"What do you mean?"

She hesitates. "I mean, let me give something up for you. You'll be gone for a year. But it gives you the chance to do something important. To make a contribution. I know how much that means to you."

"But what kind of contribution is it?"

"You're the lawyer. You tell me." She leans closer, and for a second I think she is going to kiss me. Then her hands are on my chest, pushing me away. "Go talk to the Judge. He's been fussing like a mother hen all day. Can't talk about anything else."

I bend down and put my lips on hers. She softens, leans into me, and pulls back. "Go on," she says.

Judge Skinner's library holds a chair not unlike my father's. But he isn't sitting. He is looking in one of his books, and it seems that even that is put on for my benefit, for as soon as he hears my step he slaps it shut and turns with eyes alight in his craggy face. "The Supreme Court," he says, and his voice polishes the words to such luster I can almost see the glow. "It's a real honor."

"I'm the understudy, from what I hear. The second understudy, in fact."

"Nonsense. You'll see Black tomorrow? You won't agree with him on every-thing, but I expect he'll do most of the talking. He's from the South. Stay off the Klan."

"I should be able to do that."

He claps a hand on my shoulder and smiles. "The Supreme Court. I doubt any of my decisions will make it there, but if they do I hope you'll look kindly on an old man's work."

I smile myself. As a senior district judge, he still sits occasionally. "I'm sure there would be nothing to do but look," I say. "Marvel, really. But so you think I should take this?"

"Of course. It's an opportunity few people ever have. To see the seat of power. To hold the levers. There's no telling what you might do."

"Marvel, I expect. Or watch, anyway." I pause. "I know it's grand, but it almost seems irrelevant. I was thinking—"

He cuts me off. "I know what you were thinking. To rush into the fire. I understand the feeling. If I were thirty years younger I'd want it myself. Self-sacrifice is a noble gesture. But it leaves only a footnote in life's ledger. Suppose I had burnt myself up as a young man. You'd never have known me. Nor Suzanne. And if you do it . . . well, I put Suzanne apart for the moment. Is that what you will leave your family, a name and numbers at the bottom of a page?"

"There's Charles."

"Your brother." He nods. "A fine chap. Shall the world remember Charles instead of you? A solid member of the Union League, they will say. A reg-ular at the Devon Horse Show. Those were the Harrisons. That is what you choose?"

"Of course not."

"The University has a statue of John Harrison," the Judge says. "I see men polishing his face of an evening. It is fine and tall, but where are the Harri-sons now? I mean no criticism. But look about Philadelphia. You will find their name in the rosters of clubs and cotillions, their image in illustrated journals of the popular press. No Harrison leads. No Harrison serves. You were made for more than that, and more is what is now offered you. You think the Court irrelevant?" His voice swells briefly, showing power and folding it under again. I know he can cast thunderbolts with that voice, for I have heard him do it, when I would cross the river from the University and walk down to the courthouse. "The man who dies young is irrelevant. And the man who stays here all his life as well. Philadelphia is not the center of the universe, much though it would like to think so. Drafting wills for the dowagers of Gladwyne is irrelevant. At the Court you would be at the heart of things." The voice folds over one more time, and now it is like a soft hand on your hair at evening. "We have read history together," he says. The books line the walls, sleeping in leather. "You know Philadelphia was the capital. For politics, and for finance as well. Washington and New York took those away. And now we have taste. It is what they left us."

"Taste is something," I say.

"Taste is a wonderful thing. But some would have you believe it is everything. One need not be a snob to be a gentleman, or an idiot to be an aristocrat. Society left governing to the little men, and that was fine as long as government left society alone. But it hasn't for the past decade, and it won't again. If we don't govern, we will be governed. If society isn't a part of government now, it's nothing. Oh, there is a war at the Court if you care to look for it. You need have no worries on that score." Something stirs in the voice, emerging from its covers, and suddenly it is as if the bustling hen Suzanne described has brushed me with a wing and knocked me clear across the room.

"Weeks on the front line, or years on the Paoli Local. Some nameless patch of foreign ground or the endless rosary of Main Line towns. A moment of death, or a lifetime of dying. Your friends may have no other path. But not you, my boy. Fate has stretched out her hand. You have been chosen."

· · · ·

Owen Roberts is not the man he was, my father says, not since he bent the knee to Roosevelt. But he is still one of us, a Philadelphian on the Court. And his farm is still seven hundred acres, pastures, field, and forest below a wooded hill.

Justice Black is another story. He has always been Roosevelt's man, eager to tear down any barriers the Constitution sets before his master. In Washington now they are talking of a system that will take money from your paycheck and give it to the government before you ever see it. They are telling farmers how much wheat to grow and fining anyone who surpasses the quota. There is an agency for everything, a rule, a regulation.

So says my father, but Black does not ask my views on Karl Marx. He studies me with shrewd hazel eyes and suggests that perhaps I'm not the right sort of guy after all. "I generally hire a Southern fellow," Black says. "And usually from Yale. I like to get the layman's perspective." After a moment I recognize this as a joke.

"Some of us from Columbia can give you that too."

"I'm sure," Black says. He gives me that appraising glance again. "And you play tennis. Well, let's walk."

We follow a path from the paddock, turning downhill toward the woods. Flowering honeysuckle sweetens the air. "I had my man picked out this year," Black continues. He is several inches shorter than me and small-boned, with sandy hair receding above a broad forehead, an open, inquisitive face. "But Uncle Sam's needs have been outranking mine. Gave him two clerks and two sons." He shrugs. "I don't complain. Every generation fights a war."

He is doing most of the talking, as Judge Skinner predicted. I try to think of a contribution, but what can I say? That working for him fulfills the duty his sons discharge overseas? I am beginning to doubt that myself. "I want 'em back, of course," Black says. "All four of 'em." We walk in silence for a moment. He wears a white shirt open at the neck and dark flannel trousers, flicking idly at bushes with a small stick.

"Nice land," he says eventually. "Pennsylvania."

"Yes, it is."

"My great uncle Clum came up here some years ago."

I warm to the subject. "I hope he found it pleasant."

"Can't say. He made it as far as Cemetery Ridge with Birkett Fry. Met some boys from the Second Vermont and didn't come back. What can I help you with?"

I am caught off guard. Old Uncle Clum was taking shape in my mind as an amiable itinerant, with muttonchop sideburns and a waxed mustache. Now the seersucker fades to rebel gray and a Bowie knife sprouts between his teeth. I push the image away to grapple with the question. "Help me with?"

"That's what I said." The stick flicks. Weeds fall. "I don't hire clerks for what they can do for me. It's what I can do for them. I won't hire a man unless I can teach him something." The stick moves a bit faster. "One fellow I taught to dress a little sharper, but I don't think that's your problem. One fellow I taught to stop calling himself by a letter. C. George Mann, he was. I made him see different." I offer a small appreciative laugh. Black snorts. "You go by Cash, eh? Interesting name."

"It's a nickname." We are back on familiar ground. "From Caswell."

"Another interesting name. But that's still not it. What do you want?"

"'To be useful." I have nothing better than this, but Black's face suggests he is not wholly displeased. "To do the right thing."

Now Black snorts again. "So does everyone. Don't get all vague and gauzy on me." He pauses and looks at me for a long moment with those shrewd eyes. The stick circles in the air. Then it descends. "Well, every man's got his purpose. Might be I could teach you yours. And I hear you've got a heck of a backhand."

. . . .

My mother holds me tight, and I can feel the relief as she lets go. I am leaving her, but I will be safe. Suzanne's release is more reluctant. There is a smile on her lips, but the sparkle in her eye is a tear and her head drops down as I step away. "Just a year," I say, and she nods without looking up.

Judge Skinner just puts his hand on my shoulder. "My boy." My father does not touch me at all.

"Hugo Black," he says, in that way he has that makes everything sound beneath you. I know what he means. I am lowering myself; it is a disappointment; I should sit on my tidy shelf until something happens to Charles.

"Yes, Father," I say. "Hugo Black. He doesn't seem so bad after all."

The corners of his mouth turn down almost imperceptibly. "So you think," he says. "Well, remember this. No man is a hero to his valet."

CHAPTER 4

THE JUDGE WAS right, it seems; the war is at the Court too. The FBI catches eight Nazi saboteurs come ashore from submarines; the President sends them before military tribunals. Their appointed army lawyers ask the Court to stop the trials, which, after due consideration, it declines to do. Six meet their end in the electric chair. In the mornings I read the newspaper accounts; at night as I lie in bed I imagine myself already inside the marble halls, debating the reach of the war power, the rights of the enemy.

When I get there, weeks later, I find that Washington is not just at war; it has been invaded. Atop the insular local population, the New Deal has already dropped thousands of bureaucrats. Now the streets swarm with uniforms, too, and government functionaries of all descriptions. Any girl who can type can get thirty dollars a week, but no one can find a room to sleep in. I survey damp and airless basements; I chat with lonely old widows and lonely younger women whose husbands are away at war. Eventually I learn that the Japanese embassy staff has left some vacancies at Alban Towers, a large Gothic building at the intersection of Wisconsin and Massachusetts avenues. The apartments are furnished in a spare Oriental style I think will fit well with a year of hard work. The dressers are small, but elegantly lacquered cherry; the lamps have rice paper shades. There are no beds, just odd mattresses rolled up in the closet. Perhaps the Japanese have taken their bed frames with them to the Greenbrier, where they are now detained with other Axis diplomats.

I choose the apartment with the best view. It has three rooms: a small kitchen with an electric stove, a sitting room, and the bedroom. The windows look east; standing where my bed will be when I get one, I can see the spires of the National Cathedral a few blocks away or gaze out over the string of embassies running downtown.

On June 13, as instructed, I head downtown myself, to One First Street. The Supreme Court building is six years old now, but it still looks brand-new. The white marble gleams. The plaza is blinding, and even at eight in the morning the heat coming off it is so intense I almost stop to cool myself in one of the pale blue fountains. Behind its double-columned portico, the Court looks like a Greek temple. So does the Philadelphia Art Museum, of course, but the Art Museum is soft gold in color and glows like an old friend. The Court is an austere white, mysterious and pure. A wide marble stair-case, flanked by enormous statues, leads up to great bronze doors. I study the steps, crisp and sharp-edged. Shoe leather will wear them down eventually. Philadelphia steps are rounded, with depressions in their centers from gen-erations of footfalls. Even soft pressure wins if maintained long enough. But for now the stone prevails.

I pause at the bottom of the stairs. I do not, I realize, know exactly where to go. My instructions were to come to the Court at eight, only that. Casting my eyes about, I see a knot of men nearby. Some of them are looking at me, making no attempt to conceal their interest.

They are surely Court workers, perhaps even my fellow clerks. I look back, trying to appear friendly and inquisitive, open to advice but not lost with-out it. Then one of the faces strikes a note in my memory. There is a certain sameness to the people here; wherever I have gone in the city, the streets are crowded with dark-suited men, brushing past me with the indifferent arro-gance of high purpose. They are largely indistinguishable, and already today I have found myself pulling up, sure I've seen a face before. This one, though, I know from somewhere other than the sizzling sidewalks. A blond forelock dipping into the eyes, broad shoulders, a swagger of athletic grace . . .

"Haynes," I call triumphantly. "Phil Haynes."

He grins and trots toward me. I have met Haynes once or twice, I think, though not for several years. There was a boat involved; the memory is vague.

But I know his family, Boston folk acknowledged tolerable by proper Philadelphia. "Cash Harrison," I say.

"Of course." He takes my hand. "You're the new Black clerk. I'm with Frankfurter."

"What are you doing here?"

"We're waiting for you."

"So you're the welcoming committee?"

"Something like that."

The other men have been drifting over. My comrades, my brothers in arms. They helped decide the saboteurs' case; they did the nation's work. One of them pushes his way around Haynes. He is smaller and pale, with black curly hair. "Gene Gressman," he says. "With Justice Murphy. Welcome."

"Thanks," I say, and shake his hand.

He looks at me a moment. "So why don't you go up and knock on the doors?"

"That's what you do?"

"Sure it is."

I start up the steps, clutching my briefcase. The Art Museum has more, but the Court's risers are higher, and I feel as though I am ascending in some more than literal way. The levers of power, the Judge said. I missed the saboteurs, but I am here now. Reporting for duty. Walking up the sharp-edged steps, knocking on the massive bronze doors . . . waiting for them to open.

The doors remain closed, though, and as I knock again the insignificance of my fist against the metal tells me I've been had. From the bottom of the stairs the clerks watch; Gressman waves at me encouragingly. I feel a light touch on my hat brim, then my shoulder. There is a yellow-gray stain on my suit. I look up and spot a bird overhead, more droppings descending.

Squash is a fast game, and I still have the reflexes. I sidestep briskly, stumble on the steps, and shoot out my arms to catch myself. The briefcase flies from my hand, and I regain balance in time to watch it coast away. In Hawaii, men slide on boards down the sides of waves, and just like that my leather case descends the steps. As it nears the bottom, Phil Haynes steps forward and arrests it with his foot. The group claps, for which of us I am not sure.

He picks the briefcase up and starts climbing. I am thinking of what I will do to him when he reaches the top, but by the time he gets to me my anger has subsided. "This is how you greet all the new fellows?"

"I'm afraid so."

"Why?"

His shrug is eloquent, dismissive. "Ask Gene. It's his tradition." I look down the stairs. Gressman's arms are folded, his eyes fixed on us. Haynes claps me on the shoulder. "Come on, I'll show you the side door."

CHAPTER 5

TWO WEEKS LATER I am at my desk in Justice Black's chambers listening to the Ink Spots lament a missed Saturday dance. The song hits too close to home to enjoy. At Merion they will be crowding the floor, and girls will sing along softly into boys' necks, and boys will sing to girls' hair. It makes no sense, now that I think about it, for the song is about *not* dancing, and the only people in a position to sing along are the ones like me. But I do not feel like singing.

The Court's term will not begin until October, and with the saboteurs' case resolved, most of the Justices are away. Even those in town seldom visit the Court. The clerks are here, some nervous newcomers like me, projecting a shell of confidence, and some old hands at the end of their year. Haynes has only a few months more experience than I do, but he has put it to good use. He walks about in seersucker and a straw boater, greeting the marshals by name. Gene Gressman has been here two years already and is staying for more; the other clerks call him Mr. Justice Gressman and joke that he should write a book about Supreme Court practice. Owen Roberts has a married couple as a permanent clerk and secretary, but they are older and no one calls them anything.

I think we should come up with a better way of welcoming the new hires, but no one asks my opinion. As that first morning taught me, we do not go in the front doors. Those lead to the public areas of the Court, the profane. Tourists wander there, looking at the statues and marble busts. They rub John Marshall's toe, where the brass will soon wear bright; they gaze at us curiously through the gates. We are angels walking, or museum exhibits come to life. I am not sure how they think of us, or if they even know who we are. Either way, we are part of the Justices' space, a sacred realm the public cannot enter. Under the watchful eye of the Court's marshals, we take the side entrance and walk down vast marble corridors with thick red carpets. The Justices' chambers lie along these halls, and also four small courtyards in the interior of the building, open to the sky. We meet the public only in the courtroom, where the two worlds come together.

But we will not be there for a while yet. Without the Justices, we rattle around the enormous hallways like coins in a jar. We lunch together in a downstairs room set aside for that purpose, or one of the interior courtyards. We stand at the bottom of the front steps and send newcomers up to knock on the bronze doors and meet the starlings. We argue about the war, whether the Russians can hold in the West and whether Midway has turned the tide in the East; we bounce balls down the long spiral staircase. And in the rest of the time, which is most of the time, we work on certs.

The certs—petitions for certiorari—are the vehicles that bring cases to the Court. They arrive to the tune of a thousand a year; on my first day in the Black chambers I was ushered into a room where they covered the floor a foot deep. Now that room is my office and the petitions have moved to my desk, or the mobile bookshelves we load with files and case reporters. For each I write a one-page memo, typed on six-by-eight paper, summarizing the facts and making a recommendation as to whether the Court should hear the case, whether the petition should be granted or denied. Mostly they are to be denied. There are many thousands of people who want their cases heard, but the Court will take only cases that present issues of great importance, when the lower federal courts cannot agree.

Knowing that most petitions should be denied does not make the work go faster, and certs are a constant part of life even for the Justices. Black consumes cert petitions like a nervous man smokes cigarettes. He carries a stack with him at almost all times and pulls one out in any spare moment—in the middle of a meal, or a walk, or as a sign that I am losing his attention in conversation.

But Black can tear through a petition in minutes and read them anywhere. It takes me substantially longer, and since my memos are confidential, I can't write them at home. I stay at work late into the evenings, tapping out memos on an Underwood I've brought from Columbia. I hide the typewriter under a coat each evening; there is a shortage, and reportedly the administration renews its supply by taking them at random from office desks. I doubt anyone will come to the Supreme Court, but there's no point in taking chances.

Thus far, the job is little like my expectations, less like my dreams. The load is crushing, but the work itself is tedious, the boredom leavened only by the knowledge that with any one of these petitions I could be making a catastrophic error. Recommend a denial and I might bury an issue of national importance. Recommend a grant and I could be humiliated when the case turns out to be insignificant.

Petition after petition they come, an unending stream. I pore over each, trying to figure out if this is the one that will ruin me, and they arrive faster than I can read them. I am drowning in paper. I have not been out to a movie since starting work. I have not been back to Philadelphia once. For the first time in my life, I am dealing with sustained and intense sleep deprivation, and handling it turns out not to be one of my strengths. I am so tired that I am imagining things. As though my mind has energy for only a limited number of faces, I think that strangers on the street are people I've seen before. At the Court I fail to recognize people whom I do in fact know. I am short on the phone with Suzanne, who wonders what I could be doing that is so important while the Justices are away. I am, in brief, a mess.

I reach to the little radio and change the station. I have brought it to keep me awake, a function it serves after a fashion. This being a Saturday night, there is the *Lucky Strike Hit Parade*. But the music annoys me. The songs are about squabbles, separation, lost love. The Mills Brothers have quarreled with Sue; that's why they're blue. She's gone away and left them just like all dolls do. Pleasant enough if you're swaying with a warm armful, just trying out the accents of grief. Less so if you have in fact just quarreled with someone named Suzanne, if you have heard that three straight weekends in Washington are not a promising sign.

Other men are around, the 4Fs and the older ones, but also the boys in uniform who haven't shipped out yet, burning with a doomed glory. And there is Suzanne, all by herself. Her friends are getting married and she has nothing to do but knock around the house in Haverford while the Judge mumbles in his study. Of course she wants to get out every once in a while, to see a movie, to ride the wood-embowered Wissahickon trails. If John Hall comes up on leave and stops by, well, they're old friends. It's only natural. It's purely innocent.

So she says, and I can't dispute it. The problem is of my making, and even as John Hall's grinning mug swims before my eyes I know her stories are mostly for my enlightenment and edification. Mostly. Would I rather have a paper doll to call my own than a fickle-minded real, live girl? I consider the possibility and decide against it. I have had enough of paper. What I want is to be out at the club, watching the sun set over the new-cut lawn, to be in a movie theater with her at my side, watching images dance across the screen heedless of the sun's height.

I take a sip of my coffee and frown at the bitter taste. I didn't drink coffee in college, or even law school, and I've picked a poor time to start. Sugar has been rationed since May, and laughing stewards in the Court cafeteria tell me not to worry because coffee is next. What I want is to be in a malt shop, hearing the last of an ice cream soda rattle through a striped straw.

Down the hallway footsteps approach, accompanied by a whistled tune. Justice Black whistles while he walks, but he has taken his family to Alabama, and this is not him, returned early. He whistles a song he calls "All Policemen Have Big Feet," which I know as "London Bridge." The one coming down the hall now is more complicated, though still somehow familiar. As I struggle to place it, the chambers door opens.

The man who enters is someone I have not seen before, but only one of the Justices would walk in so casually. Neatly trimmed silvery hair, a suit of English cut, features that resemble Claude Rains.

I hurry to switch off the radio. "Are you looking for Justice Black?"

The man smiles. "No, I wouldn't think to find my brother Black in chambers at this time of evening. He keeps banker's hours." He crosses to the desk and offers a hand; I rise to shake it. "Felix Frankfurter," he says, the voice lightly accented.

"Caswell Harrison," I answer. "Justice Black works at home." I have not seen much of Black, but even so I feel a loyalty to him.

"Working at home is an easy way to slack off," Frankfurter says. He touches his lapel. "Like working in casual clothes."

I am wearing a suit myself, so I merely nod in response. "And Hugo would not be listening to such jaunty music," Frankfurter continues. He inclines his head toward the radio. "No, I stopped in to welcome a new colleague. But what are you doing here so late?"

"Certs," I say. He smiles, and I continue. "It takes me forever to get through them, and at the end I don't even know if I've done it right. It seems a big responsibility."

The silvery head nods. "The Court is a place of great responsibility. It is a temple of truth. We who work here must dedicate ourselves to worship and service." Suddenly he is leaning closer and his eyes are searching mine and the words come louder. "And if you have come here for any other purpose you will be disappointed."

I hold his gaze, mystified. "I can assure you I have not, Mr. Justice."

For another moment Frankfurter's face quivers. Then whatever it is leaves him and he smiles again. "Do not worry yourself about the certs. If you're not scared stiff to begin with, you might as well fold up. But having once plunged in, to question your fitness every day—you know, that way madness lies." He pauses. "I used to pick Brother Black's clerks, when I was still a professor. Good Harvard men, but none of them any finer than you, Cash."

I frown at the nickname. "You know me?"

There is ease and pleasure in his face now. "Knowing things is my business. And Herbert Wechsler and I are good friends. Do not doubt yourself. You are one of us now."

"A little too late, maybe. I feel like I missed the action."

"You wish you'd been here for the saboteurs' case," he says. "That's the spirit. We served law and war together."

I remember the news stories. A tribute to democracy, the papers said.

Proof that in the citadel of liberty, law and justice still function. "And now I'm doing certs."

Frankfurter leans across the desk, taking hold of my elbow. "Perhaps you feel useless," he says. "Sidelined. Many do, even among my Brethren."

"I was supposed to fight," I tell him. "I flunked the physical." I feel a small sense of shame at the admission, but also some relief. Now it is out in the open.

Frankfurter nods. "Your ankles. I have heard. Well, I will not be carrying a rifle either. But we are still part of the struggle."

"I don't know," I say. "I have classmates in uniform." Bill Fitch, with his curls cut short. His father pulled strings to get him into the Army Air Force, I heard, thinking he'd be safer. "I think about what they're doing, and all this seems . . ."

"So far removed? It is not, though. You read what happened. The enemy came to kill our fellows, and we meted out his fate. It is the stroke of a pen, not a sword, but the same responsibility." Something kindles in his eyes. "You must be willing to do it, Cash. That is what it means to be a judge. You cannot write that opinion unless you would pull the trigger yourself."

"I'm not going to be writing opinions, though. I'm just a clerk."

Frankfurter's smile has a different aspect now, one conspirator to another. His shirt is fine white cotton, his cufflinks onyx. "Oh, clerks can be influential," he says. "If I could be my brother Black's clerk for one year, the law would be much improved. I won't keep you from your work. But I will advise you to enjoy some music while you labor. And if you would like variety, you might try standing. I always write standing up at a lectern. It stimulates the flow of blood to the head. I learned it from Holmes; that's the way he wrote."

He walks out. After a moment's thought I resume my seat and turn the radio back on. Before me on the desk lies a paper in which a farmer argues that he should be allowed to grow wheat free from government quotas. It is the kind of case the Court would have jumped at five years ago, when it was doing battle against the New Deal. But then Roosevelt announced his plan to pack the Court with his sympathizers. Owen Roberts changed sides, and the rest of the old guard stepped down or died. The Four Horsemen are long gone; of the nine Justices now sitting, Roosevelt has appointed seven. In their eyes, there is nowhere the arm of Congress cannot reach. Still, I think this petition is worth hearing. It will be my first grant recommendation, and just typing the word makes me nervous.

I push the typewriter away and lean back in my chair. Despite Frankfurter's advice, I am second-guessing myself. Not just on the petition, but on the whole matter of coming here. The work is not what I thought it would be. And Washington is not Philadelphia. Neither is any other place in the world, of course, but Washington is not in a particular, distinctive way. It has customs and culture of its own. People are too busy to talk, or they speak only of politics and can't be silenced. And underneath the chatter and ostentatiously hurried walk runs another thread, one I cannot quite grasp. I see it here at the Court and outside, too. Frankfurter's strange allusions, the way a man looks at me on the street. Something is happening that I do not understand.

CHAPTER 6

THE NEXT DAY at noon I am working on certs when I hear a shuffle of steps and the familiar notes of "London Bridge." I look up as the door opens and Black enters, felt hat on his head, battered suitcase filled with petitions of his own. He deposits the hat and suitcase without a word, gathers up his mail, and proceeds to his private room. Ten minutes later his head pokes through the door. "Seems a shame to waste the sun," he says. "Come on, Cash, what do you say?"

"What?"

"You say 'what'?" He walks to my desk and leans toward me. "Is that supposed to be funny?"

I sit bolt upright. "No, Justice. I just—I don't—"

Black interrupts. "Call me Judge. That's what the Constitution says."

"Yes, Judge. I don't know what you're talking about."

"Tennis, son." Black sits down on the corner of the desk; I edge back. "They weren't lying about that backhand, were they?"

"I suppose it depends on what they said."

"That's a good answer. Now you're getting funny."

"But Judge, I have twenty certs to do today."

"And that one's bad. Why do you swoop after you soar? A man needs exercise. You'll do more work, and you'll do it better."

Are these the predicted results of exercise, or an unrelated command? I cannot tell, but I grab my hat and follow him out the door.

We proceed to the Court's basement garage. "I'll drive this time," Black tells me. "You can once you know the way." He pulls out into traffic. "People seem to feel uncomfortable with me behind the wheel. I guess they think a Justice shouldn't be driving himself. I don't mind, of course, but if it makes you feel better . . ." His voice trails off as he changes lanes rapidly. I grip the seat, thinking that his companions' discomfort has a different source.

Black drives as though only speed and not direction is essential to travel and tends when talking to lose track of his surroundings. It is a relief when he makes a rapid turn into a driveway half hidden by overgrown privet. Gravel crunches under the wheels. "Stay away from that tree," he warns, gesturing toward a buckeye at the edge of the drive.

"The nuts fall?"

He shakes his head. "Birds. They'll get you every time. Deadly stuff. Eats through the paint in minutes."

I nod. Bird droppings are playing a larger-than-expected role in my Supreme Court clerkship.

Black pulls his briefcase from the backseat and shuts the door loudly. He spreads his arms to encompass the house standing before us. "What do you think of the old place?"

I am unsure what to say. *Small* is my first thought, a red brick Federalist with two dormer windows emerging from the tiled roof. It would be fair-sized for a Philadelphia row house, but standing alone in Alexandria it is a good deal less impressive. By Haverford standards it is a cottage. Black smiles. "You can't see what I've done to it." He leads me around the side, gesturing. "Used to be a slave shanty here. Knocked it down myself." Another wave directs my attention to a sprawling garden. "And that was the house next door. I bought that, knocked it down too, and now we're in business."

"I'm amazed you have the time, Judge," I say.

"There's time for everything worth doing," he answers. "Problem is there's too many things not worth doing competing for that time. You know anything about a garden?"

"I see you've got roses," I say. "And wistaria." The familiar purple trail creeps along the top of the wall. "Named for Caspar Wistar, properly pronounced to rhyme with malaria, not diphtheria."

"What?"

"He was a Philadelphian. We keep track of each other."

"You do?"

"It's what Judge Skinner always told me. He was a friend growing up."

"Oh," says Black, nodding. "Old Sam Skinner." There is amusement in his voice, but no warmth. He points to a different vine. "Well, what do you have to say about these?"

My knowledge is exhausted. "Those are grapes."

"Scuppernong," Black pronounces with enthusiasm. "From Alabama." He plucks a clump, large and bronze, and hands me one. "Squeeze it out into your mouth. Not the seeds." With a practiced motion he flattens a grape against his teeth, extracting the pulp and leaving the seeds in the empty skin. Mine explodes against my lips, viscous and sweet. I pick a piece of pulp from my face, and Black laughs. "You'll get the hang of it." He opens the garden gate. "And now it's time for the main attraction."

When we get around the back, I can see why the house is so small. In addition to the half-acre garden, Black has a clay tennis court. "Designed it myself," he says. "Now you can show me that backhand I've been hearing about. There's some clothes in the house. I think you're about Sterling's size."

Black isn't particularly good, but he is serious about his game. "The Senate doctor told me no man in his forties should play singles, so I waited till I was fifty," he tells me cheerfully. "I can still beat both my sons. And now that I've switched to an Eastern grip I think I'm safe for another five years."

Not from me. Black and I have similar styles—we are both retrievers, cautious, letting the other man make the mistakes. But my shots are better and I am faster. I win the first set we play, 6–2. Black leans on the net post, gasping. "Let's try it again. I think I can beat you." His wife, Josephine, has come and gone, her sky-blue eyes flashing amusement, but their five-year-old, little JoJo, is still watching from the shade of a peach tree. "Go get us some V8," he calls, and she scampers off, blonde and precious. "My orange juice is over Hitler's rooftops," Black says, quoting a War Information poster. "V8's better for you anyway."

By the second set I have learned to anticipate his only dangerous shot, a tricky forehand sliced down the line, spinning so it curves out of the court.

I am serving at 4–1 when he tries it in desperation. I am there in plenty of time, sliding into position on the red clay, racquet accelerating into the stroke . . . and suddenly I am on my back, looking up at the sky. I turn my head slightly to the left. The wall I collided with is inches from my face.

"Sorry," Black calls. He walks around the net, hand raised in apology. "Not a lot of space there. You're not used to it."

"That's okay," I say. I flex my fingers experimentally. Nothing's broken, but I've lost some skin from the knuckles. "I think I'll call it a day."

"No you won't," says Black. His voice is no longer apologetic. "You'll keep going."

"My hand's a little sore."

"You think you can quit and it won't matter," Black says. "What's a tennis game? Give up and go on. But one day you'll find something where if you don't keep going, you might as well be dead. That's what I'm training you for."

I look at the spots of blood on my knee. "I wanted to talk about some of the certs, Judge." I rack my brain for a viable case. "There are these children who don't want to recite the Pledge of Allegiance."

"We'll get to that," Black says. "Right now I want to see that backhand."

• • • •

It is getting dark as we go to shower, and by the time I am dressed again Black is out in the garden, watering. In the twilight he names the plants for me as he goes. "Those are turnips," he says, "and rhododendrons here. Rosa rugosa— easy to take care of." A glossy beetle clings to a pink petal, and he strikes it to the ground and stamps on it. "Where I'm fighting the Japs."

A flicker of annoyance passes through me. "To save the roses," I say. It is all irrelevant: the certs, the tennis, the flowers.

Black turns to me with a look that suggests I have his full attention. "Do what you can," he says, "with what you have, where you are." A moment, and he's back to his task, shifting the nozzle with a practiced flick of the wrist. Arcs of water hang unsupported in the air, glistening and falling. Black coils the hose. "You see how I'm doing this," he says. "Set it right, it'll coil itself next time. Let it go wrong once, it wants to do that forever. You'll understand when you have children."

A grill is heating on the porch. Black ties an apron around his waist and puts steaks down to sizzle. He tends them with a parent's care, flipping, prodding, sprinkling spices. By the time he lifts them off, I can see they are ruined. "Here, lamb," he says, as Josephine joins us.

"Thank you," she says, smiling with real gratitude as he offers a plate. But she raises her eyebrows at me as I take my first bite and stifles laughter at my reaction.

"A doctor fellow told me to eat steak every day," Black says. "I've done my best to follow his advice."

"It keeps him young," Josephine says. I nod, cut another piece, and move it to the opposite side of the plate. She smiles. "A perfect stranger came by here once, you know," she says. "He just rang our doorbell and asked if this was a public court. I told him no. But Hugo saw him over my shoulder and offered to play." She tucks a strand of hair behind one ear, a girlish gesture. In New York, the women have started using dye, one of many things that are not done in Philadelphia. In Washington, the propriety is debated, but Josephine abstains. She is more than a decade younger than her husband, but her hair has gone mostly gray, almost white in places. Still, when she turns those blue eyes on you it is easy to see how Black decided no other woman would do. Her attention pours out hungrily; it makes you feel that you are the most important person in the world.

"I beat him, too," Black adds. He has almost finished his steak. "So, Cash. Better than an afternoon of certs, isn't it?"

My feelings are mixed. "They'll still be there tomorrow, though."

"Exactly." He exhales with satisfaction. "Cash is just about a match for Sterling," he says to Josephine. "And of a size. Couple times there I thought it was him on the other side of the net." He doesn't notice her face change. "The backhand, though . . ."

At first I cannot figure out why she is looking at me that way. Then I understand. I wore the whites of her drafted son. We are of a size, we move the same way across the tennis court. She is wondering why I could not put on the uniform instead, wondering if some magic can still exchange our fates. And I have no answer, no reason it should be him and not me, only that my chance to take his place fled when the doctor smiled through his beard and shut the folder on my war.

"He'll be back soon," I say, and the lie tastes like metal on my tongue.

Josephine ignores that. She has risen from the table and is at the kitchen window, looking out into the garden. There is the twilit tennis court, there are the roses and rhododendrons. But I know she is seeing something else. The camouflage netting of a Tiger tank, the backswept wings of a Stuka. Her son in olive drab and the glinting tip of a Japanese bayonet. On the sill her hands clench and release, grasping for something that isn't there. "If it's not him, it's someone else. Someone else's mother." Her eyes turn down. "Someone else's son. I can't wish that on them." Her voice drops to a whisper. I can barely hear, but she is not speaking for me. She is speaking for the fates, who hear even the faintest words. "But I do."

Black steps to her and puts a hand on her shoulder. "Lamb," he says. When she turns, her face is empty, and she walks right past him, out of the room and up the stairs.

There is nothing I can do for Sterling, but suddenly I feel it would be enough just to suffer with her. I want to beat my head against the wall, feel blood run down my face. Anything to be a part of the struggle. But I am on the sidelines, and grief is a place she goes alone. "I should go."

"Sit down," Black says. He comes back to the table. "She has moods sometimes." He takes the steak from Josephine's plate to his own, cuts a piece, and begins chewing as though it is the most important thing in the world. "First case I had, you know what it was about? A litter of pigs."

"At the Supreme Court?"

"No, son." Black rolls his eyes. "When I was in Birmingham. I got my start as a lawyer there. Some fellow's sow wandered onto my client's land, paid a visit to his hog."

"I should—"

"Then she left, of course. Females. But I got him half the litter. Pressed the hog's parental rights."

"I've got to get back to the certs," I say.

Black chews for another moment, looking at me. "They'll be there tomorrow."

"And so will new ones. Sorry, Judge, I'm not as fast at it as you are."

Finally he nods, releasing me. "Keep at it. You'll get better. Remember, exercise helps." He raises his fork, a chunk of leathery meat speared on the tines. "And you should eat more steak."

CHAPTER 7

"YOU DOING OKAY, buddy?" Phil Haynes's fine features crinkle with concern.

I look around the lunchroom. "Of course I am." At a table in the corner, Gene Gressman sits by himself consuming simultaneously a thick sandwich and the day's paper. The noises he is making suggest that each is subject to the same lip-smacking appraisal, or perhaps that there is some degree of confusion between the two. "It's just . . ."

"What?"

"What am I doing here?"

"You're eating lunch."

"Yeah." I poke a slice of chicken with my fork. "And I'm playing tennis. And doing certs. It doesn't add up to much."

"It's still summer," he says. "The good cases will be coming. And certs are important. There's the Pledge of Allegiance . . ." His voice trails off. "Something else is on your mind."

I nod, confessing.

"What is it?"

"I don't even know, really."

"You can tell me."

I hesitate. "Something just seems off."

"What do you mean?"

I bite my lower lip. How to express it, when I don't fully know myself? "You remember when I first got here, you told me the cafeteria was no good, I should go out for breakfast?"

Haynes nods.

"So I went to Eastern Market." The market is one streetcar stop past the Court, a large brick building a few blocks east of the Capitol. Crates of apples and peaches crowd the sidewalk, green lettuce lies on beds of ice. "There was a guy there."

"Several, I'd expect."

"Not in the market, in the back. I went out the wrong door, ended up by the loading docks. And he came in after me. Guy in a gray suit."

"So?"

"He looked at me funny."

"Well, you weren't supposed to be there."

"It wasn't that kind of a look." I try to bring the scene back in my mind. "It was more like he was scared. And he didn't tell me I shouldn't be there. He just turned right around and walked away. Ran, almost."

Haynes lifts a beet to his mouth. The fork clicks on his teeth. "I gotta say, pal, you're not making a whole lot of sense here."

"Well, I remembered him because it seemed so odd. That he'd be scared of me. And then last night I saw him again."

"Really?"

I nod. After dinner at Black's house, I went back to the Court and spent an hour doing certs. When I left, my head filled with legal argument, I walked four blocks toward the trolley before I realized I'd forgotten my hat. I turned around to go back, and there was a man half a block or so behind me. He turned too, ducking away. I only caught a glimpse of his face, but something seemed familiar. And then, as he moved out of the streetlights and vanished into the shadow, I realized what it was. The gray suit receding, passing from one pool of light to another. That was the man from Eastern Market.

"You might have noticed," Haynes says, "that there's more than one guy with a gray suit in this town."

"I really think it was him."

"So you think he was following you? Why would anyone do that?"

"I don't know. But we just had the saboteurs' case here. What if there are more of them?"

"Oh," says Haynes. He nods his head. "I get it now. You feel like you missed out. You want some connection to the war. So you imagine the Nazis are after you."

"Someone is."

"Or maybe you're worried you don't deserve to be here. Black made a mistake in choosing you. You think everyone's staring at you, like they know you don't belong."

I frown. "I don't think that about everyone." On the other side of the lunchroom, Gene Gressman's newspaper rustles. Suddenly I am sure he is listening to us. I lower my voice. "But right now, for instance—"

Haynes doesn't let me finish. "Something like that. You're inventing things to make yourself feel special." He flutters his fingers in the air. "People following you. You must be important if they're doing that, right? It helps you feel like you deserve the job." I must look skeptical, for he leans closer and puts a hand on my arm. "You're here for a reason, Cash. Don't ever doubt that."

"I'm not doubting it," I say. "But the way that guy looked at me, there was—"

Haynes interrupts again. "No, there wasn't." His smile is back, easy and confident, and he pats my shoulder encouragingly. "Trust me. No one's trying to get you." He picks up his own newspaper, scans the headlines, and grunts.

"What?"

"Two Japs shot trying to escape from a camp in New Mexico. Look, you need a little break. Drive back home for the afternoon."

"I have too much work."

"Justice Black will understand. Say you need to see your girl. It'll do you a world of good. Just do me a favor, pal. Don't go around telling too many people you've got Nazis on your trail."

CHAPTER 8

HAYNES IS RIGHT about one thing, I decide. It is time to get away from the Court, to get back to something I understand. Three hours' drive to Haverford, another three for the return—I won't have much time there, but it will be worth it to see the look on Suzanne's face.

But she is not home. Gone into town, the housekeeper says, but expected to call in. "Tell her to meet me at the eagle," I say. Already my plan is coming apart. Another half hour to drive into the city, who knows how long before Suzanne gets the message. I assured Black I would not fall behind on my cert work. As I get back into the car, I feel a twinge of pain in my neck.

Montgomery Avenue takes me east toward Philadelphia, right past the Merion Cricket Club. A pair of stone pillars marks the gate; behind them I can see the red brick of the clubhouse, the peaked windows with cricket bats crossed in stained glass. The flags are flying, the white MCC on a field of dark maroon, and next to it the stars and stripes. Off to the right lies the great lawn, chalked for tennis. For a moment my shoulders loosen. Everything feels right again.

I remember the childhood Easter egg hunts on the great lawn, my first steps on the squash courts, the afternoons spent watching our stars. And the evenings, with the red summer sun sinking low and the voices of the young at play rising from the deep-shadowed lawn. The brick glowed; the day's heat ebbed from the wooden decks. Inside old men read in silence, sunk into leather chairs, wreathed in smoke from pipes and cigars. We were the boys in white ducks, the girls in flowered dresses, gardenias in their hair. We ran about the clubhouse laughing madly; we turned audacious waltzes across the ballroom; we wandered outside into the heavy dusk, alone or in pairs, losing ourselves in the scent of cut grass and the small white flowers of the privet. I felt sorry that my dancing friends would become the fat Scotch drinkers who eyed us from tables, the old men shivering in their red-striped club blazers, the widows with gorgeous jewels and crumpled paper skin—sorry, though in my heart I still believed it impossible. I never wondered what they thought watching us.

The past gains sweetness as it recedes, our golden cohort forever on the edge of adulthood. That was summer, burnished by loss. Those things are no longer in my world, replaced by hours in the law school library, caustic professors, memorized rules. And now the sweltering streets of Washington, the cool marble corridors of the Supreme Court. A strange man behind me on the street. Summer and then fall and now the smoky taste of winter in the night.

Coming up on the river, I can see willows standing along the bank, boathouses, and on the water itself an eight-man shell skidding like a bug. There is the familiar golden temple of the Art Museum, and the silhouette of Center City, John Kelly's brickwork rising crimson against the blue.

It isn't a Manhattan skyline; no buildings go any higher than the peak of William Penn's hat, where he stands atop City Hall. Nothing in the world passed Penn's hat until 1908, when the Singer Building went up in New York. Now the point that marked Philadelphia as the top is a self-imposed limit holding us back. But that is the idea. "The city does not know what it is now," Judge Skinner told me. "Only that it is not New York."

I park the car near Suburban Station, step out onto Pennsylvania Boulevard, and head east. This is the way I used to walk to the Judge's courthouse, when I would come from the University to see him hurl lightning across the room. Philadelphia runs twenty-four blocks east to west, people say, but only five north to south. Every place you hear of—every club, restaurant, theater, and shop—is just around the corner. It is enough to make you wonder what's in the rest of the city. But Philadelphians do not wonder. We stay in the great country to which we owe our allegiance, which stretches five blocks by twenty-four and out along the railroad tracks, the Main Line colonies and the Center City motherland. And all around us, like the black space of a photographic negative, lies the vast, unapproachable America that tells us who we are not.

One block south to Market Street. Already I can feel sweat starting on my face. The heat grips you and wrings your water out; it pulls damp spots onto the hatbands and jackets of passersby. Now I stand before the granite mass of Wanamaker's Grand Depot. Inside, the marble floors are cool. The central atrium rises seven stories, a tower of air carved from the stone. It is home to the world's largest pipe organ, brought from the St. Louis World's Fair. By the console on the ground floor is a ten-foot bronze eagle, which I admire for almost an hour before Suzanne arrives.

She is wearing a deep green skirt and has pinned her hair up. It is a more serious style, but she isn't old enough to look serious. She just looks beautiful.

"Cash!" she cries as she approaches. "What are you doing here?"

"I wanted to surprise you."

"Well, you did." She throws her arms around my neck and kisses my cheek. "What shall we do now?"

Her hair smells like a summer in Maine. "I don't have very much time."

Suzanne does not seem to hear me. "I know," she says. "We'll go up to the Crystal Room and have tea."

I can feel my face tightening. "I can't. I have to go back to Washington."

"You just got here."

Haynes was right, I realize. The work is important. There will be big cases. Even the certs matter; they're my chance to help decide which cases the Court will hear. "No, you just got here. I've been standing around for an hour."

A different look comes into Suzanne's eyes. "Well, I didn't know that."

"What were you in town for, anyway?"

"Shopping."

"You don't like to shop."

"There's not much to do with you away." She shakes her head. "Cash, this isn't what was supposed to happen."

"What do you mean?"

"I know we're at war, and you're doing something important, and it's not just drive-ins and ice cream sodas for anyone anymore. But I miss you. I miss your voice and your hands and the way I feel in your arms. I was so scared for you, and then I was so happy, and now it seems like all this was just another way of losing you."

She turns away. From behind I can see her long and slender neck, a curl of hair that has escaped the bobby pins and lies, fernlike, on the nape. Suzanne dabs at her eyes and I look off to the side. Men in uniform pass in the background.

"I know it's hard," I say. "It's hard for me, too. But this is my chance."

"Your chance for what?"

"To do something more."

Suzanne turns back now. Something flickers in her green eyes. Before I can tell whether it's pity or anger or sorrow, it is gone again. "My father said that to you," she says. "I mean, the Judge did. But you know, Cash, everyone wants something more. It's not what people want that makes them different. It's what they're willing to give up."

"I want to do something that's mine," I say. "That my father didn't give me, or your father for that matter."

"Something that's yours." There is an odd high note in her laugh, one I can't recall hearing before.

"What?"

"He's good." She shakes her head. "A nameless patch of foreign ground or the Main Line rosary. I heard that speech. He practiced it on me. Working at the Court is wonderful, and I'm glad you're doing it, but that's not what's yours."

"What is, then?"

Suzanne hesitates a moment, her lips parted. "I am, Cash." Now her eyes are pleading. "I'm what's yours."

I don't know what to say. Behind the face I know, I can suddenly see other faces I remember. Here is Suzanne Skinner, the little sister of my best friend, Bob, who tagged along with us to movies, and I see her round and serious face set in defiance when we tell her to go home. Here is Suzanne Skinner, the little girl running along the dock at Northeast Harbor, and I see her eyes go big as she wraps skinny arms around her knees and jumps off the end in a shrieking ball.

The Judge's house and my father's were near each other, on the leeward side of Smallidge Point, and the dock was sheltered enough that you could swim if you were brave, for a little while at least, until the sea reminded you that you were a creature of warmth and air and light and had best be getting back to your own world. Year after year we tested our endurance against the cold and sailed to the islands and roasted corn and lobster. Year after year we played tennis and explored the pine forests and bicycled to Jordan Pond when the salt sea's chill was too great. And it seemed timeless, for although we grew bigger and stronger, we were still children, and children never foresee childhood's end.

But then came a summer when the air changed, or I did, and certainly she did, and we were not children anymore. Bob was in town and we swam in the ocean, though she no longer jumped in a shrieking ball. We wrapped ourselves in towels against the cold, and when we were warm enough we lay on our stomachs on the dock, with our heads turned to the side, so that I studied her damp cornsilk hair and she looked out over the water. And then we lay on our backs, with our arms at our sides, and the sun in the blue sky coaxed a sweet resiny smell out of the pine boards and shone so bright that my closed eyelids glowed as though crowned with halos.

I tasted the salt on my lips and in the back of my nose, and I lowered my eyes to where the glow was less. Then I opened them just a slit, looking down my nose through the drops that still clung on my lashes, and I saw my hand, and another hand next to it. And I thought for a while about how close they were, and how all of the years we'd lived and all the miles we'd traveled had brought us to this spot and this second and not a couple inches closer.

You can say that about any moment in your life, of course, and any place you are, but it seemed true for this one, which was full with something as though the past had piled up inside and waited to burst out into the future. But it was still waiting, and the fullness made those inches seem very important, so important they couldn't be crossed in the second it would take to put my hand in hers. So I shut my eyes again and let my hand lie there and almost jumped when I felt her fingers on my palm.

I opened my eyes fully, and she opened hers, and she smiled quickly at me. It was the same smile I had been seeing for fifteen years, but it was different, and the face was different, which I had been seeing for fifteen years. Her hand stayed there just long enough to show me it wasn't an accident. Then she was pushing herself up and diving off the dock so that as I struggled to a sitting position and shielded my eyes from the sun I could only see the water falling back on the spot she'd gone in.

But I remembered her hand in mine.

And I remember that face that smiled at me on the dock, which is now the face looking at me in Wanamaker's, and I wonder at how the connection between two things that are so distinct can be so hazy, for I find I don't really know how we got from there to here.

"I'm what's yours," Suzanne repeats, and in her face I see all the faces.

"And I'm yours," I say, and I lean forward and kiss her quickly. Then I step back, and before she can contradict me or tell me not to promise what won't come true, I'm away and out the door.

The hot air hits me like a wall, and I think again of the waves lapping the dock at Northeast Harbor, the warm water lying atop the cold. Sometimes it was just a skin that you'd pierce without noticing, sometimes a thicker layer, like a cloudbank afloat. But if you dove more than a few feet it would get cold indeed, till it took your breath and you'd have to turn back. That was how that summer felt, as though each day was a step further into a realm that chilled me with awe. But now there is nothing but heat, and I am stepping from the cool of memory back to the present, to the world where schoolchildren refuse to recite the Pledge and Justice Black asks to see my backhand.

CHAPTER 9

HAYNES WAS RIGHT about everything, I decide on the drive back. I didn't have any time to see Suzanne, but just being back in the familiar world of Philadelphia was enough to calm me down. Of course the work is important. And of course my suspicions were silly. Why would anyone want to follow me?

In Washington I reach to put the key in my apartment door and it swings open at the touch. All my calm vanishes in an instant. The Nazis have come for me after all. This is it. There will be a trench-coated figure seated at the table, a Luger and a glass of my Scotch in the pool of lamplight before him. "Ve haff a proposition, Mr. Harrison." I back halfway down the hall before I reconsider. If they are clever enough to get past the doorman and enter my apartment, they are probably clever enough to lock the door behind them. Leaving it on the latch is the mark of an overworked and tired man, not a Nazi superspy. The mark, in fact, of someone like me.

Slowly I push the door open and creep inside. My heart beats a little faster as I flick on the light, but sure enough, the apartment is empty. I set my hat on the rack, shrug out of my jacket, and loosen my tie. I open the sliding paper screen that serves as a closet door and take down a coat hanger. Then I stop. There on the floor of the closet is a muddy footprint. I step into it, trying to remember how that might have happened, and my shoe doesn't fit. And for a long time, I stand like an idiot inside my closet, looking down at the print of someone else's shoe on my waxed cherry floor.

. . . .

The next morning I go straight to the Marshal's office. In deference to Haynes, I do not mention Nazis. I feel like I'm being followed, I say. I wonder if someone could check that out.

The Marshal is a kindly looking man, middle-aged and quilted with comfortable flesh. His haircut suggests a military background; his tone is reassuring. "We observe everyone on the Court grounds," he says.

Would it be possible, I inquire, to have someone with me elsewhere?

Now there is an edge of suspicion in his voice. "We provide security details for the Justices," he says. "If they request. You clerk for Justice Black, is that right?"

"Never mind," I tell him. The last thing I want is the Marshal informing Black that his new clerk is exhibiting the onset of dementia praecox. I walk back to my desk and sit down in front of a pile of cert petitions. Then I notice a new piece of paper, a handwritten note. *Meet me at the Uptown*, it says. *Eight p.m.*

I do as much work as I can in the morning, which is little enough, and get Black to stop the tennis early by losing the third set so abjectly he shakes his head in disappointment. "I thought you were learning something." And by a quarter of eight, with a tightness in my belly attributable only in part to the indigestible steak lodged there, I am standing in front of the Uptown Cinema on Connecticut Avenue.

The theater has a Deco brick facade and a marquee promoting *Mr. Lucky* in large black letters. Double glass doors show my reflection. Across the street the hill falls away toward Rock Creek Park; down Connecticut to the right is the National Zoo. Evening is a feeding time, and primal cries rise above the traffic. I look from side to side along the street and am caught by surprise when Gene Gressman walks out from the box office with a tub of popcorn in one hand.

"You're a trusting sort," he says. "To come here all alone."

"What makes you think I'm alone?"

Gressman laughs and dips his hand into the popcorn. "Ah, Cash. Don't try to be someone you're not." He chews in silence for a moment, watching me. "This is the part where you ask me why we're here."

"Why are we here?"

"Because it's not safe to talk at the Court."

"What?"

He gives a surprisingly full-throated laugh. "No, I just wanted to see a movie. You like Cary Grant?"

"Doesn't everyone?"

"Well, come on. I got you a ticket." He shakes the popcorn bucket at me and takes a step toward the doors.

I remain where I am. "No, really, why are we here?"

"We're going to see a movie," Gressman says. His voice has grown more serious. "Then we're going to talk."

The theater is huge; it must hold a thousand or more. The walls are lined in cloth and the seats are red velvet, even up in the peanut gallery, where Gressman leads me. We are almost alone in the balcony, twenty feet above the main floor.

Mr. Lucky gives us Cary Grant as the draft-dodging gambler Joe Adams, falling for the society heiress he's set out to fleece. I understated it, answering Gressman's question. I love Cary, with his tumbler's walk, his nimbus of poise and grace. Nothing about him is accidental; all is chosen, created, crafted with purpose. We watch as Joe abandons his schemes and turns his gambling boat into a war relief vessel, sailing for ravaged Europe instead of the beaches of Havana. By the end he has made himself a hero, stepping out of the fog into her arms as she waits on the dock.

"Reminds me of you, in a way," says Gressman, as the lights come up.

"Thanks," I say. "I've always liked his style."

The laugh is softer this time. "Not Cary. The society dame. Who can't see what's going on. But whoever's playing you might not be as soft-hearted as Joe Adams."

"What are you talking about?"

"I know some things. Who's following you, for one."

"So you were listening to us."

"It pays to keep your ears open."

Gressman's tone is unapologetic and his aftershave excessive. I have not even fully forgiven him for the stunt with the doors, but it is bad form to hold a grudge. And I want to hear what he has to say. Someone believes me. "All right, who is it?"

He leans in close, giving me a good whiff of Old Spice, and lowers his voice. "Nazis, looking for revenge."

"Jesus! I knew it."

Gressman laughs again. "You're obsessed with the war, aren't you? You're missing what's going on here."

"What's going on here?"

"Nothing with the Nazis."

"Then who?"

"The FBI."

"What? Why would they follow me?"

"Think about it." He leans back in his chair. "I was here for Pearl Harbor, you know. You must have still been in school."

"Columbia."

He nods. "I don't know what happened in New York, but there was panic here. Crowds running around, troops in the streets. We thought there would be another attack. We thought it was part of something bigger. There were soldiers around all the main buildings. People were hoarding food. And then for weeks afterward there was hysteria about spies. The FBI picked up a lot of people. Mostly aliens, mostly out West. But they grabbed some here, and they put some of the ones they didn't grab under surveillance. Citizens, too. I thought I saw some guys tailing me for a while."

"You did?"

"Sure. It actually makes sense for them to worry about the clerks. There are no confirmation hearings for us, no background checks; the Justices just bring in whomever they want. So now we're at war and the brass gets antsy, they ask Hoover to send some guys out. See who you're meeting with."

The lights are up now. We are totally alone in the balcony. In the theater below a uniformed usher sweeps candy wrappers down the aisle. "You really think the FBI would be worried about me?"

I didn't intend a comparison, but Gressman evidently perceives one.

Something flashes in his eyes. "Right," he says. "I'm a pinko from Brooklyn, but you. Why would anyone check you out? Maybe they just want to know where you got that suit."

There is a sharpness in his tone that I cannot account for. "There's a man in town," I say.

"Of course there is." Whatever it was passes across his face again and is gone. "Look, it's not you. I expect they watch everyone for a bit. It's just that you noticed."

"Maybe," I say. "But would they go in my apartment?" I explain about the footprint.

Gressman considers for a moment. "Interesting." He taps two fingers on his lips. "I don't know. But then again, how do you know how long the print's been there? Maybe it's from months ago."

I close my eyes, trying to remember. It's true; I can't swear I saw the floor clean before. Maybe when the manager carried out that folded mattress . . . "But what if it's not?"

"Well, it could be someone else. Lots of people would love to know what's going on inside the Court. There's plenty of money to be made if you know how cases are coming out."

"There is?" I have a hard time seeing how to turn a profit on Constitutional interpretation.

"Sure," says Gressman. "You know what's going to happen to some corporation, you can trade its stock. The boring business cases, that's where the money is. And there have been leaks. Sometimes Drew Pearson predicts results in the paper. Maybe they're trying to see if you leave confidential memos in restaurants."

"I'm very careful with Court papers," I say.

"Looking for leaks," he says. "You know, if that's what it is, it might be worth trying to catch them."

"How?"

"I've got an idea. I'll let you know when I figure it out."

"Okay." I pause a moment. "Hey, why do you do that thing with the doors?"

"The welcoming committee? Just to take the starch out. Show you you're no better than the rest of us."

"And why would I think I was?"

"Why, indeed?" The bitterness is back. "I can tell you, your pal Haynes took it pretty hard."

"Phil? Oh, he's okay."

"So you think. I have another tip for you. Figure out who your friends are."

"Phil Haynes is a good guy."

"Because he went to school with you?"

"No, he didn't. But we know some of the same people."

"Oh, well, in that case." Gressman shakes his head. "You may not know him as well as you think." He claps me on the shoulder and stands up. "Come on. We'll talk more tomorrow."

CHAPTER 10

I SIP MY coffee. It is bitter and growing cold, but I find I like it anyway. It helps me stay focused during the cert work, which has grown less terrifying and correspondingly more boring. Still, there's a reassuring rhythm, like the repetitive strokes of a squash practice. Reading petition after petition, like hitting shot after shot against the wall, knowing that nothing about them will ever change, but I might slowly grow to better fit that world.

"Have a nice time in Philadelphia?" Phil Haynes is at my door, jaunty in his boater.

"Yeah," I say. "That was a good idea. But someone broke into my apartment while I was away."

Haynes looks genuinely troubled. "How do you know?"

"The door was unlocked. And there was a footprint in my closet."

"So someone with a key." His skepticism is returning. "That sounds like the super."

"Or someone with a lock pick."

"Come on, Cash."

"Gene Gressman believes me."

"He does?"

"Well, he thought it was the FBI."

Haynes shakes his head. "You want to know something about Gene Gressman? Follow me."

We proceed down the hall to the Murphy chambers. Haynes pokes his head in the door to verify that Gene isn't there, then steps inside. "Hi, Rose," he says to the secretary. "We'll just be a second." He walks to Gene's desk. "Look at this."

"What?" It is a photograph, apparently clipped from the paper.

"Those are the Nazi saboteurs," Haynes says.

He is right; I recognize the picture now, the eight resigned faces. "So what?"

Haynes tilts his head toward Rose and waves me outside. "What?" I repeat in the hallway. "Are you saying he's a Nazi?"

"Of course not. But what kind of a guy keeps their picture on his desk?"

"I don't know. Did you ask him why?"

Haynes shakes his head. "I'm just saying you might not want to rely too much on his opinions. He's not . . ."

Before he can finish the sentence, Felix Frankfurter rounds the corner. He smiles at us. "Cash," he says. "I've been hoping to see you."

"Why is that, Justice?"

"The Pledge of Allegiance," he says. "The Court should not consider this case at all. But I fear there are votes to take it up."

I try to remember my memo about the petition. I recommended a denial, I think, on the grounds that the issue was settled. Of course children can be required to pledge allegiance. The Court itself said so, just two years ago. Frankfurter wrote the opinion. Now that I think about it, though, the fact that the children's lawyers thought it worth filing a petition must mean some Justices have changed their minds. "I haven't discussed it with Justice Black."

"You know we live by symbols," says Frankfurter. "The flag covers us all."

"Yes, Justice." It is the only response I can think of.

"I brought the Brethren together for the saboteurs' case," Frankfurter goes on. "When it seemed they could not agree. And not with logic or doctrine, Cash, but with love of country. We must not fail now."

"No, Justice."

"Those men were enemies, Cash. They got what they deserved. We could do nothing else. Law is a tool to administer justice. And when it does not serve justice . . ." He hesitates. "Well, justice must be served."

"What was that about?" I ask Haynes, when Frankfurter has left us.

"He's a patriot," says Haynes. "He's concerned. With good reason, I'd say. If you feel like your work's not important, you could always try talking to your boss about the Pledge."

. . . .

But Black is not in when I return to chambers. I am at my desk wrangling with cert petitions when Gene Gressman appears. "Take a walk with me." We go to his office.

"Did you find what you needed?" Rose asks me.

"Yes," I say. Gene looks at me curiously. "So what's the plan?" I ask, before he has time to say anything.

"Right," he says. "The plan. We just have to think logically. What do they want? Let's say they're not the FBI. They're following you because you're a new clerk. So most likely they're looking for information. And we know already that someone has a way of getting information out of here. Sometimes a decision will get reported in "Washington Merry-Go-Round" before it's handed down. So if we find the leaks, we find out who's after you."

"Drew Pearson's not going to tell you his source," I say.

"Of course not. We have to make whoever it is reveal themselves."

"How do we do that?"

"If you were going after inside information, where would you start?"

"With the clerks?"

"No. You'd follow the clerks too, probably, but I think you'd start with the printer's office."

I nod my head. Clarence Bright on Eleventh Street prepares the Court's opinions. He is the first one outside the Court to know how a decision will come out; his office is the first place the opinions could be intercepted. And it is open to the public. "So you want to talk to him?"

"Better than that. I say we give him a fake opinion. If it leaks, we know it's him, and then we have leverage. We can make him give up whoever else is involved."

"But then we need a fake opinion."

"Yes. And something leakable. Something interesting. Fortunately, we have it."

There is only one case that has been decided. "The Nazis?"

"Bingo. That'll get out if anything does."

"But it's over."

"The Court's going to reconsider," he says. "Two of them are still in jail. They'll be released. The military trial was unconstitutional."

I consider. It is not a bad idea; surely someone who gets his hands on that information will not be able to resist spilling it. "And you think you can write a fake opinion saying that?"

"Sure. I have the argument Kenneth Royall made for them. You should have seen that guy. Six foot five if he's an inch, covered in medals and ribbons. They thought a military lawyer would roll over, but he wasn't about to. They undercut him every way they could. Gave him only tax lawyers to help out. Did everything but order him to lose." Gressman chews his lip, recollecting. "He knew it, too. You know the quills they give out?"

"Yeah." At each argument, a ceremonial white quill is placed on the counsel tables, a memento for the lawyers. At firms I have seen them displayed on desks, usually in glass or pewter cups, a subtle advertisement of distinction.

"He finishes his argument," Gressman says, "looks down at that quill, and just pushes it away."

"Huh," I say. We look at each other in silence. "What did it feel like?" I ask. "Working on that case."

"What do you think?"

I am almost embarrassed to say it. "Like flying?"

Gressman's face shows incredulity, then something more like pity. "No, Cash," he says. "Francis Biddle came to see Justice Roberts a couple days before the argument."

"Oh, I know Francis," I say. I saw him often enough growing up, though not since he moved to Washington to join the administration. Now he is Roosevelt's Attorney General. "He's from Philadelphia."

The incredulity returns. "He argued in a white linen suit, you know. Like he was at a cocktail party with his pals."

I am not surprised; the informality is typical of Biddle. "Maybe he felt confident."

Now Gressman smiles. "Oh, I'm sure he did. I didn't tell you why he came to see Roberts. It was to let us know that FDR would kill them anyway. No matter what the Court said. So what it felt like, really, was murder."

I say nothing. Gressman lifts the photo from his desk and points to one of the faces. "Say hello to Herbie Haupt," he says. "An American, by the way."

Haupt looks to be about my age, maybe younger. He has a brilliantine wave to his hair and appears to have been arrested in a letterman's sweater.

"Of course he looked different after they shaved his head. For the metal cap. That's what you wanted to be here for."

"He's a Nazi."

"He was," says Gressman. "Maybe." He looks at me in silence for a moment, "Well," he says finally. "Don't worry. This is a two-front war. We've still got the Japs. And you'll have your chance to see what it feels like."

CHAPTER 11

I SQUEEZE MY temples with thumb and forefinger. I am working without the benefit of coffee. Rationing was announced last week, as the cafeteria stewards predicted, and a wave of panicked last-minute buying has drained the city dry. Though I knew coffee only briefly, I find I miss it terribly, like a summer romance. But I do not think that lack fully explains the headache I feel.

Gressman's description of the saboteurs' case is disturbing. Not at all what I imagined. Maybe that just means Haynes is right: maybe I shouldn't trust him. But if I can't trust him, why did I sign on to his crazy scheme to find whoever's following me?

When Black comes in, I follow him to his office. He smiles at me. "Looking for some exercise?"

"I was wondering about the saboteurs' case," I say. "Was that an easy one for the Court?"

Black gives me a curious look. "I can't tell you about the deliberations. I'll tell you something else, though."

"What?"

"I was thinking about Pearl Harbor on the way in this morning. I was in my car when I got the news. I pulled over to the side of the road; I just couldn't believe what I was hearing. But you know what I thought when I got my wits about me?"

"What?"

"I thought, 'Thank God it's finally happened.'" He pauses. "It was a good thing. They set us back, but we've still got our carriers. And now we're coming. Pearl Harbor brought the country together. It got us into a frame of mind to win a war that we were going to have to fight one way or another. We lost good men, but their deaths were worth something. War demands sacrifice, and that was theirs. But when American boys are dying like that, we can't get too upset about Nazi spies. That case was a chance to show how serious this is."

He looks at me, waiting for something. "You're right, Judge," I say.

"And they weren't innocent." I have the sense he is no longer speaking for my benefit. "I've seen some bad cases. I prosecuted four years in Jefferson County. The Bessemer cops had a perfect arrest record. Any crime there was, they'd bring me some colored boy who'd confessed. I could have got convictions, of course, but I told them I wouldn't try a case on a confession alone. And then I got a grand jury together, and we investigated that police department and cleaned 'em out."

I nod. "It wasn't like that," Black says. "We found their dynamite, you know. We found their uniforms." He sits behind his desk, a sign that the conversation is over. "War demands sacrifice," he repeats. "Every generation's got to learn it."

• • • •

Outside my office window there passes the familiar parade of pedestrians, the office workers and the government girls. But as I look through the glass I am seeing other images. Herbie Haupt with his head shaved bare, Kenneth Royall pushing away the quill. I remember Black spraying his garden, the lazy arc of water hanging in the air until a flick of his wrist cut it off at the source. It stayed there for a second after his attention turned, floating like an afterthought, then it had fallen to earth and was gone. Not completed, just gone.

Black has a role for Haupt to play. His life fits into the larger story, a warning to America, like the lives lost at Pearl Harbor. But for Herbie there is no larger story. It ends here, jagged and incomplete, as it did for all the other young men who died, the twenty-four hundred at Pearl, the thousands since, the millions the war might claim before it is over. All of them the stars of their own movies, all unable to imagine that it could just go on without them.

"Hey there," says Gene Gressman. I turn to see him holding a sheaf of papers, our mock opinion. "Tell me what you think."

I take the sheets. He's written it as a Murphy opinion, and sounds just like the Justice: ringing phrases, slightly vague. *The Constitution is made for war as well as peace,* fake Murphy reminds the reader. *It is not merely for fair weather.*

It's a good impersonation, better than it needs to be for our purposes. In fact, it's almost convincing, which gives me another twinge of a headache.

"Gene," I say, "you've got a flair for this."

"Where do you think Murphy gets it?"

I raise my eyebrows. "Really?"

Gressman shrugs. "He lets me do some drafting." Vague envy stirs within me. Black has not discussed the matter, but I have not been given the impression that my duties will include any work on Court opinions.

"Mr. Justice Gressman," I say.

He shrugs again. "Come on. Let's get it into the pipeline."

Clarence Bright is a small man with a pencil mustache, chain-smoking Luckies from a white pack behind the counter. A sign on the wall promises the fastest service in town, and he gives us the same assurance. "No problem, my friends. It will be ready to go in three days."

"Excellent," says Gressman. He leans forward confidentially, waving smoke from his face. "I must stress that this opinion is extremely sensitive. That's why we're delivering it ourselves instead of the messengers. No one can learn about it."

"No need to worry," says Bright. He spreads his hands and narrowly misses Gressman with an ash. "I divide all the opinions. Three or four parts, one for each printer. And the end, where it says *affirmed* or *reversed*, I keep that for myself. No one knows." The hands come down to the counter, and he leans forward himself. "You can be sure."

"Ah," says Gressman, patting Bright's hand. He is not as good at this as Frankfurter, I think; he has chosen the hand that holds the cigarette. Bright looks dismayed at the interruption, then reaches across with his other hand to make the switch and takes a quick puff. "No one but you," Gressman says into the smoke. "Very good, my friend."

For the next three days we watch the papers assiduously, but there is nothing from Drew Pearson, nor from anyone else. I stand in the doorway of Murphy's chambers and watch Gressman flipping disconsolately through the *Times-Herald.* "We need to go," I tell him.

"Go where?"

"To pick up the opinion."

"Oh," he says. "Do you think we should?"

"Are you kidding? If we don't get it, he'll probably send it here. How would you like Murphy to see your drafting? Or Frankfurter?"

Gressman is out of his chair with unusual speed, grabbing his hat and rushing past me. "Hadn't thought that far ahead," he pants as we stride down the street. "I was sure by this point we'd be confronting him with the evidence."

"The only evidence there is now is that opinion," I say. "And it's against us."

Gressman nods, puffing. His feet splay and his weight rolls side to side as he walks. When he begins a trot, the effect is even more pronounced.

"Did you take a physical?" I ask.

He shakes his head, unable to speak. I am mildly pleased to note I am not short of breath. Tennis is less of a workout than squash, but the amount Justice Black plays, it is enough.

"Why not?"

Gressman looks at me in exasperation, but he slows down enough to talk. Perhaps he is glad of the excuse. "Didn't need it," he says. "Bad heart. Well established. Could drop dead any moment."

"Really?"

He shrugs. "Sort of. Close enough they didn't have to look at me." The awning of Bright's shop nears us. "Not a bad thing to keep in mind, anyway. Makes you enjoy life more. Have you done what you wanted with the time you've had?"

"No," I say. "No, I haven't."

Clarence Bright hands us a package wrapped in brown paper. "Here you go," he says cheerfully. Gressman takes it and turns to leave. Bright's voice follows us from out of a cloud of smoke. "My friends," he calls.

"What?"

"There is the matter of my fee," says Bright. "I understand the opinion is sensitive and you are not following the standard procedures, but I am usually paid at this point." Frowning, Gressman walks back to the counter and takes the piece of paper Bright holds out. The news is not good. He turns a stricken face to me. Like the need to pick up the opinion, this contingency has apparently been overlooked. "Shall I send a bill to the Clerk of Court?" Bright asks.

"No," says Gressman quickly. "Don't do that."

"We'll just handle it now." I take out my wallet. Gressman looks relieved, then slightly annoyed.

"I can't pay you back," he says when we're outside.

"It's nothing," I say. The very casualness of the response seems to gall him.

"It's not nothing," he says almost truculently. "I owe you."

"Don't be silly," I say. "You're helping me." I have not thought much of it before, but of course this is true, and as I put it into words I feel a rush of genuine gratitude.

He brightens perceptibly. "So I am." For a few blocks he is silent, then he speaks up again. "Well, it's not the printer."

"Are you sure? Maybe he figured out what we were up to."

"No, he's solid. I can tell."

Back at the Court, we trot across the marble steps to the side entrance. Their corners are still sharp, but the building no longer intimidates me as it once did. For all its imposing starkness, it is starting to feel like home. "So what's our next move?"

"I don't know. I need to think."

"What do I do with the opinion?"

"Keep it. You paid for it."

That evening, I return to my apartment in good spirits. The whole escapade has the feel of a college prank, and the mock opinion in my briefcase is an amusing souvenir, like a stolen mascot. I double back a few times as I walk, but notice no trailing figures. Perhaps they have given up. The mail carries a dinner invitation from Cissy Patterson, the owner of the *Times-Herald*, which lifts my mood further. In law school I found that New York society was not open, but Cissy's parties are the best Washington has. Perhaps Francis Biddle has put in a word. Even Suzanne, calling from Northeast Harbor, is agreeable on the phone. I will do my best to get back home over the coming months, understanding that things will get busier when the Court starts hearing cases in October. Without doubt I will be back for Christmas, and then we will be halfway to the end. This separation is a minor hiccup on the way to a house in Center City. I drink a glass of Scotch and fall asleep in a warm haze.

CHAPTER 12

THINGS ARE DIFFERENT in the morning. Instead of Cissy's invitation, I have her newspaper. The Japanese are driving our Marines back on Guadalcanal; in the west, teenage girls behind antiaircraft guns stand between the Panzers and Stalingrad. They stand for an afternoon. I walk half a block toward the Capital Transit streetcar then dash back to the apartment as though I've forgotten something. Just outside the lobby a gray-suited man ignores me assiduously.

"We'll find them," says Gressman. "I have a new idea for you."

"You do?"

"Yes. Why don't you go take a walk? Maybe check out Lincoln Park."

"You're awfully peppy for a man with no coffee."

Gressman's eyes shift away and then back. "Just trust me," he says. "Take a walk. It'll do you good."

As he instructs, I wait ten minutes and then leave the Court, walking slowly. I head down East Capitol Street. Summer is fading into fall, but the sun is still bright and the sidewalk bustling. As I near the park I see Gressman sitting with a newspaper. He folds it up as I pass.

I stop before a sculpture of Lincoln, arm outstretched over a former slave. A lunchtime crowd has gathered, girls in skirts and blouses, cups of chicory and sandwiches wrapped in waxed paper. I look around as though appreciating the scene. There is Gressman, half a block away, fussing with a shoelace.

And there is the man in the gray suit, over on the other side of the statue.

I have figured out Gressman's plan now. He is trying to watch my watcher. But I do not know if he will make the identification. The crowd is pretty thick, and though Gene has a good legal mind, he is no one's idea of a spy. I turn my gaze more directly on the man. He looks down and starts to walk away. Gressman is still tying his shoe, glancing my way with what he evidently thinks is sly circumspection.

The man has almost left the plaza. With a few steps, I come up behind him. "You," I say.

He turns around. Just as at Eastern Market, he seems afraid of me. He shakes his head, though it is not clear what there is to deny, and steps back.

"You won't get anything from me," I say. I have marked him for Gressman now, and I do not feel scared anymore. I feel angry. Rats, scampering after crumbs of information. "You might as well give it up."

He backs away, still looking at me. Or not quite. He is looking behind me, off to my left. It takes me a second to figure out what that means, and a second is too long. Something hits me from behind, hard, in the middle of my back. A lowered shoulder, I guess. I stumble into a woman, spilling her cup. The man with her sees an opportunity for gallantry. "Watch it, pal."

I ignore him, spinning around, looking for whoever struck me. A man in blue pinstripes is striding away. Before I can move to follow him, someone else pushes me. Not the would-be knight errant; it's another one of them. A whisper hisses in my ear. "We know what you've done."

"What?" I turn around again. The crowd is full of blank faces.

"I said, watch it, pal." There is soup on his jacket, pale shards of poultry, tricolored vegetable cubes, and a gleaming curl of pasta.

"Not you." I try to wave him away, which only angers him further. He takes a step closer.

There's another push in my back, driving me into the soup knight. Another whisper hissing in my ear. "Trader."

"What?" The word makes no sense, but he doesn't stick around to clarify it. I spin again, pointlessly. There could be three of them or there could be twenty-three, coming in to jab and fade away. For a moment I bounce back and forth like a pinball. Then it is over and I am standing by myself, scanning the crowd in vain. Sir Chicken Noodle grabs the back of my collar. I turn to see his fist cocked. "Someone pushed me," I say. "I'm very sorry."

He scowls and lowers his hand. "You're getting off easy."

"Yes," I say. "I'm sure I am." There is no sign of Gressman, nor anyone I recognize among the passersby. I dab ineffectually at his jacket with my handkerchief. "My apologies to you both."

· · · ·

Gressman is not there when I get back to the Court, and I sit in Black's chambers for a while, waiting. There is more than one, and they are not as passive or fearful as I thought—that, or fear drives them further. But what is there for them to be afraid of? I am the one who should worry. And Gressman, who's gone after them. As the minutes tick by, I grow uneasy. Gene can't run; he can barely manage a brisk walk. He would be helpless in a fight. And neither he nor I have any idea who these people are. The knock at the door triggers a flood of relief. "You're back."

But it is Phil Haynes whose face peers in at my call. "How are you doing?" he asks.

"Fine," I say.

"You sure?" He is wearing a seersucker suit; his face is tanned. I am put in mind of Northeast Harbor, roast corn and the last clambake of a waning summer. "You look a little worried." His eyes go to my desk. "Certs got you down? Or do you still think people are following you?"

Looking at him, I can almost see the ocean in his eyes, smell the salt spray. The effect is haunting. "You wouldn't believe me."

Haynes frowns. "Try me. If something's bothering you, I want to know."

"Well," I say. "It's not my imagination."

"You see someone else you recognized?"

"More than that." I hesitate. How to describe what just happened? "There were several of them. They were working together."

Haynes nods. "How do you know?" he asks, and I am about to start telling the story when over his shoulder I see Gene Gressman appear in the doorway.

My face must change, for Haynes turns around. "Oh," he says. "Hello,

Gene." He turns back and gives me a small shake of his head. "Later," he says softly.

"Hello," Gressman says. He winks at me. "So, Cash, you had a question about antitrust?"

"Antitrust?" Gressman nods encouragingly. "Oh," I say. "Right. Yes, I did."

"Later," Haynes says again, walking out.

"So what happened with you?" Gressman asks.

"A question about antitrust? You don't want to talk in front of Phil?"

"I don't."

"Why not?"

"First, I don't like him. Second, he's one of the Happy Hot Dogs."

"The what?"

"Frankfurter's boys. He has his network. Former clerks, students, protégés, they're all over the place. Doing his bidding."

"He doesn't seem to trust you, either."

"Well, he shouldn't. He's not my friend." Gressman hesitates a moment. "He's not yours, either."

Again the ocean comes to my mind, glimpsed through goldenrod on rocky hills. "You don't get to decide that."

"I'm not deciding, Cash," Gressman says. "Just reporting." Another pause. "So what happened?"

"You saw, right? They pushed me. And they were saying things."

"What kind of things?"

"Crazy stuff," I say. "It didn't make any sense. Something about knowing what I'd done."

"Huh," says Gressman. He frowns. "Why'd you start something with them anyway? That wasn't the plan."

"I wanted to be sure you saw them," I say. "You could just pretend to be tying your shoelace, you know."

"It really came untied."

"You could tie your shoes carefully before you go out on a spy mission."

"Hey," says Gressman. "I had that guy before you pointed him out. And I followed him back without anyone spotting me."

"Back where?"

"Well, that's the funny part."

"What?"

"Would you believe the Department of Agriculture?"

I look at him. "No."

He shrugs. "That's where they went. The guy in gray, a couple more that met up with him. And it wasn't to lose me. They showed ID, they knew people there. You were being tracked by certified Grade A New Deal bureaucrats. I'd say economists by the way they walked. But maybe lawyers."

"Of course," I say. "They must have figured out I've been growing too much wheat. Seriously, what could that be about?"

"I don't know," says Gressman. He taps a thoughtful finger on his lips. "Maybe we've been looking at this from the wrong end. I have another idea."

"What?"

"Give me a little time to figure it out. You can't hurry genius."

"No," I say. "But I can hurry you."

"Patience," says Gressman. "All in good time."

CHAPTER 13

CISSY PATTERSON IS late to her own party. Once this might have been whim, when she was one of the Three Graces of Washington and balls held in her honor went on like as not in her absence. Now her triumvirate is the Three Furies of Isolation, and it is work that detains her. She is tramping through the newsroom, copyediting on the fly; she is inserting barbed jabs at her rivals and spicing the gossip on page three. Emeralds drip from her wrists and throat; a string of short-tempered poodles trails behind her, snapping at reporters. Soon a car will take her to Dupont Circle. She will recite to her maid a string of numbers, signifying the articles of clothing selected for the night. She will fortify herself with a drink and perhaps a pinch of cocaine. And she will descend the marble staircase to sniff eagerly at her guests like the half-crazed bitch she is.

Or so Drew Pearson tells me as we wait in a sitting room. It is not the customary way to describe one's host, in my experience, and I say so. "A bit tendentious, maybe?"

He sips from his martini. "Of course, I'm biased," he admits. "I know her." Pearson is a solid man with something truculent in his eyes, a well-trimmed mustache, and receding hair. I have seen him before at Black's house, where he sat in the garden drinking and swapping stories with Justice Douglas. He is from Philadelphia, like me, though he seemed not to care when I pointed it out.

I take a cautious taste of my Scotch. "How did you make her acquaintance?"

"The usual," he says. "Dinner party. Married her daughter." He rises abruptly and strides from the room. I have to follow quickly to catch his words. "Divorced her. One thing FDR forgot in the New Deal, the agency to protect you from ex-mothers-in-law."

"I suppose it's natural there would be hard feelings after the split," I call after him.

"Wasn't that," he answers. I catch up. We are in the foyer now, eye to eye with marble busts at the foot of the stairs. Caesar Augustus, I think, and another I cannot place. "Scipio Africanus," Pearson says. "The conqueror of Hannibal." A Gobelin tapestry on the wall depicts a hunting scene, and animal heads are mounted along the stair. "It looks like they came out of the weaving, doesn't it?" Pearson asks. "But they didn't make it far through the house. It's a dangerous place."

I blink, mildly surprised. "This house?"

"Cliveden on the Potomac. Of course it's not the house you have to worry about; it's the people. Crawling with isolationists. And Cissy. She shot all these herself."

"Oh," I say. Few women hunt, in my experience, but those that do seem to enjoy it a great deal.

Pearson makes a pistol of his thumb and forefinger. "She's got you in her sights now. She wants something from you. Better watch out."

"I don't mean to be rude," I say, "but I'm surprised she still invites you to her parties."

"She likes sparks," Pearson says. "She hopes I'll take a swing at one of her fascist friends. I might do it, too, with enough of these." He raises his empty glass. "I'll see you later. We're at the same table."

. . . .

Dinner awaits Cissy's arrival. I have never seen Cliveden, but this place is indeed a mansion. It raises itself up grand red-carpeted stairs; it spreads marble wings as though to embrace the circle. In the dining room flowers bedeck the tables; in the ballroom candles flicker in crystal chandeliers. Guests have scattered themselves about. Bill Douglas is here, and Francis

Biddle. Justice Black is not. Then there are diplomats, military men, and reporters, vaudeville entertainers passing from room to room, a jazzman at the piano, and a magician in the parlor.

In the library, I find Biddle inspecting the bookshelves. He smiles at my approach, something welcoming, something indulgent. He is, I realize, an example of what Judge Skinner described to me, society taking part in governance, for the Biddles are Philadelphia's First Family. But Judge Skinner would not approve of the side he has taken. He has thrown his lot with the New Dealers, and I have not seen him since the November evening in '36 when he led a line of men down Broad Street to City Hall, singing Roosevelt campaign songs. I watched them go from the windows of the Union League, where my father and the Judge clutched their *Literary Digest*s in icy disbelief.

Biddle's hair is thinner now, and he parts it on the side and combs it over the top.

"Ah, Cash," he says. "Pleasant to see you."

"But not a surprise, I think. I should thank you for the invitation."

He shakes his head. "Believe me, Cissy doesn't ask my opinions on her guest list." He turns back to the books.

"Looking for yours?" Biddle wrote a novel, *The Llanfear Pattern*, about a Philadelphia man who tests convention and subsides. I remember my father and the Judge debating how the ending was meant to be taken.

"No." He laughs softly. "I've given her copies, of course, but it wouldn't be flattering to find them here."

"Why not?"

"These are just for decoration," he says. "There's a company that sells them by the yard." He pulls one out. "See, the pages aren't cut."

"So," I say. "Why do you suppose Cissy invited me?"

"No idea, I'm afraid."

"Drew Pearson suggested it was for some sinister purpose."

Again Biddle gives his soft and pleasant laugh. "Don't pay too much attention to him. They've hit a rocky patch these past few years. Cissy's not at her best in relationships of mutual dependence. Not with Drew, or her daughter either." His face brightens. "I met her in Jackson Hole, at Struthers Burt's

ranch. It was a grand time, and I think it left her with a soft spot for Philadelphia. Or Philadelphians."

I frown. If he is offering this as an explanation of my presence, it does not
seem adequate. Biddle does not notice my expression. "She had a way with
the horses," he continues. "And the cowboys. There was this one chap, Cal . . .
well." He raises his eyebrows, then tilts his head to the side. "She must be here
now. I believe they're calling us for dinner."

. . . .

The dining room is red-tapestried, with a white marble fireplace. As he said,
Pearson is at my table; so are Francis Biddle, Cissy's brother Joe, and an army
colonel named Richards. Of Cissy there is still no sign.

There is a general din of conversation in the room. At our table I catch fragments from Pearson and Joe while trying to talk to the woman next to me,
a dark and attractive functionary from the Spanish Consulate. I am making
very little progress with my description of Philadelphia clubs. Either she
cannot hear me, or she does not care.

"So they crank them down to the horizontal and open up," Pearson says.
"Of course, they've got fragmentation rounds, not armor-piercing shells."

I make another attempt. "There's one we call the State in Schuylkill," I say.
"No other authority is recognized."

Now I have caught her interest; she leans forward and smiles. Red lips curl
back and even teeth glint. "You are separatists?" The idea seems to excite her.
"Like our Basque, yes?"

"Not exactly." The State in Schuylkill is nominally a fishing club, though
like most such organizations its purpose is to facilitate an escape to fraternal
society. Tracing its origins back to a treaty with the Lenni Lenape, it asserts
independent sovereignty over its castle. But not in any meaningful sense. "It's
just that the club officers have governmental titles. There's the governor, the
sheriff, so on."

Her face falls. "But what is the point?"

I hesitate. Removed from the Philadelphia soil in which they flourish,
the customs seem wilted and insipid. Indeed, what is the point? "There's an
annual dinner. We plank shad."

Her expression is blank. Either the construction exceeds her grasp of English, or she thinks it does not answer the question. Upon reflection, it does not seem much of an answer to me, either. "And the government does not mind this, this rebellion? Mr. Biddle is not concerned?"

I look across the table at Biddle, who gives a permissive nod. It occurs to me that he and Pearson share more than their tidy mustaches. Without Biddle's comb-over, they would have the same hairline, too. It may be a reason they enjoy spending time together, so that each can congratulate himself on avoiding the other's fate.

My Spanish friend awaits a response. "Oh, no," I say. "We've never caused any trouble." A coincident silence gives everyone at the table the benefit of my next line. "Except in the matter of the Fish House Punch." This is a guaranteed laugh-getter at any Philadelphia gathering. Fish House Punch has the reassuring taste of lemonade, but it is insidiously strong and best not drunk unless one has a full evening to devote to the enterprise. Among the unaccustomed, its force has produced plenty of scandalous tales for the society pages. The table is dead silent. Even Francis Biddle's smile is one of sympathy, rather than amusement.

I feel my face reddening. Suddenly I am wishing I had not come to this party. A Merion dinner would look much the same on the surface, but I would understand everything that went on below. I can tell you what it means that a man lives in Haverford, not Devon; that he has joined the Philadelphia Club and not the Union League; that he plays the right wall and not the left in doubles squash. But Washington is impenetrable. Its signs are illegible to me; they are the alphabet of power, which Philadelphia spurns to cover its loss. We have our secrets, but the biggest one, I see now, is that no one else cares, and that is a secret we keep only from ourselves.

A waiter takes away my plate, still half-filled with leathery meat. Cissy obtained beef, but not a choice cut, and the braising was an inadequate disguise. The Spaniard smiles at me, murmurs something, and leaves the table. The apocalypse is complete.

"Thirty-seven batteries," says Pearson to Joe Patterson. He has the tone of a man making a clinching point. Dimly I realize he is talking about the story I read in Cissy's paper, the Panzers on the outskirts of Stalingrad, the high school girls behind their useless antiaircraft guns. But he seems to have more details. "Not a one stopped shooting until it was destroyed. Those are the Reds you want to bleed white, Joe."

Patterson sighs. He is one of the richest men in the country. He owns the *New York Post*, and other things. There is American Fruit; there is the New York, New Haven and Hartford Railroad. But the railroad went bankrupt in 1935, and Joe seems to be on the decline as well. His hair is cut short in a youthful style, but it is mostly white and it gives him an air more of bemusement than vigor, like a tolerant grandfather costumed by the children. His uniform is from the last war and it is approaching the limits of what alterations can achieve, stretching taut across his belly. "No one likes war, Drew," he says. There is a strange rasp to his voice. "But if it's Russian girls or American boys . . ." He makes a vague gesture with his hand and drinks from his wineglass.

Colonel Richards steps in. His face is tan and his brass buttons sparkle in the candlelight. "I'd say if their girls fight that well, they don't need our help."

Part of me is glad to see that I am not the only one whose remarks can fall flat. Patterson is peering down into his glass, but Pearson has the look of a man whose mind has turned to violence. "English boys," he says. "French. Jews of every age and description."

Patterson's face has a sad puzzlement, as though he believes we should all be friends and cannot understand why we must disagree. His breath rasps slowly out; he says nothing. Richards does not give up. He raises his glass with a smile. "To our gallant allies. Long may they fight." There is a murmur of assent from some at the table, who I assume have not been following the conversation. Pearson actually makes a move to get up out of his chair. Francis Biddle surveys it all with the calm equanimity of a man attending a slightly dull matinee. I have a sudden unwelcome image of the Russian girls, watching their shells bounce off the tanks and reloading while the turrets sniffed toward them.

Before Pearson can do anything, Richards slides out of his seat and moves to the empty one by my side. "So," he says. "I hear you're at the Court."

"Yes."

"An upsetting place to be right now, I'd imagine."

The sudden sensitivity surprises me. "I'm not sure what you mean."

Richards presses on. "An independent Court," he says. "The Constitution gave us that to protect us from dictators. And now it's just a tool for the Democrats."

Here is a theme I have heard often enough in Philadelphia. But it is not one I can engage in now. "At the Court we try to stay out of politics."

"Quite right." Richards leans closer to me. "But patriotism is not politics." There is an intensity to his gaze. "People ask me if I am a Democrat or a Republican. I say country before party. I am an American first."

There is something conspiratorial in his smile. Now I think I recognize the rosette in his lapel. "America First is a party," I say.

"Not anymore," says Richards. "Not since Pearl Harbor." He sighs. "Taft might have kept us out, but that was it, of course. There's no going back now. Who'd have thought the Japs would save the Jews? Jesus wasn't good enough for them, but now Tojo is their messiah. Thanks to Comrade Roosevelt, of course."

Again I have the sense that I am missing something. It feels like a rush event, the brothers of St. Anthony Hall dropping allusions I cannot grasp. I did not make the cut then, and it seems I am not making it now. Richards is waiting for a response. I wonder how much I have drunk. The way the waiters keep refilling the wineglasses, it is hard to keep track. It sounds to me as though he has just suggested that FDR knew the attack was coming, or even brought it on. I fumble for an anodyne phrase. "At least it brought us together."

"Of course," says Richards. "Of course we were all united. No one thought of anything but America. But for them it was about unity behind the Democratic Party. They used the crisis to push their own agenda. A foreign one. Socialist."

I try to think of a noncommittal response. "I certainly know some people who feel that way," I say. "The State in Schuylkill . . ." At the annual dinner, the traditional toast to the President has been replaced by one to the Constitution. But Richards does not let me finish.

"Exactly," he interrupts. "A club. I was in the Fly at Harvard. A small group of men can do a lot."

But I have abruptly lost interest in the conversation. John Hall used to come back from Harvard and rhapsodize about the Fly Club; I need no more stories about the joys of men who really understand each other. "Yeah," I say. "They can plank shad."

Richards frowns at me. I stand up and look around the tables, hoping to catch sight of my vanished senorita. From the next room there comes a rough chorus. I think I can pick out Haynes's voice. I take a step to peer through the doorway and there he is, his blond hair falling over his forehead, his cheeks flushed with drink. And who is that next to him, arm in arm? Richards must have put John Hall in my mind, for I would swear that is him, green jacket damp with sweat, Army tie askew. They put their heads back and bay out the words. "Oh, Harvard's run by millionaires, and Yale is run by booze. Cornell is run by farmers' sons, Columbia's run by Jews." The end of the line is almost lost in a swell of applause from the parlor, evidently at the conclusion of a magic trick.

Richards is grasping my arm and saying something. I turn back to him. "I'm sorry, what?"

"Clubs," he says. "It's not democracy that keeps the government in line . . ."

And then everyone falls silent, for the guests part like water and Cissy Patterson arrives at our table.

CHAPTER 14

CISSY HAS DARK hair set in waves and something hungry about the mouth. She has donned emeralds, or, if what Pearson said is true, left them on. "Now, Bill," she says to Colonel Richards, "don't hang on our guests." He stands with the rest of the table, and she acknowledges us with a wave. "Hi, Francis."

Biddle makes a small and courtly bow. "You've been missed, Cissy. Out sharpening the knives for us?"

Cissy shakes her head. "Don't you see what's happening, Francis? Boys who love this country are dying across the sea. And men who don't are taking it apart piece by piece."

"We all love America. We may have different ideas of what it stands for."

"It doesn't stand for dictators. How can you go on like this? I wake up screaming."

"I try to get my screaming done during business hours," says Biddle, rising in my estimation.

"You supported T.R.," says Cissy. "You were there in Chicago, like me. *We stand at Armageddon and we battle for the Lord.* I get chills just remembering. Well, now you have to choose which side you're on."

"We're all on the same side, Cissy," he says mildly.

"That remains to be seen." She turns her eyes to me. "Mr. Harrison." There is a force in her gaze. "I am glad you're here."

"I appreciate the invitation."

She rests her hand lightly on Joe's shoulder. It is a tender gesture, which does not seem to come naturally to her, and that itself adds poignancy.

"You may be sure you are among friends," she says. She pats Joe's shoulder again and he touches her hand briefly, his face soft. Then she is gone to another table. Richards nods quickly to us and follows her.

Silence hangs for a moment, then Biddle breaks it. "Politics always puts me in the mood for dancing." He takes his wife's hand. "Care to join us?" The invitation is general. Joe remains seated, cradling his glass, but everyone else seems glad enough to go.

The ballroom is pink and white, with gold taffeta chairs along the walls. There are full-length mirrors at opposite ends, and the candles in the chandeliers glint in an endless row. "You shouldn't take what Cissy says too seriously," Biddle tells me. "She's never forgiven FDR for what he did to Joe."

"What was that?"

"Well, Joe had been editorializing against Lend-Lease and all that. But when Pearl Harbor came he snapped right around. Went to see the President and said, 'I'm yours to command. Just tell me what to do.' And FDR looked at him and said, 'There's one thing you can do, Joe. Go back and read your editorials for the past six months. Read every one and see what you think.' Joe never got over it."

The explanation should not surprise me, but it does. "So it's personal? All this stuff about dictators?"

"Oh, I suppose she means some of it. But no one complains about the dictator they like. Roosevelt's gotten on her bad side. With Joe, and the cherry trees."

"The cherry trees?"

"Around the Tidal Basin. When she heard he was going to cut some down for the Jefferson Memorial she got her friends together and they went out and chained themselves to the trees. FDR had them taken away. He's got a picture of her on his desk, kicking in the arms of the Capitol police. You can see her panties." Biddle allows himself a chuckle and pauses for reflection. "Those trees aren't so popular now. The day of Pearl Harbor some energetic idiot chopped a few down. I was in Detroit, talking to the Slav-American foundation when I got a note . . ."

I was at Columbia, daydreaming about Suzanne. My mind drifts back. The innocence of those days, the certainty that no one could touch us. Not here in America, safe behind our oceans. Ideals are free to the invulnerable, but now we must decide whether we will pay their cost. Biddle is still talking, but I stir myself to action. No one wants to dance with me. But if Haynes is around here, perhaps he can explain what is going on.

But he is not, not anywhere I can find him, anyway. Nor is John Hall. Perhaps it was a hallucination. Instead I find Drew Pearson, nursing another martini. "I warned you, didn't I?"

"About what?"

"These people. This house."

"Francis Biddle seems to like them well enough."

Pearson shrugs. "Oh, Biddle likes everyone, because no one can hurt him. He doesn't understand how serious this is. He thinks they're amusing."

"And you don't?"

"Do you? You've got a pretty good perspective, I'd think. From the Court. You know what's happening."

But I don't, I want to protest. My mind is struggling against a tide of wine. Still, perhaps this is an opening. "So do you, it seems."

Pearson raises his eyebrows. "How's that?"

"The decisions. You seem to know before they come out."

"Oh, you know." His tone is elaborately casual. "A man's got to have friends. You ever find something weighing on your mind, I'm ready to listen. Give me a call."

Power and secret knowledge, I think. That is the currency of Washington, and he is right; I hold some. Coins with unfamiliar faces, rough and strange in my hands. "Do other clerks do that?" I remember him drinking with Douglas in Black's garden. "Justices?"

It is like a steel shutter coming down. "That's not what we talk about." He looks at me appraisingly, then shakes his head. "You're not in the game yet." He shrugs, changing the topic. "You haven't seen that Richards around, have you? I think I owe him a punch in the nose."

"I haven't."

"Well, I'll find him sooner or later. You should go home." He nods as though he has considered the advice and confirmed its wisdom. "Go home while you still can."

I stand alone in the foyer. People pass all around me; the air is filled with laughing chatter, piano chords, and distant song. There is no one I know here, no one who wants to help me. Perhaps I should go home.

"Pick a card." A man in a cheap tailcoat and checkered vest holds a pack toward me. He has a pinched and foxy face, an unctuous air. One of Cissy's entertainers, spotting me as a wallflower.

I push his hand away, annoyed. "No thanks, I'm trying to quit."

He fans the deck in his hand. "Come on, any card."

"I don't go in for parlor tricks."

"Is this a parlor?" A wave of his arm takes in the sweep of the stairs, the spread of the hall. "Is this a trick?"

"Looks that way to me." I step past him.

"Wait." His hand taps my shoulder. "Your card. Was it the jack of diamonds?"

"I didn't take a card."

"Didn't you? What's in your pocket?"

I take it out without bothering to look. "Yes, jack of diamonds. Very clever. If you'll excuse me, I need a drink."

The man bows ingratiatingly. I step to the bar. "Scotch." *Smoke on the tongue*, Judge Skinner said to me, *fire in the throat*. I see him measuring it out in fingers from his crystal decanter, sitting back in the library among his books. *Slowly, Cash; it's waited a long time for you*. The Judge could help me understand this world. The Scotch cannot, though I give it a second chance and then a third. People wheel past, their voices indistinct. I need to work tomorrow. Pearson was right, I think, as I struggle to make my good-byes. I should have left a long time ago.

Outside, the night air is still humid, thick and cloying. Traffic buzzes through Dupont Circle, a river of noisy lights. A deep breath does nothing to clear my head but succeeds in making plain the extent of my intoxication. I reflect for a moment. Walking back to my apartment will not be pleasant, but vomiting in the back of a jolting taxicab would be worse. I put one foot in front of the other. Why did I let myself get this way? There was the waiter who kept refilling my wineglass. The Scotches that were supposed to help me think. And, more realistically, the desire to escape my thoughts for a while. To forget the dinner conversation with Richards, the embarrassment of Fish House Punch, the realization that I am totally out of place here.

Coming up on the bridge across Rock Creek, I realize I have made at least one good decision tonight, not to try the taxi. Even the walk is beyond me. I step quickly off the sidewalk, into the brush, and spend an unpleasant few moments reviewing my dinner. The steak is still tough. I bend over, hands on my knees, catching my breath and spitting unidentifiable substances. And as I step back into the streetlights I remember one more thing I was trying to forget. Someone is following me.

The realization is no great accomplishment, because I all but bump into him. It's the first of my new friends, the man from Eastern Market. He's wearing a blue suit now, but easy enough to recognize this close up. An economist, probably, who doesn't really know what he's doing, who thought he'd lost me and hurried to catch up.

He stops dead and blinks at me. Revulsion overtakes alarm. A fair enough reaction, I suppose, but I've had enough of mysteries, enough surprises, and this look of disgust is the final insult. In a moment it all boils over. I haul off and punch him in the face. Not hard enough to knock him down, but it sends a flash of pain through my hand and I can see the sting in his eyes. "Leave me alone," I yell. He still looks horrified, though the hand over his mouth makes it a bit harder to tell. Blood is coming through his fingers. I spit one more item on the ground and start over the bridge.

Now he's got a reason to look scared, I think. That guy won't be following me anytime soon. Maybe I should have done this long ago. There is a sharp pain in my hand; there is a general sense of unwellness that ebbs and flows. But there is also a small satisfaction warming within me. And then I see the shadow coming up along the pavement at my feet.

My satisfaction cools fast, freezes to a solid lump of dread. *No one's trying to get you*, Haynes said. But that was wrong. I start to walk more quickly. Here on the bridge a scuffle could turn deadly in an instant. Up and over the side with him! It's hundreds of feet down. A second shadow starts to gain on me. I break into a run, pumping my arms. The shadows accelerate too, rushing past me, arms flailing. I stop and they stop; I wave and they wave back. I turn my head, and only a row of streetlamps stands behind me. Otherwise the bridge is empty. It is me, always me, only me. I wave again, try a dance step with my new companions. Me, myself, and I. By the time I reach the end of the bridge, I am laughing like an idiot.

Of course, that's where they're waiting for me.

CHAPTER 15

I WAKE IN my own bed. The pillowcase is stiff with blood. Mostly from my nose, I think, though there's a fat patch on my lower lip over the left incisor and a coppery taste in my mouth. I swing my feet to the floor and stand up slowly. The pain of the hangover is something I've felt before, but this time it's joined by several more discrete aches, the traces of fists or shoes. I was beaten last night, and probably kicked as well. I remember a crowd forming around me as I came off the bridge. No words, just a blow from an unknown quarter. And then more of the same. How I got home I have no idea.

I walk gingerly to the bathroom and run a shower, avoiding the mirror. I don't want to know what I look like. The hot water is restorative, and there's no blood on the towel when I dry my face. I take that for a good sign and step to the mirror to see how much of the damage remains. And I realize that it wasn't *trader* the man said to me in the scrum at Lincoln Park. They have left the right word for me. The glass is fogged, inscrutable, but one thing is clear. One word scrawled in soap. *Traitor.*

It makes no sense. For a moment I just stand there, blinking. I rub at the letters with the heel of my hand, then a wet washcloth. My face emerges from the clouds. I don't look too bad, all things considered. Not nearly as bad as I feel, anyway. Coffee is still unavailable, but I'm not sure my stomach could handle it even if I had some. I make a cup of tea and eat a piece of dry toast. I am going to be late to work.

Downstairs, the doorman looks at me skeptically. "Sure you should be out of bed, sir?"

My face isn't that bad. "Did you see me last night?"

He nods. "Your friends brought you in. Soused, if you'll forgive me. They said you got in a fight."

I feel my jaw. "I did. With them. Do you remember what they looked like?"

"Not like they'd been in a fight." His tone is apologetic. "I'm afraid you got the worst of it."

"Yeah, I'd actually figured that out already. I mean, can you describe them?"

He shrugs. "Suits. Seemed nice enough. Said you weren't usually like this."

"Oh, that was decent of them."

He nods seriously. Perhaps the fat lip is muffling my tone. "They seemed worried about you."

"Yeah," I say. "Me too."

Outside I give a quick look about, but no one is there. There is no chance of making it to the Court at my usual time, so I stop by the local precinct house. The desk sergeant looks at me with the same expression as the doorman. "Ah, Mr. Harrison," he says when I introduce myself. "I believe I've seen your name before."

"What?"

"In last night's report." He shakes his head. "Tsk tsk, Mr. Harrison. A fellow has to know his limits."

"I was attacked," I say. "By a group of men who've been following me for weeks."

He smiles. "Oh, were you?" He slaps his papers, smile gone. "That's not what it says here."

"What does it say?"

"Drunk and disorderly. Started a row."

"No, they started it." A small part of me concedes that technically this may not be true, but overall I am surely in the right. "I want you to find the men who did this."

He shakes his head. "It happens, my friend. No need to make up stories to excuse it. You'll not be charged."

"I'm not making up stories. I don't know what you have in your reports, but writing something down doesn't make it true."

The sergeant leans across the counter. "Let me tell you something," he says, "one man to another. You won't get any better until you accept responsibility for your actions." I can smell whiskey on his breath. Or maybe that's still me.

At the Court, the marshals look at me a touch longer than usual. I decide not to engage them in conversation. Instead, I go to my office, sit down at my desk, and groan. The light is paler now, but the view is the same as when I started: a pile of cert petitions, a set of memos to write. Six-by-eight boulders to push up the hill. But work is the least of my worries. Who can I turn to?

Judge Skinner is the one I really want to call. He'd believe me; he could help me. I imagine him leaning back in his chair and putting his feet up, the craggy face splitting in a smile. I get as far as picking up the phone, but then I stop. I can't tell him what's going on. He'd be worried; he'd insist I come back immediately. I can't call him unless I'm going to give up. And despite all that's happened, I'm not ready for that quite yet.

Then there is Phil Haynes, with his seaside tan. He couldn't tell me I was imagining things anymore. But as I told Gene Gressman, we know the same people. Word would get to Philadelphia, and again they'd want to pull me back.

It leaves me with Gene. And as I sit there wondering whether I can make it down the hall to Murphy's chambers to see him, he appears in the doorway, rapping his knuckles on the frame. "Hello," he says. "We're visiting everyone in this neighborhood with an important message. No doubt you are a busy person, so I'll be brief. Perhaps you would like an informative pamphlet?"

I stare at him blankly.

"Jehovah's Witnesses," he says. "They've got two cases coming up. You might want to take a look at the briefs in between your parties."

"Come in. We've got to talk."

He takes a seat on the corner of my desk. The gesture is an odd echo of Black. They are nothing alike in most ways, but they have the same sort of easy intimacy. "Worried about how your boss is going to vote?" He smiles. "I've got him in my pocket on these." Then his face changes. "Hey, you look terrible. What happened?" He leans in for a closer look. "You don't smell so good, either."

"Those guys attacked me."

"With a Manhattan?"

"It was Scotch. At the end, at least. But no, they attacked me with their fists. And maybe their feet. I can't remember everything."

"That would be the Scotch," Gene says helpfully.

"I suppose. But what am I going to do? I thought they were economists."

"They are," says Gene. He is silent for a moment. "Bet you never saw the punch coming."

"No, I didn't. Why?"

"Because it was the invisible hand."

Again I look at him blankly. "What the hell, Gene? I just got beaten up. They could have killed me."

"Exactly. But they didn't."

"So?"

"So they're not going to. Still, they were upset enough about something to punch you out. Maybe just because you socked one of them. But I think it's because we're on the right track."

I move my jaw from side to side, testing the soreness. "Doesn't feel that right to me."

"Trust me," says Gene. "They're worried because we're getting closer."

"How are we getting closer?"

He pauses. "Well, we know they're economists."

"Oh, good." Something about his irrational optimism seems familiar. "Have you been drinking?"

"That's yourself that you're smelling."

"I don't smell of coffee."

Gene stands up from the desk. "I actually have a little more work to do with these Witness cases. You ought to take a look at them. Don't worry about the economists. I'm on that too."

"Your energy is miraculous."

He looks down for a second. "Seriously, I think this is good news for us."

"Sure. Gospel. Next time I hope they share it with you instead of me."

"As long as it's informative pamphlets," he says, pausing at the door. Then he gives me what looks like a Nazi salute and is gone before I can ask for an explanation.

I turn my attention back to the desk, first to lay my head down for a few minutes, then to read the cases that are coming. One is about door-to-door leafleting by the Jehovah's Witnesses; another is about their children reciting the Pledge of Allegiance in school. But there are many more. They have snuck up on me while I was distracted, an insidious paper army. There is the case about the farmer who grew too much wheat, which I recommended the Court should hear. There are cases about the meaning of federal statutes; there are disputes between corporations, the boring cases the clerks hate. And as I get toward the bottom of the pile, I can see that Gene was right when he said the Japanese were coming. There are suits to challenge the evacuation of the coast, the detention in camps. I wonder if I will make it through the year. My empty coffee mug sits forlorn on the desk. I wonder if I will make it through the next hour.

"There you are, Cash," says Black, emerging from his chambers. I start upright, then regret the movement. I hadn't even known he was in. "Thought for a second there you were ducking me. Come on, what do you say?"

The drive over is bad, but the tennis is worse. I can't move fast enough to get to Black's shots, and when I do, I can't hit them. Pain in my hand makes it impossible to maintain a proper grip on the racquet. Black wins the first set 6–0 and calls a halt midway through the second. At the net he looks at me with concern. "Have an adventure last night?"

"A little too much to drink," I say. There is nothing Black can do for me, no point in getting him involved.

He nods. "One thing I used to do when I was a kid," he says. "Carry a roll of pennies in your hand. Gives your punch more weight."

I just look at him.

"Someone hit you, Cash," he says. "Which tells me you didn't hit him hard enough first."

"I guess not."

"Course you're still going to hurt your hand that way. You want to play tennis the next day, probably better to give 'em your elbow." He demonstrates a roundhouse strike. It looks like a chicken wing flapping.

"Thanks, Judge."

"Not really anything you can do about the hangover," he continues. "Except not drink so much."

"Yes, Judge."

He grills the steaks outside, as usual, but Josephine and I watch from the kitchen. Like the rest of the house it is small, modest, not what I would have expected from a Supreme Court Justice. Four wooden chairs with wicker seats circle a cherry table. Yellowed recipes are tacked to a corkboard on the wall, spotted with the evidence of attempts at their execution. Black needs no paper for the steaks, though; he has that routine down by heart. He meddles enthusiastically, opening the grill again and again, no doubt thinking he's making things better.

Josephine looks out the window over the sink. It is warm enough inside the house, and she's wearing a light sweater, but still she clutches her shoulders against a chill. "I'm not used to the winters," she says. "I get these feelings in the fall. When it starts getting dark early and the cold comes on. Do you feel that way? That something is ending and you won't be warm again for a long time?"

"I feel like something's beginning," I say. I hope this might make things look brighter for her, but it's also true. Fall is when the school year starts.

"The Court starts up," says Josephine. Her tone displays no enthusiasm for the idea. "He wasn't sure he wanted the job, you know. I encouraged him to take it. I thought he'd be home more. The Senate was a prison."

"He does try to leave early," I say. "I see how hard he works, to be able to come home."

"To come home and play tennis with you. Oh, he's always worked hard. I made my peace with that. You get used to most things. We start out tender, but we get better at protecting ourselves. We understand what the world has given us, and what it won't. And you get to a point where no matter what happens, you can accept it. I felt that way, I really did."

"But you don't now?"

She turns to me, and in her eyes I see it again, the plea that rose there when she saw me in Sterling's tennis whites. "When you have children it's all different," she says. "The tender part of you, that you've spent so many years learning to protect, it's out there all alone and there's nothing you can do." She wraps her hands around her shoulders, one body she can hold.

I am silent a moment. "It's getting better," I say. "Already things are getting better."

"I'm sure you're right," Josephine says. "But I get these feelings in the fall. That it's still a long night ahead, and lots of things left to happen before the dawn."

When Black returns with the steaks, I do my best to distract her. I mug over each bite as much as I dare; I try to steer the conversation to innocuous subjects. But Josephine's eyes keep going to the empty chair at my right.

Black notices. "With Cash here, we've got one boy, anyway."

It is a disastrous intervention. Josephine's mouth goes tight and her face pales. The idea of having only one boy is worse than the fact of two being away. The single empty chair takes on a dread significance. She stands up, blinking fast.

"I didn't . . ." Black begins. But she is out of the room before he can finish. There are two empty chairs now. Black's eyes flit from one to the other; his tongue darts over his lips. "I don't suppose I ever told you about my first love," he says to me.

I open my mouth, unsure of what I am going to say. I am thinking of the dinners at my own house, two chairs that might as well have been empty. My father and my brother, two silent men named Charles. I sat there with my mother while they nodded at each other and signaled James with a raised eyebrow. And I can do that for Black, I can be his companion among the empty chairs, but he is not the one who needs my help. It is Josephine, and I can do nothing for her but remind her of the boys she can't bring home.

"An Orthodox girl, if you can believe it," Black is saying. "Well, she was too different in the end. Now, Josephine's family was different too. Fancier."

"You have to go to her."

He shakes his head. "Don't worry yourself." His face is casual. I can see why he was such a good trial lawyer; the expression is almost convincing. But when I place a hand on his arm the muscles are rigid, and he pulls back. "My doctor told me no man should play singles in his forties," he says. I've heard the joke before, but I don't let on. It is the least mercy I can show. "So I waited till I was fifty." His laugh is threadbare.

"I should leave."

"No." Now it is his hand on my arm. "There's nothing to be done."

"Do what you can."

He clears his throat. "Well. Maybe I can save some of this for lunch tomorrow."

I look at the steak on his plate. "That's a fine idea." When he has left, I push back my chair and bury my own steak deep in the garbage bin. Then I stand where Josephine did and look out the window into the dark. There is a yearning pull within my chest, as though something calls to me from the night. I strain my eyes, trying to make out a shape, but all is formless black.

"Daddy?"

I turn my head. JoJo is at the kitchen door in her nightgown. "Hi there," I say.

She looks around briefly to verify that no better option is available, then turns back to me. "I'm scared."

I drop down into a squat, bringing my eyes level with hers. "What is it?"

"Monsters," she says softly. "In the garden."

"That was a dream," I tell her. "There are no monsters in your garden."

She looks carefully at my face. "Are you scared of something?"

I consider. "No." Nothing she is scared of, anyway. Not dark, not monsters. But something out there has concerned itself with me.

"Who hurt you?"

"What?"

"I heard daddy say it. While you were showering. He said you'd gotten into trouble."

"It's nothing," I say. "Don't worry."

Her face is serious. "I know there are bad men, too."

"Not here," I say. "All the bad men are very far away. You don't need to worry about any of that."

She frowns, unconvinced. "My brothers are fighting them. We talked about it in school."

I stand up, claiming the authority of height. The world is safer than she knows, with her fears of monsters in the dark. Safer, and more wicked, and senselessly cruel.

"Listen, JoJo. Anytime you're worried there are bad men around, you just sneeze. And if anyone's there, you'll know because they'll say, 'Bless you.'"

"Why will they say that?"

"It's the rules." I reach down to ruffle her hair, feel her forehead warm and smooth. "Everyone has to follow the rules."

CHAPTER 16

BLACK IS IN earlier than usual the next morning, whistling "London Bridge" and tossing his hat on the coatrack with a jaunty flick of the wrist. "Hey there, Cash," he says. "How's your face?"

"I'm all right, Judge."

"Good." He steps to my desk and seats himself on the corner. "Thought I should tell you, I've changed my mind about the Witness case."

"What?"

"The flag salute. We had that issue a couple of years ago. I was for it the first time, but I've changed my mind."

"Why's that?"

He raises his hand in a stiff-armed salute. "Doesn't look good, does it? Little children. Other people make them do that, not us."

I nod. The meaning of Gressman's gesture is becoming clearer.

"Felix wrote that one," Black continues. "Wanted to show how much he loved America, press for unity with war on the horizon. But all it did was turn people against the Witnesses. We have law to protect us from our best instincts as well as our worst." He pauses for a moment. "You don't want to forget the people in these cases. They taught you to read cases for the law, didn't they?"

I nod. Cases are like stories, and before Columbia I read some in the leather-bound books of Judge Skinner's library and marveled at them. And then I learned that the people and the happenings in a case are just a pool of muddy water where the law swims like an elusive fish, which glints as it turns and vanishes again. At Columbia they taught us to seine that pond, to let the water slip away and hold only the bright fish in our minds.

"Felix came out with all those things about living by symbols and honoring the flag," Black says, "and everyone thought he meant the Witnesses didn't love their country. It drew a line and put them on the other side."

"So now you're voting the other way?"

"Douglas, too. Murphy. And I expect Jackson. The Witnesses are going to win this time." Black rises to his feet. "There's real people in these cases," he says. "And you should never forget that. They like tapioca, and they can't stand onions, and they wake in a dark night and don't know where they are or why. You don't want to stop seeing their faces."

"Yes, Judge."

"One more thing."

"What?"

He leans down closer to me. A lock of hair falls across his forehead, still damp from the shower. "I want to thank you for last night. Taking care of JoJo."

"Of course, Judge."

"And Josephine." He puts a hand on my shoulder. "You were right."

. . . .

When Black has gone, I walk over to Murphy's chambers. Gressman sits among a pile of papers, wearing a distracted air.

"How did you do it?"

He looks up, startled. "What?"

"Black just told me he's switching in the Pledge of Allegiance case. Showed me the salute like you did."

"Oh," says Gressman. "That." He nods. "It's what he wanted to do anyway. He just hadn't realized it yet."

"How so?"

"Black wants to be one of the good guys. I just showed him how."

"And Frankfurter doesn't?"

"Of course he does. The problem is he's already sure he is. So you can't reach him." Gressman waves his hands over the papers. "Anyway, good thing you came by. I wanted to see you. Had a brain wave."

"About the Witnesses?"

"No, the guys who beat you up. I know what's going on."

I look at him skeptically. He has on yesterday's suit, and among the papers I see a ceramic mug. I sniff the air. "Is that coffee?"

"Who's asking?"

"I am. Where'd you get it?"

"The thing about this rationing, Cash," Gressman says. "It's not about the coffee, *per se*. There's a shortage of cargo space from South America, that's all. The boats are all full of oil and rubber."

"So?"

"So this was trucked from Mexico. It's not subject to rationing."

"That's the most ridiculous thing I've ever heard."

"Well, that's what the man said."

"What man?"

Gressman hesitates for a second. "As I was saying, I've figured something out."

I am undeterred. "It looks to me like you've got enough to share."

"I need it, Cash. I draft opinions."

"You're not drafting any now," I say, taking a step closer. "Don't think I won't knock you around if I have to."

"Look, it's not easy to get. I think they have some trouble at the border."

"I bet they do."

"It's just for when I'm up all night. And I've been drinking it for years. You'd do much better getting used to not having it. Or try chicory."

I take another step toward him. A desk drawer is half open. "You've got a can in there?"

"Come on, Cash. Like you said, I'm helping you." I pause. What he says is true. "And I really have figured something out."

I decide to give him a break. "Okay, spill."

Gressman takes a deep breath. "It's Frankfurter."

"What?" I shake my head in disgust. "Hand over the coffee."

"No, listen to me. I stayed here all last night and read through Murphy's conference notes. Even he notices, almost, in that half-conscious way of his. Something's pushing people. Even Murphy a couple of years before I got here, he voted funny in a couple of cases."

"Funny because he agreed with Frankfurter instead of you? You're nuts. Every Justice tries to influence the other ones."

"That's not what I mean. Yes, of course Felix yammers on in the constitutional cases. I'm not talking about them. I mean the ones where the money is. The business cases, like I told you before. Sometimes they come out wrong, but mostly it's just that the Court is hearing them when it shouldn't. They're granting cert petitions that should be denied."

"And Frankfurter's making them?"

"Not directly. That's the genius of it. It's the clerks. It can't be anything else. Felix is there in conference giving his lectures on constitutional law, but underneath the clerks are making recommendations to grant the business cases, and they're slipping by."

"But if it's the clerks, what does that have to do with Frankfurter?"

"You know how he is with the clerks. And who else could be influencing them?"

I am silent a moment. It is true that Frankfurter talks to the clerks of other Justices, certainly more than any other of the Brethren. And it is true that the recommendations of clerks carry weight on cert petitions, perhaps more than anywhere else. But still . . . "I don't buy it," I say. "He talks to me plenty, and he's never said a word about cert petitions. Not the business cases, anyway."

"Well, maybe he really likes you," Gressman says. "That's good. We can use it."

"But why would he be doing it?"

"He knows how the cases will come out. He can tell other people. Some bureaucrat somewhere, some businessman. Someone who could be useful. They trade the stock ahead of the decision."

"What does that do for him?"

"It lets him control them afterward. He wants to be the puppet master. That's how he thinks of himself. He says all these things about how judges must avoid any extrajudicial considerations, but he's in it up to his neck."

There is a flaw in his logic. I step to the desk. "Gene, you've forgotten why we started with all this."

"I have?"

I pick up his mug. There is about half a cup left. "You have. What does Frankfurter have to do with the Agriculture men?"

A troubled expression comes over Gressman's face. I can see the coffee has driven him fast along a narrow track. "Happy Hot Dogs," he says. "I'm sure he's got former students there."

"Yes, but why would he have me followed? He knows how the cases are coming out. Even if everything you say is true, it makes no sense."

Gressman opens his mouth. Defeat looms on two fronts, and he cannot decide where he should resist. Finally he chooses. "He's still up to something. I know it. The grants are all wrong."

"Maybe. But he's not following me." I drain the mug. It is dark, strong, and sweet. "You need to think a little harder."

But I get no more theories from Gene Gressman in the days that follow. He is working on the cases. He is championing the rights of the Witnesses; he is honing his arguments for the Japanese. I try to follow his example, submerging myself in work. Perhaps he was right: no one wants to hurt me. There's a logic to what he says. Whoever they are, they had their chance and didn't take it. And now they seem to be gone. No one is following me. The days turn cold and dwindle to dusk. Our marines hold Guadalcanal; Rommel's lines break at El Alamein.

It is good news, all of it. And if the men who followed me have lost interest, that does not mean I must. Gene Gressman and I can piece this together somehow; we can unravel the mystery. Later. Right now I am not thinking of Pacific isles or the deserts of Egypt; I am not thinking of men behind me on the street or children raising arms to their flag. I am thinking of the winter dance at Merion, the holiday lights in Rittenhouse Square. It is Christmas, and I am going home.

CHAPTER 17

THE CLUBHOUSE GLOWS in the winter light. The setting sun touches the bricks with rose and gold; it warms the two flags flying near the gate. Suzanne and I pick our way through shiny black cars to the door. The older members have dined downstairs on filets, which the club must have moved heaven and earth to obtain. The younger set is arriving for drinks and dancing, neither of which is rationed.

We can hear the band as we ascend the stairs to the ballroom, the slow lilting tones of a woman singing of a carousel, a chestnut tree. "I'll Be Seeing You." The dance floor is crowded, uniforms jostling against evening wear. Some people just have them made, the rumor goes. Not Billy Fitch, though. His face moves past us, pale and serious, close-cropped hair above shadowed eyes. John Hall couldn't leave Washington; some urgent business detains him. I make a point of mentioning this to Suzanne, but she shrugs impatiently, brushing a wave of hair off her forehead.

I steer her across the floor, then to the bar as the music fades. We still move well together. The bartender's Victory Suit makes me conscious of the width of my lapels, my now-forbidden vest.

On the balcony there is a briskness and clarity to the air. Beyond the great lawn a dying fire grips the trees where crows gather. I feel I can see farther, as though the cold hones me. As I told Josephine, I still live on the academic calendar and my seasons are backward, the smoky scent in the night a promise of renewal.

Suzanne clutches her shoulders, bare in a white silk gown. I drape my jacket over her. "It's been a really busy couple of months," I say. It is in the nature of an apology. The press of work has kept me confined to Washington. The fall dance has come and gone at Merion, and the colors from the leaves, and John Hall has been about while I draft my memos in the marble tomb of the Supreme Court. But now I am here and he is not. "We're working on the Pledge of Allegiance case."

"Is it really appropriate for you to say 'we' when you're just a clerk?"

I am taken aback. "Well, I'm part of it. I help Justice Black decide."

Suzanne drinks off her champagne. "I'm sorry," she says. "I'm in a mood."

I put my hands on her hips, under the jacket. "We don't have to talk about the Court." The blond wave has fallen across her face again. Lots of girls are trying the style, but she really does look like Veronica Lake. I bend and kiss her cheek. "We don't have to talk at all."

She wriggles in my arms. "Not here. My brother's right inside." I turn and see Bob's head moving through the crowd. He isn't in uniform. I guide Suzanne around the edge of the room, out down the stairs. From the driveway, a path leads through the bushes to the flagpole. It stands in a small clearing, a seat ringing its base. It is getting too dark to read the inscription on the square pediment, but I know what is written there. Nineteen names in alphabetical order, Lovell Barlow to Emanuel Wilson, and on the fourth panel one line, *They Died for Their Flag*. That is what the Great War cost Merion.

I lean into Suzanne, pressing her back against the pole. I want to join my body to hers, to weld us together beyond the power of any war to separate. She kisses me. I put a hand under her dress and she slips her head away. "No," she says. I lower my head and kiss her neck, her shoulder. "You think it will make me yours," she says. "But that's not what it does."

"What, then?" I move my hand. "This?"

Suzanne's tone changes. "No, Cash. Loving me. Loving me would make me yours." I take three words of breath. Suzanne puts a finger to my open mouth, then pushes it shut. "You'll catch flies." She tugs her dress down. "Now's not the time. But if my disarray isn't too evident, perhaps you'll give me the honor of a dance."

I take her hand, leading her out through the bushes. The night is cold and dark around us, and again I remember Northeast Harbor. Just a few days after she put her hand in mine on the dock we were out sailing, lolling on a fitful breeze near Sutton Island. There were a couple more islands below us to the south, but to the east the bay opened up and there was nothing but ocean, and you understood how people could think they'd fall off the edge of the world if they went too far.

It's hard to tell distance on an ocean like that, and the thunderheads massing out over the bay started coming in on us while I was still thinking they might pass by up the coast. Suzanne and I reached the same conclusion at the same time, and without a word we were suddenly very busy coming about and pointing the boat homeward. But even what breeze we'd had was gone, like a small animal scared off by the approach of something much larger. The water was flat. "We can run before it a while," Suzanne said. "Once it gets closer."

I didn't think much of this idea, but I nodded. We floated for a spell in the calm, almost dead in the water, while a dark unnatural green spread across the sky. We were hundreds of yards from the mouth of the harbor, where we could find some shelter, with tiny Bear Island in our way. We could pass behind it in some safety, perhaps, but it would still be a long reach in.

After a bit we got the first stirrings of the storm and the sails filled and the boat began to move across the water at a good clip. Then the rain started falling, with a couple of hailstones rattling on the deck for good measure, and I could see we were in a race we were going to lose. "We can't make it back," Suzanne said. She had to yell for me to hear her, and the point was clear enough that it didn't merit discussion. I nodded. Her face was pale in the gloom. Bear Island was coming up, and I pointed at it. It held nothing but trees and a fog bell, but there was a sandy patch of beach on the south side where I thought we might get ashore without damaging the boat too badly.

Suzanne nodded too. We turned the boat straight inland and ran it up on the beach with a grinding noise that made us both wince. Then we jumped out and dragged it from the water while the green sky went black with rain and dark waves heaved themselves out of the ocean to fall upon the shore and burst in spray. We ran for cover into the trees, already soaked, and huddled in what shelter we could find while great sheets of water sluiced past.

Suzanne crouched down in a ball at the foot of a big pine and hugged her knees to her chest. She was shivering, and I could hear her teeth clicking against each other as I bent near. I leaned over her and put my arms around her and tried to hold her still. We stayed like that for what seemed like an hour as the trees creaked above us, my face in her hair and the water cold on my back but warming between us where we pressed together. After the storm weakened enough for us to talk, Suzanne slipped out of my arms and turned to me and put a hand up to my face.

"You'll take care of me," she said. It wasn't a question; she said it like it was something she'd just learned. She brushed my hair back out of my eyes. "You'll take care of me if something happens."

"What else could happen?" I asked, and I laughed a little, because it was starting to seem like a fine adventure, and I'd enjoyed holding her in my arms.

"I don't mean here," she said. She pointed with one finger, her arms still tight across her chest, past the island and the sea and the summer and out into the world beyond. "I mean out there. It's something I know about you now. And I'm glad I know it."

I didn't say anything to that. It was 1935, and plenty of things were happening out there. My family didn't have much to fear, and I didn't think Suzanne's did either, but I didn't need to ask what she meant. Instead I nodded and reached out and took her in my arms again for a while. And when it seemed clear that the storm had passed, she squeezed my hand and we got up and walked through the trees back down to the beach, still holding hands. And we pushed the boat into the water and sailed for home.

I am thinking of this as I walk through the Merion brush with her hand in mine, and I wonder if she is too, if she thinks of that day like I do. Under the moon her face is rounder and soft, letting me see how much nineteen is still a child. The light and warmth of the clubhouse is almost a shock, like her house felt when we finally burst through the door, still in our wet clothes and shivering again. I decide that a drink is the remedy, and a brisk restorative dance.

Later we stand on the balcony again. Other couples huddle together nearby, talking in quiet tones. Suzanne clutches my jacket around her with one hand and holds her fourth glass of champagne in the other. "I hate seeing everyone in uniforms," she says. "I hate this war. Oh, why didn't you come back to Philadelphia?"

There are patches of snow on the great lawn, and a few dead leaves blowing across the grass. "I know I haven't been back much," I say. "It just got very busy all of a sudden." There is no answer. "It's important work," I say. The words sound thin. "Like your father said."

For a moment she says nothing. She just looks at me, her slender body swallowed in the jacket. "Have you ever seen your death, Cash?" Her voice is quiet. "Soldiers do. There's a ball of fire, or a Japanese plane. There's a roaring sound. Then just blackness. At least that's what they tell girls, to make them surrender. To give themselves up. But you can't tell the girls that, can you? What do you say to them? To the girls you have in DC?"

"I don't have any girls in DC"

"I think everyone should have someone else. So if one person lets you down, you aren't all alone."

"I don't know what you're talking about," I say.

"It's so silly," she says. "We think we can control things. We think we know what's going to happen."

"I don't think that."

She goes on as if she hasn't heard me. "All our plans. What do they say about mice and men?"

"Suzanne," I say.

She shakes her head. "Don't say you love me. I won't believe it. Say you're coming back. Say you're coming back now, and I'll do whatever you want." She takes half a step into me. I feel the soft pressure of her breasts against my chest, the delicate bones of her back under my hands. Her heartbeat echoes through my body, rapid, like the wings of a bird. And I know I can't do it. There is still a mission for me; there is a duty unfulfilled.

"There's something strange going on at the Court," I say. "It's hearing cases it shouldn't. And some people are following me. I need to figure it out."

The pressure stops. "What do you mean, following you?" Her voice is sharp. "You never told me anything about this."

"I didn't want to worry you."

"That's ridiculous. Will it be better that I didn't worry when I hear that you've been kidnapped or garroted or whatever?"

"See, this is why I didn't tell you. They're Agriculture guys. Nothing's going to happen to me."

Suzanne squints her eyes shut. I see the child there again for a second, eyes closed in tiny fury—*I'm going with you!*—and then it is gone and she is a young woman in pain. "I can't go on like this," she says. "I need you to come home. I'm not strong enough for this. Maybe you are, but I'm not."

"Yes, you are."

"No. I thought I was, but I'm not." Suzanne lifts the champagne glass to her lips and seems surprised to find it empty. She lets it fall to the floor, where it breaks with a small tinkle. "I feel sick when I think about you, Cash. Seasick, like there's something skewed in the world and I can't get my balance. Like each day coming is a wave that makes it worse. And I can't tell if the wave is regret or love or guilt. I can't even tell them apart."

"You're drunk," I say.

"I am. But it doesn't change anything. It doesn't change the future. It doesn't change the past. People change, but we only change in one direction and never go back."

I find I do not like the tack the conversation is taking. "What do you mean?"

She looks at me and there is the challenge in her face, and then it slips away and there is just a pleading. "You can't expect me to be like you. You don't need people. I do."

"Of course I need people," I say.

She pays no attention. "It would have been different if I'd known you were in danger. I could have been like a war bride. But you only talked about tennis."

"What are you talking about?"

"You'd have to understand," she says. "If I did something I shouldn't. If I maybe kissed someone."

I take a step back. She holds her hands out to me, as if she's reaching through water. And I remember how I would lean out from the dock after she vanished into the ocean, looking for her and seeing first only the deep green, then bubbles, then her white hands and shoulders as she rose and broke the surface, a pale girl gliding toward the sun. I remember the moment on the dock, a couple of days after the storm, when I reached out to her. For all that her hand was hot, I trembled as I took it, and for all that her lips were warm, my teeth were chattering as we kissed. And when our lips met I felt as though I'd been underwater for a long time, straining toward the light and had just broken out into the air and sun. It felt like the air was bursting out of my lungs and the bursting out itself was a relief, even though I knew what I wanted was the breath that was yet to come.

At dinner she was flushed and giggling, and that night for the first time the Judge asked me what I would do with myself. And for the first time he opened a leather-bound book and read me a story in which the law glinted like a fish and was gone.

Now she is reaching out; she touches me, and she is the one who trembles. But I am not ready for the touch. I am thinking of how she smiles into my kiss, the corners of her mouth upturned like a cat's, of how she puts her hand over my heart. I am thinking of her doing all this with someone else—with John Hall!—and the pain is extraordinary.

"You'd understand," Suzanne repeats. It is like a brick in my chest. I step back again.

"I'd try," I say. "I don't know."

It is the only answer I have at the moment, but of course it is the wrong one. Suzanne gives a little gasping sob and my mind changes in an instant. I put my arms around her, but she slips free and hurries down the stairs. I stand holding the empty jacket. With honking cries, a bird passes invisibly above.

After a moment I go into the ballroom, but she isn't there anymore. I get a Scotch and watch the kids dance. It is a scene from my youth, the men at the tables, the children out on the floor. But now I am one of the men who watched us, and I know what they thought. They thought that we would die, and they wondered whether to be happy that we didn't know it. There is Bill Fitch, now flying an Army bomber; there is Ralph Hays in Navy blue. *How would you live if everything recurred?* A philosophy professor asked us to contemplate this at Penn. It is a child's thought, I see now, that the present will never end. How do you live knowing it won't return, that everything happens just once and rolls away into the past? Suzanne was right; we only change in one direction and never go back. I have a sudden memory of how she used to tug on my sleeve when we walked. For a moment it is almost paralyzing.

You see time's knife unsheathed. That's how the Judge described getting older, one evening over glasses of fire and smoke. But it is not just time; there is the war, too, pushing everything faster, accelerating the reckoning that awaits us all. I see in my mind the narrow band of names around the base of the flagpole. We will need more space this time.

That is where I find her, standing by the flagpole looking at the names. She puts out her hand without looking up, and I take it. Then she is in my arms. "Take me home, Cash," she says. "Just take me home."

. . . .

The next day is bright and cold and I am sitting on the porch with a mug of coffee when I see her little red coupe coming up the drive. I have been thinking that I am big enough to excuse a misstep. After all, I reason, am I not at least partially in the wrong myself? Didn't I force this separation on her, which she never wanted? And didn't I make eyes at the senorita at Cissy's house, try to impress her with my tales of Fish House Punch?

I am ready for a tender reconciliation, but Suzanne is all business.

"The Judge agrees with me," she says. "You should come home."

"What do you mean?"

"Quit the job. It's not worth it. You're in danger."

"I don't think I am," I say. "And I need to stay there. The Court is the only place I can figure out who's influencing the clerks."

"What makes you think anyone's influencing them?"

"I told you, they're the only ones who could be making the Justices agree to hear these cases."

"But why does anyone have to be influencing them? Maybe they're doing it on their own. Maybe they're part of it."

The idea has not occurred to me. "But the Justices hire their own clerks. No one could put their people in there." Even as I say it, I realize this isn't true. Most Justices have professors they rely on . . . and, I remember, Frankfurter himself has done a lot of the selection where Harvard men are concerned. What had he said to me that first evening? *I used to pick Brother Black's clerks. . . .* Perhaps Gressman was right about him all along.

Suzanne sees my frown. "Not all the time, maybe. But sometimes. And maybe they help their odds by taking out some of the clerks they don't like."

"But that's silly," I say. "No one's taking out the clerks."

"Oh, really? Didn't you get this job because Black had two clerks drafted away before they could start?"

My frown deepens. I have put the fate of the first two hires from my mind, perhaps because it undermines my own sense of merit, but what she says is true. It is worth looking into, I think. I will have to find out if anything similar has happened with other Justices.

"You see?" says Suzanne triumphantly. "They must have someone in mind for that slot. You probably only made it into the job because no one found out who you were in time. And now . . ."

"What?"

"Now they're probably looking for some other way to get rid of you. I'm serious, Cash. I want you to quit."

"And so does your father?"

"He does."

I am silent a moment. It is hard to feel threatened on a Haverford porch, but the peril seems more real as Suzanne lays it out. As best I can remember, I have never rejected the Judge's advice. I have never gone against the urgings of that powerful voice. And I have never regretted any of the decisions we made together. But as I think about it, that history itself strengthens my determination to stay. Now the Court is a place I have chosen on my own; now it is truly mine.

"I have to stick it out," I say.

Suzanne looks dumbfounded. "Did you not hear what I said?"

"I did," I say. "But what are you suggesting? That I leave Justice Black so they can put someone disloyal in with him? Or another poor sap who might get taken out? I can't do that. At least I know to watch my back." She says nothing. "We've got two weeks now," I say. "We'll enjoy it. The spring won't seem so long. And if I don't figure it out by then, I'll come home."

Suzanne's face suggests that she does not find this much of a concession. "Of course you will."

"So there we go."

Her expression wavers between mutiny and contrition. "I'm having trouble with this. I told you. I don't know if I can stand it."

"Sure you can," I say. "You told me why yourself."

"Why?"

"Because now you know I'm in danger."

. . . .

We have two weeks together. There is hot cider and carriage rides, mulled wine and the tip of her nose cold against my neck. "It is proposed to give an Assembly," the invitations always read. But there is no proposal this year; the Assembly is suspended for the duration of the war. There is a shortage of men for even the private cotillions. I go to a few, some with Suzanne and some without her. I watch the old ladies in their jeweled collars, arranging terrapin bones in neat circles on their plates, the older men with shiny pinpoint eyes in alabaster faces that redden as they drink. Suddenly I am eager to get back to the Court.

CHAPTER 18

I SIT AT my desk in Justice Black's chambers. Before me is a list of twelve names. I add one more: Jake Porter. Then I lean back, put my feet up, and look out the window. Bundled against the weather, a young couple stroll arm in arm down First Street. Am I in danger? So Suzanne said, and I agreed, and my words sounded fine in the Haverford sun: dashing, fearless, even gallant. But it has been weeks since that afternoon, and in the marble confines of the Court, in the shadows of evening on the way home, the idea is more troubling.

No one is following me anymore; I am pretty sure of it now. But since my return from Philadelphia I have been looking into Suzanne's theory, that someone is influencing the selection of clerks. Gathering information on this year's crop is easy enough. A new caution shadows my conversations with them; some may be disloyal, and I do not know who to trust. But there is room enough in the ordinary exchanges of the day to figure out whether they arrived here by some unusual stroke of luck.

Finding this out for the clerks of prior years is harder. And then there is the most difficult task: identifying the men who never made it here. They are the crucial ones. If clerks have been intercepted on their way to the Court, it supports the theory that someone is manipulating the hiring. And it is the replacements for those clerks who are most likely to be agents of the enemy.

I cannot ask the current clerks about this. I see no way to do it without tipping my hand to any disloyal element, and besides, I doubt that any of them would know. Instead I exchange gossip with secretaries and messengers; I trade jokes with marshals who have seen it all. And when names come up I add them to the chart in my desk.

All around me, the Court goes about its business. Cases are argued, opinions are drafted. The Witnesses win the right to knock on doors; the Pledge case is coming up. To me it is all a background hum. Black does not need me to write opinions, and my attention is on the clerks. By March I have what I think is a comprehensive list. In recent years there have been seven cases when a Justice's first choice did not join him. Add in the draft and the total grows to thirteen. It is an ominous number.

"Holmes always worked standing up," says Felix Frankfurter. "As I told you on our first meeting."

I spin back to the door. There he stands, in a gray pin-striped suit, his shirt crisp and white. "Elevating the feet has a soporific effect," he says. "But you are displaying energy. You have been busy. Gathering information, I suspect."

I slide a cert petition on top of my list of names. "Working," I say.

"And what have you learned?"

I hesitate.

"Ah," says Frankfurter. He steps into the room. "Come, Cash. We need have no secrets from one another. I will tell you something. Just now I passed Bill Douglas in the hall, and he said that Hugo would not go with me on the flag salute."

"Oh."

"You know that already. You are counting votes, I think. Well, I can do that too. And I see how it is shaping up." Frankfurter pauses. "You understand, Cash, how important it is for a judge to put aside his personal desires. Most of all his desire for approval from his crowd. A judge can have no loyalties except to abstractions, to truth and justice. Oliver Wendell Holmes knew that. A great Justice like Holmes never once in his career committed an absurdity. Your Justice is about to commit one here. It is a pity, because he has been moving toward the status of the great."

"That's kind of you to say."

Frankfurter waves his hand, as though brushing away a fly. "Kindness is no concern of mine. But loyalty is. Your Justice perhaps does not appreciate the significance of the oath. But it means something. It matters. *One nation, indivisible, with liberty and justice for all.*" He pauses, reflecting. "Do you know that they asked the Japanese to declare their loyalty? To renounce allegiance to the emperor, to say they will fight for America?"

"Why did they do that?"

"Why indeed? I just had dinner with the Francis Biddles. He wants to send them back to their homes. He thought that the disloyal ones would volunteer themselves, a hundred or so, and we could keep them in the camps and return the rest to the coast. And do you know what happened?"

"What?"

"Thousands said no. Biddle is not a bad man or a wrong-doing man, but a heedless fellow, because he does not take things with sufficient seriousness. He is an amateur. Too la-de-da. And la-de-da is not good enough in wartime. Now the President is talking of forming a battalion from those who said yes." Frankfurter shakes his head.

"What's wrong with that?"

"Those ones worry me more," says Frankfurter. "The army is just where a disloyal man would want to be."

I remember the doctor in Philadelphia, smiling through his beard. "Maybe they want to help," I say, and Frankfurter dismisses me with a look.

"Now, Cash," he says. "Why do you suppose your Justice has changed his mind? Has he been reading the newspapers instead of the Constitution?"

"I don't know," I say. My eyes stray to the door. Gene Gressman is passing by in the hall, and when he looks in and sees Frankfurter he stops for a moment, clicks his heels and raises his arm. I remain silent, but something must show on my face, for Frankfurter turns in time to catch the end of the display. When he wheels back to me, his cheeks have gone white and his eyes are blinking furiously.

"It is a Roman salute," he says. "Not that it matters. The arms will be raised, Cash, to one flag or another. We will live under our symbols, or we will die beneath someone else's." He bites his lip and turns away, shaking his head. At the door he pauses. His face is still white and his mouth is pale. "La-de-da is not good enough in wartime," he repeats.

. . . .

When he has gone, I wait a few minutes and go in search of Gressman.

"What were you thinking?" I ask.

He shrugs. "Nothing wrong with winding up Felix. It distracts him from his scheming."

"If you say so." I look at his desk, piled high with papers. "By the way, I think I've figured it out."

"What?"

"What's going on with the clerks."

Gressman raises his eyebrows. "Really? I kept trying with that, but I couldn't make it work. The pieces wouldn't fit together."

"You were looking in the wrong place." I tell him Suzanne's theory, and the evidence behind it. "Seven clerks intercepted. Thirteen, if you count the draft."

"Hmm." Grudgingly, he is impressed. "You have the names?"

I hand over the list and he reads it, nodding. "Jake Porter, that could be blackmail. There was talk about him at Michigan. But I don't know. Seven is an awful lot, Cash. You think they can just talk people out of taking a clerkship?"

"I don't know. Maybe some of them were genuine. But I think the replacement clerks are the ones we should be suspicious of."

"Oh, I know who we should be suspicious of."

I have identified two replacements among the current crop. "Who?"

"Haynes, for sure. Philbin. Beaver. Maybe Davis. He's got a funny look to him."

His list does not match mine. After a moment I realize why. "Gene, you've just named all the conservatives."

"I left out you, didn't I?" I let it pass. "Well," he continues after a moment, "I call 'em like I see 'em."

"In case you're interested, the ones here now who weren't the first choice are Davis and Ingalls."

"I said Davis had a funny look."

I see no point in pursuing the topic. "Are you worried?"

"About being blackmailed?"

"About being drafted. About anything."

"I have a bad heart." He pounds a fist on his chest. "It keeps me healthy."

"I'd heard the effect was rather the opposite."

"It means I don't have to worry about lead poisoning," he says. "I'm a real 4-F."

"So am I," I say. The words open a hollow in me. "But I'm worried."

"Someone's learned your secret shame?"

"The two clerks Black hired before me were drafted before they could start."

"Ah," says Gressman. "Indeed." He nods. "To lose one clerk is a misfortune. To lose two seems like carelessness."

It is not the response I was hoping for. No one is following me anymore, and it is getting late in the term to reap much benefit from replacing me, but Gressman's cavalier tone still rankles. "Can you give me anything other than a joke?"

"It's an epigram. Adapted from Oscar Wilde. You may call it a bon mot, if you wish."

I shake my head, annoyed. "I should have drunk all your coffee when I had the chance. What are you in such a good mood about?"

"The Japs," he says. "*Hirabayashi* briefs just came in. We have good facts. The Court's going to say the evacuation was unconstitutional. I'm going to win this one."

"No, you're not," I say. "Don't you read the papers? They asked the Japs in the camps if they were loyal, and thousands of them said no."

He shrugs. "If they put you in a camp, you might start saying some funny things too. Have you read the briefs?"

"No. I've been working on this. Remember when you were helping me?"

Another shrug. "I told you, I tried. Couldn't make it fit. But now you have a new idea, good. Let's switch off. You think about the Japanese; I'll look for the enemy among us."

· · · ·

Hirabayashi v. United States is not an easy case. Military authorities imposed a curfew on the West Coast Japanese Americans, then removed them from their homes, ordering them to report to Assembly Centers for transport to Relocation Camps. Gordon Hirabayashi broke the curfew and refused to assemble. For this he was convicted in federal court. Now the ACLU has chosen him to make their challenge to the exclusion orders.

They have chosen him because he is clearly loyal. He is an Eagle Scout, a baseball fan, no threat to the security of the coast. Good facts, as Gressman said. But the Court cannot decide for him alone; it will decide for everyone excluded. And how do we decide?

I use the methods my professors taught me. The lawyers have brought me a story, of a man who walked into the FBI office and told them he would not go. Through those murky waters I draw the seine of intellect. I am looking for the bright fish of the law, but I find nothing. I am lost; I am adrift in an endless sea, and there is no law, neither in the sun-dappled shallows nor the dark abyssal depths. There are only men.

I see only faces. I see Gordon Hirabayashi with his merit badges and scout kerchief. General John DeWitt with his ribbons and his medals. American soldiers, standing in the camp guard towers and crossing Pacific beaches. The earnest young men of the ACLU. And Congress and the President and the Department of Justice.

Here is how to decide a constitutional case, Justice Roberts once said. Lay the statute alongside the Constitution, and see if they fit. But he must have been joking, I think now. There is no law that will decide this case. The only question is whom to trust. If these people are dangerous, they can be excluded. If they are loyal, they cannot.

There are the faces in the story, and there are the voices in the briefs. Whose word will we accept? The Japanese are loyal, the ACLU says. There were no acts of sabotage on the coast before the evacuation. There have been none in Hawaii. The evacuation was driven by racism and fear-mongering.

We did not know, says the Department of Justice. We could not know. They worship the emperor as a god. They sent their children to Japan for schooling. If no sabotage occurred, might that not mean that they were gathering for a concerted blow? Evacuation was a reasonable measure. After all, it is milder than the draft.

The Pacific Coast states take a stronger tone. These people are disloyal, they say. They are not like us. They do not assimilate. They have their own religion, their own language schools; they sent tinfoil home before Pearl Harbor. Before the evacuation there were radio signals from the coast and lights flashing messages to ships at sea. Raids on Japanese businesses found dynamite, guns, and ammunition. And on the loyalty questionnaire they admitted it all.

CHAPTER 19

ON EACH OF the courtroom tables, as tradition demands, the white quill pens repose in their inkstands. The lawyers ignore them, focusing instead on their papers, leaning toward each other for whispered consultations. The clerks have the privilege of their own gallery, a small alley connected to the Justices' chambers by a short corridor but sealed off from the public by brass grillwork. The view is not great, for we have to contend with the marble columns that run along the sides of the room, and only about half of us can see all of the nine high-backed chairs behind the bench. Justice Black is hidden from my view, but I do see tall and dapper Harold Evans of Philadelphia and a cluster of men I take for representatives of the ACLU. At the government's table, the military uniforms of War Department lawyers mingle with the morning coats and pin-striped trousers of the Solicitor General's office. I recognize John Hall and feel a flash of anger that nearly brings me around to the ACLU side. He does not notice my glare.

Harold Evans rises to the podium to open for Hirabayashi. "The question in this case is whether the military can confine citizens to their homes, and then later order them to leave those homes, to leave the states in which they have always lived. The military cannot do that. The Constitution protects civilians from military authority outside an active theater of operations."

Frankfurter is first to speak. "So you would have us rule that the Pacific Coast was not a theater of operations."

"Yes. Pearl Harbor, where the Japanese attacked in December, is twenty-four hundred miles away. Midway, which was under attack in June, is thirty-three hundred. Attu, where they made a landing in June, is twenty-six hundred miles from the Pacific Coast. There was never any danger of invasion."

Douglas stirs. "Isn't that a question for the military, not for judges?"

Evans hesitates a moment. He looks as though he is starting to miss his corporate practice. "The facts speak for themselves," he says. Douglas grunts, not in an approving way. It is the noise he makes when clerks speak to him in the hallways.

At my side, Gressman looks stricken. "If we don't have Douglas, we have nothing," he says.

"What's this 'we'?" I ask. Gressman turns away and punches at the shoulder of Vern Countryman, the Douglas clerk, who is hiding his rangy frame behind what we call the Douglas column. It blocks Douglas's chair from view, and his clerks use it for cover when they want to watch an oral argument. Douglas is of the mind that clerks with time to watch arguments need more work, and if he spots them will send a messenger with some contrived rush assignment. Countryman ducks his head and shrugs.

Evans seems to have nothing more to say. He stands with a small smile, projecting the proper Philadelphian's air of obscure superiority, a confidence whose basis is no longer evident.

"Are the facts speaking?" Haynes whispers to me from the other side. "I don't hear anything."

"So," Justice Black says encouragingly. "You want the judges to say whether this military decision is reasonable?"

"Yes," says Evans. He starts to life again, as though he has remembered the point he wanted to make. "These orders were issued in bad faith. General DeWitt was influenced by pseudo-patriotic groups and the economic power groups wishing to acquire Japanese-owned land for a song. They beat the drums of hate against the Japanese race. General DeWitt was not free of these views himself. Testifying to Congress about the American citizens, he said, 'A Jap's a Jap. A piece of paper doesn't change that.' Race prejudice, not military necessity, was the reason for these orders."

"General DeWitt may have made a mistake," says Black. "But even if he did, isn't much more required to show bad faith?"

"There is ample other evidence that race hostility and prejudice were the driving forces. There is no doubt that most of these people are loyal Americans."

Douglas is shaking his head. "Some of these people are surely loyal Americans. But that does not affect the soundness of the military judgment. The judgment was that the disloyal could not be identified in sufficient time."

"The FBI was arresting suspects hours after Pearl Harbor," Evans says. "Evacuation took six months. The transfer from relocation centers to the current detention camps did not even begin until May. There was ample time to consider these people on their own merits as individuals." He pauses a moment and gives his conclusion. "Neither race nor color has military significance."

"Thank you, counselor," says Chief Justice Stone. "General Fahy, we'll hear from you."

I have seen Charles Fahy argue a few times before. We call him Whispering Charlie. Most people couldn't get away with a delivery that forces listeners to concentrate in order to make out the words, but as Solicitor General he commands enough respect that we make the effort. He is a short man who stands stock-still while arguing, only seldom disagreeing with Justices. "Concede every point but the one you need," Black told me once. That is Fahy's style. For emphasis he will sometimes take a step away from the podium and make a slow up-and-down movement of his clenched hands.

"The central issue in this case," Fahy says, "is the war power of the government. How far may it go to protect the nation? We all remember Pearl Harbor. We remember what followed. Imperial Japan threw us back on every front. It was the most serious threat that had ever faced the United States.

"Now, what of the West Coast? It is the part of America closest to the battle sites in the Pacific. And it is a location of manufacturing enterprises, of ships and airplanes. The military authorities bear the responsibility not only of protecting American citizens but of protecting these vital elements of the war effort."

"And would you allow judges to review these military orders?" Justice Murphy asks.

"I would," says Fahy. "An exercise of military authority must be reasonable. But these orders are certainly reasonable. One hundred twelve thousand ethnic Japanese lived on the West Coast, concentrated in areas of key strategic importance. One-third of these are enemy aliens. Of the American citizens, perhaps ten thousand were sent back to Japan for part of their education. As a group they have not assimilated."

"So you maintain it was necessary to evacuate them all?"

"I do not," Fahy says. We all lean in closer. "I maintain that necessity is not the test. The matter could have been handled in other ways. Perhaps those other ways would have been preferable. But it cannot be said that the evacuation from the coast was unreasonable in view of all the circumstances."

"What of the detention in camps of which Mr. Evans spoke?"

"Detention is not at issue in this case, Justice Murphy. Hirabayashi was never in a camp. He was charged with failing to observe the curfew, and that is all that is before the Court."

Fahy pauses for a moment and goes into his conclusion. "We understand that many of the evacuated persons are loyal. We regret the inconvenience caused to them. But all Americans, of Japanese origin or not, must be prepared to make sacrifices. In time of war, it is not enough to say, 'I am a citizen and I have rights.'" The hands go up and down, fists clenched. "One must also say, 'I am a citizen, and I have obligations.'"

CHAPTER 20

IT IS AN easy case, Black tells me after the Justices have conferred. They will consider only the curfew, not evacuation, and curfew is a reasonable exercise of the war power. Every Justice is agreed.

Gressman is crushed. For two days he says nothing at all. Then he begins to plan a dissent. "I can still get three or four to sign on," he says. "It'll be a warning to the government that the curfew is as far as they can go. They'll close the camps."

This prediction strikes me as unlikely in the extreme, but I find I do not care much one way or the other. I am nearing the end of things here. Fall is my time of beginnings, but spring smells of mercy and reprieve. The air is warm, blowing down the Mall toward the Capitol and the Court, coming up off the river with a green, wet scent. Two weeks after the *Hirabayashi* argument, a flight of P-38s catches Yamamoto's transport in the air over the Solomons. A year and a half after Pearl Harbor, the mastermind is dead, and from one lump of coral to the next, the Marines make their way toward Japan's Home Islands. There is no doubt now that we are winning.

Everything is coming to a close, and it was not as dreadful as we feared. I will go back to Philadelphia; the ordinary world will resume; my sojourn in this city of mysteries will be over. There were strange doings; there were puzzles we never figured out, but it is all ending well enough. I still get invitations to Cissy's dinners. I still go from time to time. Colonel Richards harangues us about the Court and the President, the socialists, the traitors. Drew Pearson harangues me about Richards and his ilk, the isolationists, the traitors. Joe Patterson mumbles and drinks his wine, looking worse each evening.

Suzanne and I have weathered the separation better than I expected. It was a test, I suppose, and I suppose we have passed it. In April, I steal a weekend and take the train up to see her. Sunday afternoon we sit on her bed. The white spread is lightly rumpled between us, blue flowers raised on its folds as though peeking through snowdrifts. There is no one but us in the house. Her father is in the city catching up on cases, and out the window the gardener clips the privet hedge with shears that by their size should be addressing the toes of Rittenhouse ladies. The Judge is in his courtroom, and all's right with the world.

For a moment I am impressed by the palpable emptiness of a big house. I think how lonely she must be here by herself. And then the emptiness impresses itself on me for another reason. Something is happening between us as we lean in to kiss. I am more aware of her body, aware of it not just as an object of yearning hypotheticals but as something warm and tangible and very nearby, pressing against me now through her clothes. Barriers are coming down, which have stood between us for years; lines are being crossed that marked the experienced from the imagined.

"In two months," she says breathily. "You'll be back." I don't know if she is asking for confirmation or suggesting postponement. Whatever she means, I say nothing; and whatever she means, she must not mean it very much, for we move on. We are deep in unfamiliar territory now, both of us breathing hard and clenching each other as for reassurance.

The gardener clips and sights along the hedge. My head comes up, and for a moment I watch him through the window, measuring lines and balance. He is looking not at what is but at what will be, not the branches in front of him but those that will grow months from now. The future is already visible to him, more real than the present. But not for me. I am caught in the instant, my vision limited to inches and seconds. Then I lift my thought; I rise above the hot, frantic moment and peer ahead. I feel suspended, motionless in space, outside of time. And what I see hits me like a physical blow.

I do not know what it is. There is a sudden vision of blackness, a sense of collision with something overwhelmingly large. For a moment, inexplicably, I am terrified. I do not know what is happening to me. A premonition? A stroke? I remember Suzanne asking if I had seen my death and wonder if that's what this is. Then she moves beneath me and shifts her weight. Whatever it was, the vision is gone. I am back to the immediate, the all-consuming instant. "Be gentle," Suzanne says. "Be slow."

I am, or I try, but soon enough everything gives way and I am falling into her, helpless and wild as the man who first stepped from a plane to the empty sky, trusting a square of silk to bear him up.

. . . .

In the weeks that follow, I am on edge. What have I chosen, what have I promised? What did I see? Suzanne is more confident and cheerful; she knows I am bound to her by honor. And Gene Gressman is working too hard to talk. He is there in Murphy's chambers when I arrive in the morning; he stays there after everyone has left, listening to jazz records and nodding to himself. "You'll see when I'm done," is all he'll say. "Why don't you have a chat with Felix? Get into his confidence. We may need it."

I have no particular desire to talk to Frankfurter, but there is not much else to do. The Justices are working on various opinions: *Hirabayashi*, or the Pledge of Allegiance, or some corporate case. Black wants my afternoons for tennis, but my mornings are free. And so I open myself to Frankfurter's society, sometimes in the halls or at my desk, sometimes in his chambers under the watchful eyes of Phil Haynes. I act friendly, admiring, eager to absorb his wisdom. Frankfurter is busy writing a dissent in the Pledge case, but he is happy to talk on any subject, himself above all.

"I almost attended Columbia myself," he says when I mention my alma mater. "I headed up to Morningside Heights to matriculate one day." For some reason the phrasing puts me in mind of salmon spawning. I see Frankfurter's silvery head surging above the traffic on Riverside Drive, leaping the uptown rapids with powerful kicks. I have to cough to cover my laughter, and Frankfurter looks at me quizzically. "A friend of mine talked me into going to Coney Island instead. 'If you're going to matriculate,' he said, 'you must have some money on you.'" Something about the way he repeats the word 'matriculate' threatens to reduce me again to giggles. I remind myself that this is deadly serious. "And then I got the flu," Frankfurter continues. "I was told to leave New York City for my health. And that is how I ended up at Harvard."

"My brother went to Harvard," I say. It is not much of a rejoinder, but the words are like coins in a jukebox. Frankfurter nods quickly and starts up again.

"There were lots of robust, self-confident creatures about. But it turned out that no one cared about your father or your face." He pauses. "This was at the law school, of course. When I tried to get a job, it was a different matter. I went out for Hornblower and Potter. I'd heard they'd never taken a Jew, and I said, 'That's the office I want to get into.' And they were willing to take me—on the condition I change my name."

That certainly never happened to my brother. I find myself at a loss. "Oh," I say. "How unpleasant of them."

"Yes," he says. "I refused, of course. 'Hold yourself dear,' my mother told me. I went to work for Henry Stimson instead. He was not yet the Secretary of War, only a New York district attorney. But a great man even then. He is handling the Japanese American problem with both wisdom and appropriate hard headedness."

• • • •

Eventually, Chief Justice Stone circulates a draft opinion for the *Hirabayashi* case. The curfew is a reasonable military measure, he says, and judges cannot second-guess the generals. There is reason to fear disloyalty, he continues, relying on the brief of the Pacific states. The Japanese have not assimilated, and they send their children to Japanese language schools. The military had to act quickly, and it did.

Now I get a chance to see what Gressman has been working on. A draft dissent comes from Murphy's chambers. All these things could be said of the Italians, it observes, with their Catholic schools. Placing our own citizens in camps . . . it bears a melancholy resemblance to the treatment of Jews in Germany.

My conversations with Frankfurter change tone. He is furious. How dare

Murphy speak to him of the Jews of Europe? What we can do for them is win this war as quickly as possible, united behind the President.

Black just shakes his head. It's a mess, he tells me. I wouldn't let them back if I was in command. Murphy doesn't understand that this is war.

In the next days, Gressman opens other lines of attack. A letter comes from Douglas, asking why we cannot say that the Army should let the loyal citizens prove themselves and return home. Vern Countryman goes from chambers to chambers with FBI reports attesting that the threat of disloyalty has been overblown. They took my law school valedictorian, he tells me. An empty chair at graduation. Called to serve his country in another place, the dean said.

It makes no impression on Black, and it infuriates Frankfurter further. Douglas is cynical and amoral, he tells me, writing for the mob outside, not the priests in the temple. The Court cannot order anyone released, loyal or not. As for the FBI . . . the generals said this was necessary. Who are we to second-guess them? Do you want another Pearl Harbor?

The Justices are as close to open war as I have seen them. Stone calls conference after conference, hoping to hammer out a compromise. Frankfurter rants for fifty minutes at a time, Black tells me, the duration of his Harvard seminars. At the end of one tirade, Douglas stands up and gives him a Nazi salute, saying "Heil, Fuhrer." Frankfurter sweeps a stack of books off the table and storms out.

But slowly Frankfurter prevails. Importuning, cajoling, begging, he goes from chambers to chambers, like the Russians retaking Stalingrad house by house. First Rutledge and then Douglas agree to join Stone's opinion. Gressman fights a desperate rearguard action. He looks awful, desolate and pale, so tired I don't begrudge him whatever coffee he has. But even Murphy finally gives in. He will write separately, but in concurrence, not dissent.

When that memo circulates, late in the evening, I go to Murphy's chambers to see Gressman. I can hear his music before I reach the door, one of the little combos he's always telling me will replace the big bands. The tune jumps around, too fast for dancing, but as I stop with my hand on the frame I can see Gressman moving to it. His head nods up and down; his glasses throw fragments of light my way. He's still thinking he can turn this around; he's convinced himself there's a way out. It's crazy, but endearing. "Got your new plan?" I'm trying to put cheer in my voice, but when he turns it drains away. His cheeks are wet. I open my mouth but nothing comes. After a moment he shakes his head and I walk on.

· · · ·

Spring is turning the corner into summer as the *Hirabayashi* decision is announced. Heat hangs like a damp blanket in the air, and shrill insects sing in the dark nights. The *Washington Post* picks up on Murphy's concurrence as a sign that some of the Justices entertain grave misgivings. It laments that the outright deprivation of civil rights we have visited upon these helpless and, for the most part, no doubt, innocent people may leave an ugly blot upon the pages of our history and urges the Court to reach the issues of evacuation and detention as soon as possible. I hope it will make Gressman feel better.

"I'm only reading the California papers," Black tells me; those ones are enthusiastic.

The clerks celebrate the approaching end of term with a happy hour in the courtyard. There are stone benches and chairs of wrought iron; there is a fountain that throws jets of water up to hang suspended in the air, fall, and return. "Sorry we couldn't go with you," Vern Countryman says to Gressman. "I bet Douglas a bottle of Scotch he'd realize he made a mistake. I figure he'll come around for the next one, though."

"You going to be here?" I ask.

Countryman shakes his head. "Army Air Force," he says. "Want to come along? Volunteers get their pick of service."

I say nothing. I have two more months with Black, and after that the future looms like a blank wall. I see Suzanne in her ball gown, pale silk and paler skin; I see her rising through the green water, wreathed in bubbles. I remember her lying on the bed, blue flowers in the sheets. And I remember that moment when the darkness reached out its hand. What is waiting for me? Law practice in Center City, the indentures and debentures of the Girard Trust, the annual proposal of an Assembly? Or is now the time to volunteer, time for shrapnel-torn Umbrian skies, for bloody Pacific coral? A moment of death, or a lifetime of dying?

Haynes walks over. A sheen of sweat puts silvery highlights on his temples and upper lip. "Unconditional surrender," he says.

Gressman looks up. "On the contrary," he said. "I have not yet begun to fight." His voice is thicker than usual. I wonder how much he has been drinking.

"You should probably start sometime soon," Haynes says. "Before there are too many 9–0 decisions against you."

"Nine–zero," says Gressman to me. "It's true. I would have liked a stronger message that the curfew's as far as we'll let them go. Why did it have to be 9–0?"

"Why?" Haynes asks. "Because there are only nine Justices. Besides, don't you think your stern concurrence is a warning? To the brink, the very brink of constitutional power."

"Shut up, Phil," says Countryman.

"To the brink," Haynes repeats. He sings it to the tune of the "William Tell Overture" and performs a mincing dance, evidently intended to suggest a man on horseback. "To the brink, to the brink, to the brink-brink-brink. Hi-yo Murphy, away!" Other clerks are looking over in curiosity. Gressman rises and takes a step toward Haynes, who cocks one eyebrow and both fists. "Try me, Gene."

"I can move Murphy," Gressman says. His words are clearer. "I can move Black. Ask Cash if you don't believe me." His voice rises. "You know who puts their own citizens in camps. There will be none of that here."

He stops. I am thinking that if he is anything like the drunks I've known back home, the next thing will be a rush of tears and broad affection. But Haynes has other plans: he gives Gressman a fist in the face. Gressman never has time to get his hands up; he takes the blow on his right cheek and sits down hard. Countryman and I look at Haynes in surprise.

He holds his hand, wincing. "He was going for me."

"I didn't see anything," I say. "Vern?" He shakes his head.

"I could tell," Haynes says.

I take a step toward him. "You can tell," I say. This close, I can smell the Wildroot Cream Oil in his hair. "You have this magical ability to tell when someone's about to hit you?"

"It's not magic," Haynes says. "It's just a matter of knowing what to look for."

"Might be worth a test," Countryman says.

At first I don't get it. Then I understand. "It's the way he was holding his hands," Haynes is saying. "He was—"

He doesn't get any further, because I swing from the hip and land a solid one in his gut. "You're not as good at that as you think," I say. He doubles over, then straightens and comes at me. Episcopal had its boxing master, and I fielded enough of his punches to slip Haynes's first shot. It glances off the side of my head. He swings again, a wild roundhouse that I duck. I bounce up and give him a jab under the eye. He takes a staggering step backward and trips into the fountain.

My hand is hurting now, but I try not to show it. Haynes rights himself and looks up in fury. "In fact, you're pretty bad," I say.

Gressman chimes in from the ground. "I'm staying. I'll be here for the next case. I'm going to win that one, and there's nothing you or anyone else can do about it."

But in that prediction, Gene Gressman is wrong.

CHAPTER 21

THE NEXT DAY, I head into work with a lighter step. Oddly enough, I find that the fight has restored my sense of well-being. There is a satisfaction in finding out who the enemy is, and also in punching him in the face. I would not have guessed that I would end up fighting Haynes, or that I'd do it on Gene Gressman's behalf. But he's a friend. He helped me, or tried to, and I helped him. I wish him luck in the next case, I think. When the Court can't duck the issue anymore, when it has to decide about the evacuation and the detention of the Japanese, I hope he wins.

I should get him something before I go, I decide. Maybe I'll stop by Murphy's chambers and ask him what he'd like. Or maybe it should be a surprise. In my experience, people are always giving each other silver hip flasks on occasions like this. Engraved, monogrammed . . . it's a little *de trop*. But maybe there's something like that with a coffee theme . . .

Raised voices disrupt my musings. They echo in the corridor. "This is a federal investigation," one man says.

"I don't take orders from you," another answers. "Or J. Edgar Hoover."

I round the corner. One of the Court's marshals is standing in the doorway to Frank Murphy's chambers. He blocks the way of a man in a dark suit with a badge in his hand. Haynes and Countryman stand nearby, their faces serious.

"What's going on?" I ask.

Countryman puts his hand on my shoulder.

"It's Gene."

"What?"

"He's dead. I'm sorry, Cash."

I do not think; I just push my way past the agent, heading into Murphy's chambers. The marshal steps forward, but then he recognizes me and lets me pass. I look wildly about for a body, a bloodstain, something to mark the enormity of what has happened. There is nothing, just Gene's scattered papers and books and a coffee mug on the desk. It looks for all the world as if he has just stepped out for a moment, and when I return to the hallway I half expect to see him standing there.

But there is only Countryman's concerned face. "I'm sorry."

I have the feeling that everything is slowing down around me. It isn't, though. Behind Countryman the two men continue their argument unabated. It is just that their words no longer register. One thought occupies my mind, so big that it is taking a long time to process. *Gene Gressman is dead. Right,* I am thinking; *right, I understand . . .* and then it slips away; I lose my grip. What is before me is too huge, too featureless to grasp.

"What happened?"

"No one knows. They found him this morning."

The world is coming back into focus, but it is different. My face feels slack; the air does not satisfy my lungs. "Why is the FBI here?"

"I don't know," Countryman says. "But the marshals won't let them in. You should go sit down, Cash. You're not looking good."

I nod my head. *Right,* I think, *right.* It slips away again. I am not looking good. I should go sit down. I walk on down the hall to Justice Black's chambers. Over my shoulder the words of the argument are intelligible again.

"So whose orders are you following?"

"Justice Felix Frankfurter's."

● ● ● ●

For hours I sit at my desk and gaze out the window, seeing nothing. Thoughts run through my mind. Gene is dead, and Frankfurter is blocking the investigation. Gene opposed Frankfurter in the *Hirabayashi* case, outwitted him with the Pledge of Allegiance, swore to undo the evacuation when the time came.

I shake my head. No one even knows how Gene died. Frankfurter is a Supreme Court Justice, and before that a Harvard professor. It's absurd to suppose that he could be involved in a crime. A murder.

You must be willing to do it, Cash. Suddenly I am hearing his voice again, foreign-inflected, pitched high with passion. *That is what it means to be a judge. You cannot write the opinion unless you would pull the trigger yourself.* I close my eyes, frowning. *What can we do for the Jews of Europe but win the war as quickly as possible, united behind the President?* What would he sacrifice for that goal? A clerk who stood in the way, who threatened his vision? *No one is innocent.*

I shake my head, pushing the thoughts away. I'm upset; I'm not thinking clearly. Of course there is some other explanation. I do my cert work in Black's chambers, eat lunch by myself, and go home without talking to the other clerks. Information comes in drips over the next few days. The medical examiners report that Gene suffered a heart attack. Natural causes, they say: stress, overwork, fatigue. The caffeine didn't help, nor the alcoholic binge that night.

It makes sense, I suppose. But I am finding it hard to shake my doubts. Not Frankfurter, perhaps. But Gene was doing other things, too. He was helping me; he was trying to find out who was manipulating the Court's decisions. Perhaps he was getting too close to an answer there.

Hoover seems to share my suspicions, for FBI men still come to the Court demanding access. But the marshals turn them away, first at Frankfurter's direction and now at Stone's. Murphy does not want them in his chambers; the Court will handle its own affairs. I go through the days in a haze of confusion. So many things point to Frankfurter. But he is a Supreme Court Justice. Maybe the examiners are right; maybe it wasn't murder at all. Or maybe it was someone else entirely. There is no one I can talk to, no one I can trust.

It is almost a relief, then, when I see Phil Haynes in the wide marble corridor and realize how pure and uncomplicated my feelings for him are. Here is a man I hate. He is talking to two other clerks, illustrating some tale with his hands and laughing. I move behind him, treading softly on the thick carpet, and bark his name.

He jumps at the sound. Alarm flashes across his face, followed by dull hostility. "What do you want?"

I think that Haynes must spend a lot of time outside. It is only June, but he is regaining the summertime tan he had when I first saw him. The even tone is marred by what's still a pretty good shiner. "I noticed that one of your eyes is not black," I say. He looks at me, uncomprehending. "It's an oversight that can be corrected."

The tough-guy response would be something about liking to see me try, but Haynes has lost some of his enthusiasm for playing tough guy with me. "How's your heart?" he asks.

For a moment I go light-headed with fury. The impulse to violence passes like an electric current up my spine. It prickles through the muscles of my back and shoulders. But just as quickly it leaves, and I feel only an unspeakable sorrow. "You'll answer for this one day," I say. Suddenly I am fighting tears.

My expression emboldens Haynes. "I'm ready now," he says.

I try to locate the reservoir of rage, but it is gone. I am deep underwater, where everything is dark and heavy, the emotion of the past days weighing me down like a blanket of lead.

"What's the matter?" Haynes says. He takes a step closer. "Having more funny thoughts?" There is an odd smile on his face. "Imagining things again?"

"What things?" I ask. I can barely get the words out.

Haynes puts his hands on my chest, pushing gently. "You know what's happening," he says. I stumble back a step, fetching up against the wall. The other clerks look troubled but make no move to intervene. "Just not where you fit in."

"What are you talking about?"

"You've forgotten who you are, Cash. Who your friends are."

This is enough to rouse me, for a moment at least. "I know my friends. And my enemies."

Haynes smiles. It is not odd now; it is the easy, confident smile I've seen so much this year. He could be standing with me on the squash court, waving cheerily from a Lightning sloop. "Don't be silly, pal. We're all on the same side here."

I look into his eyes. Suppose Gene did die of natural causes. Getting punched in the face probably didn't help with that. Violence wells inside me again. It will not be boxing; I am going to throw myself on him and beat his skull on the ground till the light leaves his eyes. Then I hear approaching footsteps, an operatic whistle. It is Frankfurter.

Haynes and I separate. Frankfurter does not appear surprised to see us together, but he does not seem to grasp the situation, either. He gives us a friendly smile as he passes; he places a hand on my shoulder and squeezes. "I've been looking for you, Justice," Haynes says, making to follow him.

I reach out. I do not trust myself to touch Haynes, but I grab the sleeve of his jacket and hold him for a moment. "You'll answer for this," I say again.

The other clerks stand silent and uncomfortable. Haynes offers me his smile. "You might consider an alienist." He pulls his sleeve from my fingers and follows Frankfurter. The carpet sinks under their feet and springs back, filling their footprints like the sea.

• • • •

It takes three days for the news to reach Haverford. Then Suzanne calls.

"What happened, Cash? I heard a clerk died. Someone called Gressman."

"Gene Gressman," I say.

"You must have known him."

"He was a friend. Probably my closest friend here."

"Gene Gressman," she repeats. It is interesting to hear her voice say his name. It brings Philadelphia and the Court together in a way I have never been able to in my mind. And yet there is something about how she says it that I do not entirely like.

"And I think maybe he was murdered."

Her voice goes half an octave higher. "What?"

"I'm not sure. But he was working on some things that I'm sure people didn't like. It just seems like too much of a coincidence."

"Have you gone to the police?"

I have thought of it, but I see no point. "They wouldn't believe me. And I don't even know who it was. I could be wrong about the whole thing."

"Then why are you still there?" she asks. "Why aren't you home now?"

"I don't know." It is true. My friend is dead, perhaps murdered. But I cannot bring his killers to justice; I cannot even be sure they exist. That feeling of weakness, as much as anything else, has kept me in DC Nothing I do can mend the broken world. "I still have work left for Black," I say. "There's no reason not to finish out the term."

"Are you crazy?" Suzanne asks. "What if he was murdered? You might get killed yourself. What makes you think you're not next on the list?"

"I don't think I'm worth killing. If I'm right about this, it was because he was going to stay longer. It was because he was influential. I'm not influential, and I'm here for another month at the most. I don't think anyone's going to be interested in me."

But in that prediction, I am wrong.

CHAPTER 22

I AM OUT for lunch the next day when a hand seizes my arm. "Come with me please, Mr. Harrison."

I turn. My first instinct is to ask who he thinks he is, but as I see his face I know. It is Clyde Tolson, the special assistant to J. Edgar Hoover. I remember him from the newspaper photos, entering the Court to watch the saboteurs' trial, always a step behind his boss. His grip is strong.

"Why? What did I do?"

"Nothing," says Tolson. "Not yet. But there is something we would like you to do."

"You could send a letter," I say. Tolson does not laugh, and when I try to pull my arm away, he does not let go. Instead, a second suited figure separates itself from the crowd and moves into place behind me. I could take Tolson by himself, I think, but not two at once.

"Please do not make things difficult for yourself," Tolson says.

"You mean difficult for you," I say.

"For yourself," he repeats.

I wave my free hand in a gesture of surrender. "Fine. What do you want?"

He maintains his grip just above my elbow. "As I said, I would like you to accompany me." He takes a step, still holding my arm. I have little choice but to follow. The second agent comes to the other side, and I am walking Spanish down the street.

Tolson has the air of a teacher hustling a refractory student to the princi-
pal's office, and as we continue I surmise it is a more or less accurate reflection of his mind. As the blocks go by, I can guess our destination. We are
headed to the Main Justice Building. We are going to see J. Edgar Hoover.

Main Justice stands on the corner of Ninth and Pennsylvania. Like most of
the federal buildings, it is gray limestone, lacking the marble splendor of the
Court. We walk through the iron gates, where reporters clustered during the
saboteurs' trial. The Supreme Court has bronze doors and marble statues, but
Main Justice's doors are aluminum, and its statues, too. They loom twelve feet
tall in the foyer, the *Spirit of Justice* and the *Majesty of Law*. Justice is a woman
standing with her arms up, as if an overzealous G-man has told her to reach
for the sky. Perhaps because of the pose, her toga has slipped off one breast. I
think it is not the best image for the Department, and I say so.

"What?" says Tolson. We stop in our progress across the foyer, but for
another second the echoes of our heels continue on. "I don't even notice it
anymore. And you, you've got other things to think about."

I shrug as best I can with only one arm free. The shock of my apprehension
has worn off. Somewhere in this building is Attorney General Biddle, and he
is Hoover's superior. I imagine calling out his name—*Save me, Francis!*—but
there is no need. I know I have nothing to fear from the government.

Hoover's office is on the second floor. We pass wall murals depicting men
with raised hands. The presence of agents pointing guns marks them as
evildoers surrendering. Like the Pharaohs of old, Hoover has his victories
immortalized. And like them, he has guardians before the inner sanctum.
In an antechamber we pass a pretty secretary and two lounging agents who
straighten at our approach. As we reach the door, Tolson releases my arm and
pats the wrinkles from my suit jacket. "Mr. Hoover is the man of the century,"
he tells me.

The man of the century does not rise at my entrance, or even look up from
his papers. He sits at a swivel chair behind a large desk. To his right the Stars
and Stripes hangs limp on a gilded post; to his left is the blue flag of the
Bureau with its golden seal. Tolson guides me to a low couch and directs me
to take a seat. He remains standing, his back against the wall.

"Mr. Harrison," says Hoover, still looking down. He reaches for a feather duster and flicks at his shoes. Finally, he favors me with a glance. "Francis Biddle gave me your name."

"That was kind of him," I say. "Though I can't yet say I'm grateful." Hoover has small ears, a flat nose, and bulging eyes. Reporters typically liken him to a bulldog, but he puts me more in mind of a toad. His blue tie matches the handkerchief tucked into his breast pocket.

"I asked him for a clerk who might be trustworthy."

"Then I take it as a compliment."

Hoover clears his throat. "You are aware, I'm sure, that my agents have had some difficulty obtaining access to the Court building."

"Yes," I say.

"It is Frankfurter's work. You know him?"

I nod. "I do."

"So Biddle said. And what is your impression?"

I am becoming curious about where the conversation is heading. "I think he is quite . . . an active personality."

Hoover leans forward, hands on his desk. "Listen to me carefully, Mr. Harrison. Felix Frankfurter is the most dangerous man in America. A Bolshevik propagandist. And now he is standing in the way of a federal investigation."

Frankfurter is a Supreme Court Justice, I tell myself. There is no way he could be involved in a murder. But Hoover is the director of the FBI, and he seems to think otherwise. "Do you think he has something to hide?" I ask.

"I do not know. But I will tell you what I do know. I know that we are at war. I heard the bombs fall on Pearl Harbor. I heard them, Mr. Harrison. My agent in charge called from Honolulu and held the phone out the window. I know that the Court has heard, is hearing, important cases related to the war. And I know that a federal employee has died under suspicious circumstances. Eugene Gressman. He was one of us, Mr. Harrison, and we will find out what happened."

I am silent a moment. The name has left me unbalanced, jerked my mind back to what I've been avoiding. It happens from time to time—there is a vague feeling that something isn't right, then I shift my attention and it looms huge and horrible in the center of my mind. My dreams are variations on this theme. A half-heard splash of waves on a prow in Northeast Harbor makes me turn my head to see a vast, dark ship bearing down; a rumbling engine in DC turns out to be a speeding black van. I wake up just before the collision, with my heart racing and the feeling that the impact has jolted me from sleep. Gene Gressman is dead. There is the urgent sense that I must do something about it, coupled with the knowledge that I can do nothing at all.

But now perhaps I can.

"And you think I can help?"

"You have access to the Court. And to Frankfurter. Both are in short supply. You could be useful to us, if you are willing."

"Oh, I'm willing," I say. "Ready and able. But what exactly do you want me to do?"

"With Frankfurter, we would like you to talk. What you have been doing, nothing more. Any sort of information could be useful. You can report directly to Agent Tolson."

"And my access to the Court?"

"That's more delicate." Hoover pushes his chair back and stands. "Come here, Mr. Harrison."

I walk to the desk. When I reach his side, I am surprised to realize that I have a good four inches on him. He looked taller in the papers. Perhaps it was that Tolson, trailing a few feet behind, was always on a lower step as they ascended the stairs. But he seemed taller from the couch, too. For the first time I realize that his desk is elevated, and the chair also. "Are you going to give me a badge?"

"Not quite, Mr. Harrison." He opens the desk drawer and retrieves a small box. There is a brush, a tray of powder, clear tape, and paper. It looks like a makeup kit, and for a moment I wonder how a disguise could fit into Hoover's plans. Then I understand. "Lifting prints is not difficult," Hoover says, opening the box. "Men are oilier creatures than you might think, even such as you and I. It is always on our hands. The human stain." He passes the brush across the tray. "Quite a break for law enforcement. You take the appropriate powder—dark for a light surface, light for a dark one—and spread a bit about. A hard surface, of course; that's the only one that will hold a print." He dabs the coffee mug on his desk. "You brush it gently until you see the pattern emerge, like this. Lift it off with clear tape, then transfer it to one of these cards." He presses the tape onto the mug, then the paper. A powdery design remains. "My thumb, it looks like. Try it at home a few times. And then perhaps see what you can turn up in Murphy's chambers. What do you say?"

I am silent a moment, considering. It is possible; I am sure of that. Once you are inside the Justices' part of the Court, there is little security. Only the marshals who smile and greet me by name. I am one of the trusted ones, the angels who can walk heaven unmolested. What Hoover asks is a betrayal of that trust, of course, but there has been a greater one, and I seek to cure it.

"Okay." I nod. "I'll do it."

Hoover smiles, looking beyond me. "You see, Clyde? Didn't I tell you he'd cooperate?"

Tolson has been silent, blending sphinxlike into the wall, but now he comes briefly to life. "Yes, Director."

Hoover pushes the box across the desk to me, along with the paper containing his thumbprint. "A souvenir for you," he says. "And one more thing. You have my prints now. And I must have yours."

"What?"

He removes an inkpad and a card from the desk drawer. "I am going to take your fingerprints. They will undoubtedly be in Murphy's chambers. We must be able to eliminate you. Your hands, please."

I hold them out, first the right and then the left. One by one Hoover takes my fingers in his soft hands, rolls them over the inkpad, and presses them into labeled boxes on the card. As he leans over his work I see a roll of fat above his collar at the back of his neck. From the wall, Tolson watches with an intensity that is almost angry. Looking at him, I am no longer so confident I could take him one-on-one.

"There," says Hoover, straightening. "Now you're mine." He licks his lips. "If they'd let me do all the clerks we'd know more. Do you have any questions?"

"No," I say. "Well, maybe one."

"What is it?"

"Have you been following me?"

The expression of surprise on Hoover's face appears genuine. He is the director of the FBI, but I do not think he is much of an actor. "No. Why would we do that?"

"I don't know," I say. "But someone was."

Hoover's eyes flit to Tolson. "Nobody today, Mr. Hoover. Not when we got him."

"Did you notice anything today?" Hoover asks me.

"No," I admit. "Not for a while now. But before."

Hoover gives a barely perceptible nod. "We'll look into it, Mr. Hoover," says Tolson.

"Very well," says Hoover. "Thank you, Mr. Harrison. For your time and your assistance. Your country is grateful."

For a moment I think Tolson is going to seize my arm again as we leave Hoover's office, but he does not. He simply walks me out to the hallway and stops.

"Can I go now?" I ask.

"The washroom first," says Tolson.

"What?"

"Your hands," he says. "You will want to clean them."

CHAPTER 23

I AM LATE back from lunch, and Black has already gone. He has placed a note on my desk. *You may be scared of my forehand, but you can't hide forever.* I tuck it inside the drawer, feeling a little rush of affection. We have played more tennis these past days, and I know if I show up later this evening there will be a steak waiting.

Black has also left on my desk Justice Jackson's draft of a majority opinion in the Pledge of Allegiance case. I should read it; I should jot down my thoughts and take them across the river to Black's house tonight. I should eat my steak and drink a beer and listen to Black talk about the old times in Birmingham. But I have other tasks today.

The Justices usually leave the main door to their chambers open, and Murphy is no exception. Inside there is one room for the clerk and one for the secretary, then the door to the Justice's office. Rose clucks sympathetically when she sees me. "I need a book," I say.

"Of course."

I walk to Gressman's desk. There is no way to start dusting for prints now; I could be interrupted at any moment. Instead I open the top drawer and take the door key he kept there. I slip it into my pocket and shake my head sadly at Rose on the way out. "No luck." Then I go back to Black's chambers and wait.

At six I decide that I may as well make some use of this time, and I start reading the draft opinion in the pledge case. Jackson is a stylist, Black has

136

told me, and the draft proves that true. The government cannot compel citizens to express belief, he writes. *If there is any fixed star in our constitutional constellation, it is that no official, high or petty, can prescribe what shall be orthodox in politics, nationalism, religion, or other matters of opinion or force citizens to confess, by word or act, their faith therein. Compulsory unification of opinion achieves only the unanimity of the graveyard.*

They are pretty words, but there is a real graveyard in my thoughts and fine phrases cannot compete. I put the pages down and watch the light fade out the window. I practice with Hoover's fingerprint kit. The brush, the powder, the tape and paper. At seven I go out and buy dinner, half a roast chicken. Back to Black's chambers, back to waiting. At ten, I think that the last clerk has left. I take out the box again. There is nothing wrong in what I am doing—indeed, it is surely the right thing. And yet I feel a twist within me as I slide it into my pocket, and as I walk down the hall the bright faces of the marshals light a fire of shame.

They are on the night rotation, only a few posted in the corridors, a few more walking rounds. No one is standing near Murphy's chambers. The sergeant gives me a sympathetic smile as he passes on his patrol. I nod my head, silent agreement with his unspoken comment: yes, we're both working late tonight. Then he turns the corner and I fit the key into the lock, slip inside, and shut the door behind me.

I stand motionless for a moment, letting my eyes adjust to the dark. I know the layout, of course, but there are unfamiliar piles of books and papers about, and I do not want to betray my presence by stumbling over them. After a minute I walk carefully to Gressman's desk and turn on the lamp. I sit down in his chair, rest my hands on the edge, and take a deep breath.

Some of the papers are new cert petitions, carefully stacked and bound, never to be opened. Murphy is not reading the certs himself; he has started borrowing memos, often mine. The books are case reporters, the records of the Court's decisions. And then there are folders, with the dates of recent terms. I open the closest one. It is filled with Murphy's conference notes, his account of the Justices' meetings, their decisions on the merits of the cases, and also whether to grant or deny the cert petitions. Gressman wasn't just working on *Hirabayashi* these past weeks, I realize. He was spending those late hours trying to figure out who was manipulating the Court. Helping me again, the charity that might have cost his life.

I open the top drawer. It is stuffed with papers, organized according to no discernible pattern. Gene believed that the materials for his current, most recent, and next upcoming project should all be within arm's reach; that was all. I sift through the layers. Here is draft after draft of the Murphy concurrence, comments written in the Justice's hand. Here are copies of Stone's opinion, with Gressman's savage criticisms in the margin. Letters from Douglas, Rutledge, Frankfurter, newspaper clippings describing the evacuation. And some handwritten sheets that have nothing but names.

I look more closely. There are names of cases from past years, linked by arrows to names of justices, linked in turn to other names, which must be clerks. Some of them I recognize; they are the replacements that fill my chart. Then, radiating arrows like the beams of the sun, is one name written in red.

Felix Frankfurter.

For a minute, at least, I puzzle over the papers. The cases are unfamiliar; so are some of the clerks. Sometimes all nine justices' names appear next to a case, sometimes as few as one. I can't put it into words, but I understand the structure he is diagramming, somewhere in the back of my mind. If I wait another minute it will come. The justices must be ones who voted together, the clerks the ones who worked for those justices. The arrows some sort of connection to Frankfurter. But the cases . . . why did he choose these ones? It is like struggling for a word, knowing its shape, its meaning, everything but the precise arrangement of letters. In another minute, I think, it will come. But when I catch my breath and freeze in the chair, muscles clenching tight, it is not inspiration that grips me. It is the sound of footsteps in the hall.

The sergeant on patrol has passed by before, I am sure, his regular tread not even registering. I notice these footsteps because they stop. Someone has paused in the corridor; someone is standing outside the chambers door. I wonder whether the light from the desk lamp is visible through the cracks; I am about to turn it off before I realize that this will just make things worse. I sit, holding my breath.

The footsteps start again. Shoes scuff on the carpet. They fade away, then come back faster. The doorknob rattles. Did the door lock behind me? It did; the knob jiggles but does not turn. Again the footsteps move away.

I need to work quickly. I can't take Murphy's conference notes; they would be missed. But I collect all that I can find of Gressman's handwritten pages. Then I take out the fingerprint kit. There are plenty of hard surfaces. I try some of the handles of the drawers. Prints come up easily, some smudged but many recognizably distinct. I transfer them to a pad, noting the location from which I took them.

The collection of tangible evidence is satisfying. In a burst of inspiration, I open the bottom left drawer to find Gene's coffee stash. If he was poisoned, it seems the most likely means. The can is empty, which itself strikes me as odd, but when I dust it, prints come up on the lid and the sides. I transfer them to the pad. Somewhere here may be the trace of a murderer's hand.

But of course most of them are his. I look at the patterns I have lifted, unique and irreplaceable, and the thought that there will never be another almost brings me to tears. Gene's phonograph is gone, and his jazz records, and his books. A man's life may be summed up in many ways, but surely this is one of the saddest, a filigree of oil and dust raised from an empty desk. I sit in the desk chair, overwhelmed with emotion. And I hear footsteps coming back down the hall.

Again, it is not the regular tread of the sergeant. Who is here this late? Then I know. I hear more than footsteps; there is whistling. A key turns in the lock, and a marshal's face appears. Behind him is Justice Felix Frankfurter.

The marshal flips on the overhead light. I am caught; there is nothing to do. I sit at the desk, blinking at them. The marshal frowns in surprise when he sees me, but Frankfurter seems to relax. With a touch and a whisper he dismisses the marshal and walks toward me, holding me in his gaze.

At the edge of the desk he stops. I should stand, of course, but I find I cannot even move. My whole body tingles with shock. For a long moment there is silence. "Well, Cash," Frankfurter says, and pauses as if in thought. "I find you working late again."

"Yes."

"But not in your own chambers."

"No."

He looks at me without comment. I decide that confidence is my best play. "I was looking for a book I lent Gene," I say. "I'm annotating Jackson's Pledge of Allegiance opinion for Justice Black."

"Ah," says Frankfurter. He raises his eyebrows. "Aristotle's *Rhetoric*, perhaps."

"What?"

"Jackson uses stylistic felicity to cloud the issues. It is a bad habit. Long years of observation of the work of this Court before I came down here have sensitized me against needlessly vague and rhetorical phrases. I am writing a dissent, you know. That is what keeps me here tonight."

I nod, bemused by the digression.

"So," Frankfurter continues. "Did you find it?"

"What?"

"Your book."

I wince. If that was a trap, he has caught me out. "No," I say. "I'm afraid the family seems to have taken it. They went so fast."

Frankfurter nods. "The customs of a desert people," he says. "There would be more time to mourn you." It takes me a moment to understand the first part of his statement, and by the time the second registers he has already moved on. "But I do not think that is why you are here."

"What do you mean?"

"It is understandable," he says. "That late at night your thoughts would turn to this room. I think you miss your friend."

"I do," I say. Relief swells like a tide. He is letting me off easy. But why should I be feeling guilty? He is the one Hoover suspects; his is the name written in red. As the fear fades, I am discovering things other than relief. Anger, even hate.

"There may be those who come for other reasons," Frankfurter continues. "You know that Hoover's men have been sniffing around. If you see anyone you do not recognize, you should alert the marshals."

I hesitate. I am not entirely sure that Frankfurter has not just threatened my life, and it might be unwise to press him further. But it seems a natural question for anyone to ask. "But Justice, why shouldn't the FBI be allowed to investigate?"

"Investigate," says Frankfurter. "There would be no matter if they wished to investigate. But all Hoover wants is to gather information to put in a file for his own use. When he heard that something had happened in Murphy's chambers I'm sure he salivated at the opportunity. He would love to get something on Frank."

"What could he get on Justice Murphy?"

Frankfurter frowns at me. "I did not mean to suggest Murphy in particular. But there is always something. Can you say you have no secrets?"

I realize that the fingerprint kit is still in my hand and slide it into my pocket under the desk. "No, Justice," I say.

"Anyway," Frankfurter says. "There is nothing to investigate. It is a tragedy. But natural causes, the examiners agree."

This is what I expected him to say, and I have thought about how it might afford an opening. "That almost makes it worse, I think. The feeling that nothing was gained with the sacrifice. Do you feel that way? Or do you think there might have been some purpose behind it?" I pause and swallow, intending to suggest deep sorrow. It is harder than I expect; I am choking on rage. "It would be easier," I say, "if I thought we'd gained something from the loss."

Frankfurter looks at me oddly for a moment. Then his face clears. "God's purpose perhaps, but not man's. I am afraid all I can draw from it is the admonition to enjoy the time we have. It is as Holmes said." He reaches across the desk. I expect him to grip my arm, or pat my shoulder, but instead he tugs my earlobe with his fingers. I look at him, baffled, still trying to hide my anger. "On his 90th birthday," Frankfurter continues. He smiles faintly. "Death plucks my ear and says 'Live, for I am coming.'" He stands before me a moment longer, the smile draining from his face. Then he leaves.

I sit there in the empty room with my dead friend's fingerprints in my pocket. And I wonder, for the second time, whether Felix Frankfurter has just threatened my life.

· · · ·

Black is in and out of chambers the next morning. Stone is calling more conferences, something to do with the Pledge of Allegiance case. Black gives me a hard look as he leaves. "You read that Jackson draft yet?"

"Today," I say. "I promise."

"I expect to see you tonight."

I nod. "Yes, Judge."

I use my lunch hour to make the walk to Main Justice.

"I'm not getting anything from Frankfurter," I tell Tolson. "But I collected some prints."

He inspects the sheets of paper, the strips of tape. "Well done, Mr. Harrison. You've a bit of the agent in you, after all."

I do not much like Tolson, but despite myself I feel a flicker of pride at his words. "I'm sure they're mostly his, though."

"Most of them are, of course. But we managed to take his prints at the medical examiner's office. We can exclude him. And if there are foreign prints, we can try to match them."

"Against what?"

"Our files. Mr. Hoover has hundreds of thousands of prints on file."

"Whose?"

"Criminals," says Tolson. "People of interest. Subversives, when we can get them. You." He smiles. "But we will exclude you as well. We will compare any foreign prints to our registry. It is a time-consuming process, but we will let you know if anything results."

"And what should I do in the meantime?"

"Talk to Frankfurter if you want. It might help. But Mr. Harrison?"

"What?"

"Try not to get in the way of the real agents."

No, I think as I start the walk back, I do not much like Clyde Tolson.

· · · ·

Later that afternoon I take a bus to Black's house. "Virginia," the driver announces as we cross the river. "Coloreds to the back." There is little rearrangement; the passengers have anticipated the shift. We do not do that in Philadelphia, I think. There is something more to the city than the Assembly, than Fish House Punch and jokes about the Scrapples eating biddle. Of course, they do not do it in Washington, either. Vaguely I remember reading something about a sit-in by Howard students in the morning paper.

"Jackson can turn a phrase," Black says about the opinion. "*Any fixed star in our constitutional constellation.* People will be quoting that long after we're dead." A flicker across his face; he regrets the choice of words. "A hundred years from now," he says. Another flicker, a look at me. "So we don't need to worry about it today. Come on. The sun'll be setting soon. Let's swing a racquet."

Exercise and food distract me. Josephine is with us at dinner, motherly in her attentions. I feel closer to her now; we are both haunted by absent young men. I understand—oh, how I understand—the pain of being unable to help, and I am glad I can give her someone to care for. "No reason to go home unless you want to," says Black. "I reckon that suit's got another day in it."

Sterling's room has not aged since he left for college. It holds a seventeen-year-old's life, and the fascinations of 1939. His bed is slightly short for me. It might not fit him either now, I suppose, nor would the room be appropriate for an Army captain. But I can understand why Josephine preserves it, the chrysalis that held a younger form. To step inside is to see that vanished boy, and I am in a mood to retrieve the irretrievable.

Seventeen-year-old Sterling was a jazz fan, like Gene, and after Black and Josephine have gone to bed I put on one of his Billie Holiday records. I turn the volume down low and lie on the floor with my head next to the turntable, looking at the ceiling. I lie there and I remember the music drifting out of Murphy's chambers and Gene bobbing his dark head, lamplight winking off his glasses. Billie's voice is cool and melancholy, teardrops you'd take for diamonds till they wet your hands. *No, no,* she says, *they can't take that away from me.* Frankfurter was wrong, I think. There is plenty of time to mourn.

CHAPTER 24

THE LAST WEEKS of the term crawl toward their conclusion. I look at Gressman's diagrams from time to time, but their sense still eludes me. I do not speak to Haynes, or any of the clerks. Frankfurter continues to engage me in conversation, gripping my arm when we pass in the halls. He tells me he is still staying up past midnight writing his dissent in the Pledge of Allegiance case.

"You look as though more than that weighs on your mind, Justice." I am fishing, of course, but it is true. Frankfurter has a haunted look. It is afternoon, and the sun streams through the windows in shafts of rich gold, but on his face there lingers, like a memory, the wan light of early morning, of moonglow and streetlamp.

Frankfurter sighs and lets his head droop. With one hand he braces himself against the wall. "Kermit Roosevelt is dead," he says. "You will have the news in a few days. The second of T.R.'s sons fallen in war. I fear not the last. I knew the Colonel. I thrilled to his speeches; I was ready to quit my job with Taft to go Bull Moosing. T.R. himself talked me out of it. You were not yet born, of course; you cannot understand the excitement we felt. The older people thought it was just rhetoric, but we who were young felt a real moral urgency. We sensed that this was something new."

Frankfurter is gathering momentum; I can tell he is on the verge of going airborne, into anecdote. But I have heard this story already. *We stand at*

Armageddon and we battle for the Lord. I weigh my options and decide to interrupt. "He died in war, at least," I say. I doubt I will do any better this time, but there is no harm in trying. "There was a purpose to it."

Something in my words seems to pain Frankfurter, and when he speaks his voice is cold and slow. "It was his heart."

"Oh," I say. I am determined to forge ahead. "Like Gene Gressman." My single-mindedness must arouse his suspicions, I think, but am I not entitled to the obsessions of grief?

"Very much so," says Frankfurter. His tone is still cold, but now there is an edge to his voice. Then he looks up, and it is gone. "Nothing ages a man like the death of a friend. I am old now, and we have a different Roosevelt in the White House. Perhaps even a better man. He has, of course, intellectual limitations. But no defect of character I wished the President of the United States did not have." The words gather speed. Talking seems to burn off Frankfurter's melancholy. "Most families peter out, even the Adamses, but they are going strong. And here we are on his Court, and I must say we are making a mess of things."

"How's that, Justice?" I ask, and he rounds on me severely.

"How's that? When a priest enters a monastery, he must leave all worldly desires behind him. And this Court has no excuse for being, unless it's a monastery. But your Justice does not think so. Really, what is the difference between Hugo Black and Louis XIV, who said 'I am the law'? Hugo does not believe in Law; he thinks it is nothing more than manipulation of language in support of a predetermined result." He pauses. "I give in to the temptation to speak openly with friends because I cannot speak to the outside world. I cannot speak for myself. As judge I have become an oracle; I can speak only for the law." He grasps me—not, as usual, by the arm, but by the hand. Something beseeching is in his face. "But you can speak for me. You can tell them how I love this country, how I love Roosevelt."

. . . .

At Main Justice, the FBI technicians are working. "A couple of foreign prints, yes," says Tolson.

"From the coffee can?"

There is a moment of silence over the telephone line. "Yes. Some of them."

"I knew it," I say. "You should work on those first."

"We have it in hand, Mr. Harrison. And what of your project? Have you made any further progress?"

"No." More silence. Tolson and I have not found much to chat about. And even if I had the inclination, I am not sure how to describe what I have been getting from Frankfurter. He passes on "in confidence" what he tells me are the opinions of other Justices, which he has clearly invented to flatter himself; he wanders off into irrelevant stories about Harvard and his childhood . . . it must all add up to something, but I cannot figure out what. "I'm only here a few more days," I say. "I'm going to push him a little harder. See what happens."

"I leave it to your judgment."

. . . .

I find Frankfurter in his chambers, revising a document in longhand. He seems pleased to see me. "Here, Cash," he says, clearing his throat. "Listen to this." As I stand before his desk, he reads me his dissent in the Pledge of Allegiance case. But I cannot listen. The thought that he may be responsible for Gene's death fills my mind, crowds out everything else. This little man with his silvery hair and steel pince-nez, who sits here and reads me his pompous absurdities. A sentence pierces my consciousness. *One who belongs to the most vilified and persecuted minority in history is not likely to be insensible to the freedoms guaranteed by our Constitution.* Then it is gone; there is just the rise and fall of his voice, the rough edge of the German accent. Finally he stops.

"Wonderful," I say. "Very persuasive."

Frankfurter nods. "There are those among my Brethren who think it is too personal."

"Oh, no," I say. "That's its power."

He smiles modestly. "I came to this country at twelve, Cash. I spoke no English. Walking around the neighborhood I thought that this man Laundry must be very rich, to own so many stores. I had to achieve what others claimed as their birthright. Ever since the first Pledge of Allegiance case I have had letters telling me that as a Jew and an immigrant, I ought particularly to protect minorities. And I must put on record that such considerations are entirely irrelevant to our work."

I strain to remember another sentence from the dissent, then realize that it doesn't matter. "Holmes could not have put it better, Justice," I say, and his smile grows. "I sometimes think it should not be that all of the Brethren have an equal vote. When some seem to have a clearer understanding of the issues."

"Ah," he says. "It is not all about the voting."

It is an opening. "What do you mean?"

Frankfurter looks at his desk, gone suddenly shy. "There is the persuasive force of the opinions, you know." I would swear he is blushing. "As your Justice found, as Gene Gressman showed."

So he knows that Gene was responsible for Black's changed vote in the Pledge case. One more reason he had to go, no doubt. I am suddenly burning with hatred. I try to transmute it to a fervent admiration. "But is persuasion all? Why should we stand by and let the cases go wrong? There must be something more that can be done."

Frankfurter looks up at me, and now there is an appraising cast to his features. "There are many things," he says, "that can be done, and should be done, but should not be talked about."

Closer, I think. "I should like to know, Mr. Justice," I say. "If it is not asking too much."

"Well," says Frankfurter. He stands and takes from his bookshelf a copy of the *US Reports*. "I write many of Roberts's opinions for him." He opens the book to demonstrate. Passages of a Roberts majority are underlined in green, and in the margin he has noted *Written by FF*. I have been thinking of making similar marks on Black's opinions, though there would be much less underlining. Still, I am disappointed and vaguely repelled.

"And that is what you do?"

"I speak to the Justices. I speak to clerks. I manage emotions. I call it personalia. It is a great talent I have."

Frankfurter is not very good at gauging his effect on other people, I think. I am torn between thinking him innocent and somewhat deluded, or conniving beyond my power to discern.

Frankfurter appears to be awaiting affirmation, but after a moment the silence grows too long for him. "So," he says. "You will be returning to Philadelphia soon."

"Yes," I answer. The clerks of my year are starting to leave. As he said that night in the courtyard, Vern Countryman will join the Army Air Force. He has told me to come by the Douglas chambers next week; he has a going-away present for me. I am not sure I will. I have skipped the farewells. There is no one I will miss. There is no one I am sure is not a murderer.

"It is a shame we did not have this talk sooner," says Frankfurter. "Perhaps we shall hear from each other in the future."

I find I am tired of the conversation. I can no longer summon the energy to try to steer it. "Perhaps."

He smiles. "Oh, I think it quite likely. You have impressed me greatly already. I will keep my eye on you."

There it is again. A veiled threat, or an awkward endearment? I cannot decide, but I hold his gaze firmly. "And I you, Justice."

. . . .

In July coffee comes off the rationing list. Like everything else, it makes me think of Gressman. Slowly, the other clerks are leaving. I work on my cert petitions and my backhand and try to talk the new arrivals into meeting the starlings. Midway through the week I remember Vern Countryman's talk of a present.

He isn't in the Douglas chambers, nor is the secretary I have grown used to seeing. There is only a dark-haired girl arranging papers on Vern's desk.

"Excuse me," I say. "I'm looking for Vern Countryman."

She glances up with a smile. "I'm afraid you've missed him." Her eyes are dark, too, with long thick lashes; in a way she reminds me of the Spanish lady at Cissy's party.

"I'm Justice Black's outgoing clerk. Did he leave anything for me?"

"He didn't leave anything I know of. Except a pile of cert petitions."

"Yeah," I say. "I've got enough of those already. Well, is Wild Bill around?"

The girl inclines her head slightly. Sunlight pulls other colors from her eyes, green and gold. "What did you just say?"

"I'm sorry. I meant Justice Douglas."

She chuckles. It is surprisingly low and somehow thrilling. "Don't worry. That's what the secretaries call him, too."

"You do?"

"They do."

I hesitate. "Who are you?"

"Clara. Clara Watson. The incoming Douglas clerk. And you are?"

"I'm embarrassed," I say. "This is Vern's idea of a practical joke."

"It's not a joke, Mr. Embarrassed." Her tone is playful, but there is an edge to it.

"Harrison. Cash Harrison. No, I mean . . ."

"You mean he didn't mention the next clerk would be a woman, so you assumed I was a secretary."

"He set me up," I say. "He said there was a present."

"Oh." She sounds less playful. "And you made each other presents of secretaries."

"No, of course not." I don't see what I've done to deserve such a hard time. "It was a trick."

"Or a test," says Clara. "So, Cash. That's quite a name. I suppose your brother is Stock?"

"Preferred Stock," I say, trying to get my bearings. "No, Cash is a nickname. And not the right one, actually. My parents named me Caswell, so I should be Cas or Cass. But my mother wrote 'Cas H' on everything I owned, and people took it from that."

Clara nods as though I have confirmed some suspicion. I try to change the subject.

"How are you getting on with Douglas? We were all a little afraid of him."

She shrugs, indicating the unreality of my concern. "Oh, I don't have any trouble with Wild Bill. I'm from Washington, like him and Vern. Vern vouched for me, you know. He said I'd do as good a job as a man, except I might not have quite the same contact with clerks in other chambers."

"That was generous of him." Columbia has women, though not many. I have heard professors complain that we lose students to Harvard because we no longer appear serious.

Clara shrugs again. Now it is the generosity that is unreal, and something in her gesture marks this as the more common pattern. "I was number one in my class. Vern was behind a woman and a Japanese boy. But he had the right temperament for Douglas. You just have to understand him."

"What do you understand?" Countryman never said much about Douglas, and I know him only as a tall presence in the halls, a dangling forelock, piercing blue eyes that thankfully seldom turn to clerks. But I have heard stories.

"He's a masterstroke on his way to cliché. He's a wolf. And before too long he'll be an old wolf, and what's more of a cliché than that? But clichés start as strokes of genius. Think of the worst one you can."

"You take my breath away," I say. Instantly I regret it. Why did that come to mind? Clara smiles as though I have pulled a frog from my pocket. I feel myself shrinking. Little boys and their treasures.

"Very good," she says. "A truly dead phrase. You hear it without thinking. But it must have been quite striking the first time. Clenched by awe. Like diving into a cold lake."

I think of the grip of the sea at Northeast Harbor, the icy realm of wonder. And Suzanne. Guilt flickers in my mind, swiftly erased by a tide of irritation. I am not doing anything wrong. It is hardly my fault that Countryman played a joke on me, that Clara misinterpreted my confusion, that one particular phrase came first to my lips.

"Now, of course, it means nothing," Clara says. The lights in her eyes are brighter, and there is something savage about her smile. "It shows only a failure of imagination. A mind stuck in the ruts of convention."

I look at her, incredulous. "You asked for a cliché."

"So I did." She nods. "Well, that's Bill Douglas. The young genius starting the downslope. Don't look so distressed. It happens to all of us. Even the golden boys, perfect and untamed. Even such as Mr. Caswell Harrison."

I have no idea how the conversation has come to be about me, and it seems powerfully unfair. Worse, I can feel that I am blushing. "I should get back to my certs," I say.

"Yes," says Clara. "You should." A silent moment passes between us, then she dismisses me. "Nice suit."

. . . .

But I do not go back to Black's chambers. I am faster at the certs now, and there are not many left, and suddenly I am filled with purpose. In some strange way, the conversation with Clara has firmed my resolve. I have had enough of feints and indirection. I want a confrontation, and I will bring it on.

I walk into Frankfurter's chambers. Haynes is not at his desk, and the secretary gets only as far as forming my name before I pass her. The door to Frankfurter's office is open and I step through it and stand before him where he sits at the desk.

"Cash," he says. "It is a pleasant surprise."

"I wanted to say something to you before I left, Justice."

"Of course. I am glad to hear it."

"I don't think Gene Gressman had a heart attack," I say. "I think it was murder."

Frankfurter's eyes shift over my shoulder. I turn, following his gaze, and for the first time I see Haynes sitting in a chair near the door. At Frankfurter's look he rises and shuts it. Frankfurter stands himself and steps out from behind the desk. The effect is as of a lizard emerging from a rock. There is a different expression on his face, and he blinks smooth, reptilian eyes. "Yes, Cash," he says softly. "It was murder. I know that better than anyone."

CHAPTER 25

HAYNES IS BETWEEN me and the door now, but I have no desire to flee. I feel no fear, only a rising excitement. The enemy has dropped his mask. I look from one to the other. Neither is a match for me on his own, but together they might prove troublesome, and one or both could be armed. The smart move is to put Haynes on the floor before they can coordinate. I take a step toward him, intending just that. He backs into a table, alarm and confusion on his face.

"Cash," says Frankfurter. His voice is sharp enough to break through my concentration. I stop and look at him. He is frowning severely. "What are you doing?"

I have misread the scene. I drop my hands to my sides. "Nothing. What do you mean?"

"It appeared for a moment you might assault my clerk. Please do not damage Mr. Haynes. He is quite valuable."

Haynes's face wavers between smirk and scowl. I do not know what is going on, but I hope my confusion comes across as innocence. "I would never do such a thing."

"I have heard to the contrary," says Frankfurter. I shake my head mildly. "I have had what we might call the ocular proof," he continues. I steal a glance at Haynes. The mouse is gone; his face is again an even tan. I look back to Frankfurter, and without conscious intent, I part my lips slightly and widen my eyes. After a second I realize that this is Suzanne's look of astonished innocence. She has used it to good effect over the years, with me and the

Judge alike. But Frankfurter is less susceptible, at least when the expression is on my face. "Don't gape," he says. "Such things occur. But I will thank you not to make a habit of it."

It seems best to change the subject. "I don't understand, Justice. What do you mean, you know it was murder?"

He steps behind the desk and sits down again. "I am a member of this Court, but I am also an observer of it. I am an observer of many things. And I can tell when influence is being exerted. Particularly when it runs counter to my own. Someone has been meddling in our affairs."

"And you think they killed him."

"Mr. Gressman would have been a thorn in the side of anyone seeking to affect the Court. He had some influence of his own. More, perhaps, he cut off access to Murphy, who would otherwise be the easiest justice to sway."

Frankfurter is surely speaking from experience. I am tempted to point this out, to give Gressman his due, but I let it pass. "Who do you think is behind it?"

"That is what I have been trying to figure out. If we may judge a thing by its effects, I would say they are conservatives."

I am puzzled. "Justice, aren't you a conservative?"

Frankfurter looks annoyed. "I am a neutral judge who does not impose his values. There is a pro-business influence at work."

It matches with some of what Gressman said, but I am not convinced. "But it was the Witness cases where he really made a difference."

Frankfurter waves a dismissive hand. "The people who would interfere in the Court's work do not care about the rights of the Jehovah's Witnesses. It may have demonstrated his ability, but the result did not matter. No, the people I speak of are those who have not accepted the New Deal. They still fight on behalf of capital, against the creeping socialism of that man in the White House."

"I don't know," I say. "Just a couple of days before he was killed, Gene was yelling about the Japanese. Everyone heard him. You can ask Haynes."

"I am aware of the incident, as I told you." Frankfurter pauses for a moment. He lays his hands on the desk. "There may be a connection. I cannot rule it out. But that is what I seek to discover. Philip has been helping. And young men of my acquaintance, scattered through the government."

"The Happy Hot Dogs," I say.

"I beg your pardon?"

"What?" I start to widen my eyes and catch myself. "Nothing."

"It's something they call us, Justice," Haynes puts in.

"The Happy Hot Dogs?" Frankfurter repeats the phrase, incredulous. "Oh," he says slowly. For the briefest instant I see the beginning of a smile, then he draws his lips together in a tight line of disapproval. "Ridiculous."

I am eager to end the digression. "You say you are investigating?"

"Yes. And you could help."

"How?"

"There are places you can go that I cannot. Nor most of my friends. Those parties you attend at Cissy Patterson's."

I look at Haynes. "Didn't I see Phil at that party?" He shakes his head, sullen. "Then how do you know I was there?"

"It was reported to me."

Dawn breaks in my mind. "You're the one who had me followed."

"I had to," says Frankfurter. "I believe some of the influence comes through clerks."

"I do too," I say. It is a great relief to be able to speak openly to someone who understands. All in an instant I have become quite fond of Frankfurter. I am on the verge of admitting that I have been spying on him in turn, for Hoover, who despises him . . . or perhaps I would do better to keep that to myself. "Your guys got pretty rough with me."

Frankfurter shrugs. "I am told you swung first."

"I might have pushed him. I don't remember."

"It is no shame," he says. "Violence may be necessary. That evening, we shall call it a miscommunication." He steeples his fingers, an almost prayerful gesture. "You can understand why I was suspicious. When a Justice does his own hiring, I am not concerned. When he relies on recommendations from others, I fear the cat's paw may slip in. I had to be sure where your loyalties lay."

"And are you?"

"Not from anything my men turned up. But I believe in your friendship with Mr. Gressman. Whoever killed him is your enemy."

"And yours."

"Yes," says Frankfurter. He smiles. "I believe there is a principle of logic by which that makes us friends. If we were not already."

I decide to make a relatively clean breast of things. "You know, Gene wasn't fond of you. He thought you were the one pulling strings."

"Most of the time I am," says Frankfurter. An element of self-satisfaction enters the smile; he is pleased with the line. I am not. I give him a flat look in response, and eventually the smile fades. "Well," says Frankfurter. "I did not agree with him on every issue. But we can all agree that outside influences are to be resisted. We can all agree that none of our family here may be touched. That is what they have done. And we must bring them to justice. Or bring justice to them. You could be quite helpful." He stops. "But I forget."

"What?"

"You are going back to Philadelphia."

In the excitement of the conversation, I have forgotten too. "Oh," I say. Once again I am standing on the street outside the Beta house, pulled abruptly back to earth, feeling the halter around my neck. But not this time. This is my decision; this is my friend. I shake my head side to side. The rope strains, snaps, slides away. "No," I say. "That's not what I'm doing."

· · · ·

"I don't understand," says Suzanne. "What are you saying?"

"Gene Gressman really was murdered. Justice Frankfurter agrees with me. And we're going to figure out who killed him."

"That's . . ." Suzanne seems to be struggling to find the right word. "That's absurd."

"Look," I say. "Someone needs to get to the bottom of this. And I think I'm the one with the best chance."

"First you wanted to volunteer. Now you're going to be a detective."

"If I have to."

"And you think you have to." There is a depth of bitterness in her voice that I have not heard before.

"Gene was my friend," I say. "I owe him."

"Cash," says Suzanne, and now I can hear the sorrow, too. "I know he was your friend. But he's dead. You can't bring him back."

"I'm not trying to bring him back. This is my duty. Because of what he did for me." Suzanne is silent. "It's a principle," I say. I am in Judge Skinner's library, eight or nine years old, and he is showing me a sheet of paper. *See how it bends, Cash? But put a crease in it and it will bear weight; it will stand on its own. That's what principles do for a man.*

"What he did for you," Suzanne repeats. There is a breathy syncopation to her words that I am pretty sure signifies tears. "Your duty. That's what you think this is about. Your honor."

At first I think she's stressing the second word, and I want to respond: of course. Of course it's a matter of honor. And then I realize her focus is on the first, that there's a different question hanging in the silence between us. *Your honor*, she is saying without words. *What about mine? What about what I did?* Agonizingly, it is like Pearl Harbor again. The things I have forgotten in my selfish rush.

"This isn't about us," I say.

"What does that even mean? I'm not worth thinking about?"

"No," I say. In my mind is tearing paper, the crackle of flames. I don't know how to explain. That duty fights with duty, that one honor tarnishes another.

"I was wrong," Suzanne says. Her voice has the same tone of discovery it did when we huddled together under the trees of Bear Island in the rain. "Thinking I could count on you. I was wrong, wasn't I?"

"Of course not." Pictures flash through my mind. Suzanne laying her hand on mine on the dock, tan and childlike; raising it to my shoulder at Merion, white-gloved and elegant. "I have to do this." Her smile, her skin. I am silent a moment, flayed by memory. Her murmurs, her cries. I had not expected this pain. "I can't be someone who sees his friend murdered and decides to let it go."

"So who will you be?"

"I don't know," I say. "I think this is how I find out."

There is a silence so long I think the connection has been lost. Then another voice comes on the line.

"Cash, what's this I hear?" It is Sam Skinner. It is the Judge.

"I have to stay in Washington," I say. "I don't know how much Suzanne has told you. But there's something I have to do."

"Your friend who died." The familiar deep voice wraps Gene Gressman in its folds. I imagine him borne heavenward on a dark velvet bier.

"He was killed."

The Judge is silent a moment. "If that is true, I would think it is dangerous for you to stay."

"That may be," I say. "But I'm not going to run from danger." And even as I say the words, I know my feelings are stronger. I am glad of the danger, I realize. I welcome it. For once in my life I am risking something.

"Philadelphia is not only safer for you," he says. "It is where your friends are. Those who love you. And we can help."

The voice has the force of something massive. It advances with a slow relentless logic, and there is nothing impressive until you try to stand in its way. Then it sweeps you aside like you were never there. "I know," I say. "But it wouldn't be the same. I don't want to hurt Suzanne—"

"Suzanne will collect herself," he interrupts. "She is upset. She has been lonely. Since her mother died, since Bob went away. Since you left. It is one thing age teaches us, that the world shrinks. But she is young for that lesson. I had hoped she might learn that families can grow as well. That I might learn it myself."

"I think I should do this." I cling to that proposition as the slow avalanche tosses me like a twig. "Gene was my friend. He got killed because he was trying to help me. And I think I'm needed."

"There are people here who need you as well. I count myself among them. We are your people, Cash. We are your family. Is this really your fight?"

They are my family. Philadelphia is my home. Washington is an alien city, it is true. But I think of my long evenings in Black's garden with him and Josephine, of Gressman knocking on the chambers door with yet another Witness joke. Who will I be? I don't know, but I know that Gene deserved better than he got. And I cannot make it right, I cannot give him the life he should have had, but I can show that his death was wrong. If I don't, no one will. "It is now," I say.

For a few seconds the Judge says nothing. I know that he is probably on the phone in Suzanne's room, sitting on the white bedspread embroidered with blue flowers. But I see him amid his books in the library, where law glints like a bright thread in man's dark tapestry. "We owe duties to the living as well as the dead, Cash," he says. "And it is only the living who can repay." The avalanche has moved on, and astonishingly I find myself in the same spot as before.

"Can I talk to Suzanne again?"

There is a pause, and a sadness in the voice when it returns. "She tells me no, Cash. I do not think she wants to hear what you have to say. And for myself, I can only say that I hope you change your mind." It is the slow protest of an old tree in high wind, the sorrow of the mountains. Then there is the creak of shearing wood, the rumble as rock moves. "Before too long. Before it is too late."

I put the phone back in its cradle. Another image rises in my mind. Once again I am watching Suzanne dive from the dock that day after she first took my hand. It comes to me, vivid and unbidden, the faint splash as water falls back on the spot where she entered, the glass-clear drops rejoining the green sea. I have replayed that scene hundreds of times in my mind. Next comes the moment when the bubbles rise, then her white hands and shoulders, breaking the surface like a seal.

But this time it does not. Like a balky projector, my mind cannot advance past that frame. I see the drops fall and the water grow still, and there it stops. And I think the Judge was wrong; I think it is already too late. She may have kissed John Hall, but I am the one who betrayed her. And that is how my thoughts end. Suzanne lifts her hand from mine; she dives into the water and vanishes and does not return.

• • • •

"Well," Frankfurter says. "It is time to consider our next move."

"I could get a job with the War Department."

He nods his head and looks meditatively at the ceiling. "The War Department certainly has a stake in the Japanese cases," he says. "And if our enemies are removing clerks through the draft, they must have some influence there. But from the Department of Justice you would have a broader perspective. You would be able to keep an eye on every case before the Court."

He is still thinking of the soldiers of capital. But it makes sense; even Gressman suspected something afoot in the business cases. And with Francis Biddle in charge I will likely have a greater freedom of movement, the opportunity to pick my work.

"After all," Frankfurter continues, "it is Justice that defends the evacuation program in court. If that is what this is about, it is as good a place as any to start."

The reference to my theory of the plot is a sop, and I feel patronized. But he is right. If Gressman was killed to protect the evacuation, those who defend it must be my first suspects. I nod in my turn. "Agreed. We need to be looking here, too. At the clerks."

"I have been thinking that myself," says Frankfurter. "Whoever was behind the murder is probably gone already. But if we screen the newcomers carefully, we may identify the bad seeds before they sprout."

"Justices who don't choose their own clerks," I say. "Clerks who weren't the first choice. Justices who can be swayed. That's what we need to look for."

Frankfurter gives the ceiling another pensive glance. "Murphy is the obvious one. He thinks of the history books; he is fond of the grand phrase and does not care much what is behind its glorious fog. And I do not think they would have acted against Mr. Gressman unless they had their own man lined up. His replacement will bear watching. For the rest . . . Black can be moved, as we've seen. But your successor is handpicked, a liberal from the South. I am confident in him. Stone and Jackson know their own minds, and Roberts has his permanent pair. Reed . . . Reed is mostly vegetable. He could be susceptible to a clever young man. I will keep an eye open there as well."

"And what about Douglas?"

"Douglas?" Frankfurter twists his mouth in displeasure. "Douglas has no care for anyone but himself. It makes him incorruptible, in a way. There is no room for another's plans. And I do not think they would send a woman." He pauses. "Although, with Douglas that might be the only way. And he has an antiauthoritarian bent that could be useful. Do you know that he has never once voted for Internal Revenue in a tax case?"

"He was all over the place with the Japanese, too," I say. "His would be a useful vote to nail down."

"You are right," says Frankfurter. "Clara Watson must be on our list. I will leave her to you, I think. I have reasons to talk to the other clerks. You have reasons to talk to her."

"I do?"

"She does not know the city. I doubt she knows anyone here. She would welcome your company."

I hesitate. "I'm not sure we really got off on the right foot."

"Nonsense," Frankfurter scoffs. He looks me up and down and smiles with approval. "Invite her to a movie. She'll be grateful."

• • • •

"A movie?" asks Clara.

"Yes," I say. "I thought you might have some questions about the clerkship."

"Indeed, I might." There are glints of light in her dark hair and flecks of gold in her eyes. "Yes, why not a movie? And perhaps an ice cream soda?"

I allow that this too is a possibility.

"A delightful prospect," she says, and smiles. "We will most of us end as clichés, wonder boy. But I find that starting with them is a poor idea. It leaves you nowhere to go."

I am puzzled. "Is that a yes?"

"Did it sound like one?"

I have to admit that it did not.

"Brilliance personified," says Clara. "You will go places in life. But not to a movie. Not with me. Not this evening."

Now I think I understand; I know this sort of banter. "Another evening, then?"

Clara frowns. It is her turn to look puzzled. "Have I encouraged you?" She sounds genuinely confused. "I don't mean to. Let me put it this way. You will not talk me into going to a movie with you. Are we clear?"

"Fine," I say. She has not left much room for a playful riposte. "Great." Suddenly I am angry. More than I should be, but the invitation was not my idea, and it is doubly galling to face rejection for something I never wanted to do in the first place. "You don't have to be snooty about it. I'm just trying to be nice."

"How generous of you," she says. "How lucky I am that everyone wants to do me favors."

"Okay," I say. "No movies."

"No," says Clara. She allows herself a small, mysterious smile. "But still a nice suit."

CHAPTER 26

A SHEET OF glass across the top of a mahogany desk shows me an inverted image of the upper half of Attorney General Francis Biddle. He wears a dark suit and vest, a speckled salmon tie. The neat mustache remains, and his comb-over is careful as ever, but a bald spot is emerging at the back.

Biddle smiles. "Well, Cash," he says. "You'd like to see how the other half lives?"

The upside-down face is distracting, and his choice of words does not help, but I retain enough concentration to surmise that Hoover has not mentioned my trips here. I think it wiser not to raise them myself. "I could learn a lot from a different perspective on the cases," I say.

"I think so," says Biddle. "Hard to beat the view from the Court, of course. Your clerkship must have been wonderful. I remember my year with Holmes. He wrote all his opinions himself, and he did it faster than anyone else. When he was finished he would invite me on walks to Georgetown or along the canal. Weekends I knocked polo balls around on the Mall."

Biddle evidently did not have a friend murdered. My feelings about the experience are a bit more complicated, but I simply nod and say, "Mmmm," as though savoring the memories.

"I never grew as much as I did that year," Biddle continues. "Holmes opened my mind and let the platitudes and prejudices of Harvard fall out. I don't think we have his equal on the Court now, but it's a solid group. Black, of course. Owen Roberts, Bill Douglas. And Felix Frankfurter. I had a very nice letter from Frankfurter when I was appointed Attorney General. 'In the words of Holmes,' he wrote, 'I bet on you.'"

I try to remember Frankfurter saying a kind word about Biddle. I fail. "He's always been very solicitous with me," I say.

"Felix collects people," Biddle says. "Generally he shows good taste. I invited him to speak at the Fly Club alumni dinner in '33, you know. Not a success, I'm afraid. Many of the members declined to attend. Sam Skinner didn't speak to me for years." His voice trails off, and he is silent for a moment; then he looks around the room as though recalling himself to the present. "So, you're interested in the Department. I think it can be arranged. You've seen what we do. A bit different from the work of the Court. The certificate the President signs to appoint a Justice attests to his uprightness, wisdom, and learning. For the Attorney General it lists patriotism, integrity, and ability. It makes for an easy joke about the qualities each one lacks, but there's truth to it as well. We represent the United States. Not a party or a faction, but the country. Roosevelt is not a superman, but he has given the people a vision of what their government could be, that it could be theirs, the government and the country alike.

"I decided as a young man that I would be one of the governing class, not just a gentleman of cultivated taste. And that's who I want with me. Not society, but those who want to serve. Do you understand me?"

I nod assent. It is what Judge Skinner said to me, so long ago. He and Biddle have different views on governance, of course, but it is interesting to see they share this much.

"Well, then," says Biddle. He follows my gaze to a photograph on the wall. A small boy with a tag on his jacket leans out the window of a train, holding an American flag. "Terribly sad," Biddle says. It is a Japanese boy. "James Rowe gave me that. The head of the Alien Enemy Control Unit. You know, the Japs actually have a much stronger sense of duty than we do. Of the obligations of citizenship."

It is a perfect opening. "Do you need anyone else there? I'm quite familiar with the cases."

"Oh, of course," says Biddle. "Indeed we do. Rowe's actually on his way out. His number came up. We could use your understanding of the Supreme Court's thinking. And you can help us work with the War Department. It's been an area of some difficulty for us." He presses the intercom on his desk and a secretary appears. "Our friend the Captain is still with Rowe," Biddle says. "Send him to my office." He turns back to me. "There's been rather a tug-of-war between the departments, but it's important that we stay in close communication. I believe you'd have an advantage in the job."

We wait. Biddle smiles at me; I look at the photograph on the wall. Footsteps come down the corridor and pause, then the door swings open.

"Hiya, Swell," says John Hall. I look at him in silence.

"Well," says Biddle. "I expect you have some catching up to do."

· · · ·

"I ought to punch you in the nose," I say when we are alone together.

"What for?" Hall's bland good looks express puzzlement easily.

"And again for not knowing why," I say. "Suzanne. Did she mean that little to you?"

"Suzanne?"

"Did you tell her you'd seen your death? Pretend you were going into combat? Let me know when the planes hit the Pentagon. When your desk gets shot down."

"No, Swell, you've got it all wrong." Hall raises his hands as if in surrender. "That wasn't me. It was a buddy of mine. He said it to all the girls, but he really was shipping out. He's dead now, if it makes you feel better. The Japs got him at Guadalcanal."

"Jesus," I say. "Of course not." There is risk and its rewards, the body that held hers now uniting itself with earth, or bobbing slowly homeward on Pacific swells.

"I didn't know you were still an item. Honest. I would have . . . said something. Hell, I don't know. But she didn't talk much about you. Really, are you still seeing her?"

The answer is no. We have not spoken since that last phone conversation, and when my thoughts stray to her I push them away as best I can. I have a job to do; I cannot spare the energy to suffer. Still, the question is an insult. I say nothing.

"Maybe that's a sore spot," says Hall. "Forget I asked. Look, we've got to work together." He puts out his hand. "Bygones?"

I let it hang there. "No one calls me Swell."

Hall smiles. "I do."

"You're going to stop. It's Cash."

"Oh, yeah. I remember that one. Very reliable, but doesn't draw much interest." He smiles more broadly, attempting to induce a matching response.

I give him none. "How's that?" I ask.

"We said it about your squash game," he says. The smile looks like it is not a part of him, but something affixed to his face with adhesive. "And a little bit the girls." He extends the hand farther. "Come on, you should hear what I get with John Hall."

"What do you mean?"

"Alco-hol," he says. "'John Hall gives me a headache,' that sort of thing. Never heard it? Never mind. Just shake my hand, will ya?"

I look from his thick fingers to his earnest eyes and back again. There was always a sharp edge of rivalry to my childhood friendship with John Hall, and nothing that has happened since has made me think more kindly of him. But he is my best source in the War Department, and I am sure I will need him. I take his hand. "Bygones," I say.

· · · ·

Biddle walks me out, pointing to murals on the wall. "My brother George did these," he says. They are triumphalist, like Hoover's, but slightly more abstract. A stylized Holmes rides a white charger against what looks to be a cloud of red tape; religious figures hover approvingly above icons of the law. "I had a bit of trouble getting them approved," Biddle says. "There was a feeling in some quarters that he'd made Christ look too Jewish."

In the entry foyer, Biddle bids me farewell. I pause, looking about the Great Hall. I have gone from one set of statues to another, from marble to aluminum. Here again they are Justice and Law, but there is a difference. The Court's lintel promises equal justice under law, the impartiality of the blind. The Department's statue wears no blindfold, for its members take sides. As Biddle said, they take the side of America, they sue for justice. I say the motto to myself as I leave. *Qui Pro Domina Justitia Sequitur.*

I say something else, too. The men behind Gressman's murder may be here. They may be in the War Department; they may be somewhere else altogether. But wherever they are, I am on their trail. I am coming for them. It isn't the weightless ecstasy of that moment when I leapt from the stairs of the Beta house. I am hauling sadness, trailing broken vows. But I am aloft. Black wings beat the air. I am coming, flying to vengeance, flying to war.

• • • •

At home there are fewer people to notify and no one's permission to seek. "Francis Biddle," says my father, his voice faint over the phone. He says nothing more. He does not need to; I can fill in the general outlines. Francis shows that even the solid Biddles can lose their heads. He has never been reliable, with his novel-writing and his Bull Moosing; he was clearly deranged by the Depression. There is rot in that family, and artistic frivolity—do I know that George is now painting impressionist tenements for the WPA?

What need not be said need not be answered, and there is no answer that would satisfy my father anyway. But later, as I say good-bye to Black, I think of another point that he might have been suggesting.

"Been an interesting year," says Black. "I hope I taught you something."

"You did, Judge."

Hazel eyes sparkle. "What?"

"My father once told me that no man is a hero to his valet."

"And?"

"You taught me it's not true."

"Shucks," says Black. "No man who's got a valet is a hero in my book."

PART II
MAIN JUSTICE

CHAPTER 27

IN SOME WAYS my job at Main Justice begins just as my clerkship did. They take me to a small room filled with stacks of paper and tell me to get to work. I am in James Rowe's office, sitting at his desk, reading his files. The man himself is en route to a Navy destroyer.

In another way, of course, this job is totally different. I am not here to get experience or a look at the justice system from the inside. I am not here to make friends or connections who can help me further down the road. I am here to find a killer, and I know already that there is no one I can trust.

The main task of the Alien Enemy Control Unit is to defend the evacuation and detention of the Japanese. More legal challenges are making their way towards the Supreme Court. *Hirabayashi* was a victory for the government, but the struggle is by no means over. Rowe's files will give me the background necessary to understand the cases still to come. And, I hope, they will help me figure out who might care about these cases enough to kill for them.

But as I start to work through them, the files puzzle. Rowe's notes are cryptic and incomplete, and arranged in no order I can discern. In places they are spiced with plainly irrelevant materials. The same folder might hold a court filing from the *Hirabayashi* litigation, Rowe's narrative of a meeting with Karl Bendetsen of the War Department, and a report on grain prices in the Midwest.

I try several boxes of files, but it is all more of the same. I find Bendetsen's name again and again, the chronicles of War and Justice; I find briefs and legal analysis; I find a report on price-fixing in the wheat industry from the 1920s.

I have seen Rowe once, a pale young man sitting at the government's table during the *Hirabayashi* argument. He did not look happy then, but he did not seem completely insane, either, which is how he comes across from the files. Hoping he's left something as a guide to all of this, I put the papers back down on the floor and open the main drawer of my new desk. Like insects fleeing the light, a few pencils roll to the back. They leave behind a smell of wood shavings and a single sheet of paper, Justice Department stationery.

Rowe has written a letter, but it is not addressed to me. It is for Attorney General Biddle, two sentences long. *I hereby resign my position as Special Assistant to the Attorney General. I do not believe that continued representation of the government in this matter is consistent with the interests of Justice.* Rowe's resignation, I think, though the phrasing is odd for a man who was drafted out of his position. But then I notice two things. The letter is undated. It is unsigned, too, but below the space for a signature someone has typed a name. And the name there is not James Rowe. It is Caswell Harrison; it is me.

I blink a few times at the paper in my hand. It could be a practical joke. For all I know, it could be a tradition in the Department. But it gives me an unpleasant feeling, and I am sitting at the desk frowning into space when the door opens and Edward Ennis steps in.

Ennis is my boss, the head of Alien Enemies, a pink-faced thirty-five-year-old with dark, expressive eyes and waves of Brylcreemed hair. There is a thick folder under his arm. "So," he says. "You're Biddle's fair-haired boy."

I shrug, getting to my feet.

"Oh, please." He raises a dismissive hand. "Sit. Now, do you know what you're here for?"

There is something challenging in his tone. I am out of place, I suppose. Inexperienced. And it is true that I would not have this job but for my friendship with Francis Biddle. But I know why I am here. I hold his eyes. "Yes."

"Good," he says. "I hope you're settling in. These cases won't be won or lost on the law. I need you to pull together the facts."

I am already regretting my answer. "The facts?"

"The facts justifying evacuation." Again there is an edge of hostility in his voice. "The facts that show disloyalty."

"Right."

Ennis hefts the folder. "That's your main job. But we've got some months for that. Here's your first assignment." The folder lands on my desk with a thud. "I want an answer this week."

• • • •

Unlike Rowe's, these files explain themselves. They are records for inmates at the Leupp detention center, a prison camp set up on a Navajo reservation in Arizona. It is an isolation center for the incorrigibles among the detainees, the worst of the worst. We send them there from the other camps in trucks with the windows painted black and hold them behind cyclone fences. The 150 military police outnumber their charges by more than two-to-one.

But how do we know who belongs in Leupp? That, it seems, is where I come in. There is a new director, appointed in the summer of 1943, and he does not know what his residents have done to warrant transfer. This is a problem. Detainees are supposed to receive hearings to determine whether the transfer was justified and when they might return, but the hearings can hardly proceed without any information about the alleged offenses. The director complains to the head of the War Relocation Authority, who sends an alert out to the camp directors. From all the camps, records flow to Washington, to the Department of Justice, to the folder on my desk. I am to evaluate the records and make a recommendation: hold this man or release him.

Easy enough, I think as I begin. It will be like cert work: synthesize the information, weigh the two sides, make a decision. But experience discourages that prophecy.

"There's something wrong," I tell Felix Frankfurter later that evening.

He tilts his head. "How so?"

"I got through about eight files today. None of them has enough to support detention."

"There is no explanation for why they are at Leupp?"

"Oh, there is. It's just not good enough." Sometimes, in fact, it is laughably bad. An informer reports that Minoru Kanno tried to organize a union among the beet farmers at the Topaz camp. I am not sure that this justifies sending Minoru to Leupp at all, but in any event the man they put in the truck was Masuo Kanno. Two of my eight are mistaken identity. The others are unsourced rumors. *It is reported*, they say, *that George Yamaguchi aided in the planning of an attack on a fellow resident*. It is believed; it is suspected; it is thought. Whispering voices, unsigned notes. How can I decide if these merit trust?

"Well," says Frankfurter. "If the government thought it was important enough to put in the files, you may presume it is reliable."

"You think so?"

"Why not? They are experts in these matters."

"I don't know," I say. "I was thinking something else."

"What?"

"I think he's testing me." By any objective standards, my first day has been disconcerting. Ennis is hostile, Rowe's papers a mess. Everything is wrong, but I take that as a good sign. I have found something at the Department of Justice. In the lack of evidence against the Leupp detainees, in the disarray of Rowe's files. It rises like a whorl of dust. The fingerprint of the enemy, trace of their invisible hand. They have been here.

"That may be," says Frankfurter. "In which case your course is clear. You must tell him to hold these men. That will prove your loyalty."

"Even Kanno? They've just got the wrong guy."

"Who knows when the mistake was made? Perhaps the records are wrong and the man is right."

"Is it fair to assume that?"

Frankfurter shakes his head. "Do you want to find who killed your friend? Or to be fair to someone you will never see?" I say nothing. "It is the right thing to do, anyway," he continues. "If there is any chance they are dangerous, they should not be released."

"I don't think that's what Ennis said."

"Who cares what he said?" Irritation rises in Frankfurter's voice. "Why should we take the risk? These people use our courts and laws as weapons against us." His tone softens. "I am not so sure Ennis is testing you. Perhaps mistakes were made. But not every error is sinister. They may be born of fear, or indifference, or sincere devotion burnished too bright." He smiles at me, suddenly avuncular. "Still, we should follow all possible leads. Perhaps you are right. See what you can learn from Rowe's papers. Talk to your friend John Hall. For my part, I have been watching the clerks. Murphy's new man arouses my suspicion. And how was your movie?"

"My movie?" The disastrous conversation with Clara returns to my mind. "We didn't go."

Frankfurter cocks his head. "Why not?"

"She didn't want to."

"She has some objection to the movies?"

"Seemed more like an objection to me."

"Not you." He frowns. "Perhaps she is cautious because she has something to hide. You must try again."

I consider the possibility. I would rather try to ferret out a conspiracy in the Justice Department. Upon reflection, I would rather do almost anything. "I must?"

"Of course. You are our best means of uncovering the truth." Frankfurter sets his mouth in a firm line. "I did not think you the sort to shrink from duty."

He is right. I nod glumly and go. The walk to the Douglas chambers is like a condemned man's march for the scaffold. But then, as I near the door, I come up with a plan.

CHAPTER 28

JOHN HALL RAISES his squash racquet, his arm floating out and up to head level. He takes two steps backward into the center of the court. Standing behind him near the right wall, I am forced to backpedal also. A final flourish in the windup takes his racquet even higher and signals the start of the downstroke. It is the Merion backswing. I have it too, but the shot he follows with is pure Harvard, a combination of wrist action and forearm rotation that generates so much power the ball comes off the wall with a higher-pitched crack than my hardest drive. Beekman Pool introduced the style, and I remember it from college matches. You can walk past a court and know that Harvard players are warming up by the sound alone.

Hall drives the ball crosscourt to the left wall, near the front. It comes off fast, hitting the front wall low above the tin and trickling into the court. A reverse corner; I anticipate it and start forward as soon as I can, but his backswing has pushed me out of position and the shot is too fine, dying almost immediately. The game is over.

"Another one for the good guys," Hall says. We shake hands. "Join me for a drink?"

"Sure," I say. It is becoming a routine: we go to the Metropolitan Club, Hall beats me at squash, and we talk over beer. Two Philadelphia boys.

In the oak-paneled bar, his tone is ingratiating. "Honest, Cash, I'm glad you're here." He takes a sip of beer. "That's the stuff. I'm glad I won't have to deal with Rowe anymore, too. He wasn't easy to work with."

"Really? I hadn't heard that."

Hall's mouth is full again. He waves his hand, indicating protest or pending clarification, and swallows audibly. "No, no," he says, "I'm sure he was fine within DOJ. But he was no good as a liaison to the War Department. Karl Bendetsen hated him. He's sure Rowe was out to sabotage the whole program."

Bendetsen. There's that name again. It fills Rowe's notes. Bendetsen hated Rowe, thought he would undermine the detention. And now Rowe is on a destroyer in the Pacific. Funny how things work out. "'Sabotage' is an ugly word," I say.

"Yes," says Hall.

"It would be disloyal," I continue.

"Yes, it would be." Hall nods as though encouraging a child. "That's the point. Bendetsen thought Rowe was disloyal."

"So why didn't you give him a questionnaire to fill out?" I ask.

"Hah," says Hall. His face assumes a hurt expression. "Try to remember we're on the same side here. You know, I wrote that questionnaire. Took me weeks."

I take a drink of my own beer. It is refreshing, but rather tasteless. Not like the Yuengling at Merion. "Well, good job."

"It was a good job," Hall says. "We got thousands of people to admit they were disloyal. That's an accomplishment, isn't it?"

"If that's what happened."

"What do you mean?"

"Seems sort of funny, that's all. That you're so worried about who's loyal and who isn't that you have to ship them all off to camps, and then it turns out all you had to do was ask."

"It's not just asking," Hall says proudly. "They had to take an oath. And say they're willing to serve."

I think that Hall's Harvard degree has not cured the streak of idiocy he displayed in high school. Or possibly the War Department has restored it. In either case, it is time to move on. "So Rowe was no good for you. Ennis was better?"

Hall shrugs. "Not really. No one in Justice has been particularly helpful." He smiles and lays a hairy hand on the bar near mine. "That's why it's nice to have you here."

Involuntarily, I move my hand away. "And how about Karl Bendetsen?"

"What?"

"Sounds like he's pretty committed to this program."

"Yes, he is."

"How far do you think he'd go to defend it? Do you think he might do something he's not supposed to?"

That gets a reaction from Hall. The dark eyes widen, the thick eyebrows edge up. Then, quickly, a pleased expression replaces the surprise. "He might. Why do you ask?"

My heart begins to beat faster. "I have an interest in the matter."

Hall looks crafty. "Is it business, or is it personal?"

I consider. "It's personal."

"I might be able to help you, then. Just to satisfy your interest. But you've got to do something for me." He is adopting a conspiratorial tone, but for a moment a genuine enthusiasm breaks through. "See, Cash, this is how it's supposed to work. I could never talk like this with Rowe."

I ignore that. Hall's affect is entirely wrong for someone discussing a murder, but perhaps he knows only part of the truth. Whatever information he has, I want it. "What do you want me to do?"

"Talk to Biddle."

"About what?"

"So we got several thousand no-nos on the questionnaire. Won't take the oath, won't fight. They're certified disloyal, right?"

"If you say so."

"I do. We're sending them to the Tule Lake Relocation Center."

"Great," I say. "So what do you need me for?"

"The ones who said yes on the questionnaire, the ones who aren't going to Tule Lake."

"What about them?"

"Well, the Relocation Authority is screwing with us. They're a bunch of sociologists. They've never understood the idea of military necessity. They want to get the detainees out of the camps. They sent ten thousand out last summer on temporary furloughs to harvest the sugar beets, and now they want to say that the ones who don't admit they're disloyal are safe to release. They're willing to let them go if they can find jobs and places to stay. Some of them are out already." He looks at me expectantly.

I do not see the problem. "So?"

Hall frowns. "Well, they might be disloyal. We've been screening them. Some of them are serious security risks."

"Even though they took your oath?"

"Come on, Cash. You know a disloyal person would lie."

"If the disloyal people lie, then who are the ones who refused to take the oath?"

For a moment, Hall looks confused. Then he shakes his head as if to clear it. "Leave that to us. The point is, we've said these people are security threats, and the Relocation Authority is letting them go. And this is where you come in. The War Department wants to know if DOJ will bring them back."

"Arrest them?"

"If you have to. You can start by asking nicely."

"I don't know," I say. I am feeling a flicker of discomfort. Surely Gene Gressman would have been horrified at the idea. In my mind I replay our plan to flush out the leak by giving a fake opinion to the Court printer. Such innocent games, when the enemy was a myth to us, the shadow of fire on a cave wall. Things are different now. Gressman is dead; the enemy is real; Hall has promised me information on Bendetsen. And if all I do is raise the issue, perhaps make a recommendation . . . The ultimate decision will still lie with the Attorney General. I sip my beer. Warmer, but still watery. "I can ask Biddle. But I can't promise anything."

"Then I guess I can't promise you anything, either. But ask. Tell him it comes from me. I'm sure he'll be reasonable. We're all Philadelphians. That's what Rowe didn't understand. We're all on the same side here."

"And if he says yes, you'll tell me what Bendetsen did?"

Again there is the widening in his eyes, the lift of the brows, followed by the crafty smile. "Who says he did anything?"

"We should play cards sometime, John." He frowns uncomprehendingly. I look at my watch. It is almost five.

"Got somewhere to be?" Hall asks. He finishes his beer and signals for another.

"I do, actually." I drain my glass and put a dime on the bar. "Let me give you something for this." Hall pushes the coin back to me.

"It's on Uncle Sam," he says. "Just talk to Biddle."

. . . .

Clara has said she will meet me in Dupont Circle. I find her by the fountain in a black dress, and together we walk up Massachusetts Avenue. The after-work crush is thinner here than downtown, where the government girls throng, but it is still a steady stream. Clara gives me an appraising glance as we pick our way along the sidewalk. "Are you sure you're game for this?" I ask. "I told you it would be risky."

"Better than a movie," she says.

I hope it will be. The last time I was at Cissy Patterson's house, Drew Pearson told me about a new sport in the capital. Put on a dark suit, he said, get your girl a silk dress, and just walk down Massachusetts Avenue until you see a crowd of people. That will be an embassy party. Tell the greeters you are with Senator Smith and smile your way in.

It seemed audacious enough to lift me from the realm of ice cream soda cliché. In the Douglas chambers, Clara arched an eyebrow as I laid out the possibility. "Were we not clear?"

"We were," I said. "No talking you into the movies. And this is absolutely not a movie."

"A fair point," she said. "Worthy of a lawyer." In the silence that followed I did my best not to show my nerves. "We are not working together anymore," she said at last. "And I should like to see an embassy."

This one belongs to Spain, according to its flags. The promised crowd mills outside; black cars drop off passengers. I take Clara's hand and lead her toward the door. "Stay close to me," I say. "We'll have to hoof it if they figure out what's up."

"Of course," says Clara. Her voice is skeptical, but she leaves her hand in mine.

There is a row of functionaries at the door. "Senator Lucas will be along in a moment," I say, shaking hands. "Last-minute vote." I move down the line. "Cloture motion. Filibuster." It is working just as Pearson promised. I am developing a smooth rhythm, barely looking up from the hands. Clara is right behind me. "Appropriations," I say. "Hearings."

"Why, Mr. Harrison." I stop cold. The voice is familiar. It matches the hand I am holding, delicate and feminine. I look up into a pair of attractive dark eyes. "So glad you could make it." She lays her other hand atop mine and leans forward. In an instant I remember her from Cissy's party. "I regret we can offer you no Fish House Punch. But you may learn to enjoy sangria."

I feel my face flush. From Clara there emanates a speculative silence. When we are through the line she turns to me. "Tell me," she says. "Do we have to hoof it now?" She digs two stiff fingers into my ribs. "What a gangster you are," she says. "You had an invitation."

It is true. "Just as backup," I say.

"Of course," says Clara. "Still, it makes the venture a little less risky, wouldn't you say? Makes you cut a slightly less dashing figure, maybe?"

I am starting to steam again. The girl has a genius for putting me in the wrong. "It's not my fault I was invited."

"No. But to pretend to me that you were not . . . I suppose I should be flattered. You wanted to put on a show for me. You were trying to impress. Does that excuse it?" She lifts a glass of champagne from a passing tray and takes a meditative sip. "Were you nervous, trying to pass for something you are not?"

I don't know what to say. "It was just fun."

"Yes," says Clara. There is something wistful in her smile. "It was fun." She sips her champagne again. "Well, I will see you later."

"What?"

"You seem to have friends here already. I am going to see if I can make new ones."

CHAPTER 29

"ABSOLUTELY NOT," SAYS Francis Biddle. He does not look up from his desk. "These are American citizens living outside the evacuated military areas. There is no legal authority to bring them back to the camps, and I will not send the FBI to do it."

There goes my information on Bendetsen, I think. Yet I am not entirely disappointed. Indeed, I am feeling something like pride in Biddle. "John Hall says the War Department thinks they're security risks."

Biddle raises his eyes to meet mine for the first time. "This doesn't come from John Hall."

"I just talked to him."

Biddle shakes his head. "John Hall confuses domination with nobility, which he was taught at Episcopal and again at Harvard. The lesson was available at Groton, too, for those who wished to learn." He shrugs. "It is one view of aristocracy. My mother raised me to be gallant, which to her meant protecting one's people. I hope to have enlarged the compass of my sympathy. As for Hall, he likes working with the Army. He likes the feeling that they will do what is necessary, that he shares the ruthlessness of the righteous. But I've known him his whole life. He would not on his own set out to hunt down citizens cleared by the Relocation Authority. This comes from Karl Bendetsen."

My heart leaps at the name. "Why would Bendetsen want it?"

"Bendetsen built his program on the premise that loyalty could not be determined. He's against anything that would call that into question. Eventually it will be undone, of course. General DeWitt is a fool and an embarrassment, and the War Department has finally realized that. He's not in charge of the Western Defense Command anymore; they've kicked him upstairs to the Staff College. The new generals will be more reasonable." He looks down again at the papers in front of him.

"Why do you think Bendetsen pushed this program in the first place?" I ask.

Biddle shakes his head. "I do not know. Possibly he believed it was necessary. Possibly he saw a chance to prove his loyalty and zeal, to overcome his origins or to curry favor with DeWitt. His rise has been rapid."

"So what should I tell Hall?"

Biddle looks up one more time. His eyes meet mine and hold them. "Tell him this department will not participate in an action that has no basis in the laws or Constitution of this land."

· · · ·

So the swap with Hall is off. Still, I am making progress. Back in my office, I spend more time with Rowe's files. I am pulling out all of Rowe's descriptions of intergovernmental meetings and putting them in order. And I can see the story of evacuation is not what I thought it was. Working on the *Hirabayashi* curfew case, I'd thought the program was generally agreed to be necessary. That was what the government briefs said. But now I can see that was not the case. There was a struggle among the departments, a fight between War and Justice. *January 4, 1942*, Rowe writes. *Meeting with Bendetsen and General DeWitt at the Presidio in San Francisco. Bendetsen claims radio transmitters operating on coast.* There is a useful fact, a token of disloyalty I remember from the amicus brief of the Pacific states. Rowe has marked it with a handwritten marginal note: *FCC RID 42-107. ONI Ringle.* His narrative continues. *Wants warrantless searches of Japanese homes. "For a warrant, you have to show a reason. We don't want to show a reason." Refused.*

But Bendetsen is not done. *January 30, 1942. Meeting with Bendetsen. Wants Bainbridge Island Japanese arrested. Told him unconstitutional, can't be done to citizens.*

February 1, 1942. Bendetsen unannounced at Biddle's office with McCloy. Jack McCloy, I think, Assistant Secretary of War. I do not know him personally, but he is a Philadelphian, and as Judge Skinner once said to me, we keep track of each other. *Biddle: DOJ will have nothing to do with detention of citizens. Unconstitutional. McCloy: You put a Wall Street lawyer in a hell of a box, but if safety of country at stake, Constitution just a scrap of paper.*

I flip the pages, looking for more Bendetsen. Through February, Rowe lobbies Biddle, congressmen, anyone who will listen. Hoover backs him up. Bendetsen is spreading hysteria, they say. There is no evidence that sabotage is threatened. *February 15, 1942. Drafted letter from Biddle to FDR. Special interests pushing for evacuation, no military necessity.* Rowe is marshalling his forces. He sounds optimistic, almost happy. He does not know how it will end.

But I do. *February 17, evening. Meeting at Biddle's house. Ennis, Bendetsen, McCloy. Explained constitutional difficulties. Bendetsen pulled out draft Executive Order authorizing evacuation of coast. "Crazy," I said. Biddle wouldn't look at me. Authorized it yesterday.* Rowe is too angry to speak, he writes. Biddle keeps his eyes on the floor and tells them to prepare the order for the President's signature. FDR has already approved. "Do what you need to," he said. "Be as reasonable as you can." In the taxi on the way back to Justice, Rowe considers resignation. Ennis talks him out of it. There will be lawsuits. Someone has to write the briefs.

And James Rowe wrote them, doing the best he could with the facts he had. It must have been an unpleasant job, but he did his duty. A loyal soldier.

I still cannot understand why he left his files in such confusion. I sit for a moment mulling it over, frowning into space. Rowe was trying to make it hard to reconstruct his thinking, I guess. But why would he do that? Or was he trying to confuse someone else, under whose eyes he was working? And in another flash of insight, I realize why the notes sound odd. There is nothing in there about the role of the man who told me to get the facts. Nothing about Edward Ennis.

"Kanno?"

The voice startles me out of reverie. When I look up, Ennis has poked his head around the doorframe. I look at him in silence and he steps into the office, closing the door behind him. "Minoru Kanno," he repeats. "What about him?"

Again there is a challenge in his voice, and it pricks me with annoyance. That, and his use of Kanno's first name. "The guy at Leupp is Masuo Kanno," I say. "And you should let him go."

Ennis nods, his face expressionless. "Yamaguchi?" he asks.

I hesitate. *Do you want to find who killed your friend?* Frankfurter asked. *Or to be fair to someone you will never see?* If I say we should hold Yamaguchi, it may prove my loyalty. It may let me get the information I need to find Gene's killer. I would be sacrificing Yamaguchi for my purposes, but they are good purposes, and if he's released from Leupp he will just be going back to Rohwer, to another camp. I open my mouth to tell Ennis we should keep him at Leupp.

But I can't. At Rohwer, Yamaguchi will at least be back with his family. "Let him go," I say.

Ennis looks quizzical. "Really?"

"Really," I say. I strive to put conviction in my voice. "If we hold the ones we don't have anything on, the courts won't trust us for the ones we do have evidence against."

"And what if we don't have evidence against any of them?"

I hold his eyes. "Then I guess we let them all go."

"You guess wrong."

"What?"

"What are we going to say? We made a mistake? We don't know what we're doing? We're at war, Cash. Is that the kind of message you want to send to our citizens, to our enemies?"

"When did this become about sending a message?"

Ennis shrugs. "We're not letting them go. Actually, they're all going to Tule Lake. We're shutting Leupp down. It was a public relations nightmare."

"Then why did you ask me?"

Now he gives me a smile, though it is not one I would call nice. "Just got the news this morning. And I wanted to see what you'd say." He turns to leave, pausing at the threshold. "Made any progress on the facts?"

"There doesn't seem to be much in Rowe's notes," I say.

"Oh," says Ennis. "I wonder why that would be."

"The Pacific states made a stronger argument. I might start there."

"Sounds reasonable."

He is giving me nothing. "It was a funny thing," I say. "Don't you think? Rowe getting drafted like that?"

"Yeah," says Ennis. "A laugh riot." Now there is open hostility in his eyes.

"Okay," I say. "Well, I'll get to work on those facts."

I look at the door for a long moment after he has gone. Rowe put nothing in his notes about Ennis because he expected Ennis to read them. Or perhaps Ennis has been through the files already, removing the mentions of his role. Perhaps he's the one who put in the wheat market analysis, throwing sand in my eyes.

It doesn't seem completely right, as I think about it. But surely I will learn more about Ennis in the days ahead. About Bendetsen there is no doubt. That is the lead to pursue, and the time has come to take advantage of my institutional resources. I pick up the phone. "How are you coming with the prints?" I ask Clyde Tolson.

"We are searching our files. There is no match yet. We will continue to look."

"And you'll let me know if anything comes up?"

"Of course, Mr. Harrison." There is a different tone to Tolson's voice. I am a Special Assistant to the Attorney General now, toiling in the same vineyard. I do not know if I outrank him, for he is an Assistant Director and can boast a closer relationship to Hoover than I have to Biddle. But when he calls me "Mr. Harrison" it sounds as though he is addressing a colleague, not sneering at a street punk. I find that I like it.

The news that they have failed to match the foreign print is less welcome, but not surprising. It tends to support my theory that the killer was one of the clerks, someone gone now with no way to trace him. Perhaps Hoover was right; perhaps they should all be printed. But the FBI has more to offer.

"I've got another question," I say. I do not know if Tolson will help, but it seems worth a try.

"What is it?"

"Do you have a file on Karl Bendetsen?"

"I am not familiar with the name," Tolson says. He does not sound surprised at the request; perhaps it is more common than I'd supposed.

"He's an Army colonel," I say. "An aide to General John DeWitt. And one of the architects of the Japanese evacuation."

"Ah," says Tolson. "He has most likely undergone a background check. We have files on many people, Mr. Harrison, and if we do not, we can open one. We will let you know in either case." There is something unsettling about his calm assurance. For a moment I wonder what they might have on me, and who might ask for it. But I put the thought aside. There is work to be done.

Half an hour later a young man comes to my office with a manila folder. I recognize him as FBI before he identifies himself as Special Agent Miller. There is a type, at least here at Main Justice: clean-shaven and well-muscled under the white shirt, dark hair parted on the left.

"From the Assistant Director," he says. I thank him and open the folder.

Karl Bendetsen is from Aberdeen, Washington. Weatherwax High School, Stanford University, Stanford Law. He is Jewish but likes to conceal that fact, a practice he started as an undergraduate seeking to join Theta Delt. From law school he went back to Aberdeen and local practice. He married his secretary. In 1940 he joined the army as a lawyer with the Judge Advocate General's Corps. He changed the spelling of his name, originally Bendetson, and began claiming Danish heritage. He became an aide to General DeWitt and a specialist on the threat of enemy aliens and native fifth columns. After Pearl Harbor, he stayed awake for forty-eight hours, setting out in memos the government's power to respond. Two months later he completed a recommendation for the evacuation and detention of American citizens of Japanese descent. He was promoted to full colonel the same day that recommendation was accepted. No known subversive tendencies or associates; no known sexual deviancy.

I am impressed that the file exists at all, but it does not give me much to go on. I study the photograph clipped to the folder. Bendetsen sits at a desk in his army uniform, dark hair slicked back. About the mouth he resembles Bogart, and I think he knows it, for in the photo he has adopted Sam Spade's calculating squint. All that is missing is the cigarette dangling from cynical lips.

I look into the pictured eyes and speak aloud. "Are you my man?" He is from the West. He could have an economic interest in acquiring Japanese land, I suppose, or in eliminating the competition of their farms and orchards. His advancement through the ranks is clearly tied to his role in the evacuation. It would be an embarrassment to see the program rejected by the Supreme Court; it might cast a shadow over his career prospects. But it does not seem enough of a motive for murder. Perhaps fear of exposure, if he thought Gressman was getting close to unmasking him. Or perhaps, I think, I am looking in the wrong place after all.

Felix Frankfurter does not share my doubts. "I understand this man," he says. "It could be him. He would go that far."

"Why do you think that, Justice?"

"He might do it for love of country alone. There is something desperate in the patriotism of the unassimilated. The refugee who has lost one home and will not lose another. The man who pushes another out of the boat fearing lest it be him instead." Not for the first time, it occurs to me that Frankfurter has a keen eye for his own traits when they occur in others. "And yet . . ." Frankfurter hesitates.

"What?"

"His interest would not extend beyond the Japanese cases. Bendetsen gives us no explanation for the range of activity, the attention to corporations."

"Maybe he got distracted when he realized there was a chance to make some money."

Frankfurter nods. "We must not discount cupidity. Surely it would be a temptation, no matter what purpose set the plan in motion. But Bendetsen cannot be a full answer. This scheme has been in place for a while. From before internment was dreamt of, if I am not mistaken. From before Pearl Harbor. Its roots go deeper than that." For a moment he is lost in thought, his face unfocused. Then his attention gathers itself to a point and aims at me. "You have turned up quite a lot of information on this man, and very quickly. Do you mind if I ask how?"

"The FBI," I say. "Hoover has a file on him."

Alarm flits across Frankfurter's face, followed by a severe frown. "He does not know why you requested it," he says. "He does not know I am involved."

"Of course not, Justice."

Frankfurter's brow relaxes; then his lips tighten. "Hoover can be useful," he says. "But do not think you can control him. And do not think he performs favors for nothing. You may find you have incurred debts that will come due at an inconvenient time."

CHAPTER 30

ONCE AGAIN, I meet Clara at Dupont Circle. She has insisted that we cannot meet at the Court; nor will she tell me where she lives so that I can pick her up in proper fashion. She is wearing a belted dress beneath her coat and has swept her hair up under a black cloche hat. Her skin, which can look olive in some lights, seems pale now, and her dark features stand out in sharp relief. "So, you have another plan for me? Dinner with a friend?"

Her tone is light and amused. Almost smug. But I do have a plan. "Yes," I say. "This time I admit we're invited." And then I point her to Cissy Patterson's house.

"That?" Her tone is different as she looks at the sweeping wings, the Italianate marble. "That is your friend's house?"

"Yes. Let's go."

She is hanging back. "No," she says suddenly. Her hand goes to her throat. "No, I don't want to."

"Are you scared of something?"

"I will go to a movie instead if you want." She is looking down and her voice is small.

"Oh, so now you think it's too risky? You want to hoof it?" I am trying for a playful tone, but I think she can hear something else underneath it, for color comes into her face and she straightens her back.

"I do not." She leaves me behind as she crosses the street.

Dinner with a friend was not a fair description, I think as I follow her, for Cissy is not really a friend, and there are many other people there. And Clara certainly seems taken by surprise. I watch as each room of the house opens before her, and I can see how her lips part for a second before they tighten. She talks to the jugglers and magicians who mingle with the diplomats and social lights; she drinks one glass of wine quickly and starts on another.

At dinner the talk is still of war. But now the news is good. The Allies advance on every front, from the Pacific Islands to the steppes of Russia. British bombs fall on Berlin, and Mussolini must accept rescue from German paratroops. "And they've let Oswald Mosley out, too," Drew Pearson says to Colonel Richards. "That must please you."

Richards ignores him. Joe Patterson is not there to support him—I gather he is unwell—but Richards has been pushing ahead on his own. For most of the meal he has pressed upon me the necessity of ensuring that the expansive government powers—wheat quotas! price controls!—ushered in by the war are rolled back when peace arrives. Did I know they plan to take taxes from our paychecks before the money even reaches our pockets? I have been ignoring him in turn, watching Clara. This environment is plainly unfamiliar to her, but she is navigating it with a certain aplomb. There is a *Times-Herald* reporter to her left who is hanging on her words, leaning in to whisper stories.

"I met my wife here, you know," Pearson says to me. "At one of Cissy's dinners."

I don't know why he's raising the topic. "Cissy's daughter, you said."

"That's right. We had an odd number, so Cissy called her downstairs and sat her next to me. I took her out afterward and gave her her first planter's punch. And the rest is history."

"How interesting."

"It's not. Not to anyone but me, and even I don't care so much anymore. But it's got a moral that you might find apropos."

"What's that?"

"Reporters are hungry men." He jerks his head toward Clara, who is spilling a lilting laugh at her *Times-Herald* companion. "Watch out."

"Oh, no," I say. "You misunderstand. I have no interest there."

"Is that what you think?"

"What do you mean?"

Pearson just looks at me. Somehow the next sip of wine enters my trachea, and he smiles more broadly as I start to cough. Clara pounds on my back with a small fist. "Are you all right?"

"He'll be fine," Pearson says. "A little trouble swallowing."

Before I can speak she nods and turns away again. When dinner is over she leaves the table, losing herself in the crowd. "Excuse me," I say to Pearson, and he nods encouragement.

As always, the house is filled with entertainers. The parlor is a smoky cabaret, jazz piano and drunken singing. A juggler is on the stairs. But Clara is nowhere to be seen. As I continue my progress, a magician blocks my way. "You seek a maiden?"

It's the guy from my first visit, I think. "Not your card tricks, anyway."

"Is this a trick?" It is the same guy; that, or they have a standard line of patter. Which also seems likely enough, as I think about it. "Are these cards?" He makes a conjuring pass, and suddenly he's holding a spray of flowers.

"Thanks, I'll take those." I pluck them from his hand.

He gives me a sly smile. "Think what you really bring her."

"What?" Something in his eyes unsettles me. I look down, and I am holding a bunch of dead sticks. A fist of bones. I can't see how he's doing it, but then I'm fairly drunk. "What is it with you?" I hand them back; in his grasp they bloom again.

"She's dancing," he says. "Go forth, young knight."

I get to Cissy's ballroom, half expecting to see Clara surrounded by admirers, but she is standing by herself. The mirrors on the facing walls hold an infinite row of solitary girls in black dresses, whom infinite boys approach with slow steps. Life's limited patterns in eternal return. I can see now the magician has left a carnation on my lapel, which emits a jet of water as I toss it away.

"Are you enjoying yourself?" I ask.

"Do you want me to?"

"Of course," I say, even as part of me realizes it isn't wholly true. I am a little annoyed, in fact, at how even here she seems to have all the answers. Beauty is the universal solvent.

"You're not sure, are you? Maybe not, if you're not the reason?"

The glass of wine in her hand must be her fourth now, but this is still pointed. "You're pretty bold."

"Would I be here if I weren't? I wouldn't be clerking at the Supreme Court. What kind of woman do you think gets that job? You think someone just called me up and offered it? It's easier with the war, of course, but it wasn't handed to me. Nothing was, except an apron." She twirls, a trifle unsteady, looks down at her dress. "And I seem to have lost that somewhere along the way."

"You've got a real chip on your shoulder, don't you? You might try being a little more . . ."

"Feminine?"

"No. You're plenty feminine." She smiles and looks down again. "I just mean that I've found things go better if you get along with people."

Clara nods. "Have you ever thought that what works for you might not work for everyone? That maybe you're in a slightly different situation than I am?"

Suddenly I feel stupid. Of course it is true. I resented her reference to the phone call, but that is exactly how I got my job. And certainly not how she got hers. I parry with a compliment, the only way I know. "That's a beautiful dress."

Clara smiles. "Thank you. It's handmade."

"Oh, so's my suit." I offer a shoulder seam for her inspection. "It makes a real difference with the stitching."

She fingers the fabric, seeming puzzled. "You don't mean you . . . or your mother?"

"Of course not," I say. "There's a man in town. What, did you . . . ?" My voice trails off. Clara is looking at me with a curious mixture of embarrassment and contempt. Others have come into the ballroom now; there is a burble of chatter all around. Somehow it only makes the lengthening silence between us more apparent. "So," I say. "How about a movie next time?"

Clara laughs. It is incredulity more than anything else, but I have caught her off guard. She gathers her face into a smile under the dark eyebrows, the multicolored eyes. "What could match this production?"

"Seriously. How about it?"

She sips her wine again and looks at me. "I must admit I was mistaken," she says. Toleration edges into her smile. "You have talked me into it."

The silence between us has a different feel now, warmer, suggestive. There is a sense of rising possibility, perhaps my favorite feeling of all. Cissy's voice breaks in.

"Cash! You've been hiding your light under a bushel." She stops as Clara registers. "And your friend."

"Clara Watson," I say.

Cissy is dripping emeralds and seems somewhat liquid herself. "My," she says to Clara. "You're an exotic, aren't you?"

Clara blushes. In an instant, every trace of confidence has gone.

"Turn your head so I can see, dear," Cissy continues. An unaccountable anxiety is creeping through me. She inspects Clara from another angle. "I was married in this room, you know. Every time we have the candles lit I remember. It was filled with flowers all across the mantles and I saw them go on forever." Her voice goes soft. "An eternity of lilies."

"How beautiful," I venture.

"Deceptive," says Cissy, still in her reverie. "Nothing goes on forever. Life consumes life. Everything we have is taken from someone else. And it will be taken from us in turn."

I am at a loss, and Drew Pearson's arrival is a relief. Until he speaks. "Oh, no, Cissy," he says. "Some things do go on forever. This story, for instance. Though like the candles it's only by virtue of indefinite repetition. Can we skip to the part about what a brute your husband was?"

Cissy's eyes sharpen. "Someday, darling, I'll play chopsticks on your bald, fat head with a meat cleaver."

"Well," says Pearson. "Till then."

Cissy turns back to us. The hate in her face is fearsome to see. That we are not its cause is small consolation, for we are still the only outlet to hand.

"What was I saying?" Cissy asks. "Ah, yes. Where is your family from?"

I can barely hear Clara's response. "Seattle."

Cissy laughs, and if I ever thought Clara's tone cutting, I can see now that she is an amateur. "No, dear, I mean what country. I don't think it's so long ago that you've forgotten."

The answer is even quieter. "Germany."

"But, *Watson*?" I say. It is not my idea of a German name, and I am about to remark on this when something in Clara's face stops me. She flushes deeper; her hand goes to her neck. She looks small and wretched, nothing at all like the serenely superior girl who mocked my ice cream and movies. It is what I wanted—I understand now that this is why I brought her here—but I don't feel triumphant. I feel protective, and sick, and very, very sorry.

"I think perhaps we'll go now," I say.

Cissy's teeth are like daggers in her smile. "But we're having such a marvelous conversation."

I am trying to think of a polite way to insist when a tumult of noise from behind Cissy spares me the trouble. There is the smack of fist on flesh; there is the crash of glassware on a marble floor. From what I can see over her shoulder it looks as though Drew Pearson has finally made good on his repeated promises to take a swing at Colonel Richards. The two of them go to the floor together as guests clear a circle. Cissy loses interest in us at once.

I turn back to Clara. There is a special kind of sorrow that comes from getting what you want and realizing afterward just how low and mean it is. I have worked hard to break something, and now that I see the aching vulnerability in its ruins I feel an irretrievable loss. I remember Pearson's stories of Stalingrad and think this is what the Panzer crews must have felt when they drew past the wrecked guns and saw they'd been fighting girls. I am comparing myself to Nazi shock troops, but at the moment that feels about right.

"I'm sorry," I say.

Clara's voice is recovering volume. "Why did you bring me here? A joke for your friends? A lesson for me, to show me how much I don't belong?"

"They're not my friends."

Yellow lights kindle in her eyes. "So?" I am getting a sense of the phrase "spitting mad" in all its original vigor. "What was it then?"

Disastrously, I decide to be honest. "You have this superior air."

Clara is almost incoherent with rage. "Of course," she says. "Of course, I must think I am better than you. Why wouldn't I, with my homemade dress and my German parents?"

"Then why did you act all mysterious? Why not tell me where you live?"

"I am living," says Clara, "at the Y." Her words are clipped and precise. "The rents are too high in this city." I look at her in silence for a moment. She continues in the same tone. "Would you like to know more about the dress?"

"That's okay," I say.

Clara ignores my words. "I made a dress because I could not buy one," she says. "And I wanted to feel pretty. Because I was fool enough to want to be pretty for you."

"You're beautiful," I say.

"And you are very stupid or very mean." She dabs at one eye, collecting herself. "You are certainly the dumbest genius I have ever met. Do you have even the slightest idea of what the world is like for someone who isn't you?"

"I'm sorry."

"Then we are not so dissimilar after all."

"No?"

"No. I am sorry, too. Sorry I ever spoke to you. I could tell what you were the first second I saw you, and I should have known better."

"That's not fair."

"Fair?" Her voice is loud and high enough to peel a few spectators away from the Pearson-Richards wrestling match. "If there is one thing I wish for you, it is that someday you learn how little you know about what is not fair."

She turns and starts walking away. "I'll get your coat," I say, but she doesn't stop or even slow. Her only reaction, in fact, is a loud "Ha!" which sounds at first like a laugh, but as I think about it later could well have been a sob.

CHAPTER 31

MAIN JUSTICE IS hollow. In the center of the building lies the Great Court, a city block in size, with scattered bushes, three cherry trees, and the raised aluminum bowl of a large fountain. Three floors up, my office window looks the other way, out onto Pennsylvania Avenue, but I can step from my desk and walk a full circuit inside. I pass Edward Ennis and the other employees of the Alien Enemy Control Unit: John Burling, pale and nervous; Nanette Dembitz, a distant cousin of former Justice Louis Brandeis. As on every floor, murals run along the walls. Our series is called *The Search for Truth*, and it canvasses methods of resolving doubt. *Brute Force, Ordeal, Tradition*. There are twenty or so, keeping pace with me as I walk in circles. *Superstition, False Witness, Magic*. They progress and improve with each step. *Intuition, Reason, Science*.

The walking helps me think. It helps ease the sting of my memories of Clara, too. She is innocent, and I treated her shabbily, and she despises me, as she should. Still, at least I have established that she is not involved. But now the circuit completes itself. I am back to *Brute Force*. Back to the beginning. Do I try again with Hall? Pursue Bendetsen? I pass the open doors of offices. Ennis, Burling, Nanette. Unknown toilers of the Antitrust Division. *Superstition, False Witness, Magic*. The *Science* mural shows a figure examining fingerprints. Perhaps something will come from the FBI labs.

· · · ·

But it does not. "We have no match, Mr. Harrison," says Clyde Tolson. I immerse myself in the work of Alien Enemies. More cases are headed to the Supreme Court. Fred Korematsu, arrested in San Leandro; Mitsuye Endo, suing for release from the Tule Lake camp. "Get me the facts," Ennis says again. Records pile in stacks on my desk. I pore through the pages. From time to time I take out Gressman's files and study his diagrams, the names inked in red. They still make no sense to me. I play squash with John Hall; I chat with Felix Frankfurter. And then one day Francis Biddle is at my door.

It is May, and spring's whisper is growing to the drone of summer. Biddle wears a linen suit and a pale green tie. "Cash," he says. "A moment."

He does not sit on my desk like Black, or even take the chair opposite. Instead he stands and looks out the window. I stand, too. "I believe that the government will lose these cases," he says softly.

"Why?"

Biddle turns back to me with a smile. His comb-over is no longer a cap, but a band across the top of his head, with empty skin in front and behind. "No aspersion on you, of course. But our position may not be as strong as some might like."

"You were against evacuation, weren't you?"

The smile drains away. I remember Rowe's notes, imagine Biddle with his face turned to the floor, not meeting Rowe's eyes. "We are defending the legality of the relocation," he says. "Not everyone agreed with it at the time. There are some in government now who would like to see an immediate release."

I nod. The Marines are in New Guinea. It is hard to see what military necessity justifies keeping the detainees from their homes.

"But the President believes we should not act before the election. That gives us six months to prepare for the return."

"Prepare?"

Biddle sighs. "There is substantial opposition to the idea that these people are coming back. They are viewed as disloyal. Most are not, of course. But in truth there is a real pro-Japanese element in the camps now. Tule Lake in particular. It must be dealt with before we can think of a general release. If disloyals return to the coast, they will be attacked, and the loyal Americans along with them."

"So what are we going to do?"

"Some congressmen want to strip citizenship from everyone who gave a 'no' answer on the loyalty questionnaire," Biddle says. "I opposed that idea. Congress will pass a law providing for the voluntary renunciation of citizenship. If the disloyals renounce, we can remove them to enemy alien camps and eventually repatriate them to Japan. The western states will be more willing to accept the return of the others once we've sorted them."

It seems reasonable enough. "Okay," I say.

"Someone will have to explain renunciation to the Japanese," Biddle continues. "The Relocation Authority has people in place for that, but they obviously didn't do a very good job with the questionnaire. Two hundred should have refused the oath, not nine thousand. Once that law is passed, you're going to Tule Lake. Air Priority One."

．．．．

As I think about it, I like the idea. In Washington all my paths have reached dead ends. I am learning nothing from Ennis or Hall; Frankfurter has discovered nothing on the Court. But there may be answers in the camps.

It takes another month for the renunciation law to emerge from Congress and gain the President's signature. In the East, the island-hopping continues. In the West, our troops enter Europe. On June 4 the Allies take Rome. The Nisei combat team, the 442nd Regiment, is part of the assault, fighting its way out of the Anzio beachhead. Orders halt it ten miles south of the city. White faces will be first along the Appian Way.

Two days later the real second front opens on the beaches of Normandy. Now the war in Europe is won too, the Allies on the western shore and a red dawn rising in the East. With his forces scrambling to defend France, there is no way Hitler can hold against the weight of the Russians. It is just a matter of time.

FDR signs Public Law 405 on July 1. True to his word, Biddle has me on the next flight to Sacramento, displacing a civilian. The DC-3's propellers chew the air, swallowing miles. We are seventeen hours in the air with three stops to refuel, from one dark coast to another across a glowing land.

Tule Lake is almost a full day's drive north from Sacramento, only four miles from the Oregon border. An Army jeep picks me up. "Going to see the Japs, sir?" my driver asks. A tag on his khaki shirt identifies him as PFC Rosen.

"You don't need to call me 'sir,'" I say. "What's your name?"

"Andrew, sir," he says, and smiles. "Sorry, but that's what they taught us. If you're worth a driver, you're worth a 'sir.'" He offers me a stick of gum and pops one in his mouth. I look at his thick-muscled arms on the steering wheel; I notice the spots of stubble on his chin, the beginnings of sideburns, the bare pink cheeks between. Nineteen, maybe.

He takes us north on Highway 99, heading for Chico. Sweat prickles under my collar and down my back. "I didn't know it was so hot here," I say. "Isn't California supposed to be mild?"

"You're asking the wrong guy, sir," Rosen says. "I'm from the East."

"Whereabouts?"

"Linwood. It's in Jersey. Down near Atlantic City. You?"

"Philadelphia."

"Oh, we're practically neighbors."

"Practically," I say. He looks so young to me. I have experienced the feeling before, of course. The child whose size and experience loom large to a five-year-old is small and vulnerable from the vantage point of ten. But I expected that this would stop at some point, that eventually I would attain the absolute perspective. It does not stop; everything remains relative, and my reference point keeps shifting. It is hard for me to accept that Andrew Rosen is old enough to drive, much less hold a gun. I shudder to think how young he and his ilk must seem to the old men who make the real decisions.

Near Burney we stop to eat at a roadside diner. The sun is setting behind mountains to the west, and when we emerge it is dark. Stars burn overhead with the intensity I associate with Northeast Harbor and remoter Maine, though I realize now they belong to all dark places equally, or not to the Earth at all. From the road I can see the distant lights of towns, almost indistinguishable from the stars above. Unbounded blackness on every side, pierced here and there by pinpoint twinkles: America the limitless.

Then we come to the camp.

Route 139 goes up a rise and turns west as it nears Oregon. A view opens up before us, a dark congregation of buildings encircled by lights. When we reach the main gate I can make them out as guard towers linked by cyclone fencing. Searchlights wander along the perimeter, and now and then a beam transfixes a desert creature, whose eyes cast back its light. Inside the gate we register at the provost marshal's office and are admitted to the administrative section. A military policeman shows me and Rosen to our lodgings.

"Colony's over there," he says, gesturing. I see another dark fence, the expanse of a firebreak, and row upon row of black tarpapered buildings glinting in the moonlight. My room has blond wood furniture from Sears Roebuck, upholstered for some reason with a pattern of cowboys and Indians. A photograph of FDR gazes benignly from above the desk. "Director'll see you in the morning," the soldier says.

"What time?" I ask.

He laughs. "Don't worry; you'll be up."

. . . .

I wake the next morning to the notes of a bugle. Reveille, I think, but the tune is unfamiliar. Unintelligible shouts and chanting carry through the wall. I stumble to the window and raise the blind. In the firebreak behind the fence, lines of Japanese men in white pants and sweatshirts conduct calisthenics. Their heads are shaved bare or down to a military stubble; most wear headbands emblazoned with the rising sun.

I jump back involuntarily. The men continue to drill. I can make out the shouts now, even if I cannot understand the words. "*Wash-sho*," they cry, raising their arms in the air. They march in columns three or four abreast. "*Wash-sho!*" Behind them are the black rows of barracks, then a level, dusty plain and hazed mountains on the horizon. The rise from which I first saw the camp is a small hill. Beyond it, unglimpsed in the night, is a sandstone butte incandescent in the dawn. It is a foreign land, so different from the electric cities of the East.

I watch for some minutes, then dress and begin to review my papers. The chanting outside goes on for another half hour. A deep silence follows, broken by the occasional rumble of engines. The camp is still mostly asleep. After a moment I become aware of a lone voice singing. A soprano. At first I think it a phonograph, but there is no accompaniment. I step out of my barrack apartment and walk to the fence. Farther across the firebreak, looking not into the administration section of the camp but out at the trackless plain, a Nisei girl stands. Her back is to me; I can see only a dark skirt, a white shirt, black hair in curls. She is singing a Puccini aria, one of the few I can recognize. *Un Bel Di.*

"Hear the national anthem this morning?" The voice startles me. I turn to face Raymond Best, the Tule Lake project director. He is in his fifties, I guess, with a high forehead and short, dark hair graying at the temples. He is wearing the pants from a windowpane-checked tan suit and a tie, but no jacket.

"That's what that was?" I ask.

"Not ours, of course. I swear I'm getting to know theirs just as well. Five-thirty every morning. They do it as close as they can get to the administrative buildings."

"Who are those people?"

"The Hoshidan. Our militants. They want to go back to Japan to fight for their divine emperor. But at least with them you know where you stand." He swallows as though an unpleasant taste has entered his mouth and looks off to where the girl is singing.

"Who's she?" I prompt.

"Oh, that's Fumiko. Nice girl. She came here with her family from Sacramento. When she heard she was going to Tule Lake she ordered a bathing suit from the Sears catalog." He waves a hand at the dust around us. "As Bogart would say, she was misinformed."

I smile at the reference. "She's quite a singer."

Best nods. "She opens the baseball games here. She was a featured soprano with the Sacramento Junior College Symphony. They had her sing the national anthem—ours—before their December 7 concert. Then this, actually. You know it?"

"Yes," I say. "*Madame Butterfly* was originally a story by a Philadelphian, you know. John Luther Long." Best looks at me curiously. "We keep track of each other," I say.

"Huh," says Best. "As a matter of fact, some of the Quakers who visited got her a scholarship to the Curtis Institute there."

"So what's she doing still at Tule Lake?"

"She's a no-no," says Best. "It complicates things." Fumiko is reaching the end of the aria. "*Tienti la tua paura*," she sings, "*io con sicura fede l'aspetto.*" Her voice rises, clear in the empty sky. *You may hold on to your fears; I, with perfect faith, I will wait.*

"She answered no on the questionnaire? Why would she do that?"

Best shrugs. "Who knows? Come on, I've got you meeting with some block managers."

. . . .

I eat breakfast in the mess hall: eggs that are shaken from powder but still seem half-cooked, a slab of Spam. I am getting my taste of army life. Best stations me in one of the administrative buildings, also stocked with blond wood Sears Roebuck furniture and a portrait of Roosevelt. The block managers come to see me, passing through a gate in the fence separating the administrative section of the camp from the sixty-four detainee blocks called the Colony. Each block contains fourteen barracks and roughly 250 detainees. Some of the managers are hostile, some polite. I say the same thing to all of them. "American citizenship gives you rights. To renounce citizenship is to surrender those rights. No one should renounce unless he wants to go to Japan and live there as a Japanese."

Responses differ. Most greet my statement with anger and disbelief. "We are Japanese to you anyway," says Tom Kurihara. "I was at Minidoka when the army came through. One of your colonels, recruiting. Do you know what he said to the boys who volunteered? That he was proud that they had chosen to fight for America and against their country."

"One colonel does not reflect the views of the United States government," I say. "I am speaking to you as a representative of the Department of Justice."

"What rights do we have here?" asks Ransaku Takei. "Three hundred of us are in the stockade. Hungry, with no food. Sick, with no medicine. Those are Americans. What are their rights? No charges, no trial. I ask any question, the administrators say, 'All detainees receive excellent medical care.' My workers have cleaned blood and hair off those walls; they have picked up pieces of baseball bats. Even in the camp our conditions are worse than a federal prison."

"I will talk to Director Best about the stockade," I say.

"The Relocation Authority officials tell me renunciation is wise," says Harry Nakamura. "They seem to think it is a good idea."

That is not government policy, and it pricks my interest. Perhaps it is incompetence; perhaps it is something else.

"Who is saying that? What are their names?"

He shrugs. "I cannot give you names. It is the men who talk to us. They come and go."

"I have no idea why they would say that," I tell him. "You will be sent to Japan if you renounce. A beaten Japan."

Harry nods. "Not everyone believes that is what the future holds."

"People who are listening to Radio Tokyo on their shortwaves? America will win this war, you can be sure of it."

"Even so," says Harry. "You must understand the minds of the people who live here. We Nisei were proud of our citizenship. The Issei mocked us for it. America, with its rights and its liberties. 'You are no different from us,' they said. 'Your skin is what matters.' And now we are worse off. If we were Japanese we might be in an internment camp, with international monitors. We would have the Spanish acting for us. But because we are Americans, we have no one to help us. We have nothing."

"You have rights," I say. "There are cases going on in the courts right now. Tell people that if they throw away their citizenship, they throw away rights."

"The idea of these rights makes life perhaps more difficult," Harry says softly. "To tell us we are enemies and lock us up, that we can understand. To tell us we are still Americans, to arrest us for refusing the draft, to make our children each day salute the flag and pledge allegiance to their jailers—it is perhaps this that people cannot bear. Renouncing citizenship could seem a relief."

"They can't make your children recite the Pledge." I say it without thinking.

"What do you mean?"

Immediately I regret raising the issue. But now there is no choice. I explain about the Pledge of Allegiance case. The fixed star of our constitutional constellation, as Justice Jackson wrote—no official can force a confession of faith.

Harry is silent for a long moment. You cannot really see the stars in

Washington, it occurs to me, not as they are above this camp; you cannot pick out the constellations that burn in this sky. "So that is what the Supreme Court has done for us," he says at last. "To protect our rights. I see. You sent us here by the thousands because we refused your oath. But the children need not recite the Pledge. Liberty and justice for all."

I say nothing. Harry nods and continues. "We are viewed with suspicion because we do not act as your culture thinks appropriate. I am in that position now. I know that I should laugh at what you have told me. You will forgive me if I find myself incapable."

"Laugh or cry, I guess," I say uncomfortably. "I can tell you this, though. There is no advantage to renouncing. You gain nothing, unless you are truly loyal to Japan."

"Ah," says Harry. "Let me show you something." He rises from the table and crosses to the door. I follow him outside to the fence in the firebreak.

"What is it?" I ask.

"Wait," says Harry. In the guard towers, flags flutter in the breeze, colors crisp against the deep blue sky. Looking down I see tiny shells studding the black sand of the firebreak. Harry follows my gaze. "Girls string them into necklaces," he says. "Very pretty." After some minutes a squad of white-clad Hoshidan passes by on the other side. When they see us, they begin to bark. "*Inu*," they shout. "*Inu*." "It means dog," Harry says calmly. "Collaborator. They call me *inu* because I talk to you, because I talk to the administrators. If I renounce I prove my loyalty to them."

"And if you don't?"

"They were not bold at first," he says. "Many joined the Hoshidan because they thought they could avoid the draft. They dared to wrestle with Boy Scouts who raised the flag, that was all. Now there are more of them and they dare more. Some men are beaten. The general manager of the co-op was killed. They are growing in power. This is the price of our American rights."

"I'll talk to the director," I say. "But I want you to tell the people in your block that renunciation is a mistake."

Harry gives me a small bow. "I will convey the words of the most esteemed Department of Justice."

. . . .

"Why do you let the Hoshidan do this?" I ask Ray Best.

"They're mostly harmless," he says. "And Tule Lake is supposed to be a segregation center for disloyals. If we didn't let them blow off steam with the marching, it might get worse. We have to handle these people carefully. An MP shot a truck driver a while back and we were afraid the place would explode."

"But they're beating other detainees," I say. "I heard they just killed one."

Best nods. "That's true. And we'd like to do something about it. But the men who've been beaten don't cooperate. We can't prove anything."

"What about the stockade?" I think I am changing the subject; Best does not.

"Oh, we've tried that," he says. "We put the leaders in there, we thought. But it's impossible to know if we've got the right guys. We've had near-riots over the stockade, and hunger strikes too. And the Spanish complain about the Issei and then we catch hell from Washington. I don't think it's worth the trouble."

"So you're going to let them out?"

Something in my tone must strike Best as odd, for he looks at me sharply. "Their ACLU lawyer was here a couple of days before you. We sent him off, but he'll be back. He's threatening to file habeas petitions. We can't defend it in front of a judge. We're going to have to tear it down pretty soon."

"Where is it?"

Best points. "Not much to see," he says. Over toward the edge of the colony there is another fence, and behind it a beaverboard wall. Farther still, and hidden from view, I can surmise a building by the flags that rise above it. "You see it's right by the barracks. Women used to come over and hang on that fence weeping and holding out their hands. They could see inside; that's why we had to put up the wall."

"Ah," I say. "Of course."

. . . .

I wake the next day to the bugles of the Hoshidan. I keep the blinds drawn this time, listening to their chants while I dress. Then there is silence, then Fumiko's voice. I step outside and she is standing by the fence again, looking into the desert. She sings a different song this morning, of skies and mountains, of dreams that see beyond the years.

I walk to my side of the fence, as close as I can come but still yards away. Her voice reaches up a yearning interval, seeking a higher register, and the song takes form within me. I can feel it move, wings beating against the cage of my bones. Fumiko casts back her head and the music pours from her. It is an aria now, a ladder into the sky, where all is blue and open and the endlessness is not desert but freedom. Her hands open and close at her sides; at first I think she is clenching her fists, but as I watch I understand the gesture is an opening, a release. She is offering something, or letting it go: a promise, a hope, a vow. "With perfect faith," she sings, "I will wait." And then she stops and there is only emptiness, only silence. It takes me a moment to remember where I am.

Fumiko turns her head; for the first time, she notices me. Her gaze drops to the ground; her shoulders tighten. My first thought is to clap, and I raise my hands, but something stops me. Instead, I reach out and take hold of the fence; I stand there with my palms against the wire, and she gives a nod that is half a bow and walks quickly away.

That day I visit the stockade. It is a camp within the camp, another barbed-wire fence, more guard towers, a single gate. The inmates regard me listlessly. Sixteen are on a hunger strike, Best tells me. If they die it will be a public relations headache.

For three more days I meet with block managers. The Hoshidan wake me each morning and I dress, waiting for Fumiko. I do not go outside anymore. I do not want her to see me watching; I do not want to feel her eyes on me. Instead I look through the window until she has finished. Then it is breakfast in the mess hall and a day of meetings. In the evenings I eat dinner with Best or other administrators, while Franklin Roosevelt smiles down from the wall. "What have you told the detainees about renunciation?" I ask Best.

"Nothing," he says.

"What?"

"Justice said not to. Apparently we made a mess of it last time."

"So you're telling me your men haven't been discussing it at all?"

"Yeah," says Best. "Why, do you want us to?"

"No. It's just that someone else told me something different."

"Could be War Department guys," Best says. "The detainees can't always tell us apart."

"Could be," I say. He finishes and excuses himself, but I stay at the table drinking coffee. In bed that night I cannot sleep, and it is not just the caffeine. Discovery thrills through me. Here are the enemy's traces, their fingerprints. I have picked up the trail again. And it seems my initial guess was right. Whatever is going on is indeed connected to the Japanese. But what could these men want? Getting more Japanese to renounce—what does that achieve? It will strengthen the government's hand in litigation, I suppose. It is tangible proof of disloyalty. But it seems an awfully small gain.

The next day I widen my net. Best has little contact with the detainees. Others have more. I go table to table in the mess hall; I seek out the Relocation Authority workers integrated into the detainee community. Ruth Fischer teaches in the high school. "Rumors," she says. "But they're not very open with me. First couple of years it was different, but not now. Maybe the younger ones."

Marvin Opler is Ray Best's community analyst, an anthropologist detailed to the Relocation Authority. "Yes, I've heard about renunciation," he says. He has enrolled his son in the Japanese nursery school. "The kids talk about the certificates."

"Certificates?"

"The ones they're given if they renounce."

I frown. "There are no certificates."

Opler nods his head in contradiction. "I've seen them. In the apartments."

"What do they look like?"

He turns vague. Fingers stroke his red beard. "Official. Stamps and seals."

"Can you get me one?"

"Hal Morita, maybe," he says. "I'll try."

Morita is willing, Opler tells me at dinner that evening. He will come to see me the next morning.

A bugle fanfare wakes me. I stretch under the coarse cotton sheets. Fumiko sings of alabaster cities; she rehearses Puccini. I eat a quick breakfast and take my seat under FDR's portrait. I wait for half an hour, then an hour. Morita is not coming, I think. It is a surprise when the knock sounds on the door. Then another when I open it to see the serious face of Harry Nakamura.

"What are you doing here, Mr. Harrison?"

"I'm having a meeting."

He looks over my shoulder. "There is no one else in the room."

"I'm aware of that." A pause. "I'm waiting for Hal Morita."

Harry nods. His hair is uncombed and his shirt rumpled. "And I am aware of that. Would you like to know where he is?"

I step back from the door and beckon him inside. "Yes, I would."

Harry sits down across the desk from me. "He is in the hospital."

"What?"

"There was an altercation in his apartment last night. He will live. But he will not be coming to talk to you."

"The Hoshidan?"

"I do not think so. I think it was men like you. And so I ask again, what are you doing here?"

"I'm advising people about renunciation," I say.

"Yes, but that is not all. What are you looking for?"

"What business is that of yours?"

"I am a block manager, Mr. Harrison. I am responsible for the safety of my residents. I am doing my job. And you are doing yours, I am sure, but I would like to know just what it is."

I take a breath. Our interests coincide, I think. At any rate, there does not seem to be anyone else who can help. "Certificates," I say. "I've heard that people are being offered certificates for renunciation."

Harry looks at me with a curious expression. "Not just for renunciation. For their land. Do you not know this?"

I ignore his question. "Their land?"

"Aliens are not allowed to own land in California." His tone is impatient. "That is why the parents' farms are all held in the children's names. But if the children now renounce, there will be no citizen to own them."

"Can't you just sell them?"

Harry smiles thinly. "We had some experience selling to our neighbors when the evacuation plan was announced. It was not wholly satisfactory. That is why there is now this government compensation program. Your program."

"There is no such program," I say. We look at each other. "Can you get me one of those certificates?"

It is his turn to hesitate. "I think so. I will try."

Two days later, word comes through Marvin Opler. Harry wants to meet with me again. He has something to show me. But for this meeting, I am the one who does not turn up.

CHAPTER 32

"WHAT'S THE RUSH, sir?" Andrew Rosen stuffs clothes into a duffel bag. "I was getting on well with one of the nurses."

"Duty calls, soldier." In the jeep I explain the gist of a lengthy phone conversation with Edward Ennis.

Eureka, California, calls itself the Queen City of the Ultimate West. In reality, it's a small to midsized fishing and logging town with a growing tourist industry. And once a year, in the summer, it gets an especially distinguished visitor. A federal judge for the Northern District of California makes the day-long drive up from San Francisco and hears cases in the Humboldt County courthouse. The local bar association welcomes him appropriately, with a clambake and plenty to drink. The cases are an afterthought, trivial and one-sided. "Guys selling alcohol to the Indians," Ennis told me. "That sort of thing. It's an excuse for a party."

This year, the visiting judge was Louis Goodman, and the cases they had for him were those of twenty-seven draft resisters from Tule Lake. Dinners and dances were planned. Upon Goodman's arrival, he appointed two local lawyers, Arthur Hill and Chester Monette, to represent the defendants. That evening, the parties began. Seventy-five guests filled Eureka's finest restaurant. They ate steaks with mushrooms, shoestring potatoes, and whole kernel corn. There was crab cocktail for a starter and green apple pie for dessert.

"I don't need the menu, thanks."

"Just setting the scene," Ennis said.

Then came the whiskey and the speeches.

Arthur Hill spoke, and Assistant US Attorney Emmett Seawell, up from Sacramento for the occasion. Prosecution and defense agreed that only in America could such people as the resisters receive a fair trial with all the protections of the Constitution. It is a wonderful thing.

Finally it was Judge Goodman's turn. "He gets up there," Ennis told me, "and says something vague about the need to be calm and just despite the war, to adhere to the principles of our forefathers. There's some confusion, as you can imagine."

The following day Hill and Monette began the process of pleading their clients guilty. Judge Goodman questioned the defendants briefly about the conditions at Tule Lake and accepted their guilty pleas. He was seen late that night in a bar, talking animatedly to his clerk. The next morning there was a new member of the defense team, a man named Blaine McGowan. Emmett Seawell did not know who he was; nor, apparently, did Hill or Monette. "Just walks into court with a string tie and a pair of alligator boots," Ennis said. "Goodman appoints him, too, and he greets his clients in front of everyone. 'Let me tell you, I got no love for Japs. But I haven't lost a case yet, and I don't intend to lose this one.'"

With Hill and Monette watching in amazement, McGowan made an oral motion to withdraw the guilty pleas. "Granted," said Judge Goodman.

"I move to dismiss the indictment," McGowan said.

"On what grounds?" Goodman asked.

"Duress," said McGowan. "Confinement without due process of law in violation of the Fifth Amendment of the United States Constitution."

"Opposition, Mr. Seawell?" asked the judge. Seawell said nothing out loud. His internal monologue was extensive, but nonlegal in nature, and mostly obscene. Arthur Hill rose slowly to his feet. "Mr. Hill?"

"We would like to withdraw as defense counsel, your honor," said Hill. "Our clients have disregarded our advice and we do not feel we can offer effective representation under these conditions."

"Agreed," said Judge Goodman. "And now, Mr. Seawell?"

Emmett Seawell did what any Assistant US Attorney would do under the circumstances. He requested a postponement and called for help. At Main Justice, he got Edward Ennis. "He was in quite a lather," Ennis told me. "Went on and on about how the judge was trying to railroad him. I told him not to worry; we had an expert in the area who could be there in half a day."

"Me?"

"That's right."

"And what do you want me to do?"

"Help him," said Ennis. "What do you think's going to happen if word gets out that the Japs are free to refuse the draft? How would that play in California?"

"What do we argue?"

"You're an expert on the evacuation, right? Say they weren't confined; the Relocation Authority would happily have released them for military service. Say that when your country calls, you go. Sixty-three resisters from Heart Mountain got sentenced to three years a couple weeks ago."

"So here we are," I tell Andrew Rosen. "Riding to the rescue." It is a distraction from my investigation, but there is nothing I can do about it. I remember the Sears upholstery of the administrative apartments. "We're the cavalry."

"Jeez," says Rosen, chewing his gum. "I guess we are." He shakes his head; muscles jump in his shoulders and upper arms as his hands move on the steering wheel.

"What do you think?"

"Permission to speak freely, sir?"

"I'm not your superior officer, Andrew. I'm not in the army at all."

"You're the cavalry, though, sir. I'm just the horse."

"Thanks," I say, unsure whether I am being mocked.

"Well, here's what I think, then. I got in this uniform through the draft. I didn't like it. I had a job. I had a girl. I didn't like being told to put them aside and pick up a rifle. But I did it. Your boss is right; when your country calls, you go. But let me tell you. If old Uncle Sam had taken away that job, taken away that girl because he didn't like my looks, put me in a camp and then said, 'Well, son, pick up that rifle, I guess you're good enough to die'—I'd spit in his face is what I'd do. A man that would go along with that kind of treatment, he's not a man at all."

"That's what you think?"

"Yes, sir, it is. But like I said, I'm just the horse."

"All right, then," I say.

. . . .

A few hours past Mount Shasta the first seabirds fly into view, high in the darkening sky, and an hour later there is the shining expanse of the Pacific under the setting sun. It is the first time I have seen sunset on the ocean, and another reminder of how far I have come from Philadelphia. Eureka hugs the coast of Humboldt Bay. I see a tangle of buildings, a calm lagoon, a clock tower with a statue above.

"Thank God you're here," says Emmett Seawell when I introduce myself. He is a fireplug of a man, short and sturdily built, with the face of a bull-dog. "Judge Goodman will know Washington is paying attention." He seems less enthusiastic when I offer him Ennis's arguments. "It's not a question of whether the Relocation Authority would have let them go," he says. "It's whether they were unconstitutionally detained in the first place. That's what Blaine McGowan is arguing. He's attacking the whole plan of detention."

I consider this for a moment. "You're right," I say. "That's not going to work."

"So what do we say?"

"We can't let this case be about the detention. We can't defend that unless we have the facts to show it was reasonable to suspect disloyalty. And we don't have those facts right now." Finding them is my job, of course, but I think it best not to mention that. When I get back to Washington I will have to take a closer look at the brief the Pacific states filed.

"And so?" Seawell interrupts my reverie.

"So we're going to have to avoid the issue."

"How do we do that?"

"I'll think of something," I say. "I'm the expert."

. . . .

"Caswell Harrison," I say. My voice sounds thin. I get to my feet, button my jacket, and step out from behind the prosecution's table. "Special Assistant to the Attorney General. With the court's permission, I will offer the Justice Department's opposition to the motion to dismiss the indictment."

"Please proceed," says Judge Goodman. He does not look the ogre Seawell described. If anything, his face conveys a quizzical air. Pale eyes, pale eyebrows, slightly protuberant ears. The clerk with whom he schemed in the bar is a pretty, dark-haired girl.

"These men were called for military service," I say. "That call had to be obeyed. Whether they were unconstitutionally confined has nothing to do with it."

"It doesn't?"

"No. The Supreme Court will tell us whether their confinement was lawful. They cannot decide on their own that the government has treated them so badly that they're now entitled to ignore the Selective Service Act." I have learned something from the Supreme Court, I realize; I have learned how to avoid hard questions. "We cannot let every man's conscience be the measure of the law. That would be anarchy."

Goodman leans back in his chair. "Or, two wrongs don't make a right?" he asks. "Well, however you put it, you have a point, Mr. Harrison. The motion to dismiss is denied. I'll start hearing testimony this afternoon."

"That was beautiful," says Emmett Seawell, clapping me on the back.

"Thanks," I say. "Well, we'll see how it goes."

"Don't worry," says Seawell. "The rest is a breeze."

• • • •

When court resumes in the afternoon, word has gotten around that interesting doings are afoot. The gallery of the Humboldt County courthouse is filled with the citizens of Eureka. Only one of the resisters is present, a man named Masaaki Kuwabara; the others remain in the county jail. Kuwabara has donned a suit for the occasion and slicked his hair back in a pompadour above his wide and placid face. He looks young to me, too, as he takes the stand.

"Did you receive a notice that you had been inducted into the United States Army?" Seawell asks him.

"Yes." Kuwabara's answer is flat.

"What did it instruct you to do?"

"To go for a doctor's exam."

"And did you report for the preinduction physical?"

"No."

"Are you willing to serve in the Army?"

"No."

"Thank you," says Seawell. "Your witness."

Blaine McGowan is older, probably nearing fifty, but he dresses with the flash of a younger man. Under the pants of his suit I can see the alligator boots I heard about. He smiles at Kuwabara but gets no response. "I'd like you to tell the court the story of how you came to be confined at Tule Lake," McGowan says. "From the beginning. Your father was born in Japan, is that right?"

"Yes," Kuwabara says. "He came to Hawaii on a one-year indenture contract. He was an interpreter on a sugar plantation."

"I object," says Emmett Seawell, rising to his feet. "The family history has no relevance here."

"Our argument is that the defendants were under such psychological strain that they could not make a voluntary decision to submit for induction or not," McGowan answers. "To understand their psychological condition, the court must hear the full story."

"I'll allow it," says Goodman.

Seawell is so surprised he forgets to sit down. After a few seconds he recalls himself. "This isn't good," he whispers to me.

"And how did your father end up in California?" McGowan asks.

Kuwabara tells his story. His father was a translator, accompanying the overseers. One day an overseer beat a sick worker with a bullwhip. Kuwabara's father took the whip and knocked the overseer unconscious. After that he had to leave, of course. The workers hid him in sugar cane and put him on a freighter to San Francisco. There he sharecropped and saved until he could afford a wife. "A picture bride," Kuwabara says, sent from Japan. There were three children, Masaaki and two younger daughters.

"What was your childhood like?" McGowan asks.

Kuwabara shrugs. "It was ordinary. My father had saved enough to buy a farm by the time I was two. He held it in my name, since he could not own land."

The Alien Land Law, I think, flashing back to Harry Nakamura in the barracks at Tule Lake. Certificates for the land. *Your program*, he said, *the government's program.* A program that does not exist. On the stand, Kuwabara is still talking. The children went to the local schools. His parents sent one of the girls to Japan for education, but she did not like it and returned to the United States. Some people shunned them, but most were accepting. They traded vegetables for meat from neighbors who hunted; they hid Easter eggs together.

"And did this change after Pearl Harbor?" McGowan asks.

"Not at first," Kuwabara says. He was seventeen at the time of the attack, a senior in high school. Like everyone, he was astonished and angry. At school they talked all day about the damn Japs. For the first time, Kuwabara smiles. "No one seemed to think I was one of them."

Then the FBI started taking the men away. They searched his house. The older sister had drawn pictures of the Panama Canal in school, and agents seized them as evidence of a plot to destroy the canal. Kuwabara smiles again, a different smile. "The drawings of an eleven-year-old girl," he says. The FBI took his father to a Justice Department camp in North Dakota. They took a busload of men from the neighborhood, everyone who had any role in the community. The man behind the wheel was the driver of Kuwabara's school bus. He could not meet their eyes. He dropped his cap to the ground as if by accident and picked it up slowly to give the wives time to say good-bye.

For weeks after, Kuwabara says, there was still no talk of evacuation. But at the end of January, things changed. When the President issued his order, they knew it was coming. Kuwabara's mother considered leaving on their own, but they heard that families were being turned back at the state line. Without his father, they did not know what to do. In March the freeze order came down, and leaving was no longer an option. They stayed, waiting for evacuation. They tended the farm. "The seasons will not wait," his mother said. "Plow, plant, weed; that is the process of life."

McGowan waits a moment before his next question. "You did not think of resisting?"

Kuwabara looks around the courtroom. Through windows on the right-hand wall, squares of sunlight fall on selected chairs in the gallery. They shift, slow spotlights traversing the audience. "*Shikata ga nai*," he says. "It is a saying. It cannot be helped; it must be borne. We could not resist the Army. A neighbor killed himself rather than go. He had fought in the Great War and thought he was dishonored. But the Citizens League told us it was a way to show patriotism. For some I think it was a relief. No one would ask us to be anything other than what we were. And we did not know what the camps would be like."

The order that applied to Kuwabara's family was issued on April 27. The Army posted notices on telephone poles. *Bring only what you can carry. Report to the Tanforan Assembly Center.* "We had eight days to dispose of everything else." There is more expression in his face now, and an edge coming into his voice. "My parents had a tea set from their wedding. We did not use it; we were saving it for a better house. It was fine china, worth over three hundred dollars. A man came by the house and said he'd pay seventeen. 'You won't get a better offer,' he said. My mother smashed the plates in front of him."

Tanforan was a racetrack. The people were lodged in whitewashed stalls that still smelled of horse urine. It was so hot that the legs of Kuwabara's cot sank into the asphalt floor. He woke up with the bed frame on the ground. The guards said they should be honored because Seabiscuit had lived there.

There are scattered laughs from the audience. "Please," says Judge Goodman. A man in a plaid shirt catches my eye and spreads his hands, palms up. Ostentatiously innocent. I raise my eyebrows and shrug. After all, it was funny. I think.

After four months in Tanforan, Kuwabara tells us, they were sent to Topaz, in Utah. They had been told that the assembly center was temporary, that the camp would be different. But the barracks were tarpaper. The walls were green pine boards that pulled apart as they dried. Dust came through the gaps and covered the furniture, the clothes, the food in the mess halls. Storms shrank the visibility inside to three feet. When they came at night, he woke up coated white with dust.

The toilets were communal, he says, all unscreened. Women brought cardboard boxes with them for privacy or tried to go when no one else was there.

Midnight became a crowded hour. Kuwabara's youngest sister began to complain. She thought she was in Japan again because none of her white friends were there. She kept asking to go back to America. His mother pointed to the flags in the guard towers. "This is America," she said. His sister did not believe her.

"Perhaps she was right," says McGowan.

Seawell stands up. "That's not a question."

"Mr. McGowan," says Judge Goodman, "please do not comment on the witness's testimony."

"I apologize, Your Honor," says McGowan.

"Bush league," Seawell whispers to me. I grunt. The aside seems pointless, at any rate. McGowan has sensibly opted for a bench trial, so there is no jury to impress, only Judge Goodman. And me; I am finding myself drawn into Kuwabara's story. His life is nothing like mine, of course. But he hid Easter eggs like I did; he went to school to learn what was right. He was called for a physical, a doctor to smile and call him son. But not to say his war was over.

Kuwabara's father joined them in Topaz in July, after six months in a Justice Department detention camp. He had aged past the point of recognition. Soon after that, the administrators came looking for men to harvest crops. They offered work furloughs, and Kuwabara got on a train to pick sugar beets.

"How was your experience harvesting?"

Kuwabara scowls. "Worse than the camp." The detainees were guarded like cattle on the trains. They went to a farm in Utah. The townspeople wouldn't let them into movie theaters or serve them in cafes. All around were signs saying *No Japs*. When no other place would take them, they slept in the jail. "I was happy to go back."

"So you went back to Topaz," McGowan says. "How did you come to Tule Lake?"

"It was the questionnaire." Kuwabara shakes his head. In February the Army came through with the loyalty questionnaire. *Will you serve*, one question asked. *Will you pledge allegiance to the United States and forswear loyalty to the emperor of Japan?* "I answered both questions no, and so did the rest of my family."

"Why did you do that?"

"For my family."

McGowan raises an eyebrow and tilts his head. People were confused, Kuwabara says. They were suspicious. The form was called an application for leave clearance, but they did not want to leave. They were not allowed to return to California, and where else could they go? He had told his family what it was like on the outside.

Then, too, some people thought the second question was a trick, that a yes answer admitted loyalty to the emperor. How else could it be forsworn? And what of the parents, who were not American citizens, who were not allowed to be? To pledge allegiance to the United States and forswear Japan for them was treason. What would happen if they did that and were sent to Japan?

Jesus, I think. Of course. Nine thousand said no instead of two hundred, Biddle told me. Now I know why the questionnaire didn't work. I remember John Hall protesting that he spent a lot of time writing it.

"So they could not answer yes to that question," Kuwabara says. He did not want to be separated from them. And he did not want to be drafted. The Army was forming Nisei suicide squads, he heard, so the white boys would not have to die. But why should he die in their place? Why should his parents lose their only son?

After they answered no, the family was classed as disloyal. They were sent to Tule Lake on a train. The people from Tule Lake who had answered yes were on trains in the other direction. Kuwabara saw them when they passed. The faces that looked like him, like the enemy. He heard them shout.

"What did they say?" McGowan asks.

Kuwabara's face is expressionless again. "They said, 'Go back to Tokyo, you goddamn Japs.'"

In Tule Lake he received the draft notice. He refused it. "Same reason I said no on the questionnaire," he explains. "My family." His father had come to the United States with only a bedroll, had worked all his life for his children's future. Kuwabara's life is not just his to do what he wanted, he says; it is his father's too. "I will not let the government take it from him." He pauses. "We Japanese go to war expecting not to come back. The white boys all think someone else will die. We do not. If I am to do that, if my father is to lose his only son, it must be for a cause I respect. When I believed in this country, I could have gone. I could have said, 'This country gave us much, and in return we gave all.' But we could not tell it that way now. It would be that my father worked for everything and it was all taken from him. And last they took his son and the future of his name. There is no honor in that. My family will not end that way."

"I see," says McGowan. He turns his eyes down for a moment, then looks back up. "Is there anything more you would like to say?"

Masaaki Kuwabara looks at me and Seawell, at the crowd in the gallery. "I forgive you," he says.

The audience erupts in hisses. Goodman pounds his gavel. "I will clear this courtroom." The crowd settles slowly. "I'm going to take a recess now," says Goodman. "We'll resume tomorrow."

· · · ·

Eureka has several hotels, but pride of place belongs to the Eureka Inn, a Tudor Revival building occupying a full city block. Emmett Seawell, Judge Goodman, and all the court personnel are lodged there, courtesy of the Humboldt County Bar Association. Andrew Rosen and I are too, which would not have been the case if DOJ were footing the bill. But Seawell has managed to get us included in the judicial party, and I am not about to complain. In the restaurant we discuss strategy over a chicken dinner. Outside of special occasions, steaks are still rare.

"McGowan's turning this into a circus," Seawell complains. "And the judge is letting him."

"Yes," I say. "I don't think Goodman is on our side."

"You don't say." Seawell looks at me as though I have professed a belief in the law of gravity.

"I wouldn't give up hope, though. What can he do? They broke the law and they admit it. So he lets them tell their stories. It doesn't matter in the end, does it?"

"Yeah," says Sewell. "How old are you?"

"Twenty-six," I say.

"I've got a couple more years under my belt. In my experience, having the law on your side isn't always enough."

"What's he going to do?" I ask. "Strike down the Selective Service Act?"

"You're the expert," says Seawell. He drains his beer. "See you tomorrow."

I turn my glass meditatively in my hand, watching the amber liquid. It is true that Goodman seems favorably inclined toward the defense, and true that the law by itself isn't always enough. Still, I have a hard time seeing what Goodman can do other than allow the resisters a forum to air their grievances.

When I look up I find myself staring into the eyes of Judge Goodman's law clerk, seated on the other side of the room. I raise my glass in her direction, and she turns away. Then she gets up and walks over.

"Enjoying your stay?"

I rise to my feet. "This is what I think of as the California climate," I say. "Nice low sixties."

"You didn't find that elsewhere?"

"Sacramento was pretty hot."

"How was Tule Lake?"

"Better," I say. "So you know where I came from."

"Of course I know. You're the Special Assistant to the Attorney General," she says. I can hear the capitalization in her voice, and other things.

"One of many," I say. "I don't think you're supposed to be talking to me. Not without the other side present. It could give me an unfair advantage."

"I don't think Blaine McGowan is going to complain."

"Probably not. Where'd you get him?"

"He's one of the judge's law school classmates."

"Is it true he's never lost a case?"

"As far as I know."

"Well then, I probably need all the advantage I can get. Would you like to sit down?"

She shakes her head. "I can stand."

"How about telling me your name then?"

"Eleanor."

"How can I help you, Eleanor?"

"Does your mother know what you do?"

I am taken aback. "What do you mean?"

"Or your girlfriend? I'm sure you have a girlfriend, with that suit. Is she proud of you?"

"What are you talking about?"

"You're prosecuting people who were drafted out of a concentration camp. Do you feel good about that?"

I didn't join Justice to prosecute them, I want to say. *It's an accident. I have other reasons for being where I am.* For a moment I think about telling her this, but I'm sure she'll only say that my reasons don't matter. "It's the law," I say. "I didn't send them the draft notices. It may be unfair, but you've got to serve when you're called."

"Even when you've been put in a camp and stripped of all your rights?"

"I don't see anything in the Constitution that says otherwise."

"We'll see about that," says Eleanor. Color has risen to her cheeks; firelight glints off her dark hair.

"You know what the law is," I say. "But you want to do what's right and the law be damned, is that it?"

"And what if I do?"

She looks like an avenging angel, terrible and beautiful, youthful and ageless all at once. I feel surprisingly tired and a little sad at my answer. "You realize that's the kind of thinking that put them in the camps in the first place. That we'll do what has to be done."

Her face grows even fiercer. "You know what I'm saying is right."

"That's the problem, Eleanor. Everyone knows they're right. We have law to protect us from our best instincts as well as our worst."

"What rubbish. Who told you that?"

"Hugo Black."

Eleanor tosses her hair. "You listen to their stories and tell me again that everyone's right."

"I know the stories. I just came from Tule Lake. Where I was telling people not to renounce their citizenship, by the way. But if these men beat the draft, the country will hate them even more."

"You beat it, didn't you?" I can feel my face flush. "That looks like a hit," Eleanor says. "The army wasn't for you, then. How do they put it? You were called to serve your country in another place."

"I flunked the physical."

Eleanor looks me up and down. "A disease of the wealthy, I expect. They had that in the Civil War. Did you hire a substitute?"

"No." I cannot keep the outrage from my voice.

"Well, someone's there in your place. Maybe one of them."

"You think I don't know that?" Josephine's haunted face comes before my mind, Billy Fitch shorn like a lamb.

Eleanor tilts her head. "More that you don't care."

"Of course I care." Other diners turn their heads. I lower my voice. "It wasn't my choice. I never said no."

"What would you say, if they took everything you had?"

"That's not the point. Letting these men go will get the Californians more stirred up. Who does that help?"

"So you'd sacrifice them for the greater good?"

"If you have to put it that way, yes."

She folds her arms triumphantly. "*That's* the kind of thinking that put them in the camps."

I shake my head. "I'm not the bad guy, Eleanor."

"Keep telling yourself that."

"You think different?"

"It's a democracy," says Eleanor. "If we don't do something about this, we're all bad guys."

. . . .

The next day we have Joe Imihara on the stand. Seawell asks him the same four questions and gets the same answers. He received a notice to report for a physical; he ignored it; he will not serve. Then McGowan takes him through the full story. When Imihara is done, Carl Suzuki follows; after him Pat Noguchi, and then more.

There are some differences. Imihara is angry; Suzuki is scared. From Bainbridge Island, we hear, pet dogs followed the army trucks to the ferries and children carried clumps of grass to remember their homes. In Hood River the soldiers wept, too; they were a local battalion and knew the people they were putting on the trains.

But the general story is the same. They were given days to dispose of their belongings and offered insultingly low prices. Many destroyed property rather than sell it. "If I hear one more time about wedding china," Seawell whispers to me. They were sent to assembly centers and then relocation camps. And after answering no to the loyalty questionnaire, they took the train to Tule Lake.

At the end, McGowan always asks them if they have anything more to say. "Good-bye, America" says Imihara. "Don't do this again."

"This is my contribution to the war," says Suzuki. "I am defending your principles." But mostly they follow Kuwabara, and what I assume is McGowan's coaching. They look me and Seawell in the eyes, nod to the gallery, and say they forgive us. The crowd goes crazy each time, but McGowan doesn't need them. He needs Judge Goodman, and the crowd's reaction probably helps.

The next day is the same. When the fifth resister says that his mother smashed a tea set, Seawell stands up. "Your honor," he says. "This is getting ridiculous. I'm willing to stipulate that every one of these men saw their family china broken. Can we move it along?"

"I will let the defense develop the facts as it deems them necessary," says Judge Goodman.

"I'm not going to sit around and waste my time listening to this again," says Seawell. He turns to leave.

"You *will* listen, Mr. Seawell," Judge Goodman says. He gestures to the federal marshal in the corner of the courtroom, who takes a step forward. Goodman speaks more quietly. "Would God I could make you hear."

I catch Seawell by the arm and pull him back down. "Wow," he says, settling into his chair. "This really isn't going well."

· · · ·

By Friday evening the testimony has concluded. I eat alone in the hotel restaurant. I am finishing an excellent grilled Pacific salmon when Eleanor comes to my table.

"What do you think now?" she asks.

"Will you sit down this time?" She does. "So you're determined to let them go," I say.

"Yes."

"You sure your judge agrees? He thought enough of my argument that he wouldn't dismiss the indictment."

"He did that because we're here till the end of the week. If he set them free the first day he thought we'd be lynched. That's one reason we're hearing every defendant's story."

"Are you serious?"

"You don't know Eureka very well, do you? I guess you got here too late for the tour. They drove their Chinese out by mob in 1885 and haven't allowed any Orientals back since. They're very proud of it."

"So this trial's just for show, huh? You always knew how it was going to come out."

"We knew what was right. These aren't the people who attacked us. They look like them, but that's not enough. We can't punish them just to make ourselves feel better."

"So how are you going to do it? They refused the draft; you can't get around that."

For the first time Eleanor seems less sure of herself. "To be honest, we don't know. Got any expert advice?"

"They said no," I tell her. "They knew what they were doing. There's no way around it." But even as I speak I wonder. That first day McGowan argued that the conditions of confinement were such that the resisters could not make a real choice. It was a ploy to get his evidence in, but it is an argument for acquittal, too. If there is no choice, there is no crime. Law forgives the help-less. "Unless you buy the idea that they had no choice."

"We'll buy it if there's nothing else for sale," says Eleanor. She rises to leave and hesitates, two fingers on the table. "Mr. Harrison, did a military driver bring you here?"

"Yes."

"Is he armed?"

"Armed? He's got a sidearm, I suppose."

"Could you arrange to have him present in the courtroom when the judge hands down his opinion tomorrow?"

"Why?"

"These people are expecting one sort of show, and we're going to give them quite another."

I think of the comforting brawn of Andrew Rosen. "I'll have him there. He won't need his gun, though."

"I hope not," says Eleanor.

"If you're so worried, why don't you leave early?"

"We'd like to. But it's not our choice. The cars all go together."

I think for a moment. "You know what," I say, "you can have my driver."

"Really?"

"Sure. If you don't mind a jeep. He's from the Presidio motor pool in the first place. Put your stuff in the back now; he'll have it waiting behind the courthouse tomorrow morning, and you can just hand down your opinion and drive off into the sunset."

"Sunrise," says Eleanor. "Well, that's generous of you. But how will you get back?"

"Emmett Seawell is headed that way, too. I can ride with him. I'm sure we'll have plenty to talk about."

. . . .

Like our hotel, the Humboldt County courthouse occupies a full block. It is impressive, with gray-sanded zinc statues of Justice on the roof and a clock tower crowned by Minerva. It reminds me a good deal of Philadelphia's City Hall with William Penn above the clock face.

Judge Goodman's courtroom is large, but it is filled to capacity when he takes the bench Saturday morning. There are the twenty-seven resisters, for one thing, shackled together in the front two rows. The remainder of the seats are filled by curious citizens. Andrew Rosen stands by the door that leads back to the judge's chambers, thick arms crossed in front of him. He sports an olive drab cap now. When worn indoors, he has explained, a cover indicates that he is bearing arms. I think the significance of the hat may be lost on some in the audience, but they will not miss the pistol at his hip.

Judge Goodman looks slightly pale, as does Eleanor. Neither appears to have slept much. "The uncontroverted facts are as follows," he reads. "Tule Lake Segregation Center was initially constructed and used for a time as a permanent relocation center to which Japanese and Japanese Americans were sent from temporary assembly centers. Sometime in 1943, the Relocation Authority decided to segregate loyal and disloyal internees. Tule Lake was chosen as a concentration center for those whose disloyalty was determined either by the government or by their own declarations. Defendants were evacuated from Pacific states to various relocation centers and removed as disloyal Nisei to Tule Lake Center. There they have been forcibly detained since their arrival."

At "forcibly detained" Seawell nudges me. I shrug.

"It is not controverted that the defendants have refused a summons to military service," Goodman says. "It is not questioned that Tule Lake Center is an area surrounded by barricades and patrolled by armed guards, and that immediately beyond the barricades, armed forces of the United States prevent the departure of any persons confined in the center."

Seawell slumps in his chair and shakes his head. "Good lord," he whispers.

"Whether such confinement is lawful or not is beside the question," Goodman continues. "Dangers to the security of the West Coast may justify the evacuation and confinement. No such dangers, however, can be cited to justify the prosecution of these defendants for refusing to be inducted. The fact that the war power may support detention does not mean that the Constitution does not apply at Tule Lake, as Mr. Justice Murphy's concurring opinion in the *Hirabayashi* case observes."

There are Gene Gressman's words, I think. The images come to me so strongly that I can almost feel his presence. Gene drafting that opinion by lamplight, falling to the ground under Haynes's fist, looking up in puzzled hurt. And me punching back for him. I am so wrapped in memory that I almost miss Goodman's next sentence. "Citizens confined on the grounds of disloyalty are under sufficient duress and restraint that they are unable to make a meaningful choice between serving in the armed forces or being prosecuted for not yielding to such compulsion. The social contract imposes obligations on citizens, but it does so in exchange for rights, and the government may not deny the rights while it insists on the obligations."

"What the hell is that supposed to mean?" asks Seawell.

"It means we lost," I say. To my surprise, I feel the corners of my lips lifting in a smile.

"The defendants are remanded to the custody of the marshal, to be returned to the custody of the Relocation Authority," says Goodman. He brings down his gavel. "Judgment for defendants; case dismissed; court adjourned." The last sentence comes out fast. Andrew Rosen has the door open, and Goodman and Eleanor are moving toward it. The crowd hisses uncertainly; the resisters sit quietly in their shackles. I get up and walk over to Masaaki Kuwabara.

"What do you think now?"

"What do you mean?"

"About your rights as a citizen. They kept you out of jail."

"I was drafted and brought into this court because I am a citizen," he says. "And I am going back to jail."

I sigh. "Would you do me a favor and tell your friends not to renounce? Not for any piece of paper someone offers them. The paper is nothing. Your citizenship protects you."

Kuwabara nods to me. His expression is the same one Harry Nakamura showed me with his farewell bow, courtly and ironic. The tone of his voice is the same, too. "I will spread that good news around Tule Lake."

CHAPTER 33

EMMETT SEAWELL DOES not travel by jeep. His car is long and black; his driver sits alone up front. In back, the seats are plush, but the air is close. As we pull out along the bay, I envy Judge Goodman and Eleanor, speeding down the highway ahead of us with Andrew Rosen at the wheel. I imagine them laughing together in the aftermath of danger, feeling the thrill of success. Seawell settles himself into the cushions and stares straight ahead. For the first few miles he says nothing. Then he looks abruptly at me. "So the judge took your jeep."

"Yes."

"Why'd he do that?"

"I think he wanted an early start."

Seawell nods once, then grunts and turns his head. For a few moments he gazes out the window. We are climbing higher, skirting the wooded mountains. On my side of the car the ocean shines beyond the flat land, winking through gaps in the trees.

"Are you going to report it stolen?" he asks.

"I gave it to him."

Seawell starts nodding again. "Of course. Remind me what you're supposed to be such an expert about?"

"The Japanese cases."

"And which side you're on?"

I look away. Seawell and I have the same view now, thick, green forest of spruce and hemlock. "We're going by San Francisco, right?" I ask.

"Maybe."

"Can you drop me at the Presidio?" I turn back toward him, but Seawell is still showing me the back of his head.

"Want to try to find your jeep?" he asks.

"There's someone I need to see."

"Of course." He turns around now, the anger on his face surprising. "I can drop you wherever you want. Any time, any place."

"What?"

"I'll drop you," he says fiercely.

"I don't understand."

"Yes, you do."

I shake my head. "I'm sorry, I don't."

He tries to hold the furious expression, but it slips away. "With a punch," he says. "Drop you on the floor. Get it?"

"Oh," I say. "Sure, I get it now. That's a good line. Like in a movie."

Seawell sighs. "No, it's just . . . you understand. What the hell was that? Supposed to be a fun-filled weekend, then Blaine McGowan shows up with his alligator boots, then you, and then the whole thing blows up in my face. Someone sabotaged my case. What am I supposed to do now?"

"Let it go," I say. I have given the matter some thought. "Don't appeal."

"Don't appeal?"

"Look, no one's going to hear about it if it's just Judge Goodman. Appeal it up to the Ninth Circuit and all the California papers will get the story."

"Main Justice is going to hear about it." Seawell sounds skeptical, but I can hear a note of hope in his voice.

"They'll hear about it from me. You did everything right. Judge Goodman just went a little nuts. But pushing this case any further will stir up more hostility, make it harder to resettle the loyal ones. Biddle doesn't want that. Believe me, I know what he thinks." Seawell is nodding more enthusiastically now. "Main Justice has no further interest in this case," I tell him. "I don't really see why it started, actually. These guys are all certified disloyal, right? What did the army want them for in the first place?"

"It was a mistake," Seawell says absently. "Administrative snafu. Draft notices weren't supposed to go to Tule Lake at all."

I am astonished. "And then you prosecuted them for saying no to a mistake?"

He shrugs. "That was a War Department decision. The principle of the thing. But that makes sense about the appeal."

. . . .

It is a detour into San Francisco, crossing the Golden Gate when Seawell would have skirted the city to the north. But his mood improves as the ride goes on, and by the time we reach the bridge, he is happy to help me. He knows the base, and at his direction the driver takes me straight to the appropriate office. "You'll talk to Biddle," he says.

I promise I will and leave him with a handshake. Then I turn to the legal offices of the Western Defense Command.

The building is white stucco with a red roof. Three palm trees stand in front. Inside, it is easy to find Karl Bendetsen. He is something of a celebrity on the base, it seems, and it strikes no one as unusual that he is receiving an emissary from Main Justice.

Bendetsen himself is somewhat more surprised. He cocks his head at me as the secretary shows me in. "I wasn't expecting you."

"I happened to be in the area," I say, offering a business card. As in the picture in Hoover's file, Bendetsen has his hair slicked back and his khaki tie tucked into a dark green shirt. A shelf behind his chair holds a radio and an empty ashtray.

He glances at my card and puts it in a drawer. "It's a busy afternoon for me."

"Looks it." Save for a daily planner, his desk is bare. I take a seat without being asked.

"What can I do for you, Mr. Harrison?"

"Are War Department men in the camps encouraging renunciation?"

Bendetsen looks at me more closely. "What's it to you?"

"I'm writing the briefs for *Korematsu* and *Endo*," I say. "I'm defending your program. I need to know what you're doing."

"Ah," says Bendetsen. He leans back. "The new and improved James Rowe."

"I suppose so."

"You didn't know him?"

"No."

"You're missing out." Bendetsen's tone turns expansive. Somehow I have put him at ease. "A character. He . . . well, it's almost funny. You should have seen him, that last meeting at Biddle's house. He got so emotional making his case, I thought he was going to cry. On and on about the Constitution this and individualized hearings that."

I remember it from Rowe's notes. "Why is that funny?"

"Well, the whole time I was sitting there listening to him, you see, I had the order in my briefcase. Biddle had approved it. The President had signed off. Poor old James got himself all worked up for nothing. It had all been decided already."

"Funny," I say.

Bendetsen shrugs. "Maybe you had to be there. So, what was it you wanted to know?"

"Are War Department men encouraging renunciation?"

"Of course not." Now he is frowning. "The War Department is against renunciation."

"You are?"

"Of course we are. Renunciation is part of Biddle's idea to sort them. Sift out the disloyal, let the rest go. And of course we oppose that."

"Why?"

"You haven't been in this job long, have you, my friend? If we can sort them now, why not before? Why not when they were still on the coast? Why remove them at all? That's what a court will ask. And what will we say?"

"That there was no time."

Bendetsen laughs and pushes back from his desk. "How silly of me to forget." He is doing some sort of Bogart impression, I think, trying to find an appropriate line. Apparently nothing comes. "No, there was time. The first trains went out in May. We had six months if we wanted individualized hearings."

"Then why didn't we do that?"

He lights a cigarette and holds the pack out to me. I shake my head no. "The military judged it impossible to determine loyalty," he says, reaching back for the ashtray. Pinned to the wall is a map of California showing the military exclusion zones. "That was General DeWitt's view."

"But that's not what Justice argued to the Supreme Court in the curfew case."

Something in my tone sparks a light in Bendetsen's eyes. Then it dies away. "John Hall is our liaison to Justice," he says. His face turns vague. "He coordinates the legal strategy. It's not really in my hands."

"You just set the whole thing up, that's all."

A great calm is coming over him. This, too, I remember from Rowe's notes. Bendetsen with his reassuring smile, saying everything in the mildest of tones. It means he has identified me as an enemy. "I am a lawyer, Mr. Harrison. I had a client. My client needed a question answered. I told them what the law would allow. I never said this was good policy."

"But you think it was right."

"It is not what I joined the government to do." He sounds innocent, surprised. "We were attacked. We had to respond. I gave a description of the law, of the powers of the President to defend the nation in a time of war. The time pressure was intense. After Pearl Harbor, I didn't sleep for days. But I didn't put anyone on a train. I wrote memos."

"Men have died because of those memos."

He is still eerily calm, just as Rowe described him. "Men are dying every day," he says. "Good men and bad. None of that is my choice. I only described the law."

I search Bendetsen's face, and it is like looking into the depths of a still sea. Down at the bottom is the Tule Lake stockade, with blood on the walls and broken bats on the floor. Figures move there. The bats rise and fall, the blue chips of wedding china leap. But they are so small, so faint, and in between are miles of water, the thick, invisible layers of the law that cushion our sight. It is so far down through the water, his smile tells me. Who is to say that those things are men at all? Who knows what they feel?

"The President approved it," Bendetsen says. "Congress approved it." His voice is soft. The waters move; the figures are obscured. There is only the smooth, impenetrable blue of the law. "If the Supreme Court thinks it's so wrong, they can put a stop to it."

I nod. I am thinking of clumps of grass in children's hands, dogs trotting after Army trucks. A mother pointing to flags in the guard towers to show her child this is still America. "Well, it's my job to see that they don't."

"Then I'm sure we have nothing to fear." He stubs out his cigarette and looks down, dismissing me. I stand.

"'A republic, if you can keep it,'" I say. "Ever heard that?"

Bendetsen shakes his head. He does not look up. "Benjamin Franklin," I say. "A Philadelphian. Not that it matters. Some old lady stopped him coming out of the Constitutional Convention, asked what the drafters had done. 'What sort of government have you given us, Mr. Franklin?' That was his answer."

"I see," says Bendetsen. He nods his head as though reaching a decision. "So we've replaced the old troublemaker with a new one." Now he looks up. "You're just another James Rowe, aren't you? All worked up over something that's been decided already."

"Oh, no, Colonel." I lean forward over his desk, doing my best to sound menacing. "I think you'll find I'm a good deal more than that."

. . . .

I sleep on the flight east, a full night's worth or more. Back in Washington, I still feel drained. What have I learned? That Gene Gressman was right about the Japanese cases, perhaps. There was plenty of time for individual hearings, Bendetsen said, time to sort the loyal from the disloyal. The evacuation is looking harder and harder to defend. And Bendetsen was right to see me as an enemy. I would send these people home if I could. Harry Nakamura and his children, Fumiko and her parents. George Yamaguchi and Masuo Kanno and all the rest. I would tear down the program on which he's built his career. He is right to fear me, if there is anything I can do.

But I am not sure there is. And none of this is going to help me figure out who would kill Gene, or who would encourage the detainees to renounce their citizenship. Or how those things might be connected.

I could report that there are strange doings at Tule Lake, I suppose. But I do not even know who at Main Justice I can rely on. I am confident in Francis Biddle, but he seems to be avoiding these cases. Ennis is a question mark; Hoover is out only for himself. Frankfurter is interested in my information, but his men cannot help. The Happy Hot Dogs do not range that far west.

Bendetsen was right, I think sadly; I am just another James Rowe. Writing briefs I do not believe, uncertain whom I can trust. I think about the letter Rowe left in my desk drawer. There is my way out, my ticket back to Philadelphia. But I am not ready to give up yet. I walk circuits around the Great Court, wishing for help. Murals on the walls show paths to truth; Gressman's files offer names and circles in red ink. And when help comes, it takes me a long time to recognize it for what it is.

CHAPTER 34

THE ENVELOPE ON my desk is yellow and bulky. It comes from the Pentagon under John Hall's name. I slit the seams with a letter opener and pull out six hundred pages of typescript. A bold legend runs across the front page. *Final Report: Japanese Evacuation from the West Coast.* It is General DeWitt's report on the evacuation.

I scan the cover letter quickly. Evacuation was impelled by military necessity. Thousands of American-born Japanese had gone to Japan to receive their education and had become rabidly pro-Japanese. Time was of the essence. The cooperation of the Department of Justice was appreciated, and great credit was due to the Japanese themselves for complying with the exclusion orders, under Army supervision and direction.

Chapter two details the need for military control and evacuation. I read it through with mounting puzzlement. Justice was indifferent to the security of the West Coast, the report says. We offered ineffectual half-measures; we refused to defer to the judgment of military officials on the scene; we withdrew in a huff if Francis Biddle's views were challenged. Whoever wrote it clearly hates James Rowe, which suggests to me that the author of this chapter, at least, is Karl Bendetsen.

Then I notice something else. Contraband was seized in spot raids, the report says, including dynamite and sixty thousand rounds of ammunition. Signal lights were often seen from the coast, and radio transmissions were intercepted. The Japanese American population was tied to the Empire by race, filial piety, customs, and culture. They were a tight-knit, unassimilated racial group. Hundreds of pro-Japanese organizations were sending tinfoil across the Pacific . . .

I stop. These are the claims that the Pacific states made in their amicus brief in *Hirabayashi*, the curfew case. The facts Ennis has asked me to find, the claims that James Rowe carefully did not make on behalf of Justice. Here they are now in the voice of the War Department, in a report that stops just short of branding the men of Justice traitors. I pick up the phone.

"Hiya, Swell," says John Hall. "Sorry, Cash. What can I do for you?"

"I've got this report," I say.

"Yeah," says Hall enthusiastically. "We finally got it out."

"Where is this coming from?"

"What do you mean?"

"The facts it gives. These aren't things the Department has claimed before."

"I know," says Hall. "But now you can."

"What?"

"Now you have the report to rely on."

"Sure," I say. The picture is getting clearer. The War Department wants a stronger brief from Justice this time. "Another thing. I see the main argument here is that there wasn't time to do individual hearings."

"That's right."

"Well, funny coincidence, I was just talking to Karl Bendetsen, and that's not what he said."

There is a long moment of silence. "What?"

"He said there was plenty of time."

Hall sounds less cheery. "What were you talking to him for? You're supposed to go through me, Cash. That's the way this works."

"Why is this report telling me something he denied?"

"He's just one guy, Cash. This is the position of the War Department. Of the United States."

"Actually, the Justice Department speaks for the United States. And I notice you had some things to say about us, too. Biddle's not going to like that."

"Yeah," says Hall. "Nothing personal, you understand."

"Not such great liaison work there, John. Not necessarily going to make us more eager to cooperate."

"That wasn't my call." He sounds positively lugubrious now. "Really, I'm just trying to help. We're all on the same side here."

"Right." I hang up the phone. Here is my brief for *Korematsu* and *Endo*, written by the helpful folks at the War Department. It is the brief they wanted Rowe to file in *Hirabayashi*, no doubt, but he would not. And now he is on a destroyer in the Pacific. I carry the report to Edward Ennis's office. "John Hall sent this over."

"What is it?"

"Justification for the evacuation," I say. "Chock full of useful supporting facts."

Ennis looks up. He is working something out; behind his eyes I can almost see gears turning. But all he says is, "Should make writing the briefs easier."

"Yeah," I say. "If it's true."

His face is unreadable. "What do you mean?"

"It's just War Department say-so. Do you believe it?"

Ennis shrugs. "Not my decision. If you're worried about it, talk to Biddle."

• • • •

But I talk to J. Edgar Hoover instead. He smiles at me from behind his massive desk, the flags limp by his sides. "It's been too long, Mr. Harrison. I'm glad you've returned."

"I'd like an investigation," I say. "Into certain claims made by the War Department."

"Indeed."

"It's about the Japanese evacuation. They're claiming radio intercepts, signal lights. Subversive activity. Does the Bureau have confirmation of that?"

"We were intimately involved in securing the coast," Hoover says. "We have the information you need."

"Okay." There is a moment of silence. "Great."

"And now it is time to talk of what you can do for me." Hoover stands behind his desk. "You are still familiar with Felix Frankfurter, I believe."

"What?"

"You have been to see him. Last week, was it not?"

"I don't understand."

"A record of his conversations could prove very valuable. A listening device—"

I interrupt. "You're asking me to bug Frankfurter's chambers?"

Hoover's face changes. As if it is a mirror, I can see myself, moving into another category, leaving the charmed circle. The confidantes, the protected. He licks his lips. "Have I been wrong about where your loyalties lie? I have been very helpful to you."

"And I appreciate that. But I'm not asking a favor here. It's my job to represent the United States government, and I want to know what the facts are."

Hoover's lips glisten. "I am not asking you a favor, either. I am asking you to serve your country. Felix Frankfurter is a very dangerous man. He is . . ."

I am out the door before he finishes. There is no way I can do what Hoover asks. But this is no impasse; already my mind is moving up the chain of command. Now it is time for Francis Biddle.

. . . .

It takes surprisingly little work. Biddle needs no help to see that the Final Report is a personal attack on him and his department. He is sympathetic when I explain that I must verify the War Department's claims, and surprised that Hoover did not jump at the chance to assist me. "We will have a word with him," he says.

Together we make our way downstairs. "How did you like Edgar's office?" Biddle asks me as we walk along the second-floor hallway, past the triumphant murals.

"It's fine," I say.

"Did you notice his flags?" We are approaching the antechamber, where the secretary sits and the agents lounge. "The Director is a man who likes his flags."

"I did see that," I say.

"Yes," says Biddle. His voice has gained volume. "It brings to mind an argument I often have with Edward Ennis. Do you think that Hoover is a homosexual?"

I blink. "What?"

"Oh," says Biddle, more loudly still. "I only mean a *latent* homosexual."

The secretary has heard the conversation, if not the words; perhaps she has recognized Biddle's voice. She emerges with a troubled look. The Director is not expecting us, she says. Will we wait for him?

"The Attorney General will not wait for the Director," says Biddle. "Even if he is not a latent homosexual."

The secretary's face goes white, then red. She dashes off. I am staring at Biddle with my mouth open. "What?" he asks equably. "I said 'if he is *not*.'"

"We have to work with him," I say.

"He works with you," says Biddle. "He works for me. And I don't intend to let him forget it."

Biddle is the first person I have seen who does not seem at least a little bit scared of Hoover. Perhaps he has nothing in his life that might go into a file. Or perhaps it is just that he is Francis Biddle, who can argue before the Supreme Court in white linen and think nothing of it. "Edgar should be very helpful," he says. "Roosevelt has given him considerable power, and we may set him after anyone we want. He is a useful tool."

The secretary returns and beckons us inside. Hoover sits at his desk and Tolson stands against the wall behind him. He glances up at our entrance, but says nothing. Biddle remains silent too, simply looking at him from the doorway. At last Hoover gets to his feet. "Mr. Attorney General," he says. "An unexpected pleasure."

It is plain that half of this phrase is true, and also plain which half. Standing, Hoover looks the same height as Tolson, presumably because Tolson is behind the raised platform on which the desk rests. But he is considerably shorter than the flags, which now do strike me as large for an office. With Biddle at my side, I am beginning to find the scene ridiculous.

"Edgar," says Biddle. "Have you met my assistant, Mr. Harrison?"

"We are acquainted," says Hoover.

"I should like you to assist him. We are in possession of certain claims made by the War Department, about activity on the West Coast prior to the evacuation. I have asked Mr. Harrison to ascertain whether they are well substantiated. He will need investigative support."

"Of course," says Hoover. "The Bureau is at your disposal."

"Yes, it is," says Biddle. "Mr. Harrison will let you know his requirements."
Hoover looks at me intently. Tolson's face is dark with anger.

Biddle turns and walks out, and I follow. "Edgar will do what he is told,"
says Biddle. "But you should not expect miracles. He cannot live up to his
reputation as a supersleuth. He spends more time on the reputation than
the sleuthing. And he can go off half-cocked, like anyone else. Before Pearl
Harbor he drew up a list of people he wanted to detain. I told him to scrap it.
He just needs a firm hand."

I am glad that Biddle has his hand on Hoover. I would not like that job
myself, and I wonder what will happen when there is a new Attorney General. But for now, the FBI is mine to command. Hoover sends Agent Miller
to my office. "I want your information on the Japanese," I say. "Anything you
have. And I need some particular facts verified." I give him the details of the
Final Report, the contraband, the signal lights, the radio intercepts. He nods
seriously and departs.

He is back surprisingly soon, pushing a cart. "That was fast," I say.

Miller gives me a wide, white smile. "There's more work to do. But I think I
got your facts. These are the reports that were generated already."

"Already?" I don't understand. "For whom?"

"The Unit. Alien Enemies." His smile is unchanged, but there is puzzlement in his voice now. "You."

I sift the files. There is one from the FCC Radio Intelligence Division,
another from the Office of Naval Intelligence, written by a Kenneth Ringle.
They bear FBI processing stamps, and the name of the recipient. Alien Enemy
Control Unit. Mr. James Rowe.

A few minutes' reading is enough to reveal their substance. Rowe has done
my work for me. There were no unauthorized radio signals, the FCC reports.
The Army radio operators were incompetent, picking up stations in Tokyo
and reporting them as Oakland. There were no signal lights from the coast.
Ringle, writing in early 1942, says there is no Japanese problem at all. There
are some individuals who might be dangerous, but they are already in FBI
custody. The evidence of disloyalty is manufactured: raids seize dynamite

that farmers use to clear tree stumps, ammunition from sporting goods stores. The loyalty questionnaire I know about already.

The pieces are falling into place. Rowe had these reports. That is the meaning of his marginalia. *FCC-RID 42-107. ONI Ringle.* He knew the War Department claims were false. He would not put them in his brief, and he was drafted for his pains.

But something still does not fit. Rowe sent these files back to the FBI; he encoded his notes. And Ennis, who should have known about all of this, just asked me to take the War Department's word with no mention of contradictory reports.

Ennis is their man. That has to be it. Rowe knew; he kept his research secret; he did what he could knowing that his boss was in War's pocket. And when he went too far and they moved against him, he left clues so that his successor might have a better chance.

Now I am exactly where he was, sitting at the same desk, reading the same reports. Faced with the same War Department lies. But Bendetsen was right to call me new and improved. I know more than James Rowe did, and I have more powerful friends. I summon Agent Miller back. "New assignment," I say. "I want you to follow someone. See who he talks to. Tap his phone if you have to."

He does not seem surprised. I take it surveillance is within his job description. "Who?"

"Edward Ennis."

CHAPTER 35

"THE WAR DEPARTMENT is trying to influence the Japanese cases," I tell Frankfurter.

He nods, looking up at the ceiling of his chambers. "I'm sure they are. But that is the way government works, my friend."

"No, they issued a report about the evacuation that's not true, and they have a man at Justice who's working for them."

"Who is sympathetic, maybe. I do not think he takes their orders."

I hesitate. I do not, I realize, know that Ennis is actually in contact with the War Department. It is what I hope to learn from Miller. "What about the certificates?"

"Intriguing," says Frankfurter. "But that is not the War Department. I believe Karl Bendetsen on that point. There may well be people trying to take advantage of the Japanese. But I doubt there is a connection to our concerns." He turns his gaze down toward me. "A yeoman's efforts. But I do not think they bring us closer to our quarry." My mood sinks. Frankfurter touches his lapel. For a reason he has not explained, he sports a white carnation in his buttonhole. "I have been making progress, though."

"You have?"

"Murphy's new clerk has departed. Mr. Gressman's replacement."

"Why?"

"He was caught leaving the building with draft opinions in his bag."

"So he was leaking information?"

"Not necessarily." The eyes are bright in the bullet head, sparkling behind his pince-nez. "I put them there."

"Why would you do that?"

"He was acting suspiciously. I misliked the people he was meeting with."

"Drew Pearson?"

Frankfurter's wave is dismissive. "Others. It does not matter."

"But then you didn't know."

"I knew enough. The next man will surely be loyal."

"But you've ruined his career."

"No," says Frankfurter. "It was handled quietly. There will be no permanent harm." I look at him in silence. The meeting is depressing me. Frankfurter has rejected my contributions, and his own reveal an alarming ruthlessness. "I have removed a potential threat," he says. "And I have other interesting news for you."

"What else?"

"About your friend Clara Watson."

The name deflates me further. "I told you, she's clean."

"Perhaps," says Frankfurter. "She lied to you, though."

"About what?"

"She is not living at the YWCA. At least, that is not where she goes when she leaves work."

"Where, then?"

"Dupont Circle."

"An apartment?"

He shrugs. "My men lose her. She seems concerned to evade pursuit. And as you noticed, they are not professionals. You might do better."

"I'm not a professional either." I could send Agent Miller, I suppose. But I have already broadened his responsibilities beyond what Biddle authorized, and Hoover will not miss a chance to punish me if he finds out.

"But you are young," says Frankfurter. "You are quick on your feet. I would like you to give it a try."

• • • •

That project will wait till the end of the day. Back at Main Justice, there is a new stack of papers on my desk. The opening briefs in *Korematsu* and *Endo* have come in, the arguments I must answer with or without the War Department's facts. It is time to meet the plaintiffs.

Mitsuye Endo I know at a glance. She is a test plaintiff, handpicked by the ACLU. As they chose Eagle Scout Gordon Hirabayashi to challenge the curfew, they have found an indisputably loyal woman to attack detention. A typist for the State of California before they let her go, a brother in the army. She has never been to Japan; she doesn't speak the language. No one could call her a threat to America. Justice offered to release her already, I see, to make the case go away, but she refused.

Fred Korematsu is different. Like everyone else, he has his Pearl Harbor story. He was parked with his girl, listening to Tommy Dorsey and looking out at the Oakland hills, when the announcers broke in. Five months later he was ordered to Tanforan Assembly Center, the dusty racetrack where Kuwabara's cot sank into the melting asphalt.

But Korematsu did not go to Tanforan. He wanted to stay with his girl, Ida Boitano, to settle with her somewhere in the Midwest. He got surgery on his eyes; he changed the name on his draft card to Clyde Sarah. When the police picked him up he told them he was a Mexican from Hawaii.

He spoke no Spanish. They were not fooled. And so he went to Tanforan after all.

From the camp he sent Ida letters. She wrote back telling him to send no more. *She was originally engaged to subject and planned to marry him*, her FBI interview says, *but she now realizes that such a marriage is impossible and that she made a big mistake. She is now sorry that she did not report subject to the proper authorities when he refused to give himself up.* That is what the girls say in this situation, what they are supposed to say.

Korematsu was prosecuted, convicted, and sentenced to probation. The judge ordered him released back into Oakland; the War Department disagreed. Military police took him from the courtroom at gunpoint. He went back to Tanforan and then to the Topaz camp in Utah. And now he asks the Court to set him free.

How to answer? That is not the question, I realize. James Rowe was not answering arguments when he wrote the *Hirabayashi* brief. He was not just resisting the corrupting influence of War, not just doing his duty. He was trying to lose. That is why he was drafted; that is the meaning of the letter in the drawer.

And that is what I want to do now. I would send these people home if I could, I thought on the plane back from Eureka, and now I can. Why not? Something is giving way inside me. Something has torn all the way through, that has been a long time fraying. For a moment I see my bathroom mirror, the single word come clean against the fog. *Traitor*. Then it is wiped away. I can send these people home with a Supreme Court decision paving the way, telling the nation they are loyal, they are like us after all.

All I need to do is figure out how to sabotage the government's position without betraying myself to Edward Ennis or anyone else. I blow out my breath in a sigh. It was beyond James Rowe's ability. But he wasn't a Supreme Court clerk, Biddle's fair-haired boy, a young genius, perfect and untamed.

The pep talk is unconvincing. Who has called me a genius recently? A girl who lied to me the last time we spoke. I put the papers down and go to find Clara.

. . . .

Waiting at the Court brings back memories, some fond, some bittersweet. Watching my briefcase sail down the steps, running with Gene to the printer's office. Black sitting on the corner of my desk. Gene swearing he'd figure it all out . . . and me raising his ghostly fingerprints for Hoover's techs.

It is still only a little after five, and Douglas clerks tend to work late. It should be no surprise that the first figure I recognize leaving the Court is Hugo Black, but still I feel a jolt as the familiar hat emerges. He is walking in my direction; as he nears I can hear his whistle. "London Bridge." I know I should turn away—chatting with a justice is not the way to pick up Clara's trail unobserved—but I can't move, and as he passes I hear myself say, "Judge."

Black starts. "Cash!" Surprise gives way to enthusiasm. "Returning to the scene of the crime?"

My laugh is forced. "How are you?" He shrugs. "How's Josephine?"

The answer flits across his face, and it is not the word that follows. "Fine." He nods, reaching for something else. "JoJo, now. She's not scared of the dark anymore, but she goes around sneezing all the time. You teach her that?"

"It worked for me as a kid."

Black laughs. "So, you're with Francis Biddle now. You learn your purpose yet?"

"I'm thinking so, Judge."

"What are you doing for him?"

"Working on the Japanese cases. Have you seen any of the filings yet?"

Black's face changes, and he takes a step back. "Oh," he says. "We can't talk about that."

"No," I say. It would be so easy; it would make everything so simple. But he would never break that rule. "I suppose not."

He must see something in my eyes, for he tilts his head, questioning. Then he slaps my shoulder. "When it's done, Cash. When it's done we'll have a beer."

I watch him walk away. He has been playing tennis; sunburn stripes the back of his neck where the skin folds as he bends to return serve. The red clay court comes back to me, the evenings in his kitchen, his story about the Pledge of Allegiance and how he'd changed his mind. Other people make children raise their arms, not us. But who puts their own citizens in camps? Black will do it, I think. He cannot save Josephine; he cannot bring his boys home, but this thing he can do. Hugo Black is the key that will open the gates of Tule Lake.

I almost miss Clara as she comes out the Maryland Avenue entrance and heads north along First Street, walking fast. She is wearing a navy pin-striped skirt with a matching three-button jacket that hugs her waist. I find myself wondering whether she made it herself, then push the thought aside. I try to imagine her as a spy, infiltrating the Court. It would be an alien world, its customs and language unfamiliar. Its inhabitants would stare, seeing her as irreducibly other. It is not possible, I think. They would not send a woman.

And yet . . . She herself said that Douglas is a wolf. She can get his attention in a way Vern Countryman could not. She is from Washington, like Karl Bendetsen. And in a way I cannot fully explain, she has given me the feeling there is something she hides.

At Union Station she boards a streetcar going up Massachusetts Avenue. And perhaps Frankfurter has put it in my mind, but I would swear that as she mounts the steps she is looking around to be sure she isn't followed.

I get a taxicab and tell the driver to hang a few cars back from the trolley. Traffic is heavy, and the trick is not getting ahead of her. My driver manages it with aplomb, slipping behind slower vehicles, changing lanes indecisively. She alights a few blocks before Dupont Circle and plunges into the crowd. This too seems a strategic choice, for as I follow her we pass several other streetcar stops.

Like Dante's vision of Hell, Dupont Circle has concentric rings, cars and buses wheeling around in a confusion of horns. Unlike Dante's, but probably true to the real thing, it is filled with bureaucrats. Blue and gray suits jostle on the sidewalks, queue up on the traffic islands between rivers of cars. Clara weaves through the crowd. She has an advantage: most of them are at least slightly reluctant to collide with her, but I receive no such solicitude. Every now and then she turns her head and I have to duck or turn myself, which makes the collisions more frequent. A fat man in a glen plaid thinks it warrants a remark. "Young man," he says, raising a thick finger. "Young man!"

I've lost her. A sea of backs ahead of me, through which bobbing faces approach. I push between a man and his wife, wondering why they're standing still, and learn the answer when I step into the street in front of oncoming traffic. Horns blare as I jump back. A car whooshes past just in front of me. Through the back window the face of a young girl stares out, pale and receding like a drowning person. "Young man," someone says. The burst of adrenaline sharpens my senses. I pick Clara out on the next ring in, packed with people. The light changes; we shift forward and cross into the circle. And I see that she is not alone.

The man is keeping pace just a bit in front of me. He has probably been with us for some time, but it is only the way he moves forward, his eyes four bodies ahead, that shows me he is following her.

Of course, I think. A Happy Hot Dog. Frankfurter still has a man in place.

He maintains his distance as they traverse the circle. Before she reaches the fountain at the center, Clara cuts back toward New Hampshire Avenue. Now I'm sure that she's trying to spot a tail, since it would have been much quicker to walk a quarter-turn around. But she hasn't made this man, nor me as far as I can tell.

The lights catch us again on the way out. He is at the back of the crowd on her island, while I'm still in the circle proper. I almost call to him, to tell him he can sit this dance out. But something stops me. His shoulders don't look right inside the suit; they bunch and swell as he moves. One arm takes the man immediately ahead and moves him aside like a child. This is no agricultural economist, no one Frankfurter would know. This man is from somewhere else.

As I watch he takes another man from his path. "Sir!" Clara is at the front, standing on the curb, waiting for the light. His hat moves through the crowd. "Watch it, pal." The plan is no longer to follow unobserved. And suddenly I am sure of what he intends. Douglas is a valuable Justice, with his anti-government tendencies. Frankfurter may indeed have picked off one of their men by arranging the Murphy clerk's exit. A packed crowd, a stumble, an accident. They want to open another slot.

I start pushing forward myself. He still has some concern for stealth, which I do not, and I move faster. I call her name, but she does not look back. "Clara!" I yell again.

I get to the curbside. The cars gush past in torrents. I think of the icy water that takes your breath on impact. My breath, her breath. Suzanne vanishes into the ocean, Josephine fades away as we reach for her. But this one will not be lost. This one I will save.

The hat is right behind Clara now; the man's shoulders gather as his arms come up. I stand there trying to calculate whether I'm sure enough about this to make it worth throwing myself into traffic. And then before I can decide I find myself off the curb and dashing across the street.

The horn distracts him, I think; or if not that, then the screech of brakes and the crunch of the fender as the car behind slams into the one that stopped for me. Just then the light changes anyway, and the crowd surges forward. Clara heads across the street. The man starts to follow, but I'm on him in seconds. I seize his shoulder and he turns. Face-to-face, he is a gorilla, suit jacket bunching above his trapezius muscles, hat riding up on his head. I realize with a flash of alarm that I haven't planned anything past this moment. "Forget it," I say. "It's off."

"What?" The puzzlement is real, but he knows what I'm talking about. He just doesn't know how I fit in.

"We're blown," I say, improvising desperately. "The FBI is all around us." He scowls suspiciously, and I push him off in the opposite direction. "Split up. Lie low. We'll contact you."

It's convincing, or convincing enough. He slopes off and I turn back to the street, trying to find the navy blazer with the fitted waist. I cross to the sidewalk, look in both directions, run one way to glance down New Hampshire and then the other to scan P Street. Nothing. Or not Clara. What I see, when I raise my eyes, is the spread wings of Cissy Patterson's house.

Not possible, I think. *Possible*, retorts a tiny voice in my head. *She hesitated when she saw where you were going; she didn't want to come here.*

It was too grand, I say. *It scared her.*

It was too familiar, the voice answers. *She knew people there already; she was scared you'd discover the connection.*

The memories of that night change their aspect in my mind like an optical illusion. Cissy with the daggers in her smile, displeased to see Clara again. The duck becomes a rabbit. The whole scene between them an act for my benefit. The beautiful girl turns into an old hag. I stand there blinking in front of the house. Then something hard is pressed into my back and a voice tells me to reach for the sky.

CHAPTER 36

IT IS CLARA. I turn around.

"Bang," she says. The suit hugs her waist; her eyes glow gold in the setting sun. "I warned you, buster." She cocks her thumb like a pistol, taps my chest with stiff fingers.

I fold them in my hand and shift her aim aside. "What are you doing?"

"I should ask you that question. Except that I know. So I will ask why."

"Why what?"

"Why were you following me?"

"I was yelling your name."

"Yes, I heard that."

"But you didn't turn around?"

"I did not wish to see you then. You recall our last parting."

"I remember saying I was sorry." A pause. "I'm still sorry. I was thought-less. I didn't want that to happen."

Clara tosses her hair. "It is what happens that is real, not what we want."

"Well, what I want is to be your friend."

"As I said. Why were you following me?"

"There was a man. He was going to hurt you."

"And you came to rescue me? That is chivalrous. Romantic, even."

I am blushing. For a moment I was sure I had saved her life. Now my certainty melts away. How can it be that once again I am feeling awkward? "You lied to me, though."

Clara tilts her head, considering. "I do not think so."

"You aren't living at the Y."

"Indeed I am."

"Then why did you come to Dupont Circle?" The YWCA is half a mile away at 17th and K.

"I have noticed that men follow me. It helps me evade them when I do not have a knight-errant to rely on."

"You should have gone to the police."

"They wouldn't help." She shrugs. "This is something that happens to girls. You would not know what it is like."

"I do, though."

"You do?"

"I know what it's like to be followed."

"What do you mean?"

"It's a long story."

"Tell me."

I look around. The sidewalk is not quite as crowded as it was, but people are still thick around us. And Cissy Patterson's house looms overhead. I look up at the columns, the American flag, the balcony where Lindbergh waved to adoring crowds. Now that I think about it, the fact that the tough was after her actually proves her innocence. An obvious point, and it makes me realize how turned around I've gotten. "Not here," I say. "Would you like to come to my apartment? It's not far."

Her eyebrows go up. "What an extraordinary suggestion."

"No," I say. "For Pete's sake. I mean . . . Forget it. How about a diner?"

"Much better."

We go half a block up Connecticut. It is still too early for supper patrons, and we have the place mostly to ourselves. A grim old lady wipes a table clear and drops menus down. "Just coffee," I say.

"I think I'd like an ice cream soda," says Clara.

"She's joking."

"I'm not."

The old lady's scowl deepens. "Coffee and an ice cream soda," I say.

"Chocolate," Clara adds. The waitress walks slowly away. "So," says Clara. "Spill."

The jukebox is playing "I'll Be Seeing You" again and again, at the insistence of a mournful girl's nickels. I put in a gleaming quarter and buy eighteen minutes of silence. My coffee comes, and her ice cream soda. And I tell her a long story. A strange pattern of cert grants. Gene's investigation and his death. My pact with Frankfurter, Haynes and the Happy Hot Dogs. John Hall and Karl Bendetsen. The draft resisters in Eureka, the lies in the Final Report, the fake certificates in Tule Lake.

By the end, her face has grown serious. "Someone's planting clerks," she says.

"I'm almost sure of that."

"And you suspected me?"

"I suspect everyone."

"Not quite." There is a look in her eyes I cannot place.

"What do you mean?"

"Not yourself."

"I don't get it."

"I'm not the spy, Mr. Genius Detective. You are."

"What? That's ridiculous. Why would I be telling you this?"

"Because the clerks themselves don't know, not all of them. I think you're one of those."

"Why me any more than you?"

"Think about it," says Clara. "They take out two of Black's selections, his usual guys, liberals from the South. And in comes you, a conservative from the North. That's a 180-degree change. Isn't it what they'd want?"

"I'm a conservative?"

"Well, that's between you and God," she says. "Or Mammon. I don't know about the Japanese cases, but if I had to guess, I'd certainly figure you for a pro-business type. And if I wanted to place those types on the Court and I could get you in with Black, I'd think I'd done pretty well."

"Really?"

"Your name is Cash."

"It's a nickname," I say. "I explained that."

"Well," says Clara. "I may be wrong. But it's a possibility worth considering."

She is right, but it brings up a problem. "Consider how? I'm not making any progress. I can't even get Hall to come clean about what Bendetsen did."

"You said he was willing to trade information for a favor."

"But there's nothing I can do for him."

"Maybe you can not do something. Stop something from happening. Something that would be bad for him."

I consider. "I don't think there's anything bad that's going to happen."

"But he doesn't know that." Clara smiles. "Think more creatively. I'm sure there's something. Everyone trusts you. You're the right sort of guy."

"Yeah," I say, uncertain. From her it doesn't sound like a compliment. "Look, I need your help. I need to make sure the Japanese cases come out right."

"And?"

"I need someone inside the Court."

She shakes her head. "You know that's not allowed."

"I don't care."

"I do. It could cost me my job."

"No one will know."

Another shake. "Why should I trust you?"

"Because I'm the right sort of guy?"

Her smile confirms that the phrase was not a compliment. "You were unkind to me the last time we met. And furthermore, you are a spy."

"I am not."

"Yes, you are. For one side or the other. You just don't know which."

Before I can come up with a response, the music starts up again. The girl at the other table gives us a look of teary defiance. She brandishes a fistful of coins. Clara rises to leave and then bends down, her hair falling almost into my face. Her last sentence is quiet. "But I thank you for the ice cream soda."

．．．．

Agent Miller reports back to me the next day. Edward Ennis has met with some Justice lawyers in his office; he has spoken to others on the phone. Nothing out of the ordinary. But he has also left work to pay some unexpected calls.

"Covington and Burling?"

Miller nods his head. "It's a law firm."

"I know that. But why is he going there?"

"I don't know. But he is. Late in the evening, too."

I frown. There is no reason I can think of for the head of Alien Enemies to be visiting a private firm, and certainly not after hours. "Let me know the next time he does."

Miller nods again. "Sure thing, boss. Anything else?"

"Yeah," I say. "There's a Douglas clerk, a girl." Clara scoffed at my warnings, made me doubt them myself. But there is no harm in being sure. "I want someone to keep an eye on her. Make sure she's safe."

He arcs a curious eyebrow. "You think she's not?"

"Let's just be sure."

· · · ·

A few days later, the phone in my apartment rings. It is just before nine o'clock. Miller is on the line, and the jolt of adrenaline I feel at the sound of his voice makes me realize I was more worried about Clara than I let myself know. But he is reporting on his other charge. "Ennis is there. What do you want me to do?"

"Just wait. I'll be right over."

I take a taxi back downtown. Covington is at 12th and Pennsylvania, just a few blocks from Main Justice. I ask the driver to leave me at 14th so that I can approach more carefully. The entrance is set back from the sidewalk, and people are still going in and out. Miller beckons to me from a doorway a few buildings away.

"Went in about twenty minutes ago," he says when I join him. "Still inside."

"How long does he usually stay?"

Miller shrugs. "An hour, maybe an hour and a half."

"Does he carry anything?"

"Just a briefcase."

"I wonder what he's doing."

Miller gives me a speculative smile. "We could ask."

I consider, then nod. Surely I would have the stronger position in a confrontation, exposing his secrets with the FBI at my side. "Let's go."

A receptionist in a green dress is working the door. She asks who we are there to see. Miller flashes his badge in response. "I'm looking for Edward Ennis," I say. Her face is blank.

"Gray suit," says Miller. "Pink cheeks. Cream in his hair. About half an hour ago."

"Oh," she says. "Mr. Arnold. To see Charles Horsky. Third floor."

Miller thanks her with a smile. "You know this Horsky guy?" he asks as we ascend the stairs.

"I know the name," I say. I've seen it before, somewhere.

Only one office on the third floor is occupied. Low voices come from behind the closed door. Miller raises a fist and looks at me. I nod and he knocks. "Open up."

The voices inside go still. "Who's there?" a man asks. It's not Ennis.

I nod at Miller again. "FBI," he says.

There is a moment of silence, then a sound as though someone is trying to turn the lock. Miller doesn't wait for a sign from me; he grabs the knob and pushes the door open. I see Ennis, off balance, stumbling back, and another man seated behind a desk. Miller steps in and I follow. Ennis is still backing away.

"So, Edward." Here I am, flanked by my forces. Now I have found him, the subtle foe, the saboteur. "Who's your friend?"

He is startled, but defiant. "Who's yours?"

"This is Special Agent Miller," I say.

Miller gives them his wide smile and a look at the badge. "At your service."

Ennis shakes his head and turns to the man behind the desk. "This is Cash Harrison," he says. "My brief-writer."

The other man looks to be in his mid-thirties. A young partner, probably, in a white shirt and dark tie, his suit jacket hanging on the door. He raises his eyebrows. "He knows how to make an entrance."

"Why are you here, Cash?" Ennis asks.

"I wanted to see what you were doing. Who are you meeting with?"

The man behind the desk stands now. "I'm Charles Horsky," he says. "Fred Korematsu's lawyer."

CHAPTER 37

NOW I REMEMBER where I have seen Horsky's name. It is on the briefs I have just been reading, the ones that say exclusion was unconstitutional, that ask the Court to set Korematsu free. The ones we are arguing against.

"Why are you talking to opposing counsel, Edward?"

Ennis's eyes shift from me to Miller. "I think you should send him away."

Miller gives me a shrug. "You're the boss."

"I'll be okay," I say. "You can go home."

Miller shuts the door behind him. Ennis motions me to a chair. "So," I say. "What are you doing with Mr. Horsky?"

"I'm helping him," Ennis says.

"Helping him?"

"Yes." There is defiance in his voice again. "And you found me out. Congratulations. Now what are you going to do? I'm too old for active duty."

"What do you mean?"

"You can't get rid of me like Rowe."

"What are you talking about? I didn't draft James Rowe."

"You're not working for the War Department?"

"No. I thought you were."

Ennis just looks at me. Horsky shakes his head in disbelief. "You two need to figure some things out."

"I'm working against them," Ennis says. "Have been for a while."

"But you kept saying these things. About holding people with no evidence. Taking the War Department's word on the Final Report."

"That was because I thought you were one of them."

First Clara, now Ennis. "Why would you think that?"

He sighs. "Rowe was against evacuation." I nod. This much I knew already. "So was I. We were working together. We thought something was fishy with his draft notice. And then you came in, some sort of personal connection. We figured War was putting their own guy in here, someone to keep closer tabs on me. So we tried to make things a little harder for you to figure out. Just gave you what War knew already."

So Rowe wasn't hiding his work from Ennis. He was hiding it from me. And the resignation letter left in my desk, a taunt to his presumed enemy. But now it is anodyne, a harmless joke. "Well, I figured it out," I say. "I got the reports. I know the War Department is lying." Ennis nods. "What do we do now?"

"I say we lose these cases."

My turn to nod. I have wanted this for a while, probably since the Eureka courtroom. We will be saboteurs in earnest. But surely this is not betrayal; surely it is the fulfillment of some duty. Karl Bendetsen was just a lawyer with a client who needed advice. Who do we serve, the lawyers of Justice? The Department, the President, America, the law? The War Department wants us to say the President can do what he wants, that government can always be trusted and judges need not look too close. Some men fear, and others use that fear for their purposes, and no one anywhere is any different, in khaki uniform or the solicitor general's morning coat. I think of the hedge around Judge Skinner's house, the gardener with his shears, the trust in Suzanne's eyes as she lay beneath me on the bed. Law requires care, too; it grows where we nourish it and dies where we cut. I will do right this time.

"Can we tell the Court the government should lose?"

"The Department can always confess error," Ennis says. "But asking them to rule against the Government is a Cabinet-level decision. We need Biddle's approval."

I nod again. "I'll talk to him."

. . . .

"Cash," says Francis Biddle enthusiastically. "How's every last thing?" He is wearing his linen suit. Insufficiently serious, Frankfurter said; too la-de-da. As I consider how every last thing is, I think that perhaps he had a point. Biddle has no idea what is going on inside his department.

"Good," I say. The picture of the Japanese boy in the train window is still on his wall.

Biddle follows my eyes. "Alien Enemies treating you well?"

"Yes. Actually I was just talking to Edward Ennis about *Korematsu* and *Endo*." He nods in a friendly fashion. "The War Department is trying to pass off lies to the Supreme Court."

"The Final Report," Biddle says. He looks concerned. "You had Hoover check out those claims."

"Yes."

"And?"

"And they didn't check out. We need to tell the Court that."

"Well," says Biddle. He strokes his mustache. "'Lie' is an awfully strong word. Remember who we're talking about here."

"Karl Bendetsen?"

"Henry Stimson. A good man. Jack McCloy."

"A Philadelphian," I put in.

"Exactly. These are men who love their country. Some of our finest lawyers."

"So?"

"I don't think we can go before the Supreme Court and accuse them of lying. We don't want to stain their reputations."

"The Final Report says there's proof of disloyalty. That stains some reputations, too."

"Yes," says Biddle slowly. "Of course, it doesn't mention anyone by name."

"You want to help them resettle," I say. "Don't you think that would go easier if the Court said the evacuation was wrong?"

"Yes." The word is drawn out over three syllables. "You know I was never in favor. It's a terrible thing."

"So we'll confess error."

"Mmmm," says Biddle. He chews his lower lip, clearly wishing I were some-place other than his office. "Charles Fahy will be delivering the argument. Whatever you work out with him is acceptable to me."

· · · ·

Charles Fahy prefers to communicate by memo, and Ennis and I spend the afternoon writing one. We outline the claims in the Final Report and the evidence that undermines them. It is bad enough, we say, that these falsehoods were presented to the Court in *Hirabayashi* through the brief of the Pacific states. But the United States government cannot endorse them. Our goal now must be to facilitate the resettlement of the detainees, and a Supreme Court decision holding evacuation unlawful would greatly assist that project.

A messenger delivers the reply an hour later. As I stand with the paper in my hand, I hear voices singing outside. The Marseillaise. I go to the window. A crowd parades down Pennsylvania Avenue, bearing a French flag and holding bottles aloft. It is the end of August, and Paris is free. I open the memo from Fahy. It is one sentence long. *The Solicitor General of the United States does not throw cases.*

CHAPTER 38

BRUTE FORCE, ORDEAL, *Tradition*. I am walking circles through Main Justice again. Nanette Dembitz is not in her office. *Superstition*, *False Witness*, *Magic*. Edward Ennis is. He looks up as I pass; we both shake our heads. So we will not ask the Court to rule against the government. I will have to write a brief that defends the evacuation. The letter Rowe left is starting to seem a more appealing alternative, the cyanide pill a spy hides for when hope is lost. But perhaps Ennis and I can figure out how to walk the line. We can guide Charles Horsky to the weak spots in our argument, tell him what to attack. The clerks will pick up on equivocations in our brief, just as Gressman did. It might still work. I can tell Clara, or Frankfurter, or even Black, if it comes to that.

Those names bring other thoughts to mind. Quitting will make it harder to ferret out the conspiracy, to find Gene's killer. Not that I have made much progress on that front. *Intuition*, *Reason*, *Science*. There is Nanette, down in the courtyard with one of the Antitrust boys. I am back to the beginning. But all of a sudden the light is on. I have been walking the paths to truth, when what I need is a lie.

· · · ·

"So about that Final Report," I say.

"How did I know you weren't just looking for a squash game?" John Hall asks. "Oh, because no one likes losing that much." He begins hitting the ball into the front corners, one after the other, driving it so that it returns to him where he stands at the T.

I ignore the jibe. "Seriously. We need to talk."

"Okay. About the Final Report. Makes a good case for evacuation, doesn't it?"

"It would if it were true."

"What's that supposed to mean?"

"It means we looked up your claims. And they're not true."

Hall's face retains its slightly condescending smile. He switches from drives to volleys, the racquet tracing a figure eight in front of him, forehand to backhand and back again. "We think they are."

"Maybe you do and maybe you don't. But the FBI and the FCC say they aren't. There was no signaling from the shore. There were no illegal radio transmissions. Biddle's going to crucify you on that report. And it's going to cost you the Japanese cases. Charles Fahy's going to tell the Justices the report's not true, that the War Department is a pack of liars, that nothing the military says can be trusted. We're confessing error."

Hall catches the ball in his hand. The smile is gone from his face. "Why would you do that?"

"Because you made a mistake, John. You or someone else. You forgot we're all on the same side. It wasn't enough to try to justify evacuation. You had to use the report to get back at Justice, at Biddle and Rowe. Well, you made it personal, and now it's coming back at you. Personally."

Hall looks at the floor, lips moving. He hits the ball into the back corner and lets it lie there. "Bendetsen," he says. "I told him. Look, Cash, you've got to help me. If Fahy tells the Court not to trust the War Department, I'm screwed. I'm the Justice liaison. If our relationship with you breaks down, it's on my head."

"Of course I want to protect you," I say. "That's why I'm here. But the FBI reports are pretty damning. Fahy's on the warpath." No one who knows Fahy would believe this description, but Hall does not. "What were you thinking, putting that stuff in there?"

"I didn't write the report," Hall says. Self-pity is in his voice. "Karl Bendetsen did. I made it better. You should have seen what they gave us."

"What they gave you? Did I get something else?"

I can see Hall hesitating. "You're here to help me, right?" he asks.

"Of course," I say. "We're Philadelphia boys."

"Okay," he says. "Bendetsen sent this over months ago. We could have given it to you earlier. But it wouldn't have helped the litigation. Justice was arguing that we needed to act quickly, and the report said that wasn't it. There was plenty of time; it was just impossible to figure out who was loyal and who was disloyal because they're all inscrutable Orientals."

"That's not what it says now."

"Exactly. We knew that wouldn't fly. Not with Justice, maybe not with the Court. So Jack McCloy brought Bendetsen to DC and gave him a good talking-to. Said the War Department wouldn't accept the conclusion that loyalty could never be determined, that the President wouldn't either. And then I rewrote it so it said that time was of the essence. We destroyed the originals, and that was that."

I can feel my mouth hanging open. "It wasn't your report to rewrite," I say. "You understand that, don't you? It was supposed to give the thinking of the military officers who recommended evacuation. You had no business changing it to make it hold up better. You lied to Justice and you lied to the Supreme Court."

"Easy, pal," says Hall. He holds up a placating hand. "Remember that we're all on the same side here. Let's stay focused on figuring out how you can help me."

"I can talk to Biddle," I say. "And Fahy. I can cool them off. But you're going to have to do something for me."

"Of course."

"What did Bendetsen do? The thing you were talking about before. Was it changing the Final Report?"

"No," says Hall. "It was something else."

"Tell me."

"And you'll talk to Fahy? You'll calm Biddle down?" He seems pleased.

I think he enjoys the idea that he is purchasing my aid by selling out Karl Bendetsen.

"I'll try my best. I think I can do it." I enjoy the fact that I am getting the information in exchange for something he had already.

"Drafting James Rowe," he says. "Bendetsen was behind that."

"I kind of figured that out already," I say. But now we are on the right track, I think. "Who else?"

"What do you mean?"

"Did he arrange for anyone else to get drafted? Maybe Supreme Court clerks who were inconvenient?"

Hall's eyes flick to the side, then back to my face. "No. He's not involved in that."

It is a very interesting answer. "You mean you have no idea what I'm talking about."

"I mean he's not involved."

I nod my head thoughtfully. Emotion is building in me, slow and immense. "I think maybe you should tell me, John, just how it is you're so sure about that."

"We're Philadelphia boys," Hall says.

"Of course," I say. "Merion Cricket." For some reason the name of Merion gives me a pang that invoking Philadelphia didn't. I ignore it.

"Well," says Hall. "I know he's not involved because I am."

I am on him in an instant, pushing him up against the wall. There is a rushing in my ears. My hands find his throat. "You killed Gene Gressman."

His fingers scrabble at my wrists. "No, Cash. We wouldn't do that."

"Don't tell me what you wouldn't do. I know what you've done."

"He was an American, Cash. We wouldn't touch him. We were getting pressure to change his draft status, but we wouldn't even do that." His face is turning a darker red; his words grow less clear.

I let him go. "What kind of pressure?"

Hall gasps for air. "What happened to Merion?"

"What happened to you? Tell me what kind of pressure you were getting."

"You know," he says vaguely. "Hints and stuff."

"From whom?"

He shakes his head. "I can't tell you that. I gave you what you asked for. Anyway, we didn't do it. He had real medical problems. We weren't going to send a guy into combat with a bum ticker." He picks up my racquet from the floor and offers it to me. "We're all on the same side."

I pick up his and in one swift motion break it across my knee. I hand him the pieces. "Don't ever say that to me again."

Hall looks down at the shattered wood in his hand. He clears his throat. "So," he says. "You'll talk to Biddle?"

• • • •

And that, I think, is all the information I'll get from John Hall. But I have mistaken him. That evening the phone rings in my apartment.

"I've got a little more to tell you," he says.

"Spill."

"I think we should talk in person."

"You think your phone is tapped?"

"Not mine," he says.

"Mine?"

"I'd rather meet in person, that's all."

"Who are these people, John?"

He ignores the question. "You know the Double Door?"

"I've heard of it." It is a club of ill repute, down on 14th street.

"I'll be there in twenty minutes."

• • • •

Ten minutes later I am climbing the dirty staircase. Inside, smoke hangs thick in the air. There is a spotlight aimed at the small stage, and a sweating man in a red suit. His face is flushed the same color. "Guy volunteers for the paratroops and gets rejected," he says. "He asks what the problem is. 'Well,' the recruiting sergeant says, 'you're blind.' Guy says, 'Oh, that's okay. I've got a guide dog.'"

The band supports him with a rim shot, but that's about it. The patrons here are mostly military, and they are looking for women, not laughs. At the table next to me, some soldiers have made the acquaintance of three WAVES. Nearby sailors do not approve. A lively discussion begins.

"Hiya," says John Hall, slipping into the chair next to me. He waves at a waitress, holds up two fingers, and nods. "Whiskey okay?"

"Fine. What do you have for me?"

"I can tell you're sore. But you shouldn't be. I just don't want you to get the wrong impression."

"Straighten me out, then."

"Yeah, lotta soldiers here tonight," the man onstage says. "I went to buy some of those camouflage pants the other day. Couldn't find any."

"This stuff about the drafting. It's on the level. It's secret, that's all."

"What makes you think that?"

"The guy who gave me the names is in the Army."

"And what's his name?"

Our drinks arrive. Hall swallows half of his. I sip mine. Whatever it is, it's not whiskey. "You wouldn't know him," Hall says. "And they use code names, anyway. He calls himself Cato."

The comic has waited long enough to be sure no laughs are forthcoming. "But you can still get four suits for a dollar," he continues. "If you buy a deck of cards." There is another rim shot from the band, and an empty cigarette pack hurled from the audience.

"How does this seem to you at all like it's on the level?" A surge in volume from the table next to us drowns my words. The debate has progressed to the finer points of interservice etiquette. I repeat the question.

"Well, I just figured it was a secret mission or something." Hall hesitates. "You know Washington. It's all politics."

"No, John," I say. He has met the enemy, but if he is one of them, he is doing a very good impersonation of an ignorant fool. And I am pretty sure he is too much of an ignorant fool to be that good at impersonations. He does not know what he has been used for. "It's politics if the law allows it. This is something different."

Hall's expression suggests that the distinction has not yet occurred to him. "Well," he says doubtfully, "it's still the higher-ups."

I change tack. "So what were they doing?"

"He'd ask me questions sometimes. About clerks, what their status was, whether I could move up the induction date. I looked into it."

"Did you ever get any questions about me?"

The smile returns to Hall's face. "Come on, Cash. You know I'd look out for you. But no. No one pushed on you."

"And who was pushing on Gene?"

"I told you, they use code names. Cato, Brutus, the Farmer."

"But you met this man. The one who calls himself Cato."

"He was in the Fly Club with me," says Hall. "No one you'd know."

"Karl Bendetsen?"

Hall actually laughs. "Bendetsen's not a Harvard man. And he's not club-bable anyway."

"I'd club him," I say. "Or punch him. Whatever you do at Harvard."

"Yeah, soldiers," the comic repeats. "Seen that Pentagon? Can't really miss it. Am I right?" There is a shouted expletive from my left, but whether it is directed at him or the navy is unclear. The comic wavers. "A woman gave birth in there once," he says. "Couldn't get out in time." His voice gains force again; this must be one of his better jokes. "Guard says to her, 'Lady, you shouldn't have come in here pregnant.' She says . . ."

He does not finish. The controversy over the WAVES has reached a boiling point. At the adjacent table the debaters burst to their feet. Others join in; the crowd swells and flows across the floor. Men stumble past us, locked in struggle. Bodies collide with tables and chairs. Hall and I hunch down, protecting our drinks. Someone's elbow hits the back of my head and I hear Hall gasp in surprise and pain.

The house lights dim and with a rustling flap a large American flag unfurls above the dance floor. The spotlight swivels onto it, and the band launches into "The Star-Spangled Banner," presto e forte. The Double Door management evidently has a plan for these occasions.

And it works. The men on the dance floor leave off pummeling each other and snap to attention. Those still at the tables rise and salute. Without conscious intent, I find that I am on my feet too, hand over heart. Only Hall is sitting, holding his glass. "Christ, John," I say. "You're the one who's in the War Department. Can't you stand for your flag?"

He turns his face to me. There is something desperate there, a plea rising from the bones and up through the skin. He puts his hands on the table and pushes himself halfway to a standing position. "Help me, Cash." It's a phrase I've never heard from him before, and he seems puzzled himself to be using it now. One hand reaches out for me, and without its support he goes facedown on the scarred wood. Now I can see the bloodstain spreading across his back. "Help me, Cash."

Men are pouring into the room. The Navy shore patrol is here, the military police. The flag flutters under its spotlight. I notice a small electric fan providing the breeze. The colors sway gently as the music fades. At my side, John Hall twitches once and is still.

CHAPTER 39

THERE IS A shivering unreality to the air as I walk from Main Justice to the Court, the chill of approaching fall. It is the same walk I took after meeting Hoover for the first time. After the first of my friends was killed. A strange thirst grips my throat. Fall does not seem like a renewal now. I flit about on my investigations, but something is waiting.

On the street are portents. A bird has stunned itself against a window and lies trembling on the sidewalk. "He's dead," a man says as I stoop over it.

"It's breathing. Its feathers are moving."

"That's just the wind." He walks away. The small body shakes. One eye blinks at me. Can it understand that I mean no harm, that I want to help? I wrap it in a newspaper and carry it to a secluded spot, a soft patch of grass under a tree. When I try to lay it down, it rolls out with its feet curled, obviously dead. There are tears in my eyes. For the bird, for Hall, for me. I cannot save them; I cannot even understand why they die. Gene Gressman poisoned, John Hall struck down in a dirty bar, a sparrow that saw only sky.

Outside the Court I stand still for a moment, composing myself. There is work to be done. Then I go to the Maryland Avenue entrance where Frankfurter's new clerk is waiting. He is not as trusted as Phil Haynes, it seems, for he ushers me to the Justice's chambers and then leaves us, shutting the door behind him.

"Well," says Felix Frankfurter. He stretches in his chair. "You need feel no regrets that you are shirking danger in this job." He stops. "I am sorry. I knew John Hall. He was a good man, as good a man as he could be."

I suppose that is true. Hall was never a very close friend, and despite all he said, our working relationship was basically adversarial. Still, we were boys together, and part of my childhood is gone with him. The innumerable Merion afternoons we spent lashing the squash ball against the wall exist in my mind alone now, and what lives in only one mind has a weak claim to reality.

"We've learned something, though," I say. "We know they were drafting clerks. We're on the right track."

"Yes," says Frankfurter. "But we suspected that already. And we knew that to do so they must have a presence in the War Department. It is confirmed, but we do not know who they are."

"Hall said they used code names. They sounded Roman. They didn't mean anything to me."

"That is a clue. Can you remember?"

"Cato," I say. "That was the Army man. Brutus. And something else. It wasn't a name. The Planter?"

Frankfurter looks at me oddly. "The Farmer?"

"Yes, that was it. How did you know?"

"I know those names." He is frowning. "They are the Anti-Federalists, from 1788. You've heard of the Federalist Papers, of course, the writings in favor of the Constitution. These are their foes. The pseudonyms of men who argued against ratification."

"What does that mean?"

Frankfurter is still frowning, but now he begins to nod. "They feared the power of the federal government. Of course. They warned it would become a tyrant. It makes perfect sense."

"How does it make sense?"

"It is as I said. These are the enemies of the New Deal. They think that Roosevelt has proven the Anti-Federalists right, that he is on the road to dictatorship. So they take the names of their prophets to fight back."

He is right; there is a sense to it. "But how does that fit with the Japanese cases? If you're worried about government tyranny, that's got to fit the bill."

"Tyranny over people like you," says Frankfurter. "They are not so concerned with the liberty of the enemy within." Bitterness enters his voice. "The unlike, the other." He waves a hand, dismissing it. "I have never believed those cases are as central as you think. This plan has been long afoot, and it has focused on the rights of capital. They may have no involvement with the Japanese at all."

"I think they do," I say. "I think that's why they killed Gene."

"Did John Hall confirm that?"

"No." In fact, I think, he suggested otherwise. The machinations he described in the Japanese cases were those of the War Department alone. "But he did say they wanted him gone."

Frankfurter shrugs. "We have discussed this before. Mr. Gressman was an inconvenience for multiple reasons. We will not know which was the motive until we find the killers."

"And how do we do that now that Hall's dead?" The information was there with him all along, within my reach on any of those afternoons at the Metropolitan Club. I burn with regret for the lost opportunity, and then shame for missing it and not Hall himself.

"John Hall was your liaison," says Frankfurter. "I am sure there is a way you can learn who he was talking to."

· · · ·

I am sure there is, but as I make my way back to Main Justice, I cannot think of it. Instead, a new question has entered my mind, calling my attention like a tap on the shoulder. *Hey*, a voice says. *Hey, pal, why wasn't it you?*

You need feel no regrets that you are shirking danger, Frankfurter said. He was trying to make me feel better about failing the physical, about not being in uniform. But it has made me feel worse, or understand why I feel bad. John Hall did not just die helping me, like Gene Gressman did. He died instead of me; he took my place.

Hall was killed for giving me information, to stop my search from progressing. But there is an easier way to do that, more direct, more certain, and more permanent. If my prying about is the problem, why kill John Hall? Why not me?

Dark suits course past me on the sidewalk. The sky is an uninformative blue. I shake my head. I can see why they struck at Gene Gressman. He was the threat; he was the obstacle. But now, surely, it is me. Hall by himself was no danger to them. In fact, he was useful.

The limestone facade rises in front of me. Main Justice has its own legend over the Constitution Avenue entrance, *Lege atque Ordine Omnia Fiunt*, Law and Order Make Everything. The statues wait in the Great Hall, but I do not go in. I am not the quickest thinker, but I get there in the end. I am more dangerous to them than Hall. If I am still alive, it must be that I am also more useful. Clara was right, I think. I am one of them. Somehow I am serving their purposes even now.

It must be through my work at Justice. Now I enter the building. Nothing else I do could be of any interest to them. It is that I am defending the evacuation and detention; that is what keeps me alive. They think I can win the cases I have just decided to lose.

I wave at Edward Ennis as I pass his office, then turn into mine and take a seat at my desk. There are papers scattered across the wood and a blank sheet of paper in my typewriter. They'd be fools to think me an irreplaceable litigator. It is probably my tie to Black. They're worried about his vote; they think I know how to persuade him. As indeed I may, if I've learned anything from Gene Gressman; I've seen it done. Of course, I will be pushing from the other side.

And if they learn that, they will surely try to stop me. But even if they think I am helping them, I do not think I will long outlive my usefulness. I am an irritant that must someday be addressed. When these cases are decided, my shield will be gone.

What keeps you safe in the world? Principles, Judge Skinner told me, creases in paper. Family, my father said, one's class and one's kind. Hard work, I thought in the blooming shell of youth. Optimism and endurance. Stay positive, stay determined. Most of all, stay young. I see now it is youth that protects you, and the innocent world in which youth lives. But I am running low on innocence. Behind the bright, familiar surface of things is a dark and formless void. I can feel it reaching for me, the world beneath this one, the realm of the other. A soldier at the door, a too-familiar face on the street. A knife in the back. The dark hand reaches out, the floor drops away.

Vertigo sweeps over me. I lean forward over the desk, my head in my hands. The only way out is to find them first, but I don't know how. And I can't slow down the cases to give myself more time. In fact, I have to move them forward. I have to write a draft of the brief by the end of the day. At least that is a distraction from these thoughts. I crank the paper down into the typewriter and try to find refuge in work.

Where is the law in Korematsu's story? Where are the bright fish? Just as in *Hirabayashi*, it is a question of whom to trust. Again I see the faces, but there are more of them now. I see Karl Bendetsen writing the brief of the Pacific states when Justice refused to stand behind his facts. I see John Hall revising the Final Report when he thought it would undermine the position of the War Department. Francis Biddle looking down, unable to meet Rowe's eyes. And what has gone on that I do not see? There are no silver glints of law here. We are in the dark caverns where sunlight cannot come and the fish are strange blind things that prey upon each other without mercy.

The main thing to do is to cast doubt on the Final Report. I insert a footnote. We endorse the Final Report as a description of the evacuation, I write. *However, the facts offered as military justification, particularly the claims about the use of illegal radio transmitters and ship-to-shore signaling, are inconsistent with information in the possession of the Department of Justice.*

For the rest, I cobble together as unconvincing a defense of evacuation as I can, hoping the Court will see it for what it is. This is what Rowe did with the *Hirabayashi* brief, and it failed then, but perhaps I will have better luck. I send the draft to Charles Fahy. Now it is time to pay a visit to the Pentagon.

• • • •

I still have nothing definite in mind as I cross the river. My first thought was to get FBI support. With a borrowed badge, I could enter Hall's office; I could pretend to be part of the investigation. But Hoover is not in a mood to do me any more favors.

John Hall's secretary is a strawberry blond holding a tissue to her nose. When I see the black dress and the red eyes, a plan starts to form. I lean close over the desk and lower my voice to a confidential tone. "I'm Cash Harrison,"

I say. "From the Department of Justice." I give her a look at my card. "I was Captain Hall's contact there. I'm sorry for your loss."

"Thank you," she says.

I look around as though checking to be sure we're not overheard. "I have an unconventional request," I say.

"What do you mean?"

"I don't know if you're aware of this, but John Hall was no ordinary lawyer."

Her lips part. "He wasn't?"

I shake my head. Whether this works at all depends on whether I have guessed right about Hall. "No," I say. "He had a secret mission."

Tears start in her eyes. "He hinted at it sometimes. I didn't know whether to believe him. I thought maybe he was just . . . talking. The way men do."

Hall has come through for me. And in a way, I suppose, I am coming through for him, too late for it to do him any good. "Oh, no. It was all true."

The secretary is biting her lip. "I hope I helped him," she says. "He said there was no one he could trust, no one he could talk to."

I can hear the words, see the look of soulful torment on his big, dumb face. A pang of loss shoots through me. I will miss that idiot. "I'm sure you did," I say. "And don't feel bad for him. He chose that life. He knew the risks. And he was one of our best." I pause to let her wipe her eyes. "John Hall was a hero," I say. "He was uncovering a nest of spies here in Washington. That's why he was killed. Now, you can let everything he worked for die with him, or you can help me."

The girl quivers with emotion, and then her face glows with resolve. She is about eighteen, I think, from God knows where. She must have felt very lucky she knew how to type when the call went out. Fifty cents an hour. And then to be assigned to the War Department, to the dashing if somewhat forward Captain John Hall . . . Well, I am lying to her just as he did, but there may be a bit more basis to my claims about serving her country.

"I need to go into his office," I say. "I know I'm asking you to bend the rules. I won't blame you if you say you can't. I'll walk out of here and you'll never see me again. And somewhere, some Nazi will wipe the blood off his knife and breathe a little easier."

The key is in her hand before I finish. She opens the door; I duck inside. She makes to follow me and I hold up a hand.

"Sorry," I say. "The less you know about this, the safer you are." It is true for her, I think, if not for me. I close the door with a confidence I do not feel, but she does not protest.

A desk and credenza dominate Hall's office. His bookshelves hold folders. On the wall is the standard picture of Roosevelt and two framed diplomas. For anyone too far away to read them, there is also a felt Harvard banner pinned to a corkboard.

Hall was a well-organized boy at Episcopal Academy, and I am glad to see that he kept this trait in the War Department. His files are tidy. But what am I looking for? I can only hope that I'll know it when I see it.

I start with the bookshelves. Hall has folders about the various legal engagements of the War Department. *Korematsu* and *Endo*, of course, as they progressed up the ladder of appeals. *Hirabayashi*, too, and the Nazi saboteurs' case. Other cases related to the detention. Newspaper clippings and magazines, all sorts of memorabilia. Photos of Hall with beribboned men in uniform.

Does it mean something? The stories he clipped, the photos he saved? Everything seems significant now, pregnant with a hidden meaning. But I cannot coax it out.

I sit down in Hall's chair and realize that I am sweating. Searching this office, entering by deception . . . inside the Pentagon, that must be a serious offense. I am violating national security laws, and Hoover will have no mercy if I am caught.

I open one drawer, then another. A bottle of whiskey, a stack of War Department letterhead, a dime-store Western. I reach for the next. My shirt is sticking to my ribs under the armpits, along the sides. It clings and releases as I pull out the drawer. A folder labeled *Final Report*.

The telephone rings and I jerk upright in the chair. I watch the phone until the noise stops, trying to slow my breathing. I am spending too much time with my hands in dead men's desks. The folder holds a copy of the report delivered to me and a letter from Warrant Officer Theodore Smith testifying that he personally observed the burning of the original version. I try to think. These are War Department machinations. The Anti-Federalists are somewhere else. Bendetsen's not a Harvard man, Hall said. Not clubbable.

The rattle of the doorknob interrupts my thoughts. I hear the secretary's voice outside the door and then another, male. "But you have a key, don't you?"

God, I think. *This is it*. I crouch down behind the desk. Stupid, pointless. I stand up again. Face the music.

". . . not to be opened," the secretary is saying. "The MPs were very clear." I have to give her credit; her voice is calmer than mine would be. A few more words I don't catch, then silence.

I pull on the credenza door. Locked. But Hall is kind enough to keep the key in the top drawer of his desk. Now it is open. The knob has the wet print of my hand. There are more papers inside. The FCC report about radio signals, the ONI one about subversives. I shake my head, missing him less. Drafts of briefs for Fred Korematsu and Mitsuye Endo, revised in longhand, crumpled and stained. Someone has been going through the ACLU's garbage. My government at work.

I stand up, put my hands to my face, and breathe into them. I still have nothing. My fingers press into my forehead. I can feel sweat trickle down the inside of my bicep as my arms drop. Look, Cash. Think.

Next to the telephone on Hall's desk is a daily planner. Would he? It is worth a shot.

I flip the pages. He has meetings recorded, golf scores, telephone numbers. Some names I recognize, some I don't. Bendetsen, Ennis, Biddle, Frankfurter. A good deal of Phil Haynes. And, at various dates and times, symbols that look for all the world like some sort of cipher. John Hall the secret agent, advertising the clandestine. But there is no way I can crack the code. Unless there's an overlapping record.

I sidle to the office door and listen carefully. There is only the clicking of typewriter keys. I turn the knob and slip out. The secretary looks up hopefully. "Did you find what you were looking for?"

"I think so," I say. "But I need your help. Did you keep Captain Hall's appointments?"

She nods, opening her desk.

"Anything for the evening of May 17?" I ask.

"No."

"July 7?"

"No."

"August 12? Last Wednesday night?"

"No." There is a squeak in her voice, and she is bending very far forward, her face hidden from view. Looking down I can see the back of her neck turning red. Now I understand what Hall was recording. Maybe one during working hours, then.

"June 24, 10 a.m."

There is the rustle of pages turning. She doesn't say a word, just slides the calendar to the side for me to see. I read the name written there.

Her voice is still shaky. "Do you need anything else?"

"No," I say. "You've done your country a great service today." In fact, there is one more piece of information I need, but there is no reason to torture her further. Somewhere in the Pentagon there is surely someone else who can tell me where to find the man I last saw wrestling with Drew Pearson on Cissy Patterson's floor. Someone else can point me to the office of Colonel Bill Richards.

CHAPTER 40

RICHARDS'S DOOR IS closed, but it is not locked. I open it and step inside before his secretary can object. His office looks much like Hall's, but it is larger, large enough that the flag standing in the corner does not look too out of place. Like Hall, he has a picture of Roosevelt, but it has been placed on a low shelf of the bookcase. On the wall above his desk is a print of a man I do not recognize.

"Hello, Bill," I say.

He is reading the Sears catalog and seems flustered at my entrance. Perhaps he has a guilty conscience, or perhaps he is embarrassed at being caught perusing ladies' swimwear. He puts down the catalog but does not stand. "Mr. Harrison," he says slowly. I cannot quite place his tone. "What can I do for you?"

"I'm here about a friend," I say. "Or two. Let's start with John Hall."

He looks at me blankly. "What about him?"

"He was working with you."

"Sometimes."

"But not on War Department business."

Richards hesitates. "Sometimes. Why are you here?"

"Why is John Hall dead?"

Now he looks puzzled. "I hardly think I'm the right person to ask. Call your priest. Or the shore patrol."

"No," I say. "I think you have a pretty good idea. Cato."

"What are you getting at?" He doesn't deny the name, and that's enough of a confession for me.

"You had Hall killed because he was talking to me. Because he was spilling your secrets."

"Don't be ridiculous." Richards shakes his head. "I didn't know he was talking to you, and why would I care if he was? I haven't done anything wrong."

"You and your Anti-Federalist pals."

"Yes." He nods. "The Anti-Federalist Society!" He widens his eyes for effect. "You've found us out! So what? We are only doing what any patriots would. Standing against dictatorship and socialism."

"You call it patriotism."

"Yes!" An edge of frustration enters his voice. "Look around you, Cash. They're ruining this country. And you're helping them. You'll see where this goes. Do you want to be the last generation to know freedom?"

"You think that justifies murder?"

"What the hell are you talking about?"

"Gene Gressman," I say. "Investigating attempts to influence the Supreme Court through clerks. Dead. John Hall. Talking to me about your little Anti-Federalist club. Dead. You want to explain that?"

"I'm sorry about your friends," Richards says. "I don't know anything about Gene Gressman. John Hall, I liked him myself. But there's nothing to explain. They got the guy."

"What?"

"Earlier today. He confessed. Pulled a knife to defend himself when the fight started, got thrown up against Hall in the scrum. Involuntary manslaughter. You have a very active imagination, Cash."

"Bullshit!" I say. I have the sense that something is slipping from my grasp. "Don't lie to me. You killed them. You or your friends. And I'm next on the list, as soon as I'm not useful anymore. Don't think I don't know it."

Richards is shaking his head. "I don't know where you're getting these ideas, but you're way off base. Yes, we tried to influence the Court. You can see for yourself it didn't work. Yes, we called ourselves the Anti-Federalists."

He gestures upward. "Patrick Henry's on my wall. No one had anyone killed. No one wants to kill you. It's harmless fun."

"Okay," I say. "If it's so harmless, tell me who the others are."

Richards shrugs. He has a smile that's halfway to a smirk. "What makes you think you don't know them already?"

"Give me their names."

"I don't betray my friends."

"What clerks did you place on the Court?"

He shakes his head. "I respect a man's privacy." The smile is entirely smirk now, as though he is telling a joke no one else can hear. "You don't need to worry about us, Cash. We're on your side. Go back to work."

Frustration builds inside me. "John Hall talked to me on the phone the night he was killed," I say. "That's how they knew where he was."

"That's not what happened."

"Entertain my fantasy for a minute, Bill. Suppose it was. Suppose my phone's tapped. And now suppose I go back home and talk up a storm about how helpful a certain colonel was. How he gave me all the names. Sold out Brutus to save his skin. Promised me more the next time we meet. What's going to happen to you then? Think your friends might start to wonder about you? Might use a knife to find out if your heart's still in the right place?"

It's the wrong tack. Richards's face hardens. "You think I'll talk if you threaten me? You have no idea of honor, do you? No idea of principle. No wonder you're so eager to follow. Just do what the boss tells you. You're a slave, Cash. You're contemptible."

His tone is sincere, so much that I feel stirrings of doubt as I leave the building. The weather has changed, rain coming down in sheets as evening lowers. By the time I find a taxi it has soaked me through. The vastness of the Pentagon fades into the dusk behind me. Richards is proud of what he is doing. He is a patriot, a man of honor, with nothing to cover up by killing Hall. Uncertainty seeps through my mind. A bad heart, an accident, an overactive imagination. Water pools on the seat beside me. Harmless fun. An innocent club inflated into a murderous conspiracy, the dark forces I chase only shadows.

• • • •

"Cash," says Felix Frankfurter. His voice is surprised. "You're wet."

"I left my umbrella at home."

"They may be acquired at the Pentagon. Even on the street, I believe."

"Does it really matter?"

"This is how one catches cold. Particularly as the seasons change. No, don't." He stops me before I can sit, retrieves a hand towel from the washroom and dabs at me, concern on his face. "Also, these chairs are mine. Louis XIV. A dealer in New York."

"I found Cato," I say.

Frankfurter's eyes spark behind his small glasses. "Who?"

"An Army colonel named Bill Richards."

"And?"

"And he admitted it. Sort of. There is an Anti-Federalist Society, trying to place conservative clerks on the Court. But he wouldn't confess to anything more than that. Nothing to do with Gene or John Hall."

"You think he was holding back."

I look down. Despite Frankfurter's ministrations, my hair is dripping. I dab at a wet spot on the chair cushion and enlarge it. "I don't know. He sounded pretty convincing."

Frankfurter is nodding. "We must proceed logically. The simplest hypothesis that accounts for all the facts. What is left unexplained, if he is telling the truth?"

"The certificates at Tule Lake."

"True." Another nod. "Something is going on there. But it may be entirely unrelated. We do not need to make your Colonel Richards a murderer to explain those."

I frown, thinking. "What about the man who followed Clara at Dupont Circle? He wasn't yours. He was going to hurt her."

"He was not mine, it is true," says Frankfurter. "But do we know what he intended?"

"He left quick enough when I told him the FBI was there."

"I might do that too if a stranger accosted me. But it is a point. And there are the deaths. Still . . ." He hesitates. "The mind craves patterns; it craves reasons. For misfortune most of all." He is looking at me in a kindly way.

"Many things go on and many can be strung together on threads of theory. But that does not mean they are connected in reality. What interest would the Anti-Federalists have in the Japanese?" I am silent. "I am sure that they have tried to influence the Court," he continues. "But they failed. Would they really think that killing Mr. Gressman would make a difference? Enough to drive them to murder? We may have leapt too quickly at that answer. There was a history of arrhythmia."

"I know he had a bad heart," I say. My hand is massaging a watermark on the silk cushion. "That's why the poison worked." Frankfurter's face shows sympathy tinged with concern. "The original Farmer," I say. "The man from 1788. Who was he?"

"No one knows. Cato was the governor of New York. Brutus was a judge. The Farmer . . . it is a matter of speculation."

"What if this one's really a farmer? What if he's got a stake in California land? That would explain their interest in the renunciations."

Frankfurter sighs. "Perhaps. A well-chosen hypothesis can explain any fact. But we should be sure first that there is indeed something to explain. And as I said, I am growing less sure that anyone would see enough gain to justify murder."

I shake my head. *Nothing to worry about*, Richards said. *We're on your side.* John Hall, too. And Haynes, now that I think of it. *It's your imagination*, he said when I asked him about the tails—a lie, of course, since he knew those were Frankfurter's men. And in the hallway, after Gene's death. *Don't be silly, pal, we're all on the same side.* Maybe they were. Suddenly I am wondering whether Gene could have been right about Haynes after all.

Frankfurter is still talking. "We are left with speculation," he says. "It is unfortunate that there is no direct proof to hand."

But perhaps there is. "Justice," I say. "Do you have something Phil Haynes touched?"

Frankfurter's eyes narrow. "Why?"

"I can settle this," I tell him. "Maybe. There was a fingerprint on Gene's coffee can. You give me something he touched, and we can see if they match."

"Who took that print?" His voice is sharp.

"I did."

"At whose behest? Who did you give it to?"

"I was working with the FBI."

"Hoover." The word is a hiss.

"I took the prints, that's all. No agent went into Murphy's chambers. No one took anything else out."

Frankfurter shakes his head. "You are playing a dangerous game. I am not sure you know how dangerous."

"Do you have something he touched?"

"Of course I do." He looks at me a moment, considering. "I do not think Mr. Haynes is a suspect. You know I hired him myself."

"Still," I say. "It's possible, right? What's the harm in trying?"

"Maybe nothing," says Frankfurter. "Or maybe you will learn that J. Edgar Hoover is not a man to trifle with." He pulls out his handkerchief and uses it to remove something from the desk. "You may try this." It is a framed photograph of the two of them. At the sight of Haynes's face I feel a surge of hatred. "The glass should be an excellent surface."

· · · ·

The next day, I take the photograph to the lab myself. We will find out, one way or the other. "Dust this," I tell the technicians. "I want to know if there's a match for the foreign print from the Supreme Court." It is my last shot, and if it does not pay off, perhaps I will give up. Perhaps they are right; perhaps this is nothing but my imagination.

In the meantime, it is back to work. My draft of the *Korematsu* brief has returned. The changes are few, but Fahy has instructed me to remove my footnote disavowing the Final Report and replace it with one of his own. *With respect to the recital of the circumstances justifying the evacuation, the views of this Department differ.* "That could mean anything," I complain to Ennis. "It could mean we don't agree that we hampered their operation and endangered the West Coast. We need something more."

"Yeah."

"So what do we do? Write another memo?"

"No," he says. "This time we'll go see him."

Fahy has Roosevelt's photo on his desk. The wall above holds the

Department's seal, an eagle atop a shield, arrows and olive branch in its talons. About the room are the usual accoutrements of scales and blindfolds. There is one bit of additional color, a Navy Cross he earned in the Great War. When this one is over, I think, we will have to change that name.

Fahy is sitting at his desk, a newspaper open in front of him. Herbert Wechsler stands at his left elbow. I remember Wechsler pacing in front of the blackboard at Columbia, chalk in hand, asking us to identify principles. At Justice he must be pacing less; three years have laid their flesh on him, drawn new lines on his face. "What is it?" Fahy asks.

"The footnote," Ennis says.

"The Final Report," I say.

There is a soft rustle as Fahy turns the page. "What about it?"

"It's lies," I say. "We need to disavow it."

Fahy sets the paper down. I glimpse the headline as he folds it over: *Polish Home Army Surrenders*. The Warsaw uprising is over and the Russians only watched. Fahy shakes his head. "I know there are some statements about disloyalty that we haven't been able to verify."

"We've proved they're false," Ennis says.

Fahy ignores him. "But doubt about loyalty is all that's needed to justify the evacuation. There was uncertainty; there was limited time."

"That's not true, either," I put in.

Wechsler steps forward. "You are not the judge here, Mr. Harrison. Nor am I. We are lawyers. We are the President's lawyers. We are working with the War Department, and I can tell you they were not happy with your footnote."

"We are not the President's lawyers," Ennis says. "We represent the United States. We don't defend something just because the President says to. And all he wants is to put off release past the election."

"The politics are not our concern," says Fahy quietly. "Only the legal justification."

"Would you trust a Republican to finish this war?" Wechsler's voice is louder. "Thomas Dewey, with all of two years as a governor?"

"So that's the reason?" I ask. I strain to remember the phrase he used in class. "The principle that transcends the result in this particular case?"

Wechsler smiles, and something in his face chills me. He opens the paper to a new page, folds it into neat quarters. "Have you heard of a place called Maj-danek?" There is death in his eyes, though his voice is calm. "It's in Poland. The Red Army took it in July. Our reporters are there now."

He passes the paper across. A line of Russian soldiers stands in front of a warehouse. The entire foreground of the photo is filled with a pile of small dark objects. I cannot recognize them. "What are those?"

"Shoes," Wechsler says. "Those are the eight hundred thousand empty shoes of people who went to the gas chambers." He looks at me with the expression he reserved for the exceptionally slow students. "Do you understand now? That's who we're fighting. That's why we have to win. And that's why I want Roosevelt in charge, not the little man from the top of the wedding cake."

The magnitude of the number stuns me to silence. But not Ennis. "That's the whole point," he says. "Not that anything we do to beat them is justified. It's that we don't do things like that. Not to innocent people, our own citizens. Never."

"I am familiar with the principle, thank you," Wechsler says. "*Ye'horeg v'al ya'avor,* as the owners of those shoes would have put it. Even under threat of death, some transgressions must be avoided. And I believe it, as a lawyer and as an American. I am doing nothing wrong here." He looks at Fahy, and Ennis and I do too.

Fahy clears his throat. He takes the paper from my hands and spreads it out again. "I will argue the case as we have prepared it," he says. I have to lean in to hear the words. "We will file the brief as it is written."

CHAPTER 41

IN THE HALLWAY, Ennis looks at me. "Maybe a memo next time," he says.

"Maybe no next time," I say. "Did I tell you Rowe left me a resignation letter? For when my continued representation of the government was inconsistent with the interests of Justice."

"He had a sense of humor," Ennis says. He pauses. "Look, Rowe didn't resign. He got drafted."

"He was thinking about it. After the meeting when Biddle signed off on evacuation. It's in his files."

"Right," says Ennis. "But I told him something. You're an American, I said. This is your country, the one that exists in the real world, not some idealized version in your mind. You're thinking about resigning now because you don't want to be in the real America anymore. It doesn't match your vision of what it should be, and you won't stand for that. But guess what? Karl Bendetsen has an America in his mind too, that doesn't match this one, and he's working very hard to make it real. If you don't want that, the real world is the only place to meet him. You can win all the battles in your mind, but the ones that count are here. This is where you can still do some good."

I think of Bill Fitch and Vern Countryman, crossing the skies on their nation's business, of Gene Gressman promising to wait as long as it took to undo the evacuation. "Maybe."

Ennis nods encouragement. "We'll talk to Charles Horsky again. Tell him to attack the Final Report as hard as he can. Fahy's not going to disavow it, but he can't defend it either. The Court may go our way."

"Maybe," I say again. And I go to my office to think about the good I can still do.

I am waiting for a phone call from the FBI lab technicians, but it does not come. Instead there is a knock at the door and the burly figure of Clyde Tolson enters my office.

He says nothing by way of greeting, and I do not stand. "Whose fingerprint is that?" he asks.

I try not to betray my excitement. "I take it there was a match?"

Tolson steps closer to my desk. "Obstruction of justice is a felony, Mr. Harrison. Whose fingerprint?"

"I'm not obstructing anything. Find your own fingerprints. No one's stopping you."

"Is it Frankfurter's? If you are covering for him, you are making a serious mistake." I say nothing. "He cannot protect you," Tolson continues.

"From you?" I remember the visit to Hoover's office. The massive flags, the raised desk. "Maybe not, but I think Francis Biddle can."

Tolson stares at me for a long moment, unblinking. "We shall see about that, Mr. Harrison."

. . . .

When he leaves, I take Gene Gressman's papers out of my desk and look at them. The circled names, the cases, the connecting lines. Haynes is there. Frankfurter too, of course, but Gene was right to see Frankfurter pulling strings. He was just wrong to think they were working together, wrong to suppose that all the distortions in the picture flowed from a single source. Finally it is coming clear to me. The War Department, the Anti-Federalists, Frankfurter too, each with a different design. They are like radio signals interfering with each other, patterns blending together into meaningless noise.

I put the papers away and walk outside. Somewhere in the static is a message, if I can isolate it. Haynes was a plant, who managed to get hired by Frankfurter. And he killed Gene. But why? And for whom? Humid air fills my lungs. Someone thought Gene dangerous enough to kill him, and then John Hall too.

And if them, surely me. Richards's reassurances mean nothing, I realize. Maybe he was telling the truth; maybe the Anti-Federalists have no desire to hurt me. But if he was no party to the murders already committed, that only means he has no way of knowing what else is planned. The ice splits; the trapdoor swings open. I look at the pavement as I walk, hearing the creak of hinges, looking for a starburst of cracks at my feet.

I have to find them first.

. . . .

"I got the results," I tell Frankfurter. "A print on the picture frame you gave me matches the one from Gene Gressman's coffee can."

"Phil Haynes," he says. The smile with which he greeted me is entirely gone. "He worked with me. Dined at my house." He collects himself. "So," he says. "I have kept my friends close and my enemies closer." He polishes his pince-nez. "The tactic is less effective if you do not know which is which."

"Where is he now?"

"New York," says Frankfurter. "Commercial litigation. But he is not beyond my reach, you may be sure."

"We need to find out who he was working for," I say. "Make him tell us before they come for me." I hesitate. "But Justice . . ."

"What?"

"Don't just use Haynes for information. Don't tell him it's okay if he talks. He killed my friend. I want him punished."

Frankfurter is smiling again, but there is nothing twinkly or avuncular about it. Haynes has sinned against him as well, I realize, and in his eyes that is perhaps more grave. "You need have no fear on that score," he says.

. . . .

The Supreme Court holds the oral argument in *Korematsu* on October 11. *Americans Blast 38 Ships off Japan*, reads the *Post*'s morning headline. The war news is all good now. The strange names we learned as the Japanese moved west in the early days are back in the paper, each bloody battle reduced to a few columns of newsprint, another landing on another little island. They are running out of men and machines; their planes are old and their pilots young. Air combat is a turkey shoot for our Hellcats. In the Marianas we down more than two hundred in an afternoon.

I sit at the counsel table with Ennis and Fahy. Biddle has not come to the argument. The evacuation was unconstitutional, he is saying now; he will not be in court to defend it. I wish he had offered us these thoughts in time to include them in the brief.

We have other supporters. War Department officials pack the front row of spectators. Uniforms to fill in the background, they tell us. To remind the Justices we're still at war.

I mutter insincere thanks. To my right I can see the clerks assembled in their gallery, Clara hiding behind the Douglas column. She is safe, at least; Miller has reported that no more apes pursue her.

"All rise," calls the marshal, and we stand as the Justices file in. They take their seats. There is Frankfurter, his face inscrutable; there is Black, and I think I catch a smile. He will come around if we can give him the truth. Frankfurter will not help me with these cases, I am sure. He will wrap his head in the flag, say that the President can do no wrong. But he will find me Haynes and the men who directed him, and that means that I can concentrate on swinging Hugo Black.

Charles Horsky is first to the podium. Military necessity did not require the evacuation, he tells the Court. There has been no proof of disloyalty; there are no facts in the government's brief that establish a threat.

Frankfurter interrupts. "Do you think we can say that there were no other facts that General DeWitt knew that we do not? Did he say he had no other facts?"

I cannot figure out where he is going with this question, and neither can Horsky. Imagining facts that DeWitt left unreported makes no sense, especially given that the facts he did report were false.

"General DeWitt issued a report that gave his facts," says Horsky. "He did not indicate that there were any others." He pauses. "Indeed, the government's brief in this case concedes that the military judgment was based on attitudes and opinions rather than objective facts. And I would like to call the Court's attention to an extraordinary footnote. 'With respect to the circumstances surrounding the evacuation, the views of this Department differ.'" He pauses again, while I think about how much better my original footnote would have sounded in the marble chamber.

"What does this mean?" Horsky opens his hands above the podium. "The government does not endorse General DeWitt's Final Report. But what do they think of it? They do not tell us. Parts of it, one might conclude, are false. But which parts? They do not tell us." Beside me, Fahy stiffens. Horsky leans forward. "They ask for trust when they are evidently concealing something. It is not the role of this Court to blindly approve the government's actions."

Ennis is smiling as Horsky sits down, and I am thinking he has done a good job. I have helped Fahy practice his argument, and he has nothing to counter the attack on the Final Report. What he has planned to say is mostly irrelevant now.

I would not like to be in Fahy's shoes, and he seems troubled, chewing his lower lip as he approaches the podium. "If the Court please," he says, "before I begin the main argument, I should like to say that the government stands undivided in support of the evacuation program."

I am taken aback. It is not the opening I have heard him rehearse. "My friend here has just suggested that some footnote in our brief rejects General DeWitt's Final Report and with it the military necessity for the evacuation. That is a neat piece of fancy dancing. The judgment of the government—not just the military, but the whole government—has always been that the measures taken were justified. We maintain that position."

Ennis's expression passes from shock to anger to sorrow. At the other table I can see consternation on Horsky's face. No doubt he is wondering if we've taken him for a ride.

"So what about this Final Report?" asks Justice Black. "Do you say the Court is required to accept the facts it asserts?"

"Not all of them, Your Honor," says Fahy. For someone making up an argument on the spot, I have to admit he is doing a pretty good job. "But the Court should consider them as evidence of what the general was thinking, his motives, and what he based his decision on."

"And you think those facts are an adequate justification?"

"We do. A complete justification."

"Does each Justice have a copy of that report?" Chief Justice Stone asks.

"I think not, Your Honor," says Fahy, "but I am sure the War Department can provide one."

"Please make sure it does," says Stone, and Fahy nods.

Beside me, Ennis lets out an audible groan. Our strategy of encouraging Horsky to attack the Final Report has backfired horribly. It has driven Fahy to provide a full-throated defense.

Justice Murphy clears his throat. "What are the facts which you think most strongly support the military judgment here?"

"Consider the whole context of the decision. If the Japanese Army had landed on the West Coast, we could not have stopped them west of the Rockies. We did not know where their navy was. We did not know they had not steamed east from Pearl Harbor and were poised to fall upon California." Fahy is trying to pivot away from the Final Report, back to the broader argument we planned, but the damage is done.

"We know where that navy is now," Murphy says. "It's in pieces on the ocean floor. How can you justify excluding these people from their homes now?"

"This Court must evaluate the order as of the time it was made."

"And yet exclusion continues. The gates of the camps are still locked, the barbed wire is still on the fences. How do you explain that? Or you would say it is not at issue in this case; it is for tomorrow."

Fahy reverts to his quietest mode.

"Yes, Justice. The question of detention is presented in the *Endo* case and not this one. As to evacuation, I say this Court must only ask whether some reasonable basis for the decision existed. If it is argued that subsequent events showed it was all a mistake, that in June the Battle of Midway turned back the threat of invasion, then this is my answer." He raises his hands, fists together. "Say that to those who turned back the threat, if they can be reached where they lie at the bottom of the Pacific Ocean, among the hulls of the warships that went down with them in that battle." It is a prepared line, its rhetorical effectiveness somewhat blunted by Murphy's use of the same image. Fahy's tone turns casual again. "At the same time, as a matter of fact, the Japanese did land upon the territory of the United States, in the Aleutian Islands. In the spring of 1942, what did General

DeWitt know? He knew Japan could project its power to American soil. He had before him reports of signal lights from the coast and intercepts of unidentified radio transmissions. He concluded that military necessity required the removal of the Japanese to the interior. That conclusion was not unreasonable."

Horsky is now openly looking at me. I try not to react. It is one thing for Fahy to respond to Horsky's attacks on the Final Report by announcing that the government generally stands behind it. But now he is asserting as fact two key elements that he knows have been disproved. I wonder why I ever thought that the War Department machinations had to be the product of some external conspiracy. This is just my government at work. Who is loyal, who is not? Who is a friend and who an enemy? Whoever they say. And the government does not make mistakes.

For a moment I have some sympathy for Richards and his Anti-Federalists. But as Frankfurter pointed out, they are not concerned with the Japanese. Limits on how much wheat we can grow, tax dollars taken from paychecks before we see them, those are the signs of dictatorship that must be fought, not camps in the desert for false Americans.

"A wiser man might not have so concluded." Murphy has not given up.

"Of course," says Fahy. "The military makes mistakes." Curious, I sit straighter. "During the invasion of Sicily," he continues, "hundreds of our men were shot down by our own forces. Someone made a mistake." Ah, I think. It is not that mistakes should be corrected; it is that the fact of some mistakes legitimates others. We won't say, *Of course they can put you in a camp; after all, they could draft you* anymore; we'll say, *After all, they could shoot you by mistake.* I slouch down again. Fahy leaves a moment of silence for other questions, but there are none. "As I have said before, the government is aware that it has called upon some citizens to bear a heavy burden. But we are engaged in a war for our very survival as a nation. And in time of war, it is not enough to say, 'I am a citizen and I have rights.' One must also say, 'I am a citizen and I have obligations.'"

It is the same closing he used in *Hirabayashi*. It struck me as sensible then, and I am surprised at the violence of the revulsion it stirs in me now. Ennis snorts. Seated among the clerks, Clara shows no reaction. At the other table,

Horsky is still looking at me. As I watch, he stretches out his hand to the white quill and knocks it to the floor.

"The case is submitted," says Chief Justice Stone.

. . . .

"What was that?" Ennis asks on the way out.

"Whispering Charlie's got a fighter's instinct, I guess," I say. "They backed him into a corner and he had to come out swinging." The guess remains unconfirmed; Fahy says nothing to us after the *Korematsu* argument. The word in Main Justice is that he is furious with Horsky, but whether it is for slighting the government's integrity or for driving Fahy to stretch the truth, I have no idea.

Whatever the case, he has cooled down considerably by the time of the *Endo* argument the next day. He is silent on the way to court and sits equally silent as we wait for the Justices to take the bench. Mitsuye Endo's lawyer is named James Purcell. Justice Frankfurter requires him to walk through the procedural history of the case in some detail, perhaps for the benefit of the spectators. Once that is done, there is little left to say. "The government concedes that Miss Endo is a loyal American," Purcell says. "And it concedes that there is no authority to detain loyal Americans. There is therefore no authority to detain her." There is silence in the courtroom. "Would you like more?" Purcell asks. Justice Murphy laughs aloud. There are no questions.

Fahy continues to look down at the table for several moments after Purcell has returned to his seat. He appears to be studying the white quill in its inkwell before him. His walk to the podium is slow. As I look at his shoulders I realize how small he is. Usually he seems larger in court; he speaks for the United States, stands cloaked in its authority. But today the cloak seems to weigh on him, pressing him down even smaller.

He spreads his hands to begin the argument, but he gets no farther than "May it please the Court."

"Do you accept your opponent's claim that this case is properly before us?" Frankfurter asks.

It is an opportunity for Fahy to try to turn the argument away from substance, to see the case decided on a technicality, but the fighter's instincts he showed yesterday seem to have vanished. He waves a hand dismissively. "I have no wish to interfere with a disposition on the merits."

"What then is your argument?" asks Murphy.

Fahy is in full-whisper mode. "The only purpose of this so-called detention is protective. The Relocation Authority is willing to let Miss Endo, or any other loyal citizen, leave. They simply want to ensure that she is going to a community where untoward events can be avoided. They have her best interests at heart and are seeking only to make sure that she relocates to an appropriate place."

"But then you are not willing to let her leave," says Justice Roberts. "You won't let her go until she agrees to go somewhere you approve of. For how long do you claim you can hold her? In her best interests, let us say, can you hold her for a quarter century?"

"No," says Fahy quietly. If he overreached yesterday, he is making up for it now.

"No?" asks Roberts. "That would be a violation? But why? There may not be any place willing to accept her for twenty-five years."

Fahy does not try a direct answer. "A great deal has been accomplished under this program for the resettlement of these people," he says.

Roberts does not relent. "And in the meantime it's okay? A little violation of the Constitution might be winked at, but not a violation for twenty-five years?"

"I think not, Your Honor." Fahy sounds almost sad. "I think no violation of the Constitution should be winked at."

Chief Justice Stone intervenes. "Your argument is that the Relocation Authority is doing good by holding these people until they agree to go to placid communities. But why does the prospect of doing good give the government authority over them? Can the government detain any one of us on the grounds that it is for our own good?"

"No, Your Honor," says Fahy. "I think not." Silence falls. Like an animal playing dead, he has stilled the enthusiasm of the Justices for aggressive questioning. He has also, it seems to me, conceded every issue that matters. Unless I am gravely mistaken, the Solicitor General of the United States has just thrown a case.

"I have a word to speak for my government now," says Fahy. "We seek no scapegoat in this case. We hope this Court will reject any theory that the government of the United States is not responsible for what, in fact, it did. No person exceeded his authority here. The program of evacuation and detention was developed and implemented by the government, and if it is unconstitutional, that is what this Court must say. We should not leave any doubt what the government of the United States has done."

Again there is silence. "The case is submitted," says Stone.

Fahy leaves the courtroom ahead of us, walking fast. "Now does he ritually disembowel himself?" Ennis asks. "I hear they need people to chop off their heads in case they don't die fast enough. If there's no one else, I understand that as a citizen, I have obligations."

"I'd think you'd be happier," I say. "He all but asked them to hold detention unconstitutional."

"It doesn't matter," Ennis says. "Roosevelt's going to let them go after the election anyway. Detention's not an issue. What matters is whether they can go home without getting lynched. Fahy stood up there yesterday and said the government had good reasons to think they're disloyal. And that's what the Court's going to say, and California's not going to take them back."

I nod my head. He's right about what matters. But maybe what the Court says can still be changed.

CHAPTER 42

FROM THE FRONT row of the balcony, I look out over the Uptown Cinema. The red velvet seats are emptying, the credits scrolling up the screen. Ginger Rogers married a Nazi, but Cary Grant got her out of it. Their ship is sailing to America; sun burns away the fog and the wind blows free. Now they are gone and I am coming back to reality, breathing a harsher air. It is how I always feel when a movie ends. I want to linger in that other world, to stay with the beautiful giants, the figures of light. Silly giants; it is so clear what they must do, and it takes them so long to figure it out. Still, there is comfort in watching the process. Perhaps when the lights come up they will show our lives as equally simple, with a swell of strings letting us know the moment has come. But the beautiful giants are gone, the little world still quiet and obscure.

The seats next to me are empty, and I cannot help thinking of Gene Gressman, how he sat beside me two years ago watching Cary. That's what gave me the idea, of course, but I've done him one better. I look from side to side, then turn all the way around in my seat to scan the back. Meeting after the movie, when everyone else has gone, will make us even harder to tail. An older couple is shuffling for the exit. And there she is, in the far left corner, rising from her seat, a black dress flowing down her like water.

"So," Clara says. "You talked me into a movie after all. For reasons of security."

There is half a smile on her face as she walks toward me, and for a moment my breath is gone. But this is business. "I need to talk to you about *Korematsu*."

Clara stops. "That's what this is about? I shouldn't even be talking to you. If Douglas found out . . ."

"Wait." I take her hand before she can turn. She looks down but does not pull away. "No one knows we're here."

"I am not so sure about that."

Perhaps she has spotted her FBI minders. I consider telling her that I have arranged protection, then change my mind. "Please. Sit down."

Tension gathers itself in her lips and flows away. "You asked me this before," she says, tucking the dress under herself as she sits. "You know I can't do it. There are rules."

"It's different now. Charles Fahy lied to the Court. The Final Report is false. They have to know that."

"Ah," says Clara. She nods. "Someone else broke the rules and now you can too?"

"I want to help the Court."

"So much care for a marble building."

"It's for the Japanese."

Clara tilts her head and looks at me curiously. "Americans," she says. "So, you had a Eureka moment."

I remember Kuwabara and his stories. Hunting Easter eggs, getting called for his physical. "Yes." Fumiko's voice rises in my mind. *Thy liberty in law.* "And Tule Lake." Something occurs to me, an angle that might work. "This must be personal for you, too."

"What do you mean?"

"You must wonder why you're not in a camp."

"What?" She sounds almost alarmed.

"Because your parents are German," I explain. "Like you told Cissy."

A stillness folds around her. "Yes," she says softly. "Why I am not in a camp. That is what I wonder."

I curse myself for bringing up that night. "Justice Black won't go along with this if he knows the truth," I say.

Clara nods. She speaks as though from a vast distance. "If he only knew, he'd do the right thing. That's what the Nisei think about Roosevelt. The way a child feels about his father. It must be a mistake. If only people knew what was happening, they'd do something. No one would let this go on."

"I have reports I want you to give him. From the FBI and the FCC."

"That's against the rules."

"I don't care."

"But I do." She turns her head toward me, present again in the theater, returned from whatever far-off place she's been. "Rules protect people. They protect the weak. Only a rule could have stopped this, something that couldn't be balanced away."

She has a point. That is what Fahy was doing in the courtroom, when he wasn't lying about the Final Report; that is the argument I prepared with him. The interests of the individual must be weighed against the needs of national security. And who can do that better than the experts, the agencies, the army? They know what must be done. But still . . . "They don't protect you if the other guy doesn't follow them."

"I'm quite aware of that." A flash of anger lights her eyes and is gone. "Your reports won't do anything."

"I know Black."

"Do you?"

"What does that mean?"

"I can't help you, Cash. I'm sorry."

"I'm sorry, too. I helped you. I saved your life."

"So you think. Does yours need saving now?"

"Maybe."

Clara frowns. "Tell me about that."

I tell her about the Anti-Federalists, Hall's murder, how it must connect back to Gene Gressman. How they've kept me alive because they think I can make Black vote for the government.

She is frowning more severely. "Perhaps. But if that's so, aren't you putting yourself in danger by doing this? By writing the brief to lose?"

"You noticed that?"

"Of course."

"Oh. Well, yes. I guess I am."

She looks at me with something like respect. "So aren't you worried?"

"We're about to find them." I explain about Haynes and the fingerprint. Frankfurter will have called him back by now. He may be sweating on the carpet as we speak.

"And that's what you're counting on? That he'll tell Frankfurter who his bosses are?"

"Sure," I say. "Why not?"

"You're putting a lot of faith in Felix." Clara tilts her head. "And what if Haynes decides to run instead?" There are silvery lights in the green and gold of her eyes. "I think you should try to figure it out yourself."

"There's no way to figure it out. I've tried everything." I know what the government has done, holding innocent people, fabricating evidence against them, manipulating the cases. But it does not lead to murder. And I know what Richards and the Anti-Federalists have done, stocking the Court with their conservative clerks, fighting the New Deal. But again it does not take me to Gene or John Hall. I am thinking now that it must be someone else altogether.

"Work it backward," Clara says. "Someone killed John Hall. Why?"

"To stop him from talking to me."

"And what was he going to tell you?"

"Something about the Anti-Federalists."

"So they're the ones behind it."

"No, they're not," I say. "I confronted Colonel Richards. He came clean about planting the clerks, and I believe him when he says he has nothing to hide."

"Maybe he doesn't," she says. "But he's not the only one. There's Brutus. And the Farmer. What about them?"

"What would they have to hide that he doesn't?"

"Killing Gene Gressman, for starters. Richards wasn't a part of that, so he's not worried about covering it up. But maybe they are."

I lean back in the seat. It makes a kind of sense, now that she says it. Keeping the identity of the Anti-Federalists a secret was the only reason to kill Hall. Richards did not care about that, but maybe the others did; maybe they had something to hide after all. Brutus and the Farmer could have ordered Gene killed on their own, the left hand not knowing what the right hand was doing.

But there's a problem with the theory. It just moves the question one step back. "Why would they kill Gene?"

"To stop him from doing something."

"What?"

"I don't know," she says. "What was he going to do if they didn't kill him?"

That is the question. Any number of things. But what might be important enough to make them turn to murder? "He thought he was going to affect the Japanese cases. And he was trying to find out who was planting the clerks."

Clara considers. "And which would it be?"

I shake my head. "Neither one works." The Anti-Federalists don't care about the Japanese, as far as I know. But neither did they have any reason to worry about being found out by Gene. Take his murder out of it, and Brutus and the Farmer have no more reason to hide their identity than Richards. We are back in the realm of harmless fun.

The puzzle cannot be solved. There's still a piece missing. That, or I'm thinking about too many pieces. The patterns are interfering with each other; I can't isolate the signal. I shake my head again, staring at the blank white screen of the movie theater. I raise my hands, palms up, spreading the fingers. There is nothing for me to take hold of.

Then I feel her fingers in my hand. I close my own around them. Clara gives me one quick squeeze. "I have to go," she says, and before I can ask why she is up from the seat and out the door, clicking down the stairs from the balcony. I give her a few minutes and head out myself. There is still work to be done.

CHAPTER 43

FELIX FRANKFURTER IS a busy man. It is two days before I can arrange an appointment, and when I enter his chambers his desk is piled high with papers. He puts down a pen as I walk in and rises to shake my hand, sleek and satisfied. "Cash, my boy."

"Justice."

"What can I do for you?"

"I was wondering if you'd had a chance to talk to Phil Haynes."

"Ah," Frankfurter says, raising his chin as though remembering. "Mr. Haynes." His face creases with displeasure, then smoothes again. "We spoke."

"And? Did he tell you who was giving him orders?"

"He did not indicate an immediate willingness to do so, no. And I did not press him on it."

"Well, you have to." I do not understand what is going on. "You have to get him back here."

Frankfurter's tone goes distant. "Private Haynes is no longer available."

"What do you mean?"

"How do they put it? He has been called to serve his country in another place." I shake my head. "I don't understand."

"He is with the Marine combat infantry now. He should be somewhere in the Pacific, making ready for the Home Islands. They are predicting a million casualties. I do not expect that he will return."

I blink. "You did that?"

Frankfurter sighs. "You could say I did not stop it. I might have, perhaps, but I am not sure it was my decision to make. And to prosecute him would be to shine a light on ourselves, too. This may be a simpler route."

"To what?"

Frankfurter's smile returns. "To justice."

I shake my head again. I imagine Haynes clutching a gunwale, tanned face gone green. The Pacific is not Northeast Harbor, and the LCI a far cry from a Lightning sloop. I see him looking up at the buzz of a plane engine, wading through shallow surf toward a coral beach. I put the picture from my mind. "But I need to find out who's behind this. I told you, I'm in danger from them."

"I do not think so." He sounds as if he is telling me a tie does not match my shirt. "If they wanted to harm you, they would have done so by now."

"They're waiting for the Japanese cases to be decided. They thought I'd help."

"No." The same dismissive tone. "Not that your work for the government was anything but excellent." He pauses just a moment longer than he would have if this were truly a compliment. "But the outcome there was never in doubt."

Suddenly I am hearing Karl Bendetsen's voice in my mind. Just another James Rowe, all worked up over something that's been decided already. "What do you mean?"

Frankfurter smiles. "We must not discuss a pending case. That is what I should say to you, isn't it? But we are past that, you and I. This Court will not go against Roosevelt. You know that as well as anyone."

"It will come out," I say. "That these people were innocent. That there was no justification."

"We are at war, Cash. Should we allow people to use our courts, our laws against us? To use the law as an instrument of war?"

"They're not the enemy."

Frankfurter shrugs. His face is the face of the law, smooth and impenetrable. "Each of us has an opportunity to serve in his own way. I told you that long ago. Those who challenge the government are not helping."

"But they're right. Isn't it your duty as a judge to say so?"

Frankfurter lifts a pen from his desk and spins it across the back of one hand. "Duty," he says. A smile plays across his face and fades. "Would you have met with Charles Horsky if you believed in duty? Would you be here talking to me, inside the Court?"

"When I first met you, you said it was a temple of truth."

The smile returns. "Ah," he says. "I was politicking then. Holmes said it to FDR. We are at war, and in time of war there is only one rule. Form your battalion and fight."

"So the government can hold innocent people?" I remember the *Endo* argument, the sad note in Fahy's voice. "You won't get five votes for that."

"Hold innocent people?" Frankfurter sounds surprised. "No. And it does not want to. Miss Endo may go. There was never any order to detain her."

"What?"

"Detention was never authorized. Congress never approved. The President never wanted it done."

"That's not true."

"I am thinking of the future," Frankfurter says. "We need to move forward. Not to revisit policy choices that were made in good faith for the safety of the nation."

There is an unusual brightness to the room, a rushing in my ears. "Men died in those camps," I say. "Men died rather than go there." Frankfurter looks at me, impassive. "That was not a policy choice. If it was unconstitutional, what we did to those people, it was closer to a crime."

Frankfurter leans back in his chair, casts his eyes toward the ceiling. He has cut himself shaving, I can see: spots of blood stipple the pink skin of his neck where the razor went too close. But there will be a high collar when he goes out, a black robe for the courtroom. "Ah, Cash," he says. "What will be gained by spending our time and energy laying blame for the past? Some people may have exceeded their authority. That is what the opinion will say." His face comes down again, gleaming and smooth. "Detention of loyal Americans was never part of the plan. But as far as the program went, it was approved by the President and Congress, and every expert consulted said it was safe, necessary, and effective."

"They said nothing of the sort. I have the reports. The FBI and the FCC. What are you relying on? Karl Bendetsen's memos?"

Frankfurter draws himself straighter. "I have the word of the Solicitor General. This is the position of the US government."

"Charles Fahy himself asked you not to do this," I say. "He asked you for an honest judgment, for the truth. What will you give him?"

"I will give him the way to move forward."

"We do not move forward by shutting our eyes to the past."

"Yes, we do." Frankfurter seems honestly puzzled at my words. "That is exactly how we move forward."

I look at him for a moment, and then I nod my head. "Of course," I say. I am thinking of Karl Bendetsen again. He didn't make the policy; he just told a client what the law allowed. No one made the policy, it seems; perhaps there never was such a policy at all. But men lay in the stockade, and blood flecked the wall, and blue chips of china danced off the ground where the wedding plates were smashed. Look forward, Frankfurter says, but what he means is look away.

I rise from the chair. Frankfurter is no longer on my side, if he ever really was. "Of course you're right," I tell him. "There was never any doubt."

• • • •

Frankfurter's clerk walks me out toward the exit, across the thick carpet, down the marble halls. We are almost there when I hear whistling and Hugo Black rounds the corner.

"Cash!" He is clearly surprised to see me. "Sneaking around without stopping in to say hi?"

"Just a little business, Justice," I say.

"Judge," he corrects me.

"Judge. I'm putting off social calls until the cases come down."

Black nods. "Quite right." But he stands there anyway. The government is losing *Endo*, I think. Those are votes against Roosevelt, even if the opinion is a lie. There must be some in *Korematsu*, too. Murphy, surely. Roberts, Douglas, Jackson. And Hugo Black makes five.

"How's JoJo?"

"Still sneezing," he answers. "I can hear her nights." He chuckles. "Looking for monsters in the garden."

"There aren't any," I say. Is he hinting something? "No monsters, Judge. Nothing to be scared of."

He laughs again and claps me on the shoulder. "You tell her that. Soon." Now he walks on; Frankfurter's clerk leads me around the corner, past the Douglas chambers. There is the person I want to see. I throw Clara a look. Five minutes later she comes to the clerk's entrance and beckons me back inside. Douglas is out somewhere and the secretary is guarding his door. We have Clara's office to ourselves.

She sits down at her desk. "What is it?"

I walk over to the window. Clara's view is the same one I used to have. Constitution Avenue out the window and a stack of cert petitions on the desk. "Frankfurter is manipulating things with these cases," I say. "I know he is. This isn't right."

Clara's face clouds. "You still want me to talk to Black." She looks at the papers piled in front of her.

"Please," I say.

Clara shakes her head.

"I know it's not proper. But the Court can bend the rules to get the right result."

"Oh, that's what they're doing, Cash. They just think the other result is the right one."

"What?"

"You see, not following the rules can fail, too."

"Just tell Black the truth."

"He knows, Cash." Her voice is soft, but the words hit like a slap.

"What do you mean?"

"All your reports, all your evidence. Murphy's been saying it. I've been helping his clerk." For the first time I notice the depth of the shadows under her eyes. "It's not that they don't know what's happening; it's that they don't care. Not for these people. There are more important things at stake."

It is what Frankfurter said. And somehow he has gotten a majority behind him.

"This is what happens to people who aren't like you," Clara continues. "When you get scared, of course they're the first to feel it."

"But Murphy has the facts on his side. What can Frankfurter say to that?"

"Frankfurter?"

"In the opinion. I can tell he's writing it."

She hesitates. "I didn't want to tell you this. I hoped you were right, that he'd come around."

"Tell me what?"

"Frankfurter's not writing the opinion. It's Black."

There is something in my throat. For a moment the words won't come. "It's Black?"

"I went to him," Clara says. "I could see that Murphy's arguments weren't working. So I told him what you said about the original version of the Final Report. That time wasn't a problem, that General DeWitt just thought no one could tell them apart."

"What did he say?"

"He said, 'Well, can you?' I was surprised. I asked him what he meant. He said, 'Can you tell them apart? If Japanese troops landed on the West Coast, could you tell who was American and who wasn't? And if some of them were fighting with the Imperial Army, out of uniform, could you tell who was loyal and who wasn't? They'd all be shot.'

"I said, 'If German troops landed and were fighting out of uniform, could you tell who was American and who wasn't?'"

"What did he say to that?"

"He said it wasn't the same thing. He said, 'Listen, DeWitt's a patriot. He's no racist. I know what it's like to be unjustly accused of that.'" She stops.

"That was it?" I ask.

"No," says Clara. "I said one more thing. I said, 'Mr. Justice, I ask you to consider that the man unjustly accused here is Fred Korematsu.'"

"And then?"

"Then he said, 'Call me Judge.' And that was it."

I put my forehead against the window and close my eyes. The glass is cold on my skin. Clara's hand touches my shoulder softly. "Poor boy." She is so close I can feel her breath against my hair as she speaks. "Sometimes there is nothing to be done."

"*Shikata ga nai*," I say.

"What?"

"Never mind." I feel tired, more tired than I have ever been. Something has hollowed me out, removed whatever vital core powered me through the earlier days. Innocence, optimism, youth. "So it's over. There's nothing to do."

She tilts her head again, eyes dark with concern. "No, it's not over. Remember what you said to me."

"What?"

"You're still in danger. You need to worry about yourself now."

PART III

THE EMPTY LAKE

CHAPTER 44

NOVEMBER COMES. THE First Army is fighting in Germany; the B-29s are bombing Japan. At Leyte Gulf, Bull Halsey and Thomas Kinkaid have destroyed the last great fleet to sail under the rising sun. The Nisei regimental combat team has spent half its strength fighting through the Vosges to free a lost battalion of Texans. And Roosevelt has won his fourth term, with the Democrats picking up four House seats in California.

I open my desk drawer and take out a sheaf of papers. They are covered in handwriting, the names of cases, clerks, and Justices. Some words are circled or underlined, connected to others by lines and arrows. Gene Gressman's notes are what I have left now. There will be no help from Black, no help from Frankfurter. I cannot affect the Japanese cases; I cannot use Haynes to find the men behind Gene's murder. All I can do is look at these notes, consult them like a holy book, as inscrutable as it is infallible. I do not know what they mean, but there must be truth in them somewhere. Because someone thought they were worth killing for.

Words, names, diagrams. Next to each case, there is a list of Justices. Sometimes all of them, sometimes as few as one. Lines link their names to those of clerks. There is something the Justices are doing, something the clerks are influencing. The voting, presumably. That is my first thought. Gressman has drawn me a picture of the Anti-Federalists' work: Justices voting for corporate interests and against the power of the federal government.

But when I call down to the library and have them send up the volumes of the *US Reports* containing the cases he's listed, I see that's not how it works. *Hamel Manufacturing v. Skyler Corporation*, for instance, has four names next to it on Gressman's chart. But it's a unanimous decision: all the Justices voted together. And it's not about the power of the federal government at all; it's a contract dispute between a mill and a clothier. *Allcom, Inc. v. Linden Brothers* has one name next to it, but the Court did not even decide the case. In the *US Reports* there is only a curt notation: *Certiorari denied*.

And then it hits me. The votes he's recording are not at the merits stage. They're votes on the certiorari petitions. That was Gene's theory in the first place, that the Court was hearing cases it shouldn't and someone was profiting from that knowledge. *The boring business cases,* he said. *That's where the money is.*

Frankfurter's talk of a conservative conspiracy crowded it from my mind, but it all makes sense now. Two plans were in motion at the same time, Colonel Richards pushing his ideological agenda and someone else using the access for other purposes. Driving the Court to hear business cases and trading the companies' stock ahead of the decisions. That's what they wanted to conceal, the thing Richards didn't know about; that's what was worth killing Gene for. Enough money at stake would provide a motive, and avoiding discovery would too. The SEC would take an interest in these men. Even without Haynes, that is something I can hang on them. If I can find them.

I spread the papers out on the desk. It all fits. The patriots and the scoundrels, one hand not knowing what the other did. None of them would care about the Japanese cases; Frankfurter was right about that. But now the picture begins to blur again. If no one cared about the Japanese cases, why did they kill John Hall and not me? What other reason could there be for keeping me alive? I lean forward, frowning. Does that mean I am in danger now? Or that I was never in danger at all?

I am so deep in thought I do not hear the footsteps in the corridor. Only when he clears his throat do I look up and see Francis Biddle standing in my doorway. "I need you, Cash," he says. "There's trouble in Tule Lake."

"What is it?"

"Walk with me."

We go down the hallway, toward the elevators. "The decisions will issue soon," he says. "The Japanese cases."

"How do you know?"

"Felix Frankfurter. He keeps us informed."

The neutral, principled judge. I shake my head. Just a bit, but Biddle catches it.

"It's in everyone's interest," he says. "We need to prepare."

"What do we need to do?"

"We're going to lose *Endo*," Biddle tells me. He pushes the call button. "Unless there's some reason to doubt loyalty on an individual basis, they can go home."

"That's fine by me."

"Me too. First floor," he says to the operator. "The War Department sees things differently, of course. They're going to try to tell the courts that they doubt everyone's loyalty. On an individual basis. But I don't think it will work." The aluminum door opens; we walk out into the Great Hall.

"That's fine by me too," I say.

Biddle swings a roll of paper, patting his thigh. "Justice takes no position on the matter. But in any event, there will be a large number of loyal detainees returning. They may face a chilly reception."

"I know," I say. We have turned down an unfamiliar hallway. Idly, I wonder where we are headed. "That's where losing *Korematsu* could have helped."

"Yes," says Biddle. "I know that. It would have been a great embarrassment for the government, however."

"So we put their lives at risk to save face?"

Biddle stops for a moment and turns toward me. "So we try to help them in a different way. Politics is the art of the possible, Cash." He starts walking again. "That was the point of the renunciation program. Segregate out the disloyal, and California will be more welcoming."

"I remember that."

"Yes." He stops again, halfway down the corridor, before the door of the Department mailroom. "You went to Tule Lake to explain renunciation."

"Yes."

"You told them what it would mean. Loss of all rights, a boat to Japan after the war."

"Yes." I look at the papers in his hand. "Are those the applications?"

"Some of them." He hands me the roll.

There are probably thirty pages. Each has a name at the top. I scan them quickly; none is familiar. Each of the applicants will receive a hearing before the renunciation is finally approved. That, I suppose, is what he has come to me for. "So what's the problem?"

"This," says Biddle. He opens the door. Sacks of mail cover the floor. I read the stamps on the bags, two words over and over again. *Tule Lake, Tule Lake, Tule Lake.* "We got five thousand applications," Biddle says.

"Five thousand?" It is not just too many; it is impossible, absurd. I am trying to think of what I could have done wrong. "How can that be?"

"I don't know," says Biddle. "I wasn't there."

"I told them not to."

Biddle shrugs. "It seems they didn't listen. There are War Department teams out there conducting hearings as we speak."

"War's in favor of renunciation now?"

"Anything to keep them in the camps, that's War's view. But five thousand is too many. Something's happened. I want you to find out what it is."

"Okay," I say. I am still trying to collect myself. This is my fault; it must be my fault. I was the one explaining it to them. But still I cannot think of what I did wrong.

Biddle puts his hand on my shoulder. It is not a pat; he is squeezing hard enough to hurt. "We've done wrong to these people, Cash. Try not to let it get any worse."

. . . .

Back in my office, I place a call to Tule Lake director Raymond Best. Best has no idea what's going on. He transfers me to his community analyst, Marvin Opler. It's simple, Opler says. Everyone's gone mad.

"What?"

"They're insane with fear," he says. "That they'll be killed if they go back home. Everyone knows the camps are going to close, and they've been hearing horror stories about what's happened to the ones released already. If they renounce, they can stay in the camps."

"Maybe that's not insane." In California, shadowy figures shoot through windows and mobs burn houses.

"Maybe not," he agrees. "Maybe some of them would be better off in Japan." It is a sobering thought. Better off renouncing all the rights and privileges of citizens, better off shipped to a country they have never seen, than back among their fellow Americans. "If the Hoshidan come out and start chanting for their emperor, they really will be killed."

"So what can we do about it?"

"You need to get renunciations from the Hoshidan," he says. "So they don't go back to California and set everyone off. And you need to talk the normal people out of it."

"Oh," I say. "Sort the loyal from the disloyal. Well, that should be no problem."

There is a moment of silence. "It might not be as easy as you think."

"I'm being sarcastic, Marvin. How am I supposed to do that?"

"Well," he says, "I have an idea, actually."

CHAPTER 45

AIR PRIORITY ONE will not do it this time. Biddle gives me a team of Justice Department officers to conduct hearings, too many to fly. We take the train instead. Outside the window, the countryside flickers like a reel of film. It flashes past too fast for sense: office buildings, houses, baseball diamonds, empty fields.

We gather in the dining car. Opler's plan is simple, I tell my team. The militants, the Hoshidan, are the ones who really want to go to Japan. They have been studying Japanese history and culture. We can test the people who are renouncing citizenship by asking them questions about these subjects. Those who do not know the answers may be acting out of hysteria. Or perhaps they have been subjected to some sort of pressure. Whatever the case may be, we will take the Hoshidan as fast as we can and hope the rest calm down when they are gone.

I look around at the faces. Twelve men, good people. I have picked them carefully. Justice lawyers I trust, Miller and some FBI agents he recommended in case things get rough. They look at me attentively. "Just the real ones," says Miller. "Sure." He cracks his smile, makes a quiet remark to the agent next to him, and everyone at his table breaks out in laughter.

Waiters bring us food. The team is swapping jokes, looking out the windows, ordering more beers. My men in easy camaraderie. The buildings of the East are gone now, vanished behind us like the works of a lost civilization.

All around are stubble fields. The sky is clear blue and endless, a space that is the end of space. Dinner ends, and still I sit by the window with a glass of Scotch, telling myself it will work. Marvin Opler knows these people; he knows how to identify the truly disloyal. My men are careful, smart. Farther west we cross rivers, and the setting sun skims with us, an orange reflection in the water, until it crashes into the black land and is lost.

"Come on," Miller says. "You're going to need your sleep."

I climb into a bunk and lie there, clutching a rough wool blanket, listening to the thrum of the wheels. Even the Hoshidan should not have been put in this position. If they are enemies now, they are enemies of our own making. But they are the problem, and if we take some, we may save the rest. We can sacrifice a few to save a greater number.

That is what I tell myself as the dark land slides by.

. . . .

The world sleeps, but we hurtle on. The coal burns, the iron wheels turn. A day, a night, another day. And finally we are disembarking at Klamath Falls. We drive into Tule Lake, a procession of black government cars through the gray plain, under the gray sky. Shouts of "*Wash-Sho*" rise about us as we enter. I kick at the frozen ground and shiver. Tule Lake in December is quite different from the place I visited in August. It is bitter cold, for one thing. The wind blows thin and empty, like the sky, like the high plains around us. Castle Rock spots the horizon with hues of the rising sun.

The people have changed, too. Everywhere now I see the *bozu* haircut on men, military short, and pigtails on the women. Everywhere are the white uniforms of the Hoshidan. They are louder in the morning; there are more of them, marching and drilling, chanting and blowing bugles. I stand outside my apartment and look through the fence to the firebreak. There are women in the columns of white, and children. I wait until the exercises have finished and listen for singing. I hear nothing.

The walk from my apartment to the mess hall is an ordeal. I pity the detainees who have to go several blocks to the latrine. In the administration building where I will interview renunciants, a pot-bellied stove blazes. Someone has nailed the lids of coffee cans over the knotholes in the pine wall. I stuff newspaper in the cracks and gaps that remain. I can still see my breath. From the wall above my desk, Franklin Roosevelt, unaffected, beams down his genial smile.

One by one the renunciants file through. At the beginning, they are all Hoshidan. In they come, with their shaved heads, their white clothes and headbands. I show them their application forms, ask them to verify the signature. I ask them if they understand what they are doing and whether they are renouncing of their own free will. I remind them that they are surrendering something of great value. I ask them my questions about Japanese history and culture. And I give them a final paper to sign. In a few weeks, or whenever the Department completes the processing, they will receive a form letter from Francis Biddle. *Your application for renunciation has been approved by the Attorney General. You are no longer a citizen of the United States of America, nor are you entitled to any of the rights and privileges of such citizenship.*

The interviews go fast. They respond curtly to my questions. "Why do you want to renounce?" I ask.

"I want to be Japanese," say the Nisei.

"I am Japanese," say the Kibei. "Japanese in my face and my hair and my heart."

I could not talk them out of it if I wanted to; there is no conversation to be had with these people. I process twenty-five the first day.

The second morning, after the bugles and the chants, I hear *Un Bel Di* soaring through the barracks. At first it is just the soprano, a single floating voice. Then I hear violins underneath, a stirring of brass, the distant boom of drums. A full orchestral accompaniment.

It is coming from my side of the fence, I realize. I track the sound to an administration building and open the door.

The Community Center looks empty. I see only a phonograph playing on a table in one corner. Motion catches my eye: a man sitting in one of the chairs, slouched in a wool greatcoat. He looks up at the sound of the door and turns away again when he sees me.

"I'm Cash Harrison," I say. "With the Department of Justice."

He turns his head back but doesn't rise. "I'm Jerry Katz. With the Tule Lake Symphony."

"Oh," I say. "I guess it's not performing anymore?"

"No," he says. "It's not."

I process thirty-two applications that day. All Hoshidan, all seething with silent hostility. After dinner I sit with Director Ray Best over a glass of Scotch. "What's happening here?" I ask.

"They're deciding whose side they're on," he says. "Japan's, it turns out. Fancy that."

"I hear there's no more symphony."

"There's no more anything Western, really. The school teaches calligraphy, Japanese, and flower arranging. Instead of the Pledge of Allegiance, they start the day with a bow to the East and a salute to the emperor."

"Are you kidding me?" I cannot understand why he is so calm. "Those are little children. American children. They're saluting a foreign enemy. Why don't you do something about it?"

"They're all going back to Japan in the end," he says. "They need to prepare themselves to live there."

I remember Marvin Opler. "Your community analyst's son is in that school."

"Not anymore," says Best. "Don't be silly." He gestures out the window. "The Nisei teenagers, I feel a little bad for them. They're American, culturally. You see the lights on in the high school? That's a dance."

Across the fence I see the building he indicates. I can hear music, now that I am listening for it. "Turn off your radio," I say. With the room quiet, the distant tune is clear. It is "Don't Fence Me In."

Best's face wrinkles in recognition. "It's number one in the country," he says. "What can we do?" He joins me at the window and takes a drink of Scotch. "Woody Ichihashi and the Downbeats," he says. "They're not half bad."

We stand in silence for a moment, listening. Through the windows of the building I can see shapes moving, couples holding hands. The music changes to *I'll Be Seeing You*, the litany of old familiar places. I think about that night at Merion with Suzanne, the leaves blowing across the great lawn, the kids dancing under the flags, lovely in limbs and eyes. It seems unimaginably distant now, though the trail away is made of tiny steps. Some big ones, too. Ralph Hays is dead, who looked so fine in his Navy blues, and Billy Fitch the pilot, and Bill's dad, who opened his wrists in his car when he heard the plane was down.

The music stops. There is a crowd of white-clad figures outside the high school, some on the porch and some entering. "It's the Hoshidan," I say.

Best nods. "They don't approve." Men in white are taking the kids outside. Some struggle. A Hoshidan slaps a zoot-suited teen across the face.

"What are you going to do?"

"What can we do?"

"Stop them."

"With what? Their police force disbanded. You want me to send my soldiers in to protect a swing band? That would turn ugly fast."

I shake my head. "This is a mess."

Best laughs. "You got that right. If you've got any suggestions, let me have 'em."

"We can take out the leaders," I say. "That's what I'm here for. We get them to renounce and we take them out of here. Truck them to the internment camp in Santa Fe."

"And you think that'll fix things?"

"It's a start," I say. "We'll see what happens after that."

The morning bugling the next day seems louder. I can see large numbers of children, old men, old women lined up in the cold. Their breath rises in columns and blends to fade united in the sky; their voices ring out to the distant mountains. "*Wash-Sho!*"

I have two more Hoshidan that day, then a woman in pigtails, then a man with longer hair. I start on the loyalty questions. "What do you think of the emperor of Japan?" I ask.

He leaps to his feet. "The emperor is a living god," he shouts. It is what all the Hoshidan have done, and the woman too, but it suits him less well. I go on.

"Do you believe Japan will win the war?"

"Yes, and I hope so too."

"What will you do if you are released from this camp?"

"I will sabotage American war plants."

I look at him. He looks back. His breath comes quickly. There is a sheen of sweat on his face. I move to the culture questions. "For what is the Ise Shrine famous?"

"Ise Jingu is the home of the Sacred Mirror. It is rebuilt of new wood every twenty years."

"What is the significance of February 11 to Japan?"

"It is *Kigensetsu*, the day when Emperor Jimmu established his capital."

He is perfect. I give him the last form. "If you sign this, you will lose your status as an American. You will be sent to Japan when the war ends. You will most likely never be allowed to return to the United States. You will lose all the rights and privileges of your citizenship forever."

He looks me directly in the face, then seizes the paper and scrawls his name. This, too, is the pattern followed by the Hoshidan. But there is a difference. The Hoshidan looked angry. The expression on this man's face is fear.

"Why are you renouncing?" I ask him.

He looks back up at me. "I want to be Japanese."

I shake my head. "Send in the next one," I say to the guard at the door.

• • • •

I have never seen her face. I have never heard her speak. But the carefully curled hair and something about the posture as she stands there in the doorway leaves no doubt in my mind. "Fumiko," I say. "Please have a seat."

I ask her to verify her signature on the application, which she does. "What do you think of the emperor of Japan?" I ask.

She does not leap, but she gets to her feet. "The emperor is a living god," she says slowly.

"Fumiko," I say. "Your citizenship protects you."

She says something I cannot hear.

"Your government will protect you," I say.

There is no answer. I look down at the papers. When I look up again there is a line down her cheek, silver, like the trail of a star. In the silence between us, a song rises in my mind, which I heard her sing through the wire fence. *Thine alabaster cities gleam . . .*

"You cannot protect me," she says. "No one protects us."

"From who? From the Hoshidan?"

"The emperor is a living god," she says, more loudly.

"Do you believe Japan will win the war?"

"Yes, and I hope so too."

I consult my quiz and skip ahead to the question about February 11. "What is the significance of February 27 to Japan?" I ask.

"It is *Kigensetsu*," says Fumiko promptly. She does not notice I have changed the date. "The day when Emperor Jimmu established his capital." The words mean nothing to her; she is reciting a formula given by others.

"This is not a voluntary renunciation," I say. "I will not approve this."

"You gave us nothing," says Fumiko. Her voice is louder still. "We have nothing left. What am I to do? If I do not renounce, I will be forced to leave Tule Lake. But I cannot go back to California. Where will I go? Who will give me a job or a place to live? My parents are not Americans. They will be held here and sent back to Japan without me. If the Hoshidan do not kill us all first."

"You're making a mistake," I say. "I won't approve it."

"Give me the paper." It is almost a shout.

"If you sign this," I say, "you will lose your status as an American. You will be sent to Japan when the war ends. You will most likely never be allowed to return to the United States. You will lose all the rights and privileges of your citizenship forever."

"Give me the paper."

Wordless, I pass it over. *Patriot dream, that sees beyond the years.* She signs, and the voice in my mind goes still. Now there is nothing but silence and the rustle of paper as I add her sheet to the pile. She leaves the room without looking at me.

"No more today," I say to the guard. "I need to see Director Best."

• • • •

"I want to talk to Harry Nakamura," I tell Best.

His messenger returns alone. "Nakamura says it will take armed guards to make him see you."

I do not hesitate. "Then send them."

They bring him in half an hour later, two burly MPs with rifles shouldered.

Harry Nakamura is all in white, his face a hostile mask under the *bozu* hair-cut. I wave the guards out of the room.

Nakamura's face relaxes. "You understand it is safer for me to come to you this way."

"Sure," I say. "Whatever you think is best. Look, I don't understand what's going on here. Why are people so hell-bent on renouncing?"

"They are scared," he says. "There are rumors everywhere. The camps are closing, we hear. Everyone will be forced to leave. But if we cannot return to California in safety, we have no place to go. America is not opening its arms in welcome. They say if you do not renounce you will be drafted. They say you must renounce if you want to stay with your parents. It seems to offer safety."

"Who is saying this?"

"The Hoshidan. They say we will be safe if we join them. That is why you see the old women with their gray hair running around in the morning. That is why you see the children."

"Anyone else?"

"I have heard that some War Department men say the same thing. And the land reclamation agents."

"The land reclamation agents?"

"For those who are renouncing. They offer compensation for the land. The certificates."

"Are they War Department? Relocation Authority?"

He shrugs. "I regret that these distinctions escape me. I cannot tell them apart."

Clearly, I will have to find these men. But in the meantime there is another problem. "The Hoshidan coach people for the hearings, don't they?"

"There is what you could call a College of Renunciation Knowledge. They send some Hoshidan in first to learn the questions. Then everyone else is prepared."

It must be stopped, but I don't know how. We can change the culture questions, but the Hoshidan will adjust in turn. The questions can hardly be considered dispositive anyway. The pledge of disloyalty the applicants recite means nothing either. As long as they sign the final form, as long as they say they are acting freely, we are bound by law to approve.

"If I get rid of the Hoshidan leaders, will that stop it?"

Nakamura shrugs, his face impassive. "Who can say what will stop this? It will help."

. . . .

I go back to my apartment and write a letter on Department of Justice stationery. "Have a typist copy this," I say to Ray Best. "Post one in every mess hall."

He looks at it curiously. "From Caswell Harrison, Special Assistant to the Attorney General," he reads. "To the leaders of the Hoshidan."

> *I know you have pressured residents of this camp to assert loyalty to Japan. This camp is part of America and the people here are Americans. Coercing them into asserting loyalty to Japan is treason. It will stop. By order of the Department of Justice.*

The next morning, the bugles are unmistakably louder. When I look out my window I see that the drills have moved along the firebreak to a spot directly across the fence from my apartment. "You should consider it an honor," Ray Best says. "They've never done that for a visitor before."

The Army trucks I have requested arrive that day. We have approved renunciation by 171 Hoshidan now, and we load them in, bound for the Santa Fe internment camp. There is a spectacular farewell. Thousands of detainees line the road as the trucks pull out. They shout "*Banzai!*" and raise their arms in the air, palms down.

"We have elected a new slate of officers," a Hoshidan tells me in his interview that afternoon. "We will not stop. We will never stop."

I end my hearings when the first man with long hair comes in, leaps to his feet, and proclaims the emperor a living god. I call Francis Biddle instead. "The people here are terrified," I say. "They don't know what to expect. They're willing to do anything to be safe, and they're making a terrible mistake."

"What would you have me do, Cash?"

"Give me a promise that no one loyal will be forced to leave Tule Lake. Give me a proclamation I can put up in the mess halls under your name."

In the silence that follows I imagine Biddle examining his fingernails. "I can't give that kind of a blanket guarantee," he says.

"Then what am I supposed to do?"

"Do what we planned," he says. "Take the Hoshidan, discourage the others. Felix says that the decisions will be coming down Monday. You only have a few days left."

"I can't do it," I tell him. "Not with the system I'm using now. I can't just go through the applications. I need the authority to send out whomever I want."

"What do you mean?"

"There are loyal Americans here," I say, "and I'm going to protect them. I need to be able to send anyone I want out to the internment camps."

"Internment camps are for enemy aliens," Biddle says. "You can't send anyone there unless they renounce."

"But anyone who renounces?"

"Them you can take," says Biddle. "It's a mess, Cash. We all know that. Do what you think is best. Be as reasonable as you can."

. . . .

"Send some MPs to get the Hoshidan membership list," I tell Ray Best. They offer it willingly, and we call them for hearings one after the other. They line up in white outside my office, and for a lunatic moment I am seeing the girls of Merion in their debutante gowns. There is no question of choosing this time, though, no worry about who to pick for that first dance across the polished floor. This time we take them all.

It is a long line of Army trucks that assembles behind the gates the next morning. There are almost seven hundred Hoshidan inside. The farewell ceremony is weaker, I think, the shouts fainter. Of course, there are a thousand voices missing from the chorus now. The test will be tomorrow.

The bugles wake me from sleep at five-thirty, as usual. I stumble to my window and raise the blind. The firebreak is filled with figures in white. More of them are children; renunciation is limited to those eighteen and older. More of them are women; we have removed only men. But I do not think, all in all, that their numbers are any less. I send the military police for Harry Nakamura.

"You have not removed the leaders," he says.

"I've sent out the whole membership."

"There are people who want others to renounce. They do not renounce themselves. They may not be obvious in their actions, but they are effective."

"Tell me who."

Nakamura's face is expressionless. "Then I would be an *inu* indeed."

"You would be helping me protect Americans," I say.

"And what would I be doing to the men whose names I gave you?"

"No more than they deserve."

He shrugs. "Perhaps. Even so, I cannot do it."

. . . .

Nakamura has his principles, I think, like creases in paper. But I need action. There is one day left before the cases come down, and I have achieved nothing. "Who would be encouraging renunciation?" I ask Marvin Opler. "Not the Hoshidan, but people trying to push the others into it?"

He scratches at his beard. "Hard to say. I have some guesses, of course."

"Could you make me a list?"

"What for?"

"I'm going to send them out to Santa Fe."

Opler frowns. "How are you going to do that?

"Get them to renounce their citizenship."

"But they don't want to."

"Well, I'll persuade them."

A troubled expression crosses Opler's face. He takes off his glasses and polishes them on his sleeve. "How?"

"Leave that to me. Can you make a list?"

"I guess so." He hesitates a moment. "The ones I'm not sure about . . . you want them on or off?"

I am not hesitating, but I pause before responding, just to make sure he hears me. "I want them on."

. . . .

Opler comes back in a few hours. He has 150 names, a daunting number. Too many, certainly, for my team of twelve. "I need more men," I tell Ray Best.

"If the Relocation Authority wants to help," he says, "you can have them."

"No, I want your MPs. I want some soldiers."

Best's expression suggests that he's never seen me before. He shakes his head. "No way. You're not taking my soldiers into the colony."

"Why not?"

"One, this isn't a military problem. And two, the place would explode."

"And what's going to happen if I go in there without them?"

A short laugh. "I don't know. I'm not advising you to do it."

"Well, I'm doing it. You can help me, or you can explain to Francis Biddle why you didn't."

"Francis Biddle?" Best curls his lip. "I don't work for Justice."

"Fine," I say. "I'll take the Relocation Authority men."

"Okay," says Best. He picks at his teeth with a matchstick. "Well, you should probably go start talking to them, then."

I go back to my apartment and sit down with Miller, looking at Opler's list—150 names. I have four agents, and maybe three lawyers bold enough to come with me. Miller screws up his face. "We can do it," he says.

"Really?"

"Sure. I can get you some local FBI, some Relocation Authority guys."

"Enough?"

"Won't need that many. We go in at night, do it quietly, no one knows what's going on. It'll take a while, but we can pull it off."

"Okay," I say. "It's got to be tonight."

"Sure." Miller nods. "I'll get on it."

Afternoon is fading into evening when he returns.

"How's it going?" I ask.

"Good," he says. "We're going to have twenty guys, maybe twenty-five. And I got you this." There is an olive bundle in his arms.

"What's that?"

"You can't be running around the colony in that suit, boss." He laughs. "Uncle Sam's your new tailor."

I put on the uniform. Then I sit in the apartment for hours, drinking coffee and looking at my feet in the combat boots, my legs in army fatigues. The body of a soldier, or the clothing, at least. And now Miller's face is in the doorway. It is time. The night will not last; the snow is starting down. Leaves dance in the wind before us as we gather at the gate. These are my men: twenty dark figures or so, some with rifles slung across their chests. I can't remember authorizing that, but it seems like a reasonable precaution. Clouds hang low over the camp; reflected searchlight beams cast a dull glow across the sky. The cold is irresistible. The uniform is no match for it, nor the borrowed Army greatcoat I pull tight around my shoulders. The air is biting me; idly, I wonder if I have a taste in the mouth of the wind. Miller looks my way. "Let's go," I say. The gate opens and we stream into the colony.

· · · ·

For over an hour we go down the list. At four-thirty, we come to Kinzo Wakayama. He lives in Ward Eight, Block Eighty-two. The ward is deep inside the colony and was once as much as three-quarters Hoshidan. Now, of course, it is almost three-quarters empty. We are working in teams of three. Miller is with me, and a local agent he turned up named Skousen. I kick the door open and Wakayama sits up in bed, blinking into our lights. "What is the meaning of this?" He wears military-surplus long underwear against the cold.

"I want you to sign this form," I say.

"What?"

"I want you to renounce your citizenship."

"Why would I do that?"

"Because you are disloyal."

Wakayama swings his bare feet to the floor. "I am disloyal because I object to this treatment? It is wrong, and you know it."

"You are confusing these people. You are leading them to renounce citizenship that is very valuable to them."

"You are the ones who taught them their citizenship is worthless."

"Sign the paper," I say.

"I will not. I am a veteran. I fought for this country. You put me in this camp. I will keep my citizenship and I will say what I please about what you have done. Is that not my right as an American?"

Miller looks at me. There is a question in his face, but I have no answer.

"You're not a real American," says Skousen. He is a small man, his narrow jaw dark with stubble.

"And you are?"

Skousen turns to me. I don't know if I give him a signal, or if he just sees something in my eyes, but suddenly he holds a gun. "You're not going to be any kind of American for long," he says. "You're going to sign this paper."

Wakayama does not seem surprised. "You will shoot me?" he asks. "Remember where you are. Remember there are only three of you." His voice sharpens. "We are more than that, even now."

Skousen reverses the pistol in his hand, gripping it by the barrel. "I might not need a shot, chum." He raises his arm.

An emotion reaches me as from a distance, but I do not move. *This man is one of them*, I tell myself. *He admits it. He has just threatened us.* I hear the light accent of Frankfurter's precise voice, his words about the saboteurs. *Those men were enemies, Cash. They got what they deserved.* Skousen draws his arm back further, raising the elbow. Something familiar about the motion transfixes me. It evokes the final flourish of backswing that distinguishes a Merion player. I see John Hall float across the squash court, racquet above him, poised for the strike. I see him slumped on the dirty table with the plea ebbing from his eyes. *Help me, Cash.* I take a step toward Skousen, reaching for the gun.

"I will sign under protest," says Wakayama. Skousen lowers his hand. I pull out a pen. And Skousen walks him away to the trucks.

Miller and I stand outside the empty apartment. The wind whistles down the rows of black buildings. Castle Rock is a dark bulk on the horizon, darker than the clouds. "What did we just do?" I ask.

Miller pulls methodically on a cigarette. The glow casts shadows off his cheekbones, pulls a gleam from his dark hair. Hoover has a definite type. "That was the right thing. You don't understand these people."

"I understand we threatened to pistol-whip a veteran to make him give up his citizenship." For a moment I long to be back in Judge Goodman's Eureka courtroom, to hear someone say he forgives me.

Miller cradles the cigarette butt between thumb and forefinger. With his other hand, he flicks it away in a shower of sparks. "He wasn't really a citizen. He's subversive."

"He fought for this country. Did you?"

"Flat feet," says Miller. "That's why I'm in the Bureau. I know, walking punchline. You?"

"No," I say. "I didn't."

"Don't feel bad for old Kinzo," he says. "You did the right thing." He turns away from me, headed deeper into the colony.

"Where are you going?"

"There's one more," he says.

"Who?" My list is complete.

"The Bureau identified him."

I shrug. "Okay." I move to follow Miller.

"You don't have to come," he says. "I can handle him on my own."

"This was my idea," I say. "I'm there with you." He shrugs in turn.

We walk for several minutes in silence, until we come to Ward Ten, Block Forty-Seven. I have never been inside the colony, but the address is familiar. I stop, puzzled. Miller is in front of me, pushing the door open. I hear voices startled from sleep. By the time I make it inside, he has them out of bed. There are three children and a woman. There is Harry Nakamura. Nothing in his face indicates that he recognizes me. "Go to Mr. Oshige," he tells his wife. He turns to Miller. "They may leave?"

Miller nods. "Our business is with you."

"What do you want?" Nakamura asks after his family has left.

"We want your signature," Miller says.

"Wait," I say. "There's a mistake here. He's not on my list."

"He's on mine."

"Why?"

"He's an agitator." Miller looks at me, shadows pooling under his cheekbones. "You know different?"

I hesitate. "Yeah, I think I do."

"Come on," says Miller. "I backed you with Kinzo." He flashes his smile. "Don't turn on me here."

I shake my head. "Opler can straighten this out," I say, and start vaguely toward the door. It's a daft idea, for Marvin Opler is on the other side of the colony fence, a long walk away, and surely curled warm in his blankets under Franklin Roosevelt's watchful gaze. But I don't make it to the door anyway, for behind me there's a sudden grunt and a thud of bodies coming together, and a clattering as something hard skitters across the floor. I look down and see a black pistol turning in small circles at my feet.

CHAPTER 46

I PICK UP the gun. It is a blued Smith and Wesson .38 Special, a standard Bureau service revolver. The same kind I saw in Skousen's hand. Across the room, Miller and Nakamura are on the floor, locked in a peculiar embrace. "He went for you," says Miller breathlessly.

I turn the idea over in my mind. It is not convincing. "And yet it looks to me like he's the one holding you down."

Miller writhes in an unsuccessful effort to free himself. Now I can see the empty holster under his coat. "He attacked me," he says. "I told you he belonged on the list. Do you believe me now?"

I shake my head. "No," I say. "Get up."

Nakamura releases him, and Miller gets to his feet, brushing dust from his clothes. Nakamura stands half a pace away. "You should choose your friends more carefully," he says to me.

"He's not my friend."

"So it would seem."

I point the gun loosely in Miller's direction. Nakamura takes another step away, clearing the shot for me. "Who do you work for?"

He laughs incredulously. "You'd take his word over mine? Look at him!"

The *bozu* haircut is a nice touch, I think. It might have saved Harry Nakamura's life in the past weeks. It might have saved mine tonight. "Who do you work for?"

"Same man as you." Miller parts his lips and widens his eyes. I couldn't pull off that look with Frankfurter, and Miller can't do it with me. He is a better liar than John Hall, but not by much. Too theatrical in his incomprehension. He flashes his white smile, and for the first time I see in it something deceptive, something unfinished.

I shake my head. "I don't work for a man." He says nothing. "So you're one of the good guys," I say. "And he was going for me."

"That's right," says Miller, but his voice has lost its enthusiasm.

"Maybe so," I say. I heft the pistol experimentally, reverse the grip. The barrel is cold in my hand. "Maybe he's disloyal. And maybe he jumped you. Hit you with your own gun. Left you to bleed out on the ground or freeze to death in some ditch. And maybe the MPs will find your body in the morning. Maybe that's how it goes. Or maybe you're working for someone else and you'd like to tell me who it is."

Miller looks at me blankly. He's trying to judge my character; he's remembering, I think, how it went with Kinzo. Finally he speaks. "You wouldn't do that."

There is uncertainty in his voice. I have gotten better at bluffing. Or perhaps it is not a bluff. My fingers tighten on the gun and suddenly I'm not so sure. "I don't think you want to find out," I say. I am realizing that I don't either. "You tried to jump me from behind. You think I'm too soft for payback?"

"I wasn't going to hurt you." The evident absurdity of the statement cracks his facade; he sounds petulant now. It is a sign of weakness and I am heartened. "I was told to get rid of this guy, that's all."

"Why?"

"He's a troublemaker." Miller shrugs. "Interfering with the renunciations."

"And you wanted them to keep going."

He shrugs again. "You had your list, I had mine."

"And who gave it to you?"

Miller looks at Nakamura. "I can't tell you in front of him."

"Sure you can."

He whispers something, frowning urgently. I take a step closer to make out his words.

It is a mistake. He jumps for the gun in my hand. I pull back, but he hits my wrist, knocking it away. Again the blue-black shape slides across the floor. I dive in pursuit, grab it, and roll into a shooting crouch. There is no target. Miller has headed straight for the door, and as I come up I see it shutting behind him.

I rise to my feet and follow. I can hear his footsteps clattering away, and I look in the direction of the noise. But the lights are weak; already he is lost in the shadows. I drop the pistol to my side and stand looking out into the night. It was not much exertion, but my heart is racing. I stand and wait for it to slow.

"You would not have struck him," says Harry from behind me.

"I wouldn't have killed him," I say. "I don't know about the hitting."

"That is why I spoke, because I know."

I peer out into the dark. "You can just tell these things," I say. "You know when someone's about to—" I do not complete the thought. There is the crack of a gunshot and a piece of wood springs from the doorframe by my head. Miller has found another gun, or a friend with one. I duck back inside the room and push the door closed. "I'd hit him now, if I could get to him."

Harry looks at me in alarm. "Who is out there with firearms?"

"My team," I say.

"And how many of them are yours?"

"I guess not all. How can I know?"

Harry nods. "There was not time to ask them questions about American history," he says.

It seems unfair. I want to explain that I did the best I could, but the conditions are poor for a discussion. There is another gunshot, deeper this time. A rifle, I think, and the bullet tears easily through the plywood and tarpaper wall. A blue-patterned plate on the shelf explodes in fragments that dance around the room.

We drop to the floor. There is another shot, and another. At least two rifles now, and plenty of blue-patterned shards. Harry's family did not smash all their china in protest, but the failure is being remedied.

"With this much shooting, Best will send the troops," I say. "They'll be here in minutes."

Another shot comes through the wall. It is lower, hitting a tea set on the bottom shelf. For a moment I wonder why they persist. Then I understand. This is not covering fire, designed to keep us inside while Miller makes good his escape. The men behind the rifles mean to kill us.

"We do not have minutes," says Harry. I hear running feet outside and know he is right. I shoot back through the wall. Judge Skinner hunts and took me once to a pistol range. *It's going to kick, Cash,* he said, and I hear his voice now and steady my hands, though it is no use to me, shooting through plywood into the night. I have no idea where the men outside are. They know that we are in the small box of the apartment, and they are working their way through it, methodical as reapers. The shots make me flinch, though they should not. The ones you hear have missed you already. I fire back one more time, wondering if moving will help my odds. They know I am on the floor. But perhaps I could crawl to a part of the room they've hit already. Part of me is pleased to note that I am still thinking calmly. The rest is thinking that all pleasure will soon be over. There is no way out of this.

I hear a creak behind me, and when I look back, Harry has pulled up the floorboards. Underneath is a shallow pit. "In the time of the stockade we hid men here," he says.

"You hid them?"

"They did not belong in the stockade," he says. "Come, there is no time."

I fire another shot out through the door and crawl toward him. We slide down into the pit and he pulls the boards into place above us. More shots go by overhead. Then they stop. In the silence I hear the distant siren of an alarm. Best is rousing his MPs. Soon they will be piling into jeeps; soon I will hear the rumble of the motors and the crunch of tires.

But first I hear the door open. I hear boots tramping above. There are two men, maybe three, tossing the furniture and swearing. "Where's the other door?" a voice asks.

Someone is standing almost right on top of me now. "I don't think there is one." It is Agent Miller, speculation in his voice. He takes another step. Dirt drops from the floorboards onto my face, into my mouth. I try to blink it out of my eyes. I am thinking furiously, as though there is still some solution to grasp, as though I can figure out how the paths I have followed have come together in the dirt of this dry lake. And then my mind goes blank. There is nothing but a flow of images. The open sky over the great lawn at Merion, the russet sweep of clouds. The raindrops falling on me and Suzanne under the trees on Bear Island, the beautiful silly giants on their lighted screens. The green and gold of Clara's eyes. The things I will never see again if Miller notices that the boards ring hollow beneath his boots.

I imagine understanding dawning on his face. I see him raising a hand, pointing downward, beckoning his men into position around us. What will happen then? Will he lift the boards to investigate? Or will he just shoot through them? I clutch the pistol at my side. If he looks first, I will get a shot off. And even if he fires straightaway, I may be capable of reply. He could hit Harry, or no one. But there are others. Their rifles will be ready. If he notices the hollow note underfoot, I will die, here in the California dirt.

But he does not. Voices are raised outside, in English and Japanese. "Get back in your apartment," Miller yells, and someone answers his yell with their own defiant tones. Harry's neighbors do not know what is going on, but they do not like white faces behind rifles. And as Kinzo Wakayama told us, three men is not many this deep in the colony. I find myself praying there are enough Hoshidan left to rush the guns.

Miller pivots abruptly. "Time to go," he says. The boots thud across the floor and out into the night. There is silence, and through it comes the rising hum of the motors. The MPs are here.

. . . .

The trucks take 125 to Santa Fe that morning. The farewell is weaker, there is no doubt. I watch them pull away, olive drab canvas stretched over steel frames, streamers of exhaust rising like breath in the still air. I think about the men hunched in the back, about Kinzo Wakayama, who fought in the war to end all wars.

Agent Miller is nowhere to be found. Two others of my team are gone, three Relocation Authority men, and two jeeps from the motor pool. And Ray Best is angry. "What are you doing?" he demands.

"This is your camp."

"And I had everything under control."

"No you didn't. You had loyal American citizens being terrorized by traitors."

"No one was shooting up the apartments and stealing my jeeps." That is what irks him the most, I think, that he will have to report loss of federal property from his care.

As for pursuit, it is out of the question. I may take my team on foot; I may pack as many as I can into our black government cars, but I will have no help from Best. "That's not my job," he says. "You're having trouble with your own men."

"Some of yours, too."

"Be realistic," he says. One hand points to the empty expanse around us. "You'll never find them."

He is right. We can notify the local Bureau branches, but if Miller and his fellows want to disappear, we will never see them again.

Harry and his family are plugging holes in their walls with cloth and sweeping up china.

"Those Relocation Authority men," I ask. "Are they the ones who were encouraging people to renounce?"

"I do not know," Harry says. "From the descriptions, perhaps. They may have been the ones asking for names of loyalists, too."

"They were doing that?" Two sets of men, I think, making two lists. "Did people talk to them?"

"Some did."

"Do you mean we've been taking out loyalists too?"

"You have taken some, yes."

"And you didn't tell me?"

"I assumed you knew. They were taken at your direction, Mr. Harrison."

"I never directed that," I say. Like his remark about the American history test, this seems unfair. "You wouldn't tell me who was encouraging renunciation, either."

He shrugs. "At the time, it was not evident which of my captors I should trust."

I take a step back. "I'm not your captor."

"You do not want to be. I can see that. But we are not only what we want to be."

I bite my lip. "Tell me about these land reclamation agents."

"They came to those who were renouncing. They offered compensation."

"There's no compensation due," I say. "That was not the government. That was people buying the land. What did they offer?"

"The certificates," Harry says. "I can find you one." He goes to a neighboring apartment and returns with a document. It looks official; there is italicized print, looping signatures, the stamp of a seal. But it is not the seal of any government.

And now I am hearing a raspy, puzzled voice, seeing a young man's uniform tight on an old man's paunch. For what I hold in my hand is a stock certificate for a bankrupt company. I have seen these certificates before; my father and his friends had plenty of them. One year, in fact, the members of the State in Schuylkill roasted their shad over a fire fed largely by the worthless stock of the New York, New Haven, and Hartford Railroad.

Joe Patterson's railroad.

CHAPTER 47

"I HAVE TO go back to Washington," I tell Ray Best. "There will be no more marching here. No more bugles. No more salutes to the emperor. These people are Americans. All of that stops."

"Or what? What can we threaten them with? They think removal is a reward."

I click my teeth together in frustration. There are no good choices. I look at him for a moment. "Put the stockade back up."

The next morning, some kids form a column in the firebreak. The MPs swoop in and grab the ones who don't run. We put fifteen in the stockade, and there are no more chants. The Hoshidan are gone, too, all we could find of them. The camp is calm again.

There are also 5,500 new-minted aliens, fruit of the hearings we conducted. I ride the train back with the boxes of renunciation forms. The sky burns overhead, scarlet and umber. At night, rain follows us across the rivers, tearing the black water to ragged silver under the moon. I look out the window until the light fails and the glass shows only my own reflection.

I reach Washington on Sunday, the day the Relocation Authority announces that the camps will be closing. Now it is official. The government gets there one day ahead of the Supreme Court, which hands down the decisions in *Korematsu* and *Endo* on Monday. I sit in the spectator gallery and listen to Black read his opinion. There was evidence of disloyalty, he says, and time was of the essence. The Court cannot second-guess the military judgment. I cannot tell if he sees me or if he can read my expression; I do not know what that expression is. I feel tired, my face slack and heavy.

Clara hunches in the chair behind the Douglas column. Next to her, the Murphy clerk sits pale and still. There are still three votes against the government. Roberts reads from his dissent, then Murphy, then Jackson. By the time Douglas starts to announce *Endo*, most of the crowd is gone. They have their story: evacuation was justified. The camps are closing anyway; *Endo* hardly matters.

When the hand-down is over I sit on the marble steps below the great bronze doors. Workers have swept the snow on the plaza into banks around the empty fountains. I see Justice Roberts making his way down the stairs, walking slowly.

"Justice," I call to him.

He stops. "Mr. Harrison."

"I admire your opinion," I say. "I just wanted to tell you that."

Roberts blinks against the wind. "You never knew the Old Court. They say we stood in the way of progress. Perhaps we did. But we stood there for liberty." He coughs. "Now we are just Roosevelt's men. It is not the Court I knew. I will be leaving at the end of the year. For all of us, there is a moment to alight the train of history. And you?"

"I don't know," I say. "I'm at Justice for a while."

Roberts pulls his coat tighter. "Tell Francis Biddle this is what his New Deal brought."

I watch him walk away, careful on the stone. He has tried to hold the line and failed. Now he is going back to Philadelphia. The dean's chair waits for him at the law school. He will take it for a dollar a year, just as the captains of industry came to Washington to serve the New Deal he flees. He will tell the students that the country around them is not the one that lives in his mind.

It is the time-honored response of Philadelphians whose wisdom the nation has rejected. At that moment I think it has much to recommend it. But I am not quite done here.

At Main Justice, the boxes of renunciation forms lie in my office, awaiting Francis Biddle's signature. I sift through them, remembering the hearings I conducted. So many answers about the Sacred Shrine, so many about Emperor Jimmu. So many scared faces. Fumiko's form is in my hands. Now it is ripping. A strip peels off the side, then another. The sound of paper tearing is a girl's voice singing. A white ribbon drops into my wastebasket. Fumiko looks out through the fence, across the desert sea. Another ribbon falls. Harry Nakamura lifts a floorboard from a shallow grave.

"Am I interrupting something, Mr. Harrison?"

Clyde Tolson stands in the doorway. I drop the rest of the form into the trash. "No."

"Good. Come with me." He does not take me by the elbow this time, but his demeanor is the same as on our first trip to see the Director. We pass the murals, the agents, the receptionist. Hoover sits at his desk on the raised platform, a little man with his enormous flags. Tolson takes his place against the wall and Hoover turns his head in my direction.

"What are you doing, Mr. Harrison?"

"I'm doing my job."

"What happened in Tule Lake?"

"Don't you know? One of your pretty boys tried to kill me."

There is a burst of noise in my left ear as Tolson slaps the side of my head. I turn and he's got his fists up in a fighting pose. "The Director asked you a question."

"It's all right, Clyde." Hoover stands, hands splayed on his desk. "We will find Special Agent Miller. But I would like to know what you think you are investigating."

I look at him a moment. The answer is pretty clear to me now. The stock certificates are just another attempt to make a quick buck, the consistent goal of Richards's Anti-Federalist friends. And if Brutus and the Farmer aren't Joe and Cissy Patterson, I'll eat my hat. I could just give Hoover their names. But what would he do with the information? Put it in a file, use it to increase his power, demand their cooperation? It would be unpleasant for them; it would be punishment of a sort. But something in me rebels at the idea. "Sorry," I say. "Couldn't hear you. Kind of a ringing in my ear right now."

Hoover smiles thinly. "You are freelancing, Mr. Harrison. You are pursuing your own agenda. I can help you with that. But I have explained already, you must do things for me in return."

"Sorry," I say again. I try to sound like Colonel Richards, the man of principle. "I don't play that game."

"How about that, Clyde?" Hoover asks. "He doesn't play that game."

"So I hear," Tolson says.

"Don't you get tired of being the straight man, Clyde?" I ask. I turn back to Hoover and try to tell myself he doesn't scare me. This small man on his raised platform with his giant flags. "I'm not afraid of you, Director." But it doesn't have quite the ring of truth I was going for. I am not Richards.

More to the point, Hoover is not me. His smile grows broader. "That's how I know you're in over your head. Say hello to your friend."

"Who?" I ask. But some primitive part of my nervous system shrieks an alarm, starts a tingling along my spine. It spreads to my shoulder blades. I know who he's talking about. I sent them after her in the first place.

"Clara," says Hoover. "Watson, isn't it?"

"So I hear," says Tolson. He smiles as though he's managed to get off a joke.

"That is the game you're playing, Mr. Harrison. You are not the only piece on the board. Ask her if she thinks you should cooperate."

"Ask her," Tolson repeats as he shows me out. But I have no intention of that. I have moved past fear to anger. Hoover can bluster, but he cannot do any real harm. He has nothing on us, and I have other questions in mind. At Dupont Circle, I see the familiar enveloping wings of Cissy Patterson's house and walk straight into their embrace.

A man in a dark suit answers the door.

"I'm looking for Joe Patterson," I say.

"Mr. Patterson is not receiving callers today."

I produce my card. "You can tell him it's not a social visit."

The man makes no move to take it. "He is not receiving callers."

I push the card forward until it buckles against his chest. "The Department of Justice would like a word with him."

He seems skeptical. "And they sent you?"

"Tell him it's about the Anti-Federalist Society. And it will be the FBI next time. His choice."

He takes my card and vanishes. For five minutes I study the columns, the balcony, the thick wooden door. Then the man returns. "Mr. Patterson is not receiving callers."

"You have my card if he changes his mind," I say.

"Ah," he says. "I forgot." He extends his hand and I take what he offers. It is my card. I look at it dumbly. "Mr. Patterson is not accepting cards."

I let him shut the door on me without another word. If Patterson stonewalls, what can I do? Turn him over to Hoover, I guess. Or go talk to a man of honor.

. . . .

Colonel Richards is on the phone when I enter his office, finishing a joke. "And she says, 'When I came in here, I wasn't.'" He laughs. Then he catches sight of me and his face changes. "Call you right back."

"So, Bill," I say.

"What?"

"You hear about what happened in Tule Lake?"

"Yes."

"For people who aren't trying to kill me, your friends used an awful lot of bullets."

He shakes his head. "That wasn't them."

"Because they would have told you? No offense, but I don't think you're getting quite the whole story here. I think Joe and Cissy have a sideline you don't know about." He frowns at the names and I continue. "They're using you, Bill. They're making a fool of you."

"A fool?" I have surprised him, but he is gathering himself. "Almost two hundred years ago, some men dressed themselves as Indians and threw tea into Boston Harbor. They were fools, surely. They deserved the scorn of people like you. But everything we are today came from their folly."

"This isn't the tea party, Bill." I take the certificate Harry Nakamura gave me from my pocket. "It's worthless stock being traded for Japanese land. That's what they didn't want me to find out about. That's why they were shooting at me." I spread the certificate on his desk. "And it's Joe Patterson's stock."

Richards looks down. "That railroad was publicly held. Anyone could own its shares."

"And they'd just decide to use them to fool people into signing away their land? That's a bit of a coincidence, don't you think?"

"The world is full of surprises."

I lean forward. "Listen, Bill. I know what's going on. You put the clerks in and they didn't affect the cases. All that effort for nothing. And someone thought, why should it be wasted? Clerks can do other things, if they're loyal to you. Press the Court to hear business cases. Tell you how they'll come out so you can buy stock. That's what Gene Gressman was figuring out. That's why they killed him. Joe and Cissy used you. They're making money off it, and you're their dupe."

"I don't think so." But he looks troubled.

"I'm going to prove it. If I live long enough. You said they didn't want to hurt me, and maybe they didn't. Not then. But they don't want to get found out, either, and if I keep coming after them, I'm pretty sure how it's going to end. Is that what your principles demand?"

Richards blinks at me. What I have said is true, I think. That is how Miller came to be shooting at an official of his own government. One step led to another; each attempt to cover up created a new crime. Swindling the detainees out of their land, putting a loyal man on the list for removal, hitting me from behind, killing us both. The stakes increased on their own; he just kept pace. "No one is going to kill you," Richards says at last. "But I will make some calls."

CHAPTER 48

I HAVE ALMOST stopped thinking of the office as belonging to James Rowe. Familiarity has made it mine. My chairs, my desk, my window looking out onto Pennsylvania Avenue. My boxes of renunciation forms, my letter of resignation awaiting a signature. I call down to the mailroom for a trolley and take the boxes to Biddle's office myself. He watches me wheel them in.

"What are these?"

"The renunciation forms."

He draws in his breath. It is not a gasp, more the preparation for a sigh. "How many?"

"Fifty-five hundred or so."

"We only got five thousand applications here." There is surprise in his voice, and something like reproach.

"There were more out there. Once the hearing teams arrived, they stopped mailing them in."

"Cash," he says. "You were supposed to stop it."

"I did everything I could." I remember Kinzo Wakayama blinking against my light, Skousen holding the gun above his head. "Maybe more than I should have."

Biddle lifts the cover off one of the boxes. He raises a handful of forms and lets them slide down over his fingers. He leans back in his chair and looks at me. Now it is time for the sigh.

"Then don't approve them," I say. "They still need your signature."

"Are they voluntary?"

"Voluntary? They said the right words. They memorized the answers. They feared for their lives."

Biddle collects himself. "The law is clear." I can almost see it, wrapping around his shoulders, covering him head to toe. He is the Attorney General again, not a worried man hiding his bald spot. "If they're voluntary, I have to sign."

He is uncapping a pen as I leave. Soon the letters will go out. I imagine them on their way to California, a fleet of paper upon the land. *Your application for renunciation has been approved by the Attorney General.* To Masaaki Kuwabara, whose father hid in the sugarcane. To Joe Imihara, whose mother was a picture bride. She crossed the Pacific in an envelope, paper made flesh by years of toil. *You are no longer a citizen of the United States.* The parents could never be Americans, but the children might be. Now another envelope comes to take that away, a two-cent stamp to ship them all beyond the sea. *Nor are you entitled to any of the rights and privileges of such citizenship.* To Pat Noguchi, who said he forgave me.

I sit in my office and spend the rest of the day waiting to hear from Richards. Then I go to my apartment and wait some more.

• • • •

I have gone to bed resigning myself to the fact that there will be no news today when the doorman buzzes. "A young lady here to see you," he says, though his tone implies pretty clearly that no one deserving of that appellation would arrive alone so late at night.

Clara toys distractedly with objects on my bookshelf. "Is this a trophy?"

"Take your coat off," I say.

She looks full at me for the first time, and I can see she's been crying. "Douglas fired me."

"What? Why?"

"He figured out I was talking to you."

I feel an emptiness open in my chest, coupled with a strange downward pull in my throat. I think, *This is my heart sinking.* The phrase has never been more vivid to me. "How?"

Clara shrugs. "I don't know." She takes off her coat and sits on the coach, hugging it to her chest. "I think someone told him. He went out this evening and then he burst back in. I was working late. He'd been drinking. He told me he couldn't employ anyone who'd go behind his back."

"Oh, no," I say. I take a seat beside her. "Oh, no." Involuntarily, my hand goes over my mouth. Some part of me is hoping this is a coincidence, random accident rather than the rebound of my attempts at protection. Some selfish part, since that makes it no better for anyone but me.

"What?" Clara asks. And the phone rings.

I answer.

"So," says Clyde Tolson. "How's your friend?"

"You've gone white," Clara tells me. "What's happening?"

"We know things about you, too," says Tolson. "We know you met with Horsky. We know what you told him. Would you like Francis Biddle to learn that?"

"I'd like you to screw yourself."

"One of the few disappointments in your young life, I'm afraid. There's someone else there I want to talk to."

I look to the side. "She doesn't want to talk to you."

Clara gestures, her hand a white moth in the dark.

"I think she does," says Tolson. "Put her on." I pass Clara the phone. She listens for a moment and hangs up. We look at each other.

"I made this happen," I say. "It's my fault. Hoover wanted me to do something for him, and I wouldn't. And so he talked to Douglas, to show me he could reach us." She says nothing. "Clyde Tolson threatened you, didn't he?"

She nods, tight-lipped.

"With what?"

A shake of the head. "What does Hoover want you to do?"

"To tell him something," I say.

"To give him names?"

"Yes."

"People who will be under his power?"

"Yes."

"You cannot do that."

"They're bad people," I say. "The people who killed Gene and John Hall." I explain what I have figured out, Joe and Cissy running their side project, committing murders to cover it up. "They should be punished."

"They should be prosecuted," Clara says. "But you don't think Hoover would do that."

"There's nothing that would stand up in court if he wanted to charge them. And they're powerful. He'd see them as prizes, probably, that he could keep under his thumb. Just use the information to make them do things for him."

She shakes her head. "Then you cannot."

"Look," I say. "Hoover can't do anything to me. Biddle agrees with me about the evacuation. But I want to protect you."

"By hurting Joe and Cissy?"

"I don't care how. That's not the point. But I'm not going to lose sleep over what happens to them. They're bad people. I'm—"

"The good guy?"

"Yes."

"Why?" The lights are coming up in her eyes. "Tell me how you sacrifice yourself for the innocent, I will agree that makes you good. But tell me how willing you are to hurt others for my sake, in my name? No. That does not make you good."

"Look, I would be happy to suffer myself if it helped you."

"But sacrificing others is the only way."

"I don't see any other."

She looks at me, quiet and beautiful. "No one ever does."

"This isn't a game," I continue. "We don't know what he'll do next."

"Oh, I know."

"What?"

"He will tell you something. About me."

I am puzzled. Miller found something, perhaps, but what? "What could he tell me?" She says nothing. "I know your circumstances are not mine."

"My circumstances," says Clara, and in her voice is a hint of that early disdain, the tone in which she spoke of malt shops and movies. "This is not a circumstance."

"What is it?"

Clara produces a mirror and compact from her handbag. She inspects her reflection and dabs at her face with a handkerchief. "I appreciate that you are trying to do the right thing."

"So is everyone."

"No, they're not. Don't be silly." She gives a last look in the mirror and tries a smile. "You see, most things can be fixed."

"What would Hoover tell me?"

"Do you have anything to drink? Oh, don't look around for a bell to ring. You must have a bottle of some sort."

"There's whiskey."

"That's fine."

I get two glasses from the kitchen, a bottle from the bar. "Here's how," says Clara. She coughs on the drink, tears starting.

"Are you okay?"

"Yes," she says. "I think I am. And now I will tell you something. I will solve a mystery for you."

"What?"

"Why I went to Dupont Circle."

"Why did you?"

"It is closer to the Y than you think."

"I don't understand."

"Not the 17th street Y. The YWHA." She reaches a hand inside her blouse, taking hold of the golden chain around her neck. A Star of David glints at her fingertips. "Wasserman," she says. "Before Watson."

Tolson's smile makes sense now. "That's what Hoover would tell me? So what? It doesn't matter."

Clara takes another drink and blinks slowly. "You are sweet to say that. But it is a luxury to think so. A luxury not everyone can afford."

I remember the empty shoes in the photograph Wechsler pushed at me. "I can afford it. We can."

Clara leans back. Her hair is in her face. "I will not argue with you now. I am tired and the whiskey is on your side."

I wait, but she says nothing more. Her eyelids flutter half-closed. "Do you want to stay here?" I ask. "I just mean I don't want to send you home like this. I swear my intentions are pure."

"You still think that men seduce women," says Clara. She opens her multicolored eyes, and suddenly she no longer looks tired. "Poor boy."

It is not like it was with Suzanne. There is no suspension, no whispered prayer for silk to stop my fall. There is only the falling, and it goes on and on, in fierce silence and sharp bursts of breath. Clara twines her fingers in mine, closes her eyes and says my name. In the morning, the pillow I hold smells of lilac and she is gone.

CHAPTER 49

THE LIGHT OF a March morning spills across my bed. I open my eyes and blink at the ceiling. Then I turn my head to the side. Under the sun, red and gold lightning flashes within the dark storm cloud of Clara's hair. Her eyelids flutter. Still asleep, she flings out her arm, searching for something, and I move aside to let her seek until I realize it's me she wants. She takes my shoulder and pulls herself closer, making a small satisfied noise in her throat. Her breath brushes my face. Then, as though the proximity has awakened her, she opens those rainbow eyes.

I should be used to this, but I am not. Her shoulders in the morning light, her hair across the pillow. Her eyes looking into mine. Months ago, with Tule Lake and *Korematsu* still fresh in my mind, I came down with a fever. I lay awake all night, burning with sickness, and as I lay there I heard her talking. In her sleep she said terrible things. She would not come again. I had failed; I was on the wrong side; I had done nothing to help those who needed me.

The fever broke some time in the early morning and I woke soaked in sweat, wrung out like a rag. Clara smiled at me. "Better?" she asked. I had to tell her. I needed to know if it was true, I said. I wouldn't blame her.

Clara just shook her head. "I didn't say those things."

"You were asleep," I said. "I heard it."

"You didn't. You were the one who was asleep," she said. "That was a night-

351

mare. It happens with fever. I know because I sat up all night." She showed me a piece of knitting. "I was watching you."

It was beyond my comprehension then, and as I look into her eyes, it still is. I cannot put it all together; I cannot grasp the arithmetic of her. It eludes me, the sum of hair and eyes and lips, of fine high cheekbones and slender hands.

Her fingers stroke my face. "My boy," she says.

· · · ·

And so we go on. Clara finds work as a typist, for which sixty words a minute will still get you twenty-five dollars a week. She sits at my table in the mornings and reads the paper. March turns to April; the Allies push on into Germany. Clara reads about figures in striped pajamas and wheelbarrows of the dead. She reads about hundreds of thousands of shoes.

Hoover makes us no more threats. His men catch up with Miller in a Santa Rosa alley and they shoot more accurately than I did that night in Tule Lake. I suppose he considers the matter closed.

I do not. I do not have FBI investigators anymore, but I use Biddle's connections at the SEC. It is an arduous process, sifting through all the trades in the stock of companies Gene Gressman identified, and harder still to trace it back to Joe or Cissy. Their complex sprawl of holdings masks responsibility. There is suspicious activity, but I cannot pin it on them. Not yet.

But with enough time I can, and it seems I will have that time. They will not try to stop me. For weeks after my return from Tule Lake I walk with one eye scanning shop window reflections, double back on my tracks. But no one is following me. Richards was right, I guess. No one is trying to kill me; for some reason, I have been spared.

Then comes the afternoon of April 12, when all the phones ring at once and a secretary runs through the halls crying out, "He's dead." The *Times-Herald* has no words on the front page, just a photograph bordered in black.

The war does not wait. The day Roosevelt dies, the Ninth Army crosses the Elbe. By the end of April, Hitler is dead. The surrender is official a week later. That evening, for the first time since Pearl Harbor, lights come on atop the Capitol dome.

At Main Justice, another torrent of letters begins to arrive for the Alien Enemy Control Unit. The renunciants are changing their minds.

. . . .

I signed against my will. My husband signed, and whatever he does, I have to be loyal to him.

I was a member of the Hoshidan and was told that unless I renounced, the US Army would draft me after the Relocation Authority forced us outside.

I never wanted to renounce. My parents wanted to take me back to Japan, and we heard Japan would not accept anyone who was an American citizen. They begged and cried. I gave in to make them happy.

The Hoshidan knew who had renounced and who had not. They threw rocks on the roof and through the window of our barracks. I was afraid for myself and my sisters.

I heard that all Japanese would be deported to Japan and the citizens forced to remain here. I did not want my family separated.

You put us there because you were scared. I forgive you for that. Can you forgive me nothing?

. . . .

"You have to help them," Clara says.

"There's nothing we can do," Francis Biddle tells me. "It's the law. They did it willingly."

Again I remember the terrified faces. The children of the picture brides. Pictures are what will be left, empty gardens, empty homes. "And we enforce the law, no matter what it is?"

"That's what the Department of Justice does, yes."

At my office there is one addressed to me personally, from Harry Nakamura. His wife renounced, he reports. *Sachiko believed the rumors. She thought that if she did not renounce she would be forced to leave the camp. Fresno is a dangerous place now. I advised her not to. I commanded. I begged. Nothing would change her mind. She was hysterical.*

Now she knows the rumors are false and that in a few moments of panic she has thrown away her happiness, her future, and her family. She tells me to go out and take our three children, that she will stay behind alone and commit suicide. She did not renounce out of disloyalty. She would never do anything against this country. Can you help us? I am sitting at my desk, wondering how to answer that question, when my phone rings. It is Bill Richards.

"I'd like to chat," he says. "But not over the phone."

I agree that this is wise. At his suggestion, we meet at the round bar of the Willard Hotel. "Henry Clay made Washington's first mint julep here," Richards says. He wipes sweat from his forehead. "Mixed it himself. There's no better summer drink."

"I'm working." This is not really true. There is nothing for me to do at Main Justice, nothing I want to do, anyway.

"Let me know if you change your mind," says Richards, signaling to the bartender. "I have some news for you."

"What?"

"Joe Patterson will see you."

"When?"

"Up to you. But I'd recommend sooner rather than later. At your earliest convenience, I would say."

I look around the room. At the round bar in the center, men in suits are drinking lunch. No one looks at us, in our black leather booth against the wall.

"What does he have to tell me?"

"I don't know." Richards sips his drink and sighs in appreciation. A fleck of mint clings to his upper lip. "I tend my business; he tends his. He just said to send you over. If you're so curious, go now."

I nod my head and get up without another word. "Good luck," says Richards, raising his glass.

. . . .

The man who answers the door at the Dupont Circle house has a different expression this time. I would not call it welcoming, but there is a note of approval. His overall tone is somber, though. When I am ushered upstairs to Joe Patterson's room I can see why, and why Richards recommended I visit soon.

Joe Patterson is not well. From the evidence of my eyes, I would say he is dying. He reclines on a chaise longue in a red silk robe, and where it falls away I can see wasted sticklike limbs. Something has happened to the texture of his skin.

"Calvin Coolidge stayed here for six months," he says. The rasp in his voice is stronger. His face still has that pleasant quizzical expression, as though he wants to be my friend and can't understand what keeps us apart. "He fed his dogs on the dining room rug. Cissy was quite displeased." He clears his throat with effort.

"I suppose you know why I've come."

"Why I sent for you," he corrects me. "I know well enough. I have principles, Mr. Harrison."

"Sure you do," I say. "Like creases in paper."

His expression grows even more quizzical. "I don't follow you."

"No, you don't. Never mind."

"I have something to say to you," he says. "And not much time to do it." Something darker glitters in his eyes. "I swore I'd outlive that bastard Roosevelt, and I made it, by God."

"So what is it?" I know I am being rude, but I do not much care.

"That I am sorry."

"For killing my friends? For trying to kill me?"

"I am sorry those things happened. I could have stopped them, if I had kept closer watch." He coughs, drowning in his own body. Soon he will escape it. "But my attention has wandered."

"You mean it was Cissy? Is that what you're trying to tell me?"

"Cissy?" He sounds puzzled. Then he nods. "Ah, the parties."

"Yes, the parties. You wanted to recruit me, is that it? Thought I'd join your little club?"

"We thought to sound out your views, yes."

"And I failed your test."

"You did not pass. You were under the sway of Drew Pearson and Francis Biddle."

"I didn't know anyone here. They're from Philadelphia."

It starts as a laugh, I think, but by the time it comes from his mouth it is a cough. "That means so much to you," he says.

"It's something."

"It is something. But perhaps not what you believe it is."

"I'll take the State in Schuylkill over the Anti-Federalist Society, thanks."

"Who says you have to choose?" He pauses. Again the laugh struggles with the cough in his throat. "We are not bad men, Cash."

"You really think that?"

"Someday you may be grateful to us."

"Why would that be?"

"We tried to influence the Court," Patterson says. "And we failed. We could not stop Roosevelt. But we have learned."

"You learned how to make a buck?"

He shakes his head. "We learned that the courts are not enough. We must plant ideas among the people. And we have. Seeds will sprout. You will see them, you or your children. When the next one comes, we will be ready. The next one who tries to crush liberty under the heel of government, to take what makes this country special. The people will be ready."

"That's a pretty speech," I say. "But it's not what you were doing. I know about the cert grants. I found the stock trades. You killed people for money, that's all."

"That was not my doing."

"But it was done."

"It was not me. I only wanted to tell you that. What happened to your friends, what happened in California, you must take it up with him."

"Him?" I do not understand. "If it wasn't you, it was Cissy. Brutus and the Farmer."

"No," Patterson says. "The Farmer, I chose that name. Silly. But Cissy had no part."

"Then who is Brutus?"

He shakes his head as though disappointed in me. "Why, the man who put you here."

"What are you talking about?"

"You still do not know?" His tone is gentle. "I thought you kept track of each other."

There is a prickle at the back of my neck. "Who?"

Something catches in Patterson's throat and his next words are barely audible. At first I am sure I have mistaken them. "Who?"

Now the words are clear. There is a hiss to them, and a look on his face that says he no longer wants to be friends. Perhaps he has had his fill of us. "You Philadelphia boys."

CHAPTER 50

WASHINGTON TO PHILADELPHIA is 130 miles or so, and you can do it in a little under three hours on a good day, with the sun out and the road dry and the engine humming along like it's glad to be on the way. Things are different if night is falling and you're half the time shaking with rage and blinded by tears the rest. And it is past dark when I knock on that familiar door in Haverford.

Judge Skinner looks surprised to see me, but he looks pleased, too. He has been out this evening but has returned. The stiff white shirt is open at the neck and he has taken off his jacket and thrown on a robe. "Cash," he says, and his voice is warm. Then the smile weakens and the voice dips half a notch to indicate disappointment. "I'm afraid Suzanne is not in."

"No, Judge," I say. "I'm here for you."

The smile returns in full force. "Well, then," he says. "Come in, come in."

I follow him to the library. There is the familiar smell of the leather-bound books, the slow drying and decay of the pages. It seemed beautiful in a sad sort of way when I realized that history itself sinks into the past, that even the law fades. It does not seem beautiful to me now.

"You must have been driving for hours," says the Judge. He motions me to a red leather chair. "I'll wager you still drink Scotch."

I do not sit. "Did you put me there?" On the way up I have given this conversation as much thought as I was able, and this is my opening move.

For the briefest of instants there is a different look on the Judge's face, one almost of alarm. Then it is gone, so completely that anyone would think it must have been a shift of the light and not something from the face itself. "Put you where, my boy?"

"The Supreme Court."

The Judge chuckles, deep and comforting. "Cash, you overestimate me. You think I can make Hugo Black hire someone? Or Herbert Wechsler pick up the phone? You flatter me. Are you sure you would not like a drink?" I say nothing. "Well, I will have a Scotch. A visit from you is worth celebrating." He turns to the crystal decanter.

"Did you put me there?"

He turns back, and his face is older. "You put yourself there, Cash. I only made a space for you."

"So you manipulated the hiring," I say. "You and your Anti-Federalist Society."

There is sorrow on the Judge's face. Only someone who knew what he was looking for would guess that under it is relief. He purses his lips and exhales. For a long time he says nothing, looking down at his hands. Then, slowly, he starts to speak. "We were men like any others," he says. "We loved our country." He is making a clean breast of things. "We were alarmed by the direction it was taking, worried that what made America special might be lost." He raises his head. "Francis Biddle invited Felix Frankfurter to address the Fly Club. Did you know that?"

"I heard."

He shakes his head. "It would not have happened before Roosevelt. Some of us met elsewhere that night. We found that we shared concerns. Roosevelt was a Fly man himself, you know. One of us. Our responsibility, in a way. We agreed that we should do what we could to preserve our country."

"You started a club."

He smiles. "It is the Philadelphia way. We knew there were limits to what we could achieve. We hoped to strengthen the will of the Supreme Court. We failed, of course. The Court gave up; it let Roosevelt do as he wished."

"Owen Roberts changed his mind."

"He did not do so willingly. The Anti-Federalists lost in 1789, and we lost again in 1935. We are only tinkering at the margins now. But we helped you, yes."

"By drafting the other clerks?

He nods.

"And did you think what you were doing to them? Are they dead now?"

The Judge sits down in his leather chair. He gazes at the fireplace. I think he is looking for something to handle, but there is no fire now and he would look silly poking at the ashes. "I don't know," he says at last, and sips his drink. "But if they are, they saved someone else's life. Perhaps yours. Men die in war, Cash. The harvest is taken in, and neither you nor I can stop it. There are graves that must be filled. Will you stand here and tell me you'd rather be in one of them?"

I ignore the question. "So you thought I'd help you? Join your society?"

The Judge looks at me and I can almost see his mind working, trying to guess how much I know. His voice is careful. "I thought your views were sound."

"Is that all? I have been thinking, Judge. I have been remembering. In 1935 Suzanne was worried. Worried about money, I realize that now." I hear her voice again, shivering in my arms under the trees. *You'll take care of me.* "But you are doing quite well these days."

"Everyone is doing better. Suzanne was a child then. What did she know?"

"She knew a certain railroad had gone bankrupt. She knew what you talked of at night. Her father, whom she loved. In 1935, you knew you had lost at the Court. Did you think of another use for the men you put there? Did you decide you should at least make some money?"

The Judge is gathering himself. "No one makes money, my boy. Wealth is not created ex nihilo. The Crash taught us that, if nothing else." He is a voice of wisdom now, speaking from the ages. "It must come from somewhere. Like anything else, it must be taken from someone. How did you take your money? That is the question."

"And you thought I'd help you take some? Tell you how the cases were coming out? All that talk about my high purpose. How special I was, what great things lay before me. While you sent me to Washington for your own ends."

His face flickers and he turns away. One more secret gone. When he looks up his expression is earnest. "No, Cash," he says. "Did I ever ask you anything? Did anyone? I put you there to protect you. To keep you safe."

"Of course." I remember the doctor's smile. "You fixed my physical first, I suppose. And then when I wanted to volunteer, you needed a little more." I am running the tally in my head. Two clerks taken to make room for me with Black. Gene Gressman and John Hall killed in my stead. Bill Fitch falling from the sky and his dad taking a razor into the car. "I never wanted to be safe."

The sharpness in my voice surprises him. "What, then?"

"I wanted to be good."

He smiles, as though recognizing a problem he can solve. "You are good, Cash. Never doubt that."

"Am I? Or am I just the right sort of guy?"

The Judge shakes his head, waving the question off. "The others tried to recruit you, but that was never the point. What I did was for you. It was all for you."

"All of it," I say, and I can see the phrase worries him. "Everything you did."

His hands go back to the decanter, still steady. "A drink," he says again, as though offering treatment for a hurt I am too proud to admit. I shake my head. "The Farmer chose his name well," I say. "He was a farmer, after a fashion." The Judge nods, puzzled at the change in direction. "You did, too."

He nods again. "Brutus was a judge."

"Robert Yates was a judge," I say, "who took the name Brutus to write against the Constitution. I'm sure that pleased you. But it is not what I meant. It is not why the name suits you."

"Why, then?"

"Who was Brutus?" I ask. "Brutus was a killer, who stabbed his friend in the back. You gave the order, didn't you?"

Again there is a flicker across his face. "What do you mean?"

"You mentioned graves, Judge. They have been on my mind. Did you go to John Hall's funeral?"

For a moment he is silent, so still he seems removed from time. "So, Cash," he says. The different look is settling on his face, as though the light in the room has changed. "There are doors we can open but never close again. Are you sure this is what you want to talk about?"

"Did you console his parents? Smile a sad smile for lightfoot lads?" The Judge says nothing. "Did you shake his father's hand?"

"I never meant for this to happen, Cash. I never said to kill anyone. I told them to do what was necessary."

"To be as reasonable as they could."

He looks at me blankly. I think. It is possible, I suppose, that the decision to kill came about somehow through the conspiracy itself, that authority diffused itself among them so that the choice cannot be laid at the feet of any one man. The Judge thought he ordered one thing, and his minions heard something else. "You had no idea it might happen?"

"I didn't know it was John Hall." The words are slow, as though each weighs an untold amount, as though each is brought forth with enormous effort. "I heard only that you had a source in the War Department. Of course I suffered when I learned who it was. I cried like a child. I would not have hurt him. He ate at my table. More times than you know, perhaps."

I let that pass. "That explains it? You didn't know it was Hall."

"But you did," the Judge says. He is bestirring himself; he thinks he sees an opening. "Did you never think you might be putting him at risk? I warned you not to stay in Washington. I said it was dangerous. John Hall paid for that. He is dead because you did not listen."

"He is dead because you killed him." The Judge says nothing. I cannot stand still for this. I pace; I look at the spines of books on the wall. "And Gene Gressman. I suppose that was easier. You knew he was no one."

The Judge looks down again. His voice is sad. "There was no choice, Cash. He was on the point of discovering us."

"Gene was nowhere near you," I say. "He thought Felix Frankfurter was behind it all."

"In a way, he was. It was that speech—"

"Shut up." I have never raised my voice to him before. I am not sure anyone has, not since he became the Judge. Suzanne perhaps, but she is different. I look at him and I remember how he first put a racquet in my hand and showed me how to spread my fingers along the grip for control. My father rode and golfed and went to Merion for the dinners, and it was the Judge who gave me that racquet and told me the grip was firm but not tight, like an honest handshake. I sit down. "You could have just stopped. You didn't need the money anymore. There was no need to kill him. He wouldn't have figured out it was you."

The Judge shrugs. "I did not know what he thought, only what I heard. You told Suzanne he was looking into cert grants. You told her he thought it was about the business cases. Philip Haynes went through his papers. The names were there. He would have figured it out."

"So that's my fault too?"

"It is not a matter of fault. Gene Gressman had to be stopped. We could not be found out."

"And after he was killed, I suppose that became even more urgent."

He is silent, and I can see it is true. More to cover up with each act. Necessity breeds necessity; death begets death. "That is how it is, Cash," the Judge says at last. His tone shifts. There is still a plea there, but now also a hint of superiority. He is telling me the hard truth. This is what lies behind the girls in their gloves and white dresses, this dark world you do not wish to acknowledge. This is what holds up the waxed dance floor. "Our safety depends on the suffering of others. Yes, Cash, even their deaths."

"So it was for your safety? You feared what? Jail? Disgrace?"

"At first it was for Suzanne. I do not expect this to move you. But you may understand how love drives us to do what we must."

"I don't understand killing people for money."

"Money," says the Judge. His voice is darker now. "You think it is nothing. You think I have sullied my hands, as you never would. Well, we are born in blood and destined for dirt. Our beginning and our end. Is it a wonder they mark the middle too? That is humanity. You cannot escape it." He pauses and looks away from me. "Except for those born late, after a fortune is made. They do not have to think about where it came from. They do not see the dirt."

"I've seen dirt, Judge," I say. My hands are balling themselves to fists. "I have lain under floorboards while the boots of your men shook it down onto my face. You have shown me the dirt."

He is silent. "I never told them to hurt you," he says at last, and the voice is soft as the ocean after a storm. "Miller did all that on his own."

"He would have killed me, though. I expected it. I lay in the ground expecting to die. So that you could trade your worthless stock for land."

"That is not how I wanted it. You know that, don't you Cash?" He looks at me intently. "What I did was for Suzanne at first. And then for you."

"You were making money for me?"

"No, Cash. Concealing it, that was for you." The Judge is holding his glass in both hands, resting it on his knees and looking down. "Because I care about you, about your opinion. It was not prosecution that I feared. Discovery, yes. But by you, not the police. I sent you to Washington to keep you safe, so that you could come back to us. To Suzanne, to me. I knew you would."

"You knew I would come back."

"Eventually. You are one of us."

He nods, but I am not seeing him anymore. I am remembering a crowd of people, a tide of cars. "Unless there was something to keep me in Washington, I suppose. Investigating Gene's death, for instance. Ironic, that, but a temporary setback. And then there was Clara. What did you think of her?"

"Clara?" His voice is all confused innocence.

"Clara Watson," I say. "Did you send that man after her?"

"Of course not." He parts his lips and raises his eyebrows. That is where Suzanne gets the expression, I guess. "Miss Wasserman is no concern of mine. Nor yours. It's not too late, Cash. You can still come home."

Is it the expression, or the name, or the suggestion itself? I do not know, but something throws a switch inside me. The Judge's voice fades out of my consciousness, replaced by a single thought. No one knows I am here, not even Clara. No one has seen my car, heard of my hasty drive up. There is a poker by the fireplace, heavy enough to drop a man with a single blow. I could reach it in one step, take it in a grip that is firm but not tight. One more step to the red leather chair and the man who sits there. He is slow now, gone to fat, and the strength of Merion is in my limbs. The door is ten feet away, the path blocked by a couch. He would never make it.

"I have come home, Judge," I say. "You have brought me back." And for the first time there is a flicker of regret across his face, a trace of fear. He has brought me back, but I am not what I was. Black wings beat, clawed hands grasp. He has brought death to his door.

There is a buzzing in my ears, a roaring pulse of blood. I can see nothing but the fireplace now, surrounded by a field of black.

I hear the Judge step toward me. "Are you well, Cash?" I turn my face up and something in my eyes stops him. He takes a slow pace back. It is what Miller saw in Tule Lake. I hear Harry Nakamura's voice in my mind. *You would not have struck him*. Well, I think, perhaps now I know better.

The Judge stands motionless in the middle of his library, the robe falling from his shoulders in supple folds. Everything seems rotten to me. The evenings with him in this room, holding forth on Coke and Blackstone before the fire, the cold, clean mornings of Northeast Harbor, with fog on the water and in the trees. The rushing is in my ears again and my tongue is thick in my mouth. There are white streaks starting on his face, below the eyes. "Yes, Judge," I say. "I am quite well. I am only thinking that I could kill you now."

"No, Cash," says the Judge. His voice is suddenly hoarse. "No, my boy. That's not what you mean."

"It is," I say. "I am wondering if that would not be the best course. If that is not what you have taught me."

The white on his face is spreading. The skin seems tighter. His Adam's apple works up and down in his throat as though knowledge is choking him.

He is looking into my eyes and seeing what Miller saw. He thinks I will do it. That much I can tell. But perhaps for men like them the eyes of other people are only mirrors, and they see what is in themselves and not in us.

It is a comforting thought, but I can feel an itching in my palm that wrought iron would soothe.

"I want you to understand that," I say. "Whatever happens, I want you to know that I'm thinking about killing you, and there's nothing you can do about it."

He takes a shallow breath and licks his lips. His eyes shift from side to side. Soon he will try to run, and I know that if he does, I will not let him leave the room.

Then there's a noise from outside, the spurt of gravel under tires as a car makes a hasty stop. And then there are light footsteps in the hall and Suzanne puts a hand on the doorframe to stop her progress and begins an excuse for the lateness of the hour. There is something about Tom, and a movie, and a car. And then she sees me, and her words tumble over each other and come to a halt, and the light flush fades from her cheeks and comes back a deeper red.

"Cash," she says. "What are you doing here?"

"Go upstairs, Suzanne," the Judge says. She looks from him to me and back again, confusion on her face. "Go upstairs," he says again, and she hears something in his voice and steps to his side.

"I will not. Not until you explain to me what is going on here."

The fog is lifting from my sight now, the room coming back into focus. I realize I am damp with sweat. "Nothing," I say. "I was just leaving."

Suzanne's head is high and her eyes are bright. "Then leave."

The grandfather clock is ticking. Leather volumes on the walls hold the heroes of history. And more mysterious, more exotic, the bright fish of the law. But law and history alike are lies we tell ourselves to explain why things should be the way they are.

"It's all right," the Judge says, and authority is back in his voice. "I'll be up in a moment."

Suzanne gives me another long look, then she turns and leaves. I hear her feet going up the stairs and at last the stalled image completes itself in my mind: I see her rising through the green water, a pale girl wreathed in bubbles. But she is not rising to me. I think of wistaria climbing the wall at Merion and the way the air got heavy when evening came. I think of the boy who learned to play there, with his grip on the racquet like an honest handshake, gliding through the days in a golden cloud of athletic virtue.

I feel no connection to him. I have crossed over, and that childhood is as far away and strange as something that happened to someone else in a land beyond the sea. That boy is not me, though I am what he became. In the end he was not spared. That boy is gone and as dead as if he'd shipped out like cordwood to feed the fires of Europe, as if Miller had lifted the floorboards and made that empty lake my grave.

"So, Cash," says the Judge. "How do we go on from here? Will you have that drink after all?"

"I will see you in jail," I say.

"Will you? What can you prove?"

"I can prove your trades." Now I know why they could not be traced to Joe Patterson.

"A man may profit from his knowledge. There is no law against that."

"There may be one against how you gained the knowledge. The Court guards its secrets."

He shrugs. "Go. Look through the records of the Philadelphia Exchange. You may find more than you expect. Your brother. Your father."

"What do you mean?"

"I am not the only one who saw a profit."

"They didn't know." I am not sure of this, even as I say it.

Again he shrugs. "So they will say. But who will believe it? An ambitious prosecutor could make his name off theirs. Off yours. There are men like that in Philadelphia now."

I am silent.

"Suzanne lost her mother years ago," he says. He has gauged my reactions and decided where to strike. "And now you would take her father? You would do that to her as well. As if you have not done enough. That is your honor. No, I think we know what you will do."

"This isn't about Suzanne," I say. But she cannot be separated from it. I shut my eyes and there is a glow on the lids, like sun falling on the dock in Northeast Harbor, like the light from a movie screen. I see a world where lines are clean and principles like creases in paper, where we are only what we want to be and nothing is accidental. Where the tracks to Auschwitz splintered under Allied bombs and there never was a camp at Tule Lake for our flag to wave above.

But in that world the Judge and I do not face each other in this room. We are out riding or sailing or sitting on the deck at Merion watching the sun set over the great lawn. The vision burns in my mind like a flame, and like a flame it weakens and dies.

And the Judge says he thinks we know what I will do.

It is a low and harmless rumble now, the voice that used to freeze lawyers in their tracks. And it was never the voice, I realize, but what stood behind it, the sword of justice and the majesty of law. Now there is an old man in a room with dusty books, and behind him the gathered shadows of hired guns and blades.

"He was the better one," I say. "The one you didn't worry about. The man who was no one."

"What do you mean?"

"Gene Gressman," I say. "He was worth ten of you, you fat old rotting fuck."

I do not have the habit of cursing, and what this lacks in fluency it makes up for in surprise. The Judge sits looking at me with his mouth open, and that is how I leave him, an old man agape in a chair with his books and his shadows. And he can call the shadows down, but I do not think he will call them on me. He still believes there is something that connects us. It will be enough to stay his hand. But I am past that belief, and had Suzanne not walked through the door I do not know what could have stayed mine.

CHAPTER 51

THE DRIVE BACK to Washington takes longer. It is pitch-dark, for one thing. But more important, I am no longer rushing to confirm my fears. I know all I need about the conspiracy and my place in it, about why Gene Gressman and John Hall are dead.

What I do not know is what to do about it.

Joe Patterson will be dead soon, too. He and Richards are mostly blameless, anyway. Responsibility lies with Judge Skinner; the dark hand I sensed reached from that Haverford porch. I have looked too far afield for the enemy. There was no one else. It was us, always us, only us.

At my apartment, the door is unlocked. I freeze on the threshold, wondering what waits within. Against my expectations, the Judge has acted quickly. What did he choose for me: a gun, a club, a knife? Then I recognize the figure at the kitchen table. I turn on the light. "Why are you sitting in the dark?"

Clara turns her eyes up. "Where were you? I was looking for you."

"I had to go to Philadelphia."

"I was looking and you weren't here."

"I know," I say. "I had to go to Philadelphia. How long have you been sitting here?"

"You didn't tell me." She has been crying. For a long time, maybe for hours.

"I found out something important," I say. "I was wrong about Cissy. I found Brutus."

"So you went home."

"Yes." There is a magazine in front of her, *Time*. On its cover is one word: *Atrocities*.

"I have made the same decision."

"What?"

"I am going home."

"To your apartment?" I do not understand.

"To Seattle."

"What do you mean?"

"This is no place for me, Cash. I can't even get a decent job."

"There are other places. There's Philadelphia."

"Philadelphia," says Clara, and she smiles. "How would they like me at your club?"

The glories of Merion rise to my mind, dinners on the balcony, sunset over the great lawn, fields of cricketers in white. They would not like Clara much there. "No one needs to know," I say.

Clara catches her breath at that and looks away, blinking as though stung. When she turns back her eyes are bright. "That's not the right answer, wonder boy. And they would. They're good at finding that out, your people."

"It doesn't matter," I say. "That's what I meant."

"Of course. That's what you meant. But it does matter." She tosses the magazine to me. "You can read here how it matters." I shake my head. "It was real," she says. "It was real and we did nothing. And yet we must have known."

I shake my head again. "We saved those people."

Her eyes go back to the magazine. "They do not look saved."

"We did the best we could."

"No," she says. "No you didn't. The boats you turned away. The trains you did not stop. There were women there. There were children."

"Wait a second," I say. "That wasn't me."

"It was your friends," Clara says. She rises and goes to the window, looking out into the night. "It was men like you. Jack McCloy, your Philadelphian."

She is right, at least in part. We have talked about this in Justice, what will be done now, what could have been done before. But it still seems unfair. We are the good guys. "We fell short," I say. "I know we did. And we probably always will. But we'll always try, too, and if we're never perfect, we can always be better."

Clara turns. For a moment there is nothing on her face. Then sadness, but so distant it is like the expression on a statue.

"Tell that to the children," she says. "The girls and boys who are puffs of smoke. Tell them you can be better. I think they will agree."

It washes over me like a wave, the magnitude of our mistakes, the utter impossibility of amends. All I have done, all I have failed to do. It is the feeling you get immediately after you cut yourself, just before the pain comes. There is the blood, there is the flesh laid open, but there is no sensation. Just a sick awareness that something's wrong, while part of your brain is still protesting that it can't possibly be *your* hand spread out before you like a gutted fish.

And then there is the pain.

"So I think I will go," says Clara. "This is not my home."

"This is America."

"Of course. It is different here. But when they come, it is always different. It is always special. Every time, again and again, it is always just this once. Just this once and the world will be saved and nothing like it will ever have to happen again. Who would say no to that? Who can say it will never happen here?"

I remember Charles Fahy putting his authority behind the Final Report, the empty files on the Leupp detainees. "I can tell you one thing," I say. I see Agent Skousen reversing the pistol in his hand, Kinzo Wakayama's fingers white on the pen as he signed his name. "It will never happen to you." I try to think what in my eyes made Skousen draw the gun and Miller afraid to call my bluff, what made the Judge think I would pick up the poker.

"No, Cash," she says. "It will never happen to you. And you should be happy about that. It means you can afford to look for the best in people. But it could happen to me, and I have to look for the worst. Roosevelt could have become a dictator. He didn't want to. But someday the people may give their trust to a man who does. You will be surprised how little they complain. Everyone likes to shout for their country. And why should you take that on yourself? Why have to worry that someone might come for your wife, for your children?"

"Because I love you," I say.

"Ah," says Clara. "There is the decisive pledge. But what recitation can prove your heart?"

Now I have nothing to say. I just look at her and after a moment she softens. "I know it," she says. "I know it, my love." For a moment I think she is going to cry, and then she masters herself and forces a smile. "But didn't I tell you? If you start with a cliché it leaves you nowhere to go."

• • • •

When she has left, I pour myself a glass of Scotch and get into bed. The night is half gone already, but it still seems an eternity until the dawn. I cannot empty my mind. The blue wedding china, the children with their clumps of grass, the dogs chasing trucks. After a few hours awake, I make another trip to the kitchen and come back with the bottle. The renunciants waiting for the ships to take them away, the piles of shoes. Suzanne and Clara, Gene Gressman and John Hall. All the people I have failed; all the people who died in my stead. It was not just a nightmare, that dream that burned through me while Clara watched. It was a prophecy. A world builds up, a world falls down. I lie in the dark, surrounded by all that is lost, waiting for nothing.

And nothing comes.

CHAPTER 52

THE SKY HAS fallen. It lies in pieces on the ground, which closer inspection proves puddles. I blame myself for not turning Joe and Cissy over to Hoover immediately, for saying the wrong thing to Clara, for being nothing but the impress of my history. I go to work and blame Charles Fahy and Herbert Wechsler. Clement spring turns merciless summer.

In August, our bombs fall. A new light sears the world. There will be no invasion of the Home Islands, no million casualties. The reprieve comes too late for Philip Haynes. A kamikaze pilot finds his troopship where it wallows off Okinawa. I have the news in a note from Frankfurter, handwritten on a black-edged card. I do not know whether he means to show regret or thinks it funny; either way, it is a ghoulish touch.

Japan surrenders on the fourteenth. As after the news of Pearl Harbor, no one knows what to do. Strong emotion needs expression and no formula lies ready to hand. Church bells ring; firecrackers explode at my feet. Strangers kiss in the street and drink strong liquor.

And the Alien Enemy Control Unit begins its final task. The renunciants are detained in San Francisco; the ships are fueling; the papers are being collated and stamped.

At Main Justice, I have my own papers. All the documents from my file on Joe Patterson rest now in a new one labeled *Skinner*. I can prove the trades, as I said. But the penalty for that is nothing commensurate to his crimes. I am not sure it even exists—and if it does, it will hurt Suzanne, and maybe my own family, too.

There is also J. Edgar Hoover. If I tell Hoover this story, he will own the Judge. For a man like Sam Skinner, that would be torture. Hoover will hurt him more than the law can. And isn't that what I want, isn't that what he deserves?

I look down to see a new letter on my desk. It is from Harry Nakamura. I open it, remembering with a sudden flash of guilt that I failed to answer the earlier one about his wife, Sachiko. It comes back to me: she renounced; she could not undo it; she told him to take the children and leave her to her death. Another problem I cannot solve. I begin to read, hoping he has found an answer on his own.

But he has not. He is writing for a different reason. He has a legal question for me, he writes. He has heard that the sole parent of children who have retained citizenship will not be deported, even if that parent renounced. *It is a matter on which I should like to be definite*, he says.

Here is a question that I can answer, a rule that is comfortingly clear. I crank a sheet of paper into the typewriter. He is right about the law, I answer, but it has no application to his case. He is the citizen, not his wife. The suicide she threatens cannot affect him one way or the other. Only if he died could it become an issue . . .

Now I understand what he is asking. I stop typing and shut my eyes. I bite my lips until I taste blood. Then I tear up my letter and write another. *I promise you your wife will not be deported. I promise you her citizenship will be restored. I promise this on behalf of the Department of Justice and the United States of America.*

It is a lie, or at best a promise I have no authority to make. We must enforce the law, says Francis Biddle. He will not raise the issue with the President. Political suicide, he says. I nod my head and smile at the phrase. And I go to see the last man I can think of who might be able to help.

Hugo Black does not seem surprised to find me on his doorstep. His face suggests he has always expected my visit. "How've you been, son?"

"Well enough," I say. Josephine, sitting in a housecoat, looks up briefly as we pass through the kitchen on the way out back. "How is she doing?"

Black pulls on his nose and sniffs. "Better with the damn war over. Soon she'll see her boys again." He plucks a grape from the vine and sucks out the pulp, using the skin to catch the seeds. I do the same. "There you go," he says, laughing. "I taught you something after all."

"I told you what you taught me, Judge," I say, and he mutters, "Well," and dips his head.

We are out in the garden among the roses now. I turn to look back at the house, trying to think of how to say what I have come for. Josephine is a shadow at the kitchen window; above her is the library, where his books sleep in their covers. Books like the Judge had, pages and pages of explanation and analysis, years of decisions that led us to horse piss in the stalls of Santa Anita, flecks of blood on the walls of the Tule Lake stockade. Even when Fahy asked for an honest accounting, the Court pulled the cloak of law over their faces.

"Did you have a hard time writing *Korematsu*?" I ask.

Black gives me an appraising glance. "I know that opinion's not what you wanted," he says. "I can read a brief. And of course there were some differences of opinion on the Court. But no, I didn't. I'm not going to interfere with the Army."

"But it's over. The camps are closing. It would make no difference to the Army. Why not just say it was wrong?"

"You said it," Black answers. "The camps are closing. We closed them. *Endo* set those people free."

"*Endo* said detention was never authorized." Black just looks at me. "That's not true," I say. "And what if it happens again?"

"It will happen again. That's the point. The government will need this power."

"What power?" I ask. "The power to lock people up for no reason?"

"The power to defend the country," says Black. His voice is soft. "You worry that the government will do wrong in the future. So does Robert Jackson. The decision lies about like a loaded gun, he said. Well, the man's got a way with words. But I worry that some judge will stop the government from doing what's needed, and I think a decision saying he can is the real loaded gun. We don't know what will happen. But we lose more if the judges get it wrong than if the government does. Do you want to gamble the country on five votes?"

"I don't think the country was at risk."

"Maybe not here. But maybe it will be next time. And think about what would have happened if the Japs had landed. No one would have known who was loyal, who was an invader. They would have been slaughtered."

I shake my head. "They were never going to land. General DeWitt . . ."

"John DeWitt is a good man," Black says. His voice is less soft now. "And a good friend. And whether he's a good general is not my business. Courts don't make war."

I suck another grape in silence. The wistaria has flowered, trailing streams of purple down the wall. "Trim that back hard and you'll get another bloom before fall," I say.

"Yeah," says Black. "I know a lot of innocent people suffered. No one denies that."

It is my opening. "Have you followed the renunciations?" I ask. He shakes his head. "In Tule Lake, the segregation camp. Over five thousand people gave up their citizenship because they were afraid they'd be forced out."

"That's a shame," says Black. "War is the sum of hardships."

"They're going to be sent to Japan. But we can do something about it." Black frowns at me. "You can."

"What are you talking about?"

"You could issue a stay, couldn't you? You could stop the deportations."

"Good lord, son," says Black. "Tell me that's not why you came here." I say nothing. He shakes his head again, a different expression on his face. "I thought better of you."

"You can do it. It doesn't matter what the law says, not if there's something you want enough." He raises his hand, but I don't stop talking. "That's what you taught me, Judge. And now I want you to do something to help people that we've wronged. Is that so much to ask?"

Black has the expression of a man trying to make a hard decision. But as I watch the struggle on his face, I realize it is not about whether he should say yes. It is whether he should throw me out right now. After a moment, he nods at the tennis court. "I think we need to get some distance between us." After another moment, I nod too.

Justice Black's problem, I think as I change into his son's whites, is that he doesn't understand weakness. He does not feel it in himself; he does not understand how it feels for others. He has never acted in panic or despair; he has no sympathy for those who do. He is content to tell stories about his good friend John DeWitt, his days of practice in Birmingham, where he wouldn't try a case on a confession alone. Suddenly I am furious. Black does not understand weakness, but that can change.

If you want to beat someone, my squash coach told me years before, play to his vulnerability. If you want to break him, play to his strength. I do not want to beat Hugo Black. I want to teach him what it is to be helpless.

Black's strength on court is his tenacity, that and his inside-out slice forehand. I construct a point to let him hit that shot, anticipate it, and rip a backhand crosscourt past him. I play that same point three times in a row to show him he can't change it. Then I return his serve with a drop shot, almost an insult, and watch him charge vainly toward the net, thin legs pumping.

"You've been practicing," he says at the changeover. "Nice shot."

"Nice try," I tell him.

I serve hard the next game, not hard enough to get the ball past him, but enough that he struggles to put it back into play. The second shot of the rallies I hit as hard as I can, cruising up to the service line and pounding his weak return. I hit two of those away from him, sending the balls skidding out of the court as he recovers from his lunge after the serve. The other two go at him and he gets the racquet up barely fast enough to deflect them to the side. I stand in front of the net waiting for him to make eye contact, then turn and walk back to the baseline to return serve. Black gathers the balls from the corners of the court, saying nothing. One has rolled out into the grass.

The third game I slow things down. We have longer rallies, forehand to forehand, and he ends two of them with winners, the inside-out slice squirting wide to my backhand. I win the game, but I hope he will think he is getting settled.

We change sides again and he places a ball on my racquet as we pass each other. "I'm sorry about Clara," he says. "Bill Douglas can be a brute."

I have planned to step up the pressure in the fourth game, and now I do. On his backhand the garden wall comes close in on the margins of the court. I move him over to that side gradually to get him within range, then slice the ball even wider. He hits the wall at a run and looks at me with something like surprise. I set the next point up the same way and he hits the wall again. This time he doesn't look at me.

Black bows his head a moment before he serves to open the fifth game. His shots are less reliable; he looks rattled. I do nothing but retrieve, spinning the ball back with medium pace, medium depth. The points are longer and he wins one of them, but the work is starting to tell. He is dripping at the changeover and stops to lean on the net post. "You can't talk to me about a case," he says.

"There's no case."

He looks confused. "Then what is this about?"

"It doesn't have to be a stay," I say. "You could talk to the President. Frankfurter does that, and Douglas. You can do it too."

Black shakes his head. "I'm a judge. That's all. If there's no plaintiff, if there's no case, there's nothing for a judge to do."

I say nothing. It is five games to none now. Black has won three points, and he does not look well. I am discovering my capacity for deliberate cruelty. It is not infinite. I tell myself that this is a lesson he needs to learn. I tell myself it is for a good cause. I tell myself the decision has been made already and now I am just carrying it out.

I serve a double fault. My concentration is slipping. There are other thoughts in my head. I see the pleading in John Hall's eyes, the silver trail down Fumiko's cheek. I see fear on the faces of Judge Skinner and Agent Miller. I hear Clara's voice. *That's not the right answer, wonder boy.* I feel her arms around me in that last embrace.

I spin the next serve in at three-quarters speed. The point settles into the routine of a drill. I move Black from side to side, hitting the ball just within his reach. He struggles, slapping it back across the net, turning a little slower each time.

When do you give up on a point and save yourself for the next one? I asked my coach that question once as we drove to a match. He nodded thoughtfully, as though giving the matter the consideration it deserved. "When you're dead, Cash," he told me. "You give up when you're dead."

Black is of that school. But it is not a choice he is making. The thing about

Black, I realize, is that he can't stop. For a long time of his life he was a speck on the horizon, and looking at him you couldn't tell if he was a man or something else, just that he was a little spot getting bigger. If he'd been a sprinter, he'd have burned out; if he'd been a boxer, he'd have gotten up one too many times, and someone would have put him down for good. But no one could do that to a lawyer, so he kept coming, and when he got where he was going he'd forgotten how to stop.

And now maybe I will show him. My shots are floating in high arcs, landing well within the sidelines, but the two or three steps needed to reach them are all he can manage. The unsteady shuffle of his feet suggests he is reaching a dangerous level of oxygen debt. I vomited once, playing John Hall, but no one ever dropped dead on the Merion courts. But then, we were all forty years younger.

Black turns one more time, stumbling as his feet drag on the clay. There is a sound behind me, once and then again. Black pushes the ball over the net and heads toward the other sideline. His face says he is learning something, pains that persist, declines that will not be reversed. He can give all he has and it will be worth nothing in the end.

The sound comes again, louder, and this time I recognize it as a sneeze. I hit the ball into the bottom of the net and turn toward the house. JoJo is sitting under the peach tree, a bowl of ice cream melting beside her. She is looking for the bad men, for the monsters in the garden. "Bless you," I say.

When I turn back to the court, Black has his hand on the rough edge of the garden wall, gripping it as though pain, too, is something to lean against. I walk over to him. "There's nothing I can do, Cash," he says.

"Yes, there is. You can order them to stop those boats."

He shakes his head. "Someone's got to follow the rules."

"You can stop them."

He turns away, pressing his head against the wall. JoJo is still watching us from the grass. Now she stands and approaches, breaking into a run as she gets closer. She throws her arms around Black's legs. "JoJo," he says. "Tell him I can't do it."

I can see that it's the truth. He could not stop chasing my shots and he cannot break the rules he has set for himself. I cannot change that; all I can do is punish him, hurt him for not being who I want him to be. I put a hand on his damp shoulder where he bows against the wall and I forgive him for what he cannot help.

"You're right, Justice," I say. He takes a long, uneven breath and before he can correct me, I change it. "Judge."

"Yes," he says. His breathing starts to slow. "I'm a judge. And what are you?"

For a moment I am angry again. What am I to ask him this favor, to ask for help, to tell him I think a wrong has been done?

"Judges don't bring cases," Black says. And suddenly I understand. The roses in the air are the honeysuckle of Owen Roberts's farm, and I am remembering our first meeting, where Black asked what he could help me with. *Every man's got a purpose,* he said. *Might be I could teach you yours.*

I am a lawyer. I have a case; I have a claim; I have a client. And I have a judge.

The only problem is that he's three thousand miles away.

CHAPTER 53

I OPEN MY desk drawer and take out the letter James Rowe left for me. I thought it was a threat at first, then a warning. Then it was a reminder of how little we understood each other. Now it is just two sentences I don't need to type myself. I sign at the bottom and fill in the date: August 18, 1945.

Francis Biddle seems mildly surprised to hear that I am leaving the Department. "I'd hoped we might have your services for another few years. There's lots of work to be done."

"Maybe," I say. "But putting people on ships to Japan won't be the last thing I do in this war."

"The war is over," he says. "Well, we'll miss you. May I ask where you're heading?"

"West," I say.

It is enough to set him going. He tells me that when disillusioned with the practice of law in Philadelphia he spent a year in Jackson Hole. "I lived with Struthers Burt at the Bar B-C, and we shot elk and watched the geese fly. Struthers was writing his first novel, and to pass the time I tried my hand at a tale of adolescence which pointed a moral . . ." He does not seem to notice when I leave the room.

On my desk is the folder labeled *Skinner*. It is thicker now; I have added to it as the weeks passed, added everything I could find on my own or wheedle from my sources at the SEC. There is enough to start a case, I think. There is enough for Hoover to use, I am sure. I pick it up and walk to the elevator. I push the call button. On the fifth floor, Biddle is probably still telling his story. Hoover and his flags wait on the second. There is law, and there is vengeance, and neither of them is justice. The aluminum doors open. "Going down, sir," the lift operator says.

I heft the folder in my hand and shake my head. "I'll take the stairs."

"That was the summer before Cissy came to Flat Creek," Biddle is saying as I walk in. He is looking out the window, but he turns back at the thump of the folder on his desk. "What's this?"

"It's for you," I say. "I have to go now."

In the Great Hall I stop for a moment. The statues look over me in silence. The spirit of justice, the majesty of law. "Philadelphia architects, you know," I say to no one in particular. "Zantzinger, Borie, and Medary." Then I get into my car and drive west.

Outside the city are rolling hills and narrow runs crossed with split-rail fences, the tactical checkerboard of the Civil War. They give way to a deep green valley and mountains of blue. I go on, up the slope past the coal towns, down through the foothills into the flatlands.

It is a week of solid driving. I cross the plains under a great open sky, the flat horizon holding in one dimension all our dreams. I see the big soft stars, the silent sunrise, the fields and the hills and the cities raised up out of the vast land. This is the country Fumiko sang of. *A thoroughfare for freedom beat across the wilderness.* Judge Skinner thought I would kill him, and Agent Miller too. I wonder what Hugo Black thought, as I ran him into the wall again and again. I wonder what he thought later, at the end. Mountains rise before me. At last I come to San Francisco, where the long gray ships lie at anchor.

Judge Goodman's courtroom is on Golden Gate Avenue, just a few miles from the docks. He has a new clerk and the judge himself does not recognize me at first. Then he does a double take. "Mr. Harrison."

I hand him a sheet of paper. "I want an emergency stay. I want you to order them not to sail."

He does not ask who I am talking about, just reads the paper. "The government will have to be heard," he says. "I take it you are no longer in the business of presenting their arguments."

I shake my head.

"Very well," he says. "We will see who is available. Nine-thirty tomorrow morning."

. . . .

The next day dawns bright and clear, and I am in Goodman's courtroom with time to spare. As soon as I see the government attorney, it seems inevitable. Seated at the counsel's table is the familiar blocky figure of Emmett Seawell.

He looks up as I enter the room. "You again?" he asks. "They didn't say they were sending anyone."

"Don't worry," I say. "I'm not your expert this time."

"Then what are you doing here?"

"I'm your opponent."

It's plain from his face that he doesn't believe me, but I sit at my table and stand when the judge enters. Seawell gives him a wide-eyed, incredulous look. Goodman just smiles. "Counsel," he says to me.

The argument is an easy one to make. It is simply Goodman's opinion dismissing the prosecution of Masaaki Kuwabara, whom I met in the Eureka courtroom. In the circumstances of Tule Lake, I say, confined behind barbed wire, the detainees could not make a free decision to give up their citizenship. I point to the Hoshidan, too; I mention the confusing information given by the Relocation Authority. Goodman nods at the right places while I speak. I have no doubt that he will rule in my favor.

"Mr. Seawell," he says, and Seawell buttons his jacket and gets to his feet.

"I have been in contact with officials of the Justice Department," he says, "and I have been instructed not to take a position on the merits of this case."

They've come round, I think; at some moment while I was chasing the sun across the plains, Fahy and Biddle changed their minds. But Seawell has not said that the Department concedes, and Goodman's face is troubled. "Then what position does the Department take, Mr. Seawell?"

"The case is moot," he says. He does not look especially happy. "The time for judicial interference has passed."

"What do you mean by that?" Goodman's tone is sharp.

"I called my superiors in Washington for instructions," Seawell says. "I was told that the sailing date would be moved forward. The ships are gone by now. They are outside the jurisdiction of this court."

Goodman does not seem to be listening anymore. He is scribbling something on a sheet of paper. I am not listening either. I am thinking of who in the Department could have ordered this. Which friend has stabbed me in the back? It could have been Ennis; he thinks that shipping the renunciants out will help the others resettle. Or Biddle, trying to spare the President political trouble in California. Herbert Wechsler—it's just his sort of move. Or Karl Bendetsen, if the idea started with War. It could be any of them.

"They've had months to file this suit," Seawell finishes.

"Here is your order, Mr. Harrison," says Judge Goodman. "The port of San Francisco has never been the most efficient, and these days it is chronically overburdened. I do not think vessels of that size could be gone by now. If you require a car, I believe I owe you a ride."

"I've got one," I say. I take the paper from his hand and run from the courtroom.

· · · ·

Driving to the docks brings back memories of my rides with Hugo Black. The streets are crowded and narrow. They bend unexpectedly; they rise and drop. I stand on the brakes and pound my horn at fruit sellers who come into view scant yards ahead. At the top of a hill the car goes airborne, soaring for a silent second above the road. But Goodman is right; the ships are still there.

I take the car down onto the dock and jump out. There are noises coming from the ships, clanking and hooting as of engines starting up. There is a crowd near the gangplanks, and as I force my way through I see Harry Nakamura and his children. I have no time to talk to them.

A military policeman on the shore blocks my way. "You can't go on board," he says. "They're sailing in minutes."

"I can," I say, "and they're not." I shove the paper in his face.

"What is that?"

"It's an order from a federal judge. Now get out of my way."

The handwritten order does not look very impressive, but it is signed and stamped and the stationery is real. He looks at me skeptically. "I'm not asking," I say.

Maybe the suit helps. He steps aside and I run across the planks.

If I'm on board, the sailors think, I must be legit. The captain knows his orders were changed and he is not surprised to see them countermanded. The engine sounds stop as I stand with him on the bridge; the vibration of the deck stills. From the dock I hear shouts.

Now there is time to find Harry in the crowd. "You see," I tell him. "Sometimes the government keeps its promises."

He shakes his head. "That was not a promise from the government."

"You believed it anyway."

"I believed it for that reason."

He is right; this was won against Justice and the United States. But I hesitate. "You give us too little credit."

"Oh, you will realize this was wrong. Someday. You are good enough for that. But realizing someday does not help the now. And I do not know what you will do the next time."

I suppose he may be right about that, too, but for now this is something. It makes no one whole; it carries no assurances for next time, but for now it is something for those who waited and believed.

The next day I am back in Goodman's courtroom with Emmett Seawell. He shows no shame, and why should he? It was not his decision.

The Department is willing to take a position on the merits now. Some individuals, it admits, may have been unable to make a true choice. But some could; some did. Those renunciations are still valid.

Goodman tells Seawell to identify those individuals. Now he looks embarrassed. "All of them." The saying it is hard, even if the decision is not his. Again I cannot guess who in Justice came up with the ploy. But I find I no longer care.

Goodman just blinks. "Very well," he says. "We will hear those cases individually. All of them. In the meantime, Mr. Seawell, you will take those people off the boats and restore them to their families."

Seawell does not object. I do not either. I have five thousand clients now, instead of one; I have five thousand files to review and five thousand hearings to prepare. It will be a lot of work, but I can do it. I can do it on my own if I have to. And perhaps I do not. When the renunciants are off the ships, I ask Goodman for a continuance. "I have to take a short trip," I say.

"Very well, Mr. Harrison," he says. "Where are you headed?"

"North."

"Cash," says Seawell as I leave the courtroom.

"What?"

"Biddle says he's opened an investigation."

"Into what?"

"I'm supposed to tell you he's opened one. That's all he said."

Judge Skinner. I nod. The machinery of law has started to turn. Who will be caught in the gears, I do not know. I throw two days' clothes into my car and start driving.

It is flat going to Redding. Then the road climbs into mountains of spruce and hemlock; a river falls in foamy torrents beside. I see again the lonely splendor of Mount Shasta; I pass Eureka to the west and Tule Lake to the east. I drive through lumber towns with blackened stumps like headstones and logs stacked like rifles, through roaring squalls of rain that leave the glossy myrtle glossier still. I stop when the last of the light has gone and I no longer trust myself to keep the car on the road.

The next morning I learn I have made it almost all the way through the mountains. The road turns on a ridge and the land falls away into a valley below. The plain rolls on for miles, lush green spotted with yellow blooms. I pull the car over, tires crunching on the pine needles that carpet the shoulder; I step out and take a deep breath of the wet air. Rain drums on the hood and rises in steam. For a moment I am consumed with the wild thought that no one has seen this sight before, that this land is entirely new. A part of the world saved just for me.

It isn't, of course. For centuries the Indians lived here. Smallpox came, and after it the wagons. White men from the East, then Japanese from the West, tending celery gardens and orchards of peach and cherry. Now those gardens are empty too, and there is me and my Packard, heading north. There are few things to be had in this world that are not taken from someone else.

So the Judge told me, and he had seen sin and struggle, and knew perhaps of what he spoke. But I stand and look through silver mist out onto the soft swelling bosom of earth below and think that some things are given.

A distant river sparkles; gauzy hills mount beyond. That way lie the sodium lights of Tacoma, the shining sound, the islands cloaked in cedar. With another day's drive I will reach Seattle in the dusk of evening, coming in with the fog off the water and the sailors who step from shadows to waiting arms.

But for a moment I stay there, suspended above the green swell of the land as though thrown up onto the crest of a wave, seeing for the first time a break in the flat horizon. For this the boats crossed the ocean, the wagons climbed the mountain pass. For this the songs were sung with desert all around. This is what is given: the promise there is still a way, if we can find it, the promise we can always be renewed.

AUTHOR'S NOTE

THERE NEVER WAS a Caswell Harrison, as far as I know, though the University of Pennsylvania does have the statue of John Harrison mentioned in chapter three. Most of the characters around whom the conspiracy plot of this novel revolves—Suzanne and Judge Skinner, Colonel Bill Richards, Philip Haynes, John Hall, and Clara Watson—are my inventions. Joe and Cissy Patterson are real people, whom I have described in a generally accurate manner, but the Anti-Federalist Society, and Joe's involvement with it, are fictional. In 1919 there was a clerk, Ashton Embry, who leaked information about pending cases to confederates on Wall Street in order to allow them to profit from the knowledge. He was prosecuted for it, but modern insider trading law did not exist at the time, and the indictment was ultimately dismissed.

In the plotline dealing with legal events, I have tried to remain close to the actual facts. The description of the Nazi saboteurs' arrest, trial, and Supreme Court hearing, for instance, is drawn from primary and secondary sources, including transcripts of the Supreme Court argument and briefs written by the parties. I have changed the timing of those events in order to make them background rather than foreground action; in reality, they occurred during the summer of 1942, when Cash has already started work at the Court.

With respect to the cases surrounding the treatment of Japanese and Japanese Americans, I have likewise attempted to maintain a high degree of historical accuracy. There was, of course, an evacuation and detention program pursuant to which roughly 120,000 people, a majority of whom were birthright American citizens, were removed from the Pacific Coast states and confined in relocation camps. I have described that program as accurately as I could, relying again on both primary and secondary sources. I have also described the well-known litigation surrounding the program—the *Hirabayashi, Korematsu,* and *Endo* cases—based on the briefs, the transcripts of oral argument, and secondary sources.

The loyalty questionnaire I describe was actually administered to detainees, with the results I recount. The Leupp Isolation Center did exist, and had the problems I describe with the inadequacy of records in support of detention. The draft did apply to Japanese Americans detained in the camps, and some refused to register. Most of those who refused were convicted, but Judge Louis Goodman, assisted by his law clerk Eleanor Jackson Piel, did preside over a trial in Eureka in which he found some innocent.

The legal world in which Cash operates is thus drawn largely from fact. Most of the things he does were actually done by Justice Department lawyers. In his work at the Alien Enemy Control unit, which was in fact headed by Edward Ennis, Cash takes over some of James Rowe's functions. The real James Rowe stayed at Justice until he volunteered for military service in 1943. Cash also takes over some of the functions of John Burling, a special assistant to Attorney General Francis Biddle, who participated in the litigation of the internment cases and wrote the *Korematsu* brief.

As in the book, there was significant division among the government lawyers who worked on these cases. Ennis, Rowe, and Burling all opposed the evacuation and detention program and expressed doubt about its constitutionality. As in the book, they clashed with War Department lawyers over the briefs filed on behalf of the United States, including the dispute over the footnote about the Final Report. The alteration of the Final Report that I describe is also historical fact, though it was not discovered until years later. The definitive source on this intergovernmental struggle is Peter Irons, *Justice at War.*

In his work after leaving Justice, Cash takes over the functions of a private lawyer, Wayne Collins. As I relate in the book, more than five thousand